RUNAWAY HEARTS BOOK ONE

J.B. LAREE

ISBN 979-8-9898953-0-4

Developmental Editor: Melissa McGovern, Memos In The Margins

Line/Copy Editor: Angela Garcia, Romance The Page LLC

❀ Created with Vellum

Sometimes, the pathways through life lead us astray.
To those who need to change course to fulfill your dreams...
do it.
You're never too late.

The *All I Want* playlist is on Spotify!

Check out the official playlist which includes songs submitted by the following readers:

Skylar (@skyendlessbookshelf on Instagram)
Luci (@luciwashere on Instagram)

CONTENT WARNING

The characters in this book face hardships, trauma, and losses that may be troubling for some readers. The full list of sensitive themes and topics can be found in the Trigger Warning located at the back of the book. Please be aware the list contains *major spoilers*.

This book contains mature content intended for 18+ readers.

1

TATUM

"Tatum."

Ugh. My skull weighs a hundred pounds, far too heavy for my neck. And I can't feel my right arm. *Did I lose it? Can I play a guitar with only one arm?*

"Tatum!"

My facial muscles seem to work. Testing them out, I scrunch my nose at a pungent odor, and the corner of my lip tugs against the rise of my cheek.

"Oh, for Christ's sake."

I lift my brows. My eyelids stretch with the motion but refuse to open. *Maybe I'm in a coma. They say you can hear people when you're locked inside your mind.*

Cold liquid and ice cubes assault my face. I gasp and roll, landing in an achy heap on the plush floor. My working hand wipes the moisture and something crusty from my lip. I squint against the offensive sunlight streaming through the window and study my fingertips. One sniff confirms I slept in vomit. Again.

With great effort, I haul myself upright and lean against the sofa, my legs bent to one side. *Where are my pants?*

"You're done, Tatum." The exasperated voice of my manager, Bette, threatens to rupture my eardrums.

A sluggish scan of my surroundings reveals a coffee table where an empty bottle of vodka sits next to an empty glass. Fresh droplets cling to the sides of it. As my eyes adjust, the rest of the hotel suite comes into focus.

I don't remember coming here last night. The last thing I recall is getting ready backstage before the show. *What city am I in?*

My gaze slides over to Bette, who towers above me in a bold red pantsuit, fists planted on her hips in her classic power pose. A sharp black bob frames the blank expression on her face. It's a look of indifference she reserves for men in the industry when she's ripping their balls out via their throats. She's never given me that look before.

"Done?" The question comes out more like a croak. *Gosh, my throat is dry and my breath reeks.*

"Done. Finished. The label is dropping you. You're fucking lucky your contract is up. Saves *me* a bitch of a PR headache after last night's shit show and *you* lots of money in legal fees. A clean break for everyone." She maintains the power pose while I try, but fail, to keep my focus on her.

Resting my head on the sofa cushion, I inhale a deep breath through my nose and try to process what this means. My dehydrated brain works overtime to string together basic thoughts.

I've been the pop star Makenzie for eight years, seven of those spent touring the world. I've recorded six albums—all of them multi-platinum—and received over thirty awards, including eleven Grammys. And it's all at an end?

"What now?" I ask.

Bette's huff echoes in the room. "For me? I've got a business to run. For you? Not my problem anymore."

Well, that gets my attention. My gritty eyelids spring open. "You're leaving me?"

"I'm a manager, Tatum. If you're no longer a star, there's nothing here to manage. It was great while it lasted—very lucrative—but this is business. We aren't friends."

Ouch.

She straightens the hem of her tailored jacket, a sign of her impending departure, and pulls a business card from her pocket. "I'll leave you with one last piece of advice." She drops the card onto my lap. "Get some help. I already called ahead. You can check in today."

With that, my manager of eight years spins on her four-inch stilettos and struts out the door without a backward glance.

Groaning, I slump onto my side, vaguely aware of a pricking sensation in my numb arm as it comes back to life. At least some part of me has the will to go on.

"Brutal," says a monotone voice from somewhere behind me, followed by the sound of clunky footsteps.

A pair of purple Doc Martens appears in my sight line before a paper cup lands on the rug, inches from my nose. My best friend and personal assistant, Maisy Donovan, tosses a towel at my chest and plops down beside me so we're lying face-to-face. She's also my makeup artist and hair stylist. I wouldn't be surprised if she's internally recoiling at the sight of me.

"Are you leaving me too?" I ask in a small, froggy voice as I wipe my face and neck.

"It's never been about the job, Tate. I'm here for *you.*" She smiles the same sad smile she's given me a lot over the years. It's one of pity, accompanied by eyes full of worry and disappointment.

We lie in silence for long seconds while I stare into her

hazel eyes, brightened by her brown, spiral curls with chunky pink highlights. With light tan skin and a smattering of freckles she covers with makeup, Maisy's a natural beauty. She inherited her White mother's pouty lips and her Black father's pointy chin.

To her dismay, one thing neither of her parents passed down to her was their height. At five feet tall, Maisy often feels overlooked, and she hides her insecurities and emotions behind a loud wardrobe, dark lipsticks, and a dry sense of humor.

She picks up the card Bette threw at me, flipping it over to read both sides.

"What is it?" I ask.

"A treatment center in upstate New York."

Based on her gentle tone, she thinks it's a good idea for me to get help. Perhaps so, even though I don't consider myself an addict.

The drinking and pills aren't a dependency. They're simply a means for escaping my own thoughts. Thoughts of loss and love and the dark-haired boy in my dreams. I could quit anytime, but I haven't been ready to confront the mistakes of my past.

Music was supposed to be enough to keep me going. To distract me from my pain. If I'm honest, the spark that ignited the pursuit of my musical dreams, and kept me chasing them, fizzled out sometime around my third album. At least, that's when I realized I've been going through the motions and don't *feel* anything anymore.

Lying on the luxury hotel carpet with dried vomit in my hair—dropped by my label and my bitchy manager—and staring into the concerned eyes of one of the few trustworthy people in my life, an epiphany slams into me.

I'm at rock bottom. And I hate it here.

"I'll go," I whisper, tracing the rim of the cup with my finger. What better time to work on myself than during my newfound period of unemployment?

Maisy shoots up and crisscrosses her legs, flashing white panties under her yellow sack dress. "Really?" she squeals in a rare burst of excitement.

I hike myself up on an elbow, sip the lukewarm coffee to clear the crud from my throat, and answer with determination. "Yes. Let's do it."

Her shoulders relax on a long exhale. "I'll take care of everything while you're away. Fuck the label. And fuck Bitchy Bette. You just focus on yourself and walk out of that place with a genuine smile and a boss attitude. Then we'll make a new plan. We're still young, Tate, and the next chapter of our lives will kick ass because *we'll* be in charge."

Maisy's motivational speech fires me up. Despite the pounding in my head, I nod. "Heck yeah, we will."

We bump fists and make explosion noises before she winces and says, "You smell so bad. Like…so bad. Please go shower and brush your teeth." She retches to prove her point.

Before I forget…

"What city are we in?"

The past several months have been one long substance-induced blur of tour buses, stage lights, and faceless audiences. No matter where I go, everything looks the same to me. Probably because I can't see straight half the time.

"New York City," Maisy says.

"How convenient," I mutter, remembering the treatment center is in New York. Also remembering social media rules the world, I cringe and cover my face with both hands. I can't imagine what a fool I made of myself at Madison Square Garden last night. I peek at Maisy through my fingers. "How bad is it?"

Foreboding lingers in the air before she answers. "It's best you don't know."

Shit.

~

I take the longest shower in history, using all the hot water in the state of New York, while listening to the morning-show hosts of a local pop station describe what an ass I made of myself last night. They're downright giddy as they recount every last detail of my disastrous performance.

Apparently, I stumbled around on stage, forgot my lyrics, humped the mic stand, and flashed a boob—full nipple. As they relish in my rapid fall from grace, I will the scalding water to liquefy all the cells in my body and wash me right down the drain.

I never want to see the mountains of photo and video evidence. The proof will only elevate my level of embarrassment, and my self-esteem is low enough already. Fame may appear glamorous on the outside, but having everyone in the world pick you apart—frame by frame and inch by fleshy inch—does real damage on the inside.

If I had listened to Maisy and avoided the media coverage, then I wouldn't be hiding in the glass shower, dreading the reality waiting for me once I leave this hotel today.

After wrapping my hair in a towel and slipping on a fluffy robe, I slam the laptop shut and pace around the bathroom while devising a plan.

First, I'll complete ninety days of treatment to appease the people who think I have a serious problem with addiction and worry about me the most. Maybe I'll get some healing out of it too. Second, I'll change my appearance, perhaps dye my hair its natural shade of brown. Finally, I'll live as a hermit in my Hollywood Hills home and write songs under a pseudonym for the rest of my life.

Yep. That's the plan.

Empowered and ready for battle, I march into the living room of the hotel suite and raise a finger in the air. "I have a plan!"

"You're not becoming a hermit," Maisy says. She doesn't glance up as her thumbs fly across her phone screen.

I crash onto the sofa in defeat and mumble "wench" under my breath.

Our mostly packed suitcases near the door await the last of my belongings, which include my small makeup bag and the crusty clothes I slept in last night—a sparkly top and a black thong. I have no idea where my pants went.

"I threw away my clothes in the bathroom trash," I say. "They were gross."

Maisy's eyes slide my way. "Seriously, Tate? People will pay good money for the shirt you wore the night everything went to hell. And your panties?" She shudders. "I don't even want to think about it. Go tie up the trash bag and stick it in the suitcase. And get dressed. We're leaving soon."

She tosses a black sheath dress and black heels onto the cushion next to me.

"Are we going to a funeral?" I ask, my eyes burning holes in the conservative garment.

"You're going to rehab." She continues typing.

"It's a *treatment center*."

"That's what they call it so people like you will actually show up."

"Why black?"

Her arms fall to her sides with a sigh. "You need to appear sleek. Put together. Classy. I can't let you walk out in leggings, your ugly Camp Heartwood sweatshirt, and a wet ponytail after last night's…performance."

"I love that sweatshirt. It's my favorite." My bottom lip juts out in a pout. I've been photographed in that sweatshirt many times. It's basically my uniform at this point.

"Your new favorite is being fresh and fashionable. Now go dry your hair."

"You're my hairstylist."

"I'm busy writing your statement. Go." Fed up with my attempts to procrastinate, which I'm known to do, she crosses the room and sits at the small desk, typing away on her phone again.

I blow-dry my blonde hair and use eyedrops to clear the redness threatening to overtake my blue irises. Dark shadows ring my puffy eyes, and my skin has certainly seen better days. It's pasty, dry, and has one too many noticeable blemishes.

From the other room, Maisy yells, "Lip gloss and mascara only! Fresh face, full grace!"

That's one of her many nuggets of beauty wisdom. She believes a natural face earns you a certain level of grace from people because they're seeing the real you. Smart. But in this case, I don't think she saw the blotchy spots on my cheeks. So, I attack them with a light dusting of powder. She'll never notice.

I stroll into the living room wearing my business attire, trash bag in hand, as Maisy puts the final touches on my statement.

"Here," she says, passing me her phone and taking the trash bag. Her head hovers next to mine while I read the drafted Instagram post.

To my fans: Thank you for your love and support over the years. Without you, my music wouldn't have wings. I'm sorry for letting you down and for my behavior last night at MSG. To put it bluntly, I'm exhausted—physically, mentally, and emotionally. I'll be taking some time off to focus on myself so I can be the Makenzie you deserve. I plan to return with fresh, new music and hope you'll wait for me. Until then, light and love - Makenzie

I blink at my friend. "How do you always know what I would say?"

She shrugs. "Because I know what you're feeling and thinking, weird as that sounds. You're a good person, Tate. The best. And your fans know it too. They'll still be here when you're ready."

The reality of my situation sinks in. The sudden knowledge of how my recent behavior will impact my career—and how I've disappointed everyone—knocks me back a step.

"What if I'm never ready? What if it's too much to handle and I leave that place with nothing left to give?" I smother a sob with my hand, and Maisy wraps me in her arms.

"You don't always have to be a giver, you know. Sometimes you have to take what you need." She releases me, having reached her hug threshold of six seconds. "Who knows? Maybe this is your chance for a do-over. Maybe it's time for the world to meet Tatum, and you can put Makenzie *and* your past to rest.

"There's no rush to figure everything out right now. Take baby steps. And the first step is to walk out of this hotel like you have your shit together. Throw a wrench in their narrative and make it a debate instead of adding fuel to the fire. By the time you finish rehab, last night will be old news, and you can start fresh."

I sniffle and wipe my nose. "It's a treatment center."

"Whatever," she sighs. "Now go wash off that powder and retouch your lip gloss. The guys are on their way up."

When I've returned from my third trip to the bathroom this morning, the luggage has vanished. My security team of two, dressed from head to toe in black, stands near the door. Marcus and Judge Ames are cousins—both with shaved heads, whiskey-colored eyes, and curly eyelashes any girl would kill for—who joined my team five years ago.

"It's madness," Marcus says, crossing his massive arms over his even more massive chest. The graphite tactical watch he never takes off gleams in the morning light.

Marcus requires precision and demands perfection in all things. He keeps schedules down to the minute, and a wrinkle wouldn't dare crease his T-shirt, much less his suits. The only visible imperfection marring his smooth, brown complexion is the silver scar cutting through one thick dark eyebrow.

Judge grunts in agreement, his arms folded in a similar pose. At six-foot-four, he's an inch shorter than Marcus but just as broad. A tapestry of colorful tattoos conceals much of his tawny skin, and the beauty mark beside his wide nose lessens the effect of the tough guy faces he makes. But I'll never tell him that.

"What's the plan?" Maisy asks, straight to business. She and Marcus have that in common.

"We found a decoy. Paid her five grand to walk toward the front door with shades on." Marcus shares a brief glance with Judge. The latter lifts one corner of his mouth in what's considered a smile coming from him. I don't like it.

"How will she convince the paps she's me?" I ask, eyes darting between the two giants.

Marcus avoids my gaze and seeks Maisy for backup when he answers. "We gave her your camp shirt to wear."

"What?" I shout. It's more of a screech, really.

Marcus responds to my outburst in his usual, bland tone. "It has to be believable, Tatum, or you'll get mobbed. We need to be strategic."

He discusses avoidance tactics and the strategy behind his planned double decoys with Maisy, who isn't at all bothered by my sweatshirt crisis.

"What about my sweatshirt? Will I get it back?" Everyone ignores me, but I have another question and raise my hand. "So, if we have a double decoy, I'm dressed like I'm going to a board meeting for no reason?"

Maisy sends me a withering glare. "We won't get away unseen. Everyone has a camera. Anyone could score the money shot."

The hairs on my arms rise when Judge winces, putting me on high alert. Where Marcus always maintains a stony expression, Judge lets his poker face slip from time to time. Like now.

"What? What is it?"

The guys exchange another loaded glance.

"Speaking of money shots…" Marcus trails off.

Maisy lets out a long sigh, which elevates my anxiety. "Judge carried you inside last night. He thought he had all the important bits covered—"

"People saw my vag?" My voice rises twelve octaves. "Now everyone's seen my tits *and* my vag?" I grab the kitchenette counter to hold myself upright as my knees weaken and my stomach churns.

Holy crap. My life is imploding. Any minute now, I expect some lady in a robe to follow me around chanting "shame" while she rings a bell in my ear.

"It was one boob," Maisy coos. "And no one saw your vag. Only your ass because you took off your pants in the car.

You punched Judge in the nuts and threatened his life when he tried to stop you from undressing."

"Oh, Judge." My apologetic eyes land on the silent man.

He grunts and shrugs as if to say *it's part of the job*. But it isn't. I've never been this person, and I'm mortified by my behavior.

Deciding the best thing I can do is shut up and let my team handle things, covering for me as they have for years, I stand aside while they finalize the details of our escape plan. Finally, we leave the hotel, spotting only a handful of paparazzi staked out near the hidden exit we chose.

We travel to the airport in Westchester County and board a private jet which carries us to a small airfield near the exclusive treatment center in the Adirondacks. After saying goodbye to Marcus and Judge outside the plane—where Judge gives me the longest hug I've ever received, and Marcus gripes about the safety risks of them not accompanying us on the ten-mile journey—Maisy drives me in a rental car to the facility.

During the quiet ride, I fight off tears. Twelve years ago, we became best friends after I moved to the small Texas town where she grew up. We haven't been apart for any significant amount of time since she finished her cosmetology program after graduation and joined me in California. Before I became famous. I'm not sure how I'll survive three long months without her.

Maisy pulls into the entrance of the facility, and we stare at the front of a gorgeous stone lodge surrounded by a dense thicket of trees. The leaves are beginning to change colors with fall approaching—my favorite time of year. The parallel of nature's forced change and my own isn't lost on me. It's necessary. Clearing out the old to make space for the new.

"Don't come in," I tell Maisy.

"I'm not getting out of the car," she says at the same time.

Our strained laughter fills the car. If we don't part ways soon, we'll sit here forever. Perhaps we're a bit codependent.

I nibble my lip and peek at her watery eyes and pursed mouth. We reach for each other and embrace, squeezing tightly.

"You'll do great," she whispers.

"I'll miss you," I croak.

She clears away the emotion rising in her throat, always the strong one. "I'll pick you up in ninety days."

"Ok," I say into her curls. "I'll be the one *not* wearing a Camp Heartwood sweatshirt."

She barks out a laugh and lets me go, then says with a straight face, "Get out."

"Fine. Love you."

"Love you more."

A valet lurking nearby, pretending he didn't witness our awkward farewell, approaches the car as Maisy pulls the trunk release. With a tip of his hat and no other greeting, he grabs my luggage, closes the trunk, and heads inside.

Okay, then.

I shut the door and wave at Maisy through the window. As she drives toward the sunset, my smile fades along with the car's taillights. Just like that, I'm left in an unfamiliar place, forced to wage war on my past and the ghosts haunting me. Alone.

2

JAKE

The sun hangs low in my rearview mirror, its soft glow crowning the landscape like a golden halo. It's a view I'll never grow tired of seeing. Inching closer to Walford, I exhale a sigh of relief when I pass the town's welcome sign. *Home, sweet fucking home.*

My ass is asleep, I'm starving, and my truck is choking on fumes.

Over an hour west of Austin, my hometown's a quiet refuge among the more bustling, touristy places in the Texas Hill Country. Tucked between low rolling hills littered with live oaks and Ashe junipers, Walford is a tight-knit sanctuary for people looking to put down roots and fly below the radar. We mind our own business here and expect people passing through to do the same.

As a land management consultant, I spend more time driving across the state of Texas than I do visiting the ranches owned by my clients. Even when I fly into one of the bigger cities, I rent a pickup truck and drive for hours between job sites, spending my nights in crappy motels that serve shitty coffee.

Sure, setting my own schedule is a perk of being self-employed. But racking up the mileage wears on me and has me reconsidering my plan to expand into other states. I've been at this for a few years now and, while the projects vary from one ranch to another, the asphalt laid out between stops never changes.

Idling in the middle of the street outside the town's only bar, my weariness returns when I notice the lack of open parking spots. For a Wednesday night, the bar is hopping. My brother, Jensen, must be mighty pleased. Bruno's Bar is his baby, born of blood, sweat, and a shit-ton of financial investment to spruce up the joint.

I stash my truck two blocks away in the alley behind Menchy's Hardware and stride down the sidewalk on Main Street, ready for a cold beer and some mindless conversation. Loud chatter assaults me when I push open the door, but it dies instantly when all heads turn in my direction. Behind the long bar, Jensen covertly grabs the remote to mute the TVs mounted on the walls. But not before I catch *her* name mentioned by a news reporter. Silence engulfs the place. Only the sound of someone's cough breaks it.

I ignore the eyes tracking me—and the fact the TVs are now playing a soccer game—as I make my way to the bar. No one in Walford gives a crap about soccer, but *everyone* cares about the woman in the news.

Larry Olson, the interim mayor and former high school principal, abandons his barstool and totters over to join his buddies, leaving the prime seat open for me. I plant my numb ass on the stool and lock eyes with Jensen. He casually snags two beers from the fridge and pops the tops before setting them in front of me.

"Hungry?" he asks.

I take off my ball cap and hang it on my knee. "You know it. I'll have the usual."

This is a bar, not a restaurant. The menu consists of hot wings, a club sandwich, a cheeseburger, and fries. My usual is the cheeseburger.

Jensen gives me a nod, then lifts his chin at a waitress, who delivers my order to the kitchen. It's a well-oiled machine around here, and the staff is aware that Jensen prefers to communicate through numbers and body language.

Words have never been his strong suit, but owning the bar forces him out of his shell. He may not be the most talkative person but, like most bartenders, he's a great listener. He's also a reliable, honest man and a quiet leader who values actions above words, and the people in this town love him.

As the whispers continue to float around behind me, Jensen presses his forearms against the bar top and captures my gaze. He knows what I heard, and he's waiting for me to ask about it. I won't. For a decade, we've played the same game, and I never take the bait.

"Her label dropped her," he mutters, keeping his deep voice low as he studies my face for a reaction.

"Don't care."

I swallow a healthy swig of my beer, cursing Jensen in my head because this isn't the mindless conservation I hoped for. I'd much rather discuss how the school's football program needs an overhaul or whose idea it was to appoint a drunk idiot as interim mayor. The latter remains a mystery.

"Rumor is she's headed to rehab," he says. The guy won't take a hint.

I can't let on how this latest development in her life affects me. It shouldn't. She deserves every ounce of misery life throws at her.

Never one to break eye contact first, I continue chugging

my beer while Jensen's piercing stare peels back my skin layer by layer, searching for any sign of emotion.

We both have dark hair and green eyes, but his are a couple of shades lighter and remind me of a jungle cat peering through the shadows, silently stalking its prey.

"I'll take my food to go," I say, maintaining a neutral tone. No chance in hell I'm sticking around so he can play the role of concerned father.

He bows his head and sighs. "Jake."

See, this is what he does. He pokes and prods and pries, hoping one day I'll slice open my abdomen and spill my guts about the girl who abandoned me. I used to tell him every-thing—go to him first when I needed help or advice. Now, my thoughts and feelings on *that* particularly sensitive subject are sealed inside a dusty tomb buried deep underground.

Our parents died in a car crash when I was fifteen and Jensen had just turned eighteen. Somehow, he became my legal guardian and spent the remainder of his senior year in high school learning to parent and become a full-fledged adult. He gave up parties and his college football scholarship to make all my dreams come true. Because he bowed out of his future plans to support mine, I became the first person in our family to graduate from college. The guy is the gold standard, and he's never resented me for any of it. But he gets mighty pissed when I don't open up to him like I used to.

Because the punk likes to pick at my scabs, he says, "Do you ever wonder if she's hurting too? If you really loved her, maybe you'd stop thinking about yourself for one goddamn minute and notice she's spent the last few years going off the rails. And it's nothing new. *Makenzie* hasn't been happy since the beginning."

I fucking hate that she uses that stage name. I'm also

annoyed by my brother's need to keep close tabs on her movements and emotional welfare over the years.

His words give me pause though. One, because he said so many of them. Two, because I haven't paid attention to anything related to her in so long, other than the massive hole she left in my chest. It's pretty hard to miss, being the size of Texas and all.

Deciding to stamp the period on the end of this unsolicited conversation, I say, "She ain't my business," then grab my second beer and settle in to wait for my food.

Jensen rakes a hand through his wavy hair in frustration. He needs a haircut, which means I probably do too, since we always visit the barber together.

Realizing he's lost the battle, he abandons me to see to his other patrons. As soon as my to-go order hits the bar, I snatch it and head out with an unwelcome sense of worry over Tatum nudging its way into my head.

As soon as I arrive home, I hustle to my office, toss the bag of food onto the oak desk, and sink into my rolling captain's chair. It's one of the few furnished rooms in the house, with boring beige walls and a single bookcase. I crank up my laptop and type *Makenzie* into a search engine.

My cheeseburger remains untouched as I scan report after report full of speculation about the cause of her public breakdown at Madison Square Garden. And the pictures and videos? It's a good thing my stomach's empty.

To most people, she appears healthy, thanks to strategically applied makeup. Makeup the old Tatum would never wear. To someone familiar with every inch of her—someone like me—she's too thin with a sickly pallor and dark shadows above gaunt cheeks.

Her hair no longer shines with its natural luster and often hangs in a curtain to shield her unfocused gaze from flashing cameras. Cameras that capture every expression, gesture, and misstep she makes. Thanks to the disaster at her recent concert in New York City, the whole world has now seen parts of her body that, once upon a time, I believed were for my eyes only. Forever.

When she first vanished from my life, I drove myself crazy with worry. No calls, no social media posts, no signs of life. Suddenly, she popped up everywhere as the biggest breakout pop sensation since Britney Spears. I gorged myself on every scrap of gossip or grainy photo that came across my newsfeed, had alerts set up on my phone and everything—a classic case of masochism. The worry transformed into a lasting anger and resentment that persists today.

When rumors of her engagement to a famous actor hit the headlines, I quit my obsession cold turkey. I canceled my cable TV, deleted all social media accounts, and subscribed to satellite radio to avoid any entertainment news during my long drives. My preferred stations play British comedy, jazz, and classic country music. When I get bored with those, I turn on an audiobook or drive in silence. Anything to keep from hearing her name.

For four years, I've resisted the temptation to look her up. Now, here I sit, scrolling through photo after photo, searching for evidence of her suffering.

A dullness lingers in her eyes, and her smiles never quite reach them. I've seen that dullness before. It's what drew me to Tatum in the first place.

My buddies and I lounge against the hood of Rock's restored 1968 Camaro, like we do every morning, listening to country music as we kill time before the first bell rings. The sun shines in the clear October sky, the air cool and crisp. And today's game day, which means short cheer skirts and early dismissal for a pep rally. The football boys are stoked.

Rock whistles low and elbows me in the ribs, drawing my attention away from my advanced calculus notes. I follow his line of sight to a vision with honey-brown hair and striking blue eyes standing on the curb. She's wearing black skinny jeans, white Converse sneakers, and a Bob Dylan T-shirt cut off at the waist. Her hands squeeze the straps of a purple backpack slung over both shoulders.

She assesses her surroundings: the students clustered by clique, laughing and smoking and making out; the portable buildings used for overflow classes because the school is too small for its current population; the enormous football stadium hulking behind the main building.

Football is a religion in Texas, and the stadium is our church. I can tell by the slight scrunch of her button nose she's not impressed.

At Brody's obnoxious catcall, her head swivels in our direction and that's when I notice it. The sadness in her eyes. I've seen that sadness in the mirror every day for nearly two years. The hint of loss dimming the irises enough to remind you that vital pieces of yourself are missing. But not so much that people who haven't experienced loss will recognize the difference.

We lock gazes. Like drawn to like. She forces a smile, then strides toward the main doors.

It registers that someone near me is talking. "—must be Pamela's niece."

"No one calls her Pamela, idiot," Rock says.

"Whatever, bro. That chick is smoking hot. I'd hit that," Brody says. He's the moron of the group and only thinks with the head that doesn't house a brain. We ignore him and stroll inside as the final warning bell rings.

Everyone in town heard Pam Wakefield's niece was coming to live with her. The gossip mill ran rampant with rumors about a troubled teen, an expelled student, a runaway, and the actual truth—the girl's parents died in a small plane crash. I found out because I do odd jobs for Pam for extra cash, and she told me herself.

Pam's younger brother hightailed it out of Walford as soon as he graduated from high school. She saw her niece a few times when the girl was little, but it's been years since they've had any meaningful contact. Because Pam is the girl's only living relative, here she is…

Tatum Wakefield. The most beautiful, sad girl I've ever seen.

Turns out Tatum and I don't have a single class together. At lunch, I find her sitting outside under a tree, writing in a notebook balanced on her knee. Her pen strokes the page at a hurried speed.

Considering my approach, I make my way over and settle beside her, wrapping my arms around my bent knees. Careful not to touch. I've been in the early grief stages myself and had many well-meaning attempts at comfort shoved in my face.

"Aspiring author?" I ask, trying to sneak a peek at her notebook but failing.

She shifts her knee, tilting the notebook to keep the page hidden from my view. A delicate floral scent surrounds her, and I have the sudden urge to bury my nose in her long silky hair and take a big sniff. *Is that creepy? That's a creepy thought, right?*

"Songwriter," she answers, eyes focused on her busy hand.

Her voice is soft and melodic, as if an angel gifted her a set of gilded vocal cords to soothe the world's aches and pains. I want to listen to her talk forever, and she's only spoken a single word.

We sit in silence for a bit until she speaks again, still writing. "Do you have a name?"

In my head, a chorus of *hallelujahs* echoes as the gates of Heaven open. A warm, inviting glow lights the path she unwittingly laid for my perfect introduction. My lips raise to one side in a knowing smirk.

"Jake." I pause for effect before adding, "Dylan."

Her pen freezes, and those sky-blue eyes snap to mine. "Liar."

I chuckle at her accusation, but I speak the truth. My mom was a huge Bob Dylan fan and named me after his son, Jakob.

"It's my middle name, actually. Jake Dylan Holloway. At your service." I smile, and she returns it, flashing perfect teeth when her bare lips part. I'd give anything to find out if they're as soft as they look.

No girl at my school has ever had my interest. There's no time for it. My entire focus is on earning top grades and enough cash to pad my college fund. My first and last kiss happened freshman year before my parents died. So, what is it about this girl?

"Tatum Makenzie Wakefield. Nice to meet you."

She sticks out the small hand holding the pen for me to

shake. I eagerly oblige, and the callouses on her fingertips graze my palm when she withdraws.

Grinning, I bob my head. "Makenzie. I like it." *Am I flirting? I'm not sure I even know how, but I'll go with it.*

She shrugs a shoulder while toying with the ends of her hair. It's so long, the glossy strands reach her waist. "Meh. It's okay, I guess. It won't make me famous."

Leaning a little closer to her, I lower my voice and ask, "Is that your secret plan? To become famous?"

"Something like that," she answers. Her body gravitates toward mine. Our arms touch, but neither of us shift to end the contact. "This little Podunk town is a temporary stopover before reaching my final destination."

Something uneasy niggles at me when I think of this girl leaving one day. "And where's that?"

"LA. Where else? I'll be on the first flight out of here after graduation." Her relaxed slender shoulders stiffen at her mention of flying. That haze of loss I managed to clear up edges its way back into her eyes.

Rather than offer her empty condolences or lob questions she's not ready to answer about her recently deceased parents, I keep the conversation light.

With my chest puffed out as if she happened upon her own personal superhero, I ask, "What can I do to help make you a star?"

This earns me a grin. A big beautiful, sparkly one that injects a flood of warmth straight into my pounding heart. I'm a goner.

It didn't take long after meeting Tatum for me to recognize all the qualities she shares with my late mother. She's kind, caring, playful, and supportive with an ability to put others at ease and make everyone feel welcome and valued. I missed having warmth and affection in my life after my mother died, and I felt like the luckiest boy alive when Tatum chose to shower me with all her love and attention.

I wanted to bottle up every good thing about her and keep it all to myself. But, also like my mother, Tatum left me. Making me the unluckiest bastard in Walford.

After inspecting several years' worth of photos of Tatum, a.k.a. Makenzie, my eyeballs feel gritty and my stomach cramps from hunger. I force down the soggy cheeseburger and fries, chasing them with a room-temperature beer. It's almost three o'clock in the morning. Thank god, I don't have to drive anywhere until Friday, and I can sleep in.

Jensen's observation appears to be spot-on. From all my diligent research, I've concluded that Tatum has been miserable since she burst on the scene as Makenzie. Maybe since she left Texas a decade ago, though I have no evidence from the missing years to support such a claim.

Fingers steepled together, I rock back in my captain's chair, smug satisfaction tipping up the corners of my mouth. Whether her unhappiness has anything to do with me is irrelevant. Justice has prevailed. As I said, she deserves every ounce of misery she suffers.

3

TATUM
THREE MONTHS LATER…

"Is there anything we need to discuss before we bring in your support team?" Cheryl, my counselor, leans forward in a chenille armchair.

The casual furnishings in her neutral-toned office are meant to help patients relax. But I'm a nervous wreck on the matching sofa, knowing Maisy and my aunt, Pam, are waiting in the hallway.

It's been ninety days since I've seen or spoken to them. Gateway Hills only allows emails, which the staff monitors to keep the residents focused on recovery. The meaningless topics permitted in our conversations included things like "It sure is cold today" and "I had sushi for lunch." Now, I get to see my loved ones' faces again and find out what's really been going on in their lives, and I've been on the verge of tears all morning.

Cheryl brushes her red hair off one shoulder and blinks at me, waiting for my reply.

"What will you say to them?" I ask, twisting my hands in my lap. Between the nerves and excitement and too much caffeine, I'm a live wire this morning.

"I won't tell them anything we've discussed in sessions. You're free to share whatever you want, and it doesn't all have to be said today. Our goal is to make sure they understand their role is to support you if or when you need them."

If or when, meaning it's time to stand on my own two feet. I've learned so much during my stay here. Well, once I got past the horrible first month. I had convinced myself I didn't have a substance abuse problem, so the withdrawal symptoms took me by surprise. Without those substances quieting my mind, the endless thoughts of everything I've lost consumed me. I didn't sleep for weeks. However, I immersed myself in the program, and armed with healthy coping methods, I'm equipped to face whatever waits for me outside the walls of this facility.

Ready to move things along, I say, "I'm good. Bring them in."

Cheryl barely turns the knob before Maisy barges through the door and tackles me on the sofa without saying a word. Her curls smother my face, blocking my view of Aunt Pam.

I grab Maisy's arms and pry her off me so I can get a better look at her. She's dressed in black pleather leggings and a cropped herringbone sweater. Meanwhile, I'm sporting boyfriend jeans and—drum roll, please—my Camp Heartwood sweatshirt. It arrived freshly laundered in an unmarked package. My guess is Judge recovered it. He's sentimental like that.

Once Maisy unglues herself from my body, I'm able to stand and face Aunt Pam. I haven't seen her in person in almost a year, since before the start of my most recent tour. Her brown bob reaches her chin, and white streaks frame her beautiful face. She has the same blue eyes and slender build as me and my dad. In her usual attire of a maxi dress and cardigan, she's more suited to the New England seaside than the hills of central Texas.

"Tatum." Her eyes glisten with unshed tears, and I rush into her outstretched arms. She pets my hair and whispers, "You're okay, sweetie. Everything is okay."

As I fall apart in her comforting embrace, I recall all the times she stepped up beside me on the jagged peak of loss. She's never judged me or showered me with empty platitudes and advice. She simply holds me, her quiet, steady presence blanketing me as I topple over the edge and plummet into grief.

Maisy wraps her arms around us. We hold each other tight and cry together, and Cheryl lets us have this moment for as long as we need.

When my crying ebbs, I wipe my eyes and say, "Let's sit."

They plant themselves on either side of me on the sofa, pressing in close, each holding one of my hands. Literally being the support system Cheryl mentioned earlier as they keep me propped up.

Cheryl reclaims her seat in the armchair, her features and voice softer than before. "I'm so glad you could make it today," she tells them. "Tatum has done a phenomenal job in the program, and her ongoing success depends on having a solid foundation and support team." She shifts her focus to me. "Tatum, is there anything you would like to share now, or would you rather discuss your short-term plans?"

I take a deep fortifying breath and clear my throat. "First, thank you both for being here. I love you both so much, and I'm sorry I put you through this. Looking back, I realize I needed the wake-up call."

Aunt Pam squeezes my hand. Maisy, who's frozen like a statue, stares at her lap while I highlight the positive outcomes from my treatment: the confidence I'm finding within myself, the fear I'm learning to overcome, the self-blame I'm working to abolish.

I'm a work in progress, but I'm more than ready to heal from the loss that led me to this place, which means no more drowning in bottles to suppress the pain. I'm determined to make amends with my ghosts. One, in particular.

I hesitate, glancing at Cheryl in search of reassurance, knowing the next part might be worrisome to them. She gives me a nod of encouragement. "So…I'm thinking of going home for a while."

"To Cali?" Maisy frowns, images of paparazzi on parade likely circling her head.

"To Dayton?" Aunt Pam asks with wariness in her tone.

Dayton, Ohio. My birthplace and where I lived with my parents until they died. The thought of returning there never crosses my mind.

"To Walford," I say.

A shocked gasp escapes Maisy while Aunt Pam squeezes my hand a little harder.

"It may seem like a really bad idea, but Walford's my home."

Although I didn't live there long, I belong in Walford, Texas. The town offers safety and privacy, and I won't have to worry about neighbors selling me out to paparazzi. It's the best place to hide while I figure out what's next for my career.

"I know…*I know* there's a history there I'll have to face. But I'm ready." I swivel my head from side to side, gazing upon their doubtful faces, and muster enough shaky confidence to declare, "It's time."

After Cheryl and I give them the highlights of my progress, I'm eager to escape from Gateway Hills, shouting quick goodbyes to the staff and bolting to the car. As we board the chartered jet at the nearby airfield, I count my blessings that I can afford such a luxury and avoid exposing myself to the world for a while longer. Flying commercial and being recognized, plus everything that comes after that, would send me into an immediate downward spiral.

I'm already anxious about spending a few days at my house in California before heading to Walford. If the paparazzi catch wind of me being in Hollywood, all hell will break loose. But I'm confident in my team's ability to conceal my movements.

Marcus, the leader of our little crew, doesn't allow chances for information leaks or mistakes when I travel incognito. The fact that he didn't feel the need to escort me home from Gateway Hills speaks to his own confidence in his logistical planning skills. Unlike the day I arrived at the treatment center, which was a last-minute decision that stressed him out, he's had time to nitpick at every detail of this trip.

Relaxing on the plane, my cheeks ache from grinning so much. When Maisy asks for the tenth time if I'm sure about returning to Walford, I smile and say, "Absolutely."

"It'll be nice having you close by since I'll be in Austin for a few months," she says.

Maisy avoids Walford whenever possible and tries to limit visits to once a year. She'd go less frequently if she could get away with it, but her mom lives there.

I sit up straighter in my seat, my interest piqued by this news. "What's in Austin?"

Her whole face lights up when she smiles. "Graham got the rest of the funding for his film. He starts shooting in Austin in two weeks and hired me to do makeup, hair, and wardrobe. The budget's tight, and he can't pay much, but I'd do it for free as a favor to him."

Graham Kingston—major Hollywood actor, aspiring director, and another important person in my tiny circle of trust. I miss him a lot, and he would be here if his schedule allowed for it.

Mindful I shouldn't scream on an airplane, I say, "Oh my gosh! That's amazing! He's wanted this for so long." Happy tears gather on my lower lashes. "I'm so excited for you both. You're a powerhouse, Maisy. You deserve everything good that's coming to you."

"Gah! I've wanted to tell you for months, but they wouldn't let us share any personal news in those stupid emails. Communists," she says, spitting the last word. Her perfect eyebrows furrow in concern. "Are you sure you're not mad? I'm not abandoning you. I just need to stay busy, and it's a great opportunity."

"Maiz." I grasp her hand. "I could never be mad at you for chasing your dreams. You've been by my side, dealing with my crap, for so long. I'd never ask you to put your future on hold while I figure mine out."

She hugs me again. It's like she became a serial hugger while I was away. Normally, she hates being touched.

"Thank you," she says. "I wouldn't have this opportunity at all if I hadn't chased you around the globe."

I grab her cheeks, squishing them together into a fish face. "Pretty sure I dragged you around the globe."

"Don't touch my face," she mutters between puckered lips.

"Never wear herringbone again. You look like a grandma."

I glance at Aunt Pam to make sure I'm not offending the more mature population. She must've fallen asleep after takeoff.

After Maisy updates me on everything I missed while on

lockdown, she follows Aunt Pam's lead and naps until we arrive at the Burbank airport. I, on the other hand, stay wide awake.

Despite my earlier confidence in my decision to return to Walford after our stop in California, I'm wondering if it's another mistake I'll be adding to my long list of terrible mistakes.

~

Outside the terminal, Marcus and Judge stand sentry by an SUV illegally parked in a rideshare zone. Wearing black suits, they scan the area for any signs of a camera.

Judge spots me first and opens the doors with a pinched expression on his face like he's constipated. Marcus rolls his eyes at his emotional cousin and steps forward to grab our luggage. Once all arms, legs, bags, and giant crybabies are loaded, we drive toward my modest home in Hollywood Hills.

"Haven't seen a camera outside the house in weeks," Marcus says from the driver's seat. Judge punches him in the arm. "Oh, yeah. Good to see you, Tatum. How are you?"

I respond primly, "I'm very well, Marcus. How have you been?"

"I've been wonderful. However, Judge had a problematic rash in his nether—"

A smack on his head cuts him off. Marcus growls at Judge, who growls back. Their face-off ends when Marcus remembers he's driving and focuses on the road.

Maisy and I suppress our laughter while Aunt Pam shakes her head and says, "You two behave yourselves and get us there in one piece, please."

Properly chastised, Marcus offers a quiet "yes ma'am."

Judge salutes.

Rolling through the iron gates of my residence, a wave of solace washes over me when the Mediterranean-style house with white stucco and a red-tiled roof appears. Nestled among a variety of palm trees, the windows at the back of my house offer a stunning view of the hills, which is the reason I bought the property. When pinks, purples, and oranges caress the gentle curves of the landscape at sunrise and sunset, I'm reminded of Walford. Of *him*.

If I could stay here while sorting out my life, I would. Despite the state-of-the-art security system—complete with perimeter alerts, video surveillance, and a safe room—that Judge had installed, the ruthless paparazzi in LA will find a way to invade my privacy. There's no way I can regroup with cameras watching my every move.

Entering the house from the garage, I breathe in the comforting aroma of coffee and leather. Candles and wax melts constantly infuse the air with my two favorite scents. I drop my purse on the granite kitchen counter, tell the group I need a few minutes alone, and make my way upstairs.

Warm hues of cream and sage decorate the master suite, which has a king-size bed, a cozy sitting area, and a large balcony facing the hills. *Tranquil* describes my sanctuary perfectly. Kicking off my sneakers, I stroll through the luxurious, marble bathroom to the gigantic closet stuffed with fancy clothes I've never worn. My preferred style leans more toward casual than couture.

Hidden deep behind a stack of chunky sweaters on the top shelf is my box of pain. It's nothing special on the outside— just an old wooden cigar box with a metal clasp—but the contents it holds are invaluable. I carry the box to the bedroom and sit on the bed, pulling in several calming breaths before I unleash the past.

Cheryl's words from one of our sessions come to mind and offer me strength. *"We grieve many things. Loss of life. Loss of love. Loss of opportunity. And there's no prescribed end date. Grief is forever. Work with your grief rather than against it. Allow it to become a part of you—to inspire you—until your grief is no longer in control."*

When I open the lid, I see my parents' faces for the first time since I closed this box many years ago. One by one, I pull out the photos and keepsakes, lightly stroking each of them with my fingertips. All the memories of what I lost—life, love, opportunity—assail me until tears stream down my cheeks. To my surprise, I'm smiling through the tears as I find some of the memories also bring me warmth and joy.

A light knock on the door interrupts my reverie before Aunt Pam's head appears. She casts a wary glance at the memories spread across the bed. "Is it okay if I come in?"

"Of course."

She approaches with caution, eyes darting between me and the reminders of my painful past.

"It's okay," I tell her. "You can look at them. I'm done hiding."

Drawing one bent leg onto the mattress as she settles beside me, she exhales a shaky breath and picks up a photo of me and my parents in one hand, covering her mouth with the other. "You look exactly like your mom. Beautiful. With your dad's eyes."

Aunt Pam studies my dad's face for a long time, indulging in her own memories while I remain silent. There was no bad blood between them after he left Walford. They simply grew apart. Life got too busy. Time moved too fast. Then it was too late.

During my childhood, their relationship consisted mostly of phone calls and holiday cards. We rarely saw each other.

Aunt Pam hates to travel. My dad traveled all the time, mostly for work. Ironically, it was a leisurely trip on a friend's small plane that claimed his and my mother's lives.

It's funny how tragedy has a way of ushering us toward new paths of happiness and purpose. If not for the deaths of my parents, I never would've met *him*. Speaking of...

The next photo Aunt Pam chooses shows a green-eyed boy and a blue-eyed girl wearing graduation caps and gowns, their cheeks pressed together, both grinning from ear to ear. Light and love explode in the aura surrounding them. I avert my eyes. My shame, guilt, and regret are too heavy to bear the sight of what I once had for very long.

I worked through my grief after my parents' deaths, choosing to focus on the love they showed me throughout my childhood and all the wonderful memories I have of them. But the poignant loss of this green-eyed boy—though he is very much still alive—is one I'll never overcome.

Aunt Pam notices my reaction, sets the photo aside, and tucks a loose strand of hair behind my ear. "You'll have to see him, eventually. There's no avoiding it."

"I know," I whisper, holding her worried gaze with mine.

"He travels a lot. Gone for days at a time," she says, always finding the silver lining. "It could be a while before you bump into him."

"You talk to him?"

I should know this, but Aunt Pam is nothing if not respectful, and she's respected my wish for her to never speak of him.

"It's a town of three thousand people, sweetie. Of course, I talk to him. Plus, he helps me manage the land."

The Wakefields have owned hundreds of acres in the Hill Country for generations. My great-grandfather was the last cattle rancher. Every beneficiary since him has leased out the land for different uses: hunting, grazing, minerals. The land generates a comfortable income with little work on Aunt Pam's part.

I decide not to ask my aunt to explain the whole managing land thing. Last I knew, Jake headed to college for a business degree. His dream was to become the brains and business acumen behind a certain musician's stardom. Not to drive around studying land. Guess that's one more thing I can add to the guilt column.

Aunt Pam picks up another photo and a blue velvet ring box. She stares at both for long seconds, her eyes turning misty. I recognize the particular brand of loss reflected in her sorrowful expression: loss of opportunity.

Saying nothing, I tug the photo from her fingers and walk over to the beat-up guitar case leaning against the wall. She watches quietly as I unlatch and lift the lid, then stick the photo inside the ripped lining. I vow to draw inspiration from it when my thoughts get stuck, as Cheryl suggested.

As for the ring, I return it to the cigar box with the other mementos.

Maisy strolls into the room as I'm putting everything away. "I put the guys to bed," she announces.

My eyebrows jump at her declaration.

"Perv," she mutters. "They both fell asleep on the couch waiting for you. Pretty sure Judge was hoping you'd tuck him in."

Aunt Pam sighs wistfully. "I love those boys."

The cousins are grown men in their thirties. But Aunt Pam has adopted our ragtag bunch of misfits as her own and refers to us all as *boys* and *girls* despite our ages. Probably because we behave like children half the time.

I waggle my brows at Maisy and say, "Hey, you're the

one who's been living here alone with them for three months. Unsupervised."

The diamond stud in her left nostril catches the light when she crinkles her nose. "Ew. Marcus's new girlfriend kept him entertained, so I spent most nights playing Scrabble with Judge."

"Did you win?" I ask hopefully.

She rolls her eyes. "Of course not."

Judge has a ridiculously vast vocabulary, which is surprising given he only reads smutty romance books hidden in dust jackets taken from thriller novels. He thinks we haven't caught on to his deception, but we have.

"So when are you flying to Texas?" Maisy asks.

I glance between her and Aunt Pam, uncertainty creeping in and making me question my decision. "Three days? That'll give me time to wrap things up here, right?"

Maisy nods. "Okay. I'm flying down with Pam tomorrow, so we'll get your old room ready. While you're here, you can respond to fan emails since the wardens at the prison wouldn't let you have access to your private accounts." She points a stiff finger at me. "And keep them short. No rambling."

"It was a treatment center."

"They were dictators."

Resting on her hands, Aunt Pam closes her eyes, likely praying for some magical being to whisk her away from us. I truly believe that, deep down, she enjoys our sisterly bickering.

"So, we have a plan. You and Aunt Pam leave tomorrow. Marcus and Judge will fly down with me and drive me to Walford—" Marcus materializes in the doorway wearing sweatpants and a white T-shirt. "Oh! I thought you guys went to bed. Come on in."

Judge shoves Marcus into the room, then skirts around him and stands next to me. He definitely needs a hug, so I wrap my arms around half his waist. He engulfs my entire body with one beefy arm and lifts me off the floor.

"Put her down," Marcus barks at his cousin. When my feet are firmly on the ground, he says, "Judge couldn't fall asleep again without hearing the full plan directly from you."

I fill them in, fighting the urge to comment on Judge's suit jacket over his striped pajamas.

"You guys are staying here while I hide out and get my shit together, right? No matter how long it takes?" I ask. The thought of them moving on turns my stomach sour.

"Language!" Aunt Pam doesn't like when we curse.

"This is your home too." I smile at them, my steadfast knights.

Judge sniffles while Marcus nods in confirmation. These guys are more than employees to me. They're my friends, and this *is* their home. They've lived with me for years, and I'm not ready for that to change.

I don't know much about their history, only the bits and pieces Marcus has shared. He's pretty tight-lipped about their past, but Maisy learned they served in the military together when they were younger.

A security agency sent them to me on contract for a tour. Called them a *bonded pair* as if these men were rescue dogs and not humans. I didn't like that one bit, and since we instantly clicked, I hired them directly and off we went.

If Aunt Pam's house had enough room, I'd ask them to join us in Texas so they could protect me from the past awaiting me there: a past with dark hair, sun-kissed skin, and forest green eyes that reveal every emotion. The emotion I'm most afraid of seeing in them is hate.

It's been ten years since I laid eyes on the boy I promised

to love forever. Of all the promises I made to him, that's the only one I didn't break. Jake Holloway is wedged so deep in my heart and soul, it's impossible to set him free. In my most desperate daydreams, I hope to find something salvageable to convince him that our love is worth saving. A tiny thread to pull. A remnant of what we once had. A flicker of the spark that ignited us.

If hate is all he has to offer me—or worse, indifference—then I've spent the past ten years of my life suffering in vain in a prison of my own regret. And I'll have to finally move on.

After everyone signs off on the plan and disperses to their rooms, I snuggle into my pillows and stare at the beam of moonlight cutting across the ceiling through the gap in the balcony curtains. A sense of peace settles over me upon realizing that since I left Gateway Hills, no one mentioned the media circus I caused or the possible death of my career.

4

JAKE

I glide on the porch swing, sipping strong black coffee from my favorite mug, my slurps the only sounds disturbing the quiet morning. My personal symphony. I'm usually awake before the sunlight peeks over the horizon, soaking up the kind of peaceful solitude only found before daybreak.

Despite being early December, the temperatures are mild enough for me to be comfortable in sweatpants and a T-shirt. Hell, we've seen Christmases in Texas where the temperatures reach the seventies, so the warm weather expected today is no surprise to anyone.

My home sits far back on my property off the county road. The sprawling ranch-style house overlooks the prettiest acreage in the state, if you ask me. I bought the place two years ago when the previous owners decided to sell and move closer to their grandkids in San Antonio.

Call it cursed fate, but I couldn't pass up the opportunity. My part of the money held in trust from my parents' life insurance policy made it possible. Thankfully, I didn't need that money for college because I earned a full academic scholarship to cover my tuition and housing expenses.

Because the house was built in the 1970s, I've spent most of my free time—what little there is—remodeling the outdated…everything. With Jensen and my friends' help, I've made good progress. New kitchen and bathrooms. Hardwood floors. We spent hours scraping popcorn texture off the ceilings in every room and ripping out ugly wallpaper.

I gutted the full attic above the main living room to make way for vaulted ceilings. Even added a loft with a huge round window, which cost me a small fortune, so I can enjoy the stunning view of my land from an elevated vantage point. The loft area itself remains unfinished and unused, nothing but naked drywall and plywood floors.

The projects keep me sane, and I'm in no rush to finish them. I can attest to the truth in the old proverb "idle hands are the devil's playground." During my last two years of college, and for a short while after graduation, I didn't work. I lived off my savings while sowing every wild oat in my path. Parties. Alcohol. A few meaningless romps between the sheets.

Everything I gave up in high school for perfect grades and *true love,* I reclaimed with a vengeance. None of it filled the void in my soulless body or empty chest.

Rock showed up uninvited at my apartment one night, told me to pack my shit, and hauled my broke ass to Walford. At Jensen's order, of course. The three of us lived in my parents' house, now Jensen's house, while I got my shit together and started my consulting business. Rock moved out when he got married.

Our other best friend, Brody Carpenter, returned to town the summer after Rock's wedding. We all went to separate colleges, but that didn't stop us from picking up right where we left off when high school ended. Without the two of them and my brother, I wouldn't be where I am today.

I mosey into the kitchen for a refill, then head to my office and go over my schedule for next week. If I leave early Monday morning, I can be back Thursday afternoon in time for the middle school football game. Rock's the head coach, and I make a show of supporting him when I can.

James Rockford Harrison III has been my best friend since we were in diapers. He's seen me through the best and worst days of my life. The least I can do is cheer on a bunch of scrawny middle schoolers while he screams at them from the sideline.

My cell phone pings. Speak of the devil.

ROCK

Saw Maisy in town last night.

Maisy's arrival is no surprise to me. She visits her mom every year before the holidays. Without fail, one of my buddies always tells me when she's here. She stays a night or two, then bails. Guess this town turns women into runners.

ME

And?

ROCK

Just saying.

ME

And?

ROCK

Heads up. In case you run into her.

BRODY

She still hot?

ME

I don't go to town on the weekends.

Thank god. I'll drag my reluctant ass to Walford for

birthday parties or special occasions on the weekends if I have to. Otherwise, if I'm not traveling, I spend all my time improving my house and property, a safe fifteen miles beyond the town's border. The fewer reasons I have to traipse around Walford, suffocating beneath the weight of my memories and the pitiful stares, the better off I am.

ME

But thanks for looking out, bud.

ROCK

<middle finger emoji>

BRODY

Answer me, bro. Is she hot?

ROCK

<middle finger emoji>

I rustle up my usual breakfast of crispy bacon and fried eggs, and down two more cups of coffee. Eager to start on the recessed lighting in my future media room, I throw on a grey T-shirt, the jeans I wore yesterday, and cowboy boots.

Two steps inside the garage—which hasn't seen a vehicle since I moved in because it's presently serving as my workshop—the doorbell rings. My boys always stroll right in like they live here, so I curse knowing it's not one of them.

Miffed at having an unexpected and highly unwelcome guest, I stomp toward the front door and spy a head of colorful curly hair through the side window. My stomach sinks, and I take a second to collect myself before I swing the door open, fold my arms across my chest, and plant a shoulder against the door frame.

"Maisy," I drawl, trying to appear casual and not the least bit shocked to see her. In truth, her showing up on my front porch has my pulse going berserk. There's only one reason she'd be here.

Her hazel eyes flash with surprise as they trace me from head to toe. "Oh. Hi. Wow."

I tilt my head and wait out her unabashed perusal. We haven't seen each other since a few months after high school graduation. Ten years ago. I've grown three inches and packed on what I call "working man's muscle" since then. Lean, not bulky.

Maisy shoves her hands in the huge front pockets of her checkered jumpsuit. "So," she starts, clearing her throat. "Tate's coming home. For a little while, at least. She'll be here tomorrow."

All the air is sharply snatched from my lungs as if the atmosphere demanded the instant return of any oxygen that I've borrowed in the past twenty-eight years. It's a miracle my body's still upright.

"And?" I manage to ask through clenched teeth.

In her no-nonsense tone, she says, "She's been through a lot and needs a quiet place to heal and figure things out. Then she'll be gone. You won't even know she was here."

I never figured things out. *I* never healed. Mainly because no one could ever give me a goddamn clue about why Tatum ghosted me. And she has the nerve to come to Walford, of all places, to recover because *she's* been through a lot? *Can Maisy tell my whole body's vibrating? I sure can.*

And it's ridiculous to say I won't know Tatum's here. Laughable, really. If I feel the pressing force of her absence every single day, I'll damn sure feel the power of her presence.

"She left. Not me," I say, grinding the words through my locked jaw.

Come to think of it, Maisy deserted me too. It's been a

decade since we last spoke. She was one of my closest friends, or so I thought. And she has the audacity to show up at my house throwing around demands when I'm the wronged party in this situation? Oh, hell no.

Maisy glances at my hands and steps back. I track her uneasy gaze to find them fisted at my sides. It dawns on me that I've taken a step forward. A step that she must interpret as threatening. I may be pissed, but I would never hurt a woman.

"Go."

In a gentler voice, with a pitying shake of her head, she pleads, "Jake—"

"Go!" It's a thunderous command, born from a place of violent pain and a decade's worth of repressed anger.

Maisy flinches, then spins around and hightails it to her car.

I slam the door shut and try to inhale deep breaths through my nose, nostrils flaring with each pull. But the air just… won't…come. My chest constricts with a tight, vise-like pressure. My vision narrows until I can only see tiny black dots. My inner ears throb, pounding like an elephant stampede. I sink to the floor and sag helplessly against the wall in my living room, clawing at my chest.

This has happened before. Many times after I lost all contact with Tatum. For nearly two years, I dealt with overwhelming panic at my dreadful imaginings of her being kidnapped, dead, trafficked, suffering from amnesia somewhere and unable to find her way home. Two years spent in pure hell because she vanished from my life as suddenly and unexpectedly as my parents did in the head-on collision that claimed their lives.

The rational part of my subconscious knew she was alive and well. Otherwise, her aunt—hell, the whole town—

would've gone into mourning. I would've mourned right alongside them. But the irrational, more desperate part of my brain believed Tatum would never leave me. Not if she had the choice.

The day I saw her—healthy, platinum blonde, and fresh as a daisy—on TV was the last time I had an episode. The last time I actually felt anything. It was the day I learned the girl I had no choice but to love didn't choose me. So I mourned alone.

Tatum became the shiny, new pop princess. I became an empty shell.

Abandoning my efforts to breathe through my nose, I heave short gasps in and out through my mouth, desperate to fill my lungs.

I'm dying. This is the big one.

Somewhere far beyond the fast rushing of blood in my head, car doors slam. Moments later, a figure appears before me, its hands gripping my shoulders.

"Oh my god. Hey, Jake? Breathe with me. Let's slow it down."

My terrified eyes make out the worried ones of Lucy, Rock's wife.

"Rock! Find a paper bag!" Lucy's a nurse. Surely, she can save me.

What seems like hours later, the open end of a paper bag is roughly jammed against my face.

"Gentle, Rock. Jesus. You're okay, Jake. Keep your eyes on me and slow it down."

I focus on her slight Spanish accent. Her straight black hair and big brown eyes. The soft whooshing of air coming from her pursed red lips. Inside the bag, I shape my mouth into an *O* and try to match my air flow with hers.

The tightness in my chest loosens. The expansion in my lungs brings sweet relief. I'm no longer pouring sweat.

"I don't like the way you're staring at my wife's mouth." Rock's gruff voice floats from somewhere above me.

Slumped against the wall breathing into a paper sack, I glance up to find him glaring at me beneath slanted ginger brows. Six-foot-five, two hundred and forty pounds of solid muscle with a sleeping baby strapped to his chest.

"Ignore him," Lucy says in a soothing tone, drawing my attention to her. "You're doing great."

"What the hell happened?" Rock asks. "We were headed to my mom's and saw Maisy in a Toyota, peeling out of your driveway like she robbed the place."

My breaths near steady, I drop the bag and grunt, "Tatum."

Those ginger brows hit his hairline. "She dead?"

"Worse," I groan. "She's coming back."

"Shit," he says. *My thoughts exactly, which is why I'm sprawled on the floor fighting for air.*

Lucy takes charge again. "Let's get you to the sofa. Rock! Bring him some water, then grab Marcella's diaper bag from the truck."

I'm better already, but I allow Rock's wife to baby me just to piss him off. I spread across half the leather sectional like a king as she stuffs pillows around me to make me more comfortable. She even pulls off my boots.

I gulp down the glass of water Rock hands over while Lucy rubs my arm. Rock sends another deadly glare my way before storming off to retrieve the diaper bag. How their daughter stays asleep, I have no idea. The man is like a bull.

Lucy settles a sleeping Marcella on a pink, padded mat on the floor. Rock takes up the other end of the sectional and pulls Lucy into his lap, facing me. Once we're all relaxed and breathing normally, Rock gets down to business.

"What the fuck?"

I repeat the brief conversation I had with Maisy.

"Wait. So, where has Tatum been all this time?" Lucy asks, eyes darting between me and her nervous husband.

This woman is as sweet and compassionate as they come, but she's the only person I've ever seen put fear in Rock's eyes. I have an icky notion his fear has more to do with a potential ban on their bedroom activities than anything else.

Lucy and Rock met in college, so she's not from Walford. And, judging by Rock's pursed lips, flaming cheeks, and guilty expression, she isn't aware of our town's best-kept secret. From the confusion on Lucy's face, it appears Rock skimmed over a few important details when he told her about my and Tatum's relationship and its unhappy ending.

People around here love to talk about Makenzie when she's in the news, but nobody speaks of Tatum being Makenzie. It's a sacred, unwritten rule in Walford. When a newcomer moves in, like Lucy, it's refreshing to have someone who doesn't eyeball me like I might spontaneously combust.

Rock's upper body inches away from Lucy, knowing he's about to have his ass handed to him by a tiny woman, but his grip tightens on her hips.

"She's Makenzie." I set the empty glass on the coffee table and sink further into my pillow nest so I can enjoy the smack down. I've never had the opportunity to witness this side of their relationship up close and personal. To see the power she truly holds over him.

Lucy's wide eyes dart between us again, awaiting further explanation.

"*Makenzie*," I repeat slowly, giving her a pointed stare and a match to light the fire.

"Like the singer?" Her voice goes call-the-dogs high. "The actual superstar?" Her dark eyebrows pull together. "I thought she's from Ohio. Tatum is Makenzie?"

I nod once, disregarding the Ohio comment.

Rock leans farther away from his wife, but his hold on her isn't tight enough. She explodes to her feet and gets right up in his face, her scowl hot enough to draw beads of sweat from his pores.

Jabbing a sharp fingernail into his stomach, she says in an eerily calm voice, "We've been together for *years*, and you never once thought to tell me your *best friend* is in love with the most famous singer in the world? I gave birth to your child, you fucker. I squirted an enema in your ass that time you couldn't take a shit after surgery."

I'm smothering my laughs with a throw pillow, but quickly shut up when Lucy shouts at me, "No!"

She sets her sights on Rock again, raising that single finger. "Time out, big guy," is all she says. And my big, brutish friend fucking *trembles*.

Marcella's crying now, all red in the face and wormy on her stomach. The energy shift between her parents must've woken her.

Lucy scoops her up and announces, "My daughter and I are leaving."

She rummages in the diaper bag for a bottle, then hauls Marcella out the back door to the porch swing. Rock and I watch her for a minute as she settles into a rhythmic swaying, her features now relaxed as she feeds their daughter.

Rock lifts his shirt to wipe the sweat off his forehead. The man's freckles are so packed together, it's like he has a year-round suntan, though right now his whole face is bright red.

"Damn. The rest of the weekend is gonna suck. No sex for me." *Called it.*

By his glum expression, I can tell he's not being melodramatic. He's cut off. And I have a feeling his punishment for keeping this major secret from Lucy is far from over.

After a prolonged silence where both of us sulk over women, Rock asks, "So, how do you feel?"

"You wanna talk *feelings*?" I ask, incredulous.

"I'm serious, man. You heard Lucy. You've been in love with Tatum—"

"You probably told her that, prick."

"—since day one. You never got over her. Now she's coming home. So, yes, I wanna know how that makes you feel, asshole."

I stare at him, mouth agape. Speechless. Are middle school coaches trained to discuss feelings these days? I mean, I guess that could've been helpful when we were thirteen and didn't know jack about dealing with hormones or processing emotions. But I don't need him bringing that shit into my house.

"She ain't my business," I say, feigning indifference.

Rock glances around at my house, up at the unfinished loft, and shakes his head. Exasperated, he says, "Man, if you say that again in my lifetime, I'll put you through a fucking wall."

He could do it too. He played tight end in college, on track for the NFL, until a horrific knee injury ended his football career. I stopped playing sports after eighth grade.

"I was there, man," he says. "Through the worst of the worst. She messed you up bad, and you never dealt with it. So how are you gonna play this?"

I pluck at my bottom lip and think. Here's where things get tricky. I refuse to let Tatum run me out of my town, although I hardly ever make a public appearance. The times I do, I definitely don't want to cross paths with her. I can't. It won't end well for either of us. Me, especially. But this is my goddamn territory, and I need to plant my flag.

Am I still in love with her? What's the opposite of love? Because that's how I feel in this exact moment, knowing she plans to stroll into town like she has a right to be here after driving over my heart a thousand times, grinding it to dust, and letting it blow away in the wind. Fuck her. And fuck whatever she's been through.

"I'm gonna work. A lot," I tell Rock, conceding the loss without attaching my metaphorical flag to the damn pole. My instinct is to duck, cover, or evade. The winter months are usually slow, workwise, but I'll deal with that issue later. "Then she'll move on again, and everything will be back to normal."

He lets out a resigned huff and runs a hand through his fiery hair. "Whatever, man. You're an idiot."

Once upon a time, yes, I was. The biggest idiot on the planet, in fact. But fool me once and all that.

5

TATUM

ME

I'm bored.

MAISY

It's a boring town.

ME

Wow. Thanks for the pep talk.

MAISY

Any time.

GRAHAM

Ignore her. She's in a mood.

ME

Moody Maisy

MAISY

We have work to do.

GRAHAM

Mini Maisy

ME

YES! Mini Maisy. I can put her in my pocket.

GRAHAM

She twisted my nipple. No more teasing
about her size.

ME

Sorry, Maiz. Love you.

MAISY

No worries, Tiny Tits Tate.

GRAHAM

HAHAHA! I'll take a T-shirt, please. Size
sexy.

GRAHAM

<GIF of a wood plank with big eyes>

ME

Ugh. Get to work. Bye.

Emails give me a major headache. My personal inbox is flooded with them. From the record label, my attorney, my accountant. A single communication from Bette with her termination notice sneers at me, like her face the last time I saw her.

Maisy read and responded to some emails in my absence, ensuring the handful of people on my payroll got their money —her included. The majority of correspondence relates to matters Bette handled as my manager. If I don't understand half of the business crap, it's likely Maisy didn't either.

I respond to my attorney with a request to schedule a video conference, figuring I need to wrap my head around the ruins of my career and what my options are. Switching over to the email account for my fans, which I've been putting off, I nearly keel over. Thousands remain unread. It'll take months to read through them and sort the good from the bad.

With a groan, I snap the laptop shut and scan my tiny bedroom in Aunt Pam's house, searching for something else to do. I've already unpacked, cleaned the entire house, and put up the Christmas decorations. Four days in hiding, and I've run out of chores to pass the time.

My first night here, I worked up the courage to open Instagram and spent an hour scrolling through the comments on the statement Maisy wrote for me. The majority of people were loving, kind, and supportive. But no matter the enormity of the outpouring of love, those few hateful comments sprinkled throughout are enough to damage a person's psyche.

Insecurity and self-doubt take root much quicker and deeper than confidence and strength. And self-doubt now has me questioning everything.

When I was a young naïve teen, all I wanted to do was share my music. I just happened to have a decent voice to showcase my songwriting. Performing is fun, sure, but the real high comes from the shared emotion blanketing the smallest venue or largest arena—the connection between song and audience.

From as far back as I can remember, I understood the power of words. How they're used to soothe, sting, bring joy, express love, break hearts. My childhood poems became angsty, pre-teen lyrics. At thirteen, I learned to play guitar and discovered the sense of euphoria from crafting melodies and knowing when you've found the perfect hook to reel people in.

For me, it's all about creation—about the satisfaction and sense of accomplishment from drawing emotion from the listener. I yearn to revive that creative headspace and start writing again. If anything, I need the therapeutic release I get from writing, now more than ever.

Aunt Pam walks past my bedroom door then doubles back when she catches me staring into space. She's been gone all day. In fact, she spends a good amount of time with her various clubs and committees away from the house, no longer the homebody she was when I first moved in with her. Suddenly having a teenager to raise forced her to engage with other parents and become more involved in the community. That involvement didn't stop after I graduated and moved away.

From the hallway, she asks, "Bored already?"

"Just thinking." Shoving the laptop off my lap, I slump my shoulders and jut my bottom lip out.

She eyes me expectantly. "About?"

After a staring at her for beat, I ask, "What if I've lost the music? What if I'm no longer worthy of my fans?"

She sinks into the bean bag tucked in the corner of my bedroom, which hasn't changed much since I left. A white queen-size bed, nightstands, and a desk are crammed into the small space decorated in monochromatic shades of blue. What's missing is my giant cork board of concert ticket stubs and pictures with friends. I guess removing the memorabilia was what Maisy meant by getting my room ready for me.

"Don't be silly," she replies. "You once told me that writing music helps you process your feelings. With all the changes in your life right now, I'm guessing you'll have lots of new feelings to work through. People relate to your songs, sweetie. That's why they flocked to you in the first place."

"Bette said it was because I'm marketable," I grumble, thinking of Bette's priorities after she discovered me.

My aunt rolls her eyes, her voice dripping with disdain. "Bette took one look at you and saw dollar signs."

It's no secret Aunt Pam never liked my former manager. She has strong feelings about the way Bette changed and exploited my appearance for commercial appeal and financial gain.

"I don't know what I want anymore." I sigh and drag my

hands down my face. This break from performing has forced me to admit many truths to myself, so I confess one of them to Aunt Pam. "I wonder what life would be like if I didn't have to share it with Makenzie."

"Give it a try," she says, lifting a delicate shoulder. "Think of this break as a clean slate. And let *Tatum* decide who wields the chalk."

As simple as she makes it sound, the thought of ending Makenzie terrifies me. Not because I'll miss being her, but because I'll disappoint the millions of fans who believe in her and have supported her over the years. A deeper fear niggles at my brain as I consider *her* versus *me*.

What if Makenzie stole my identity? What if Tatum doesn't exist anymore? I've been putting on the face of someone else for my entire adult life, at least to the public. It wouldn't surprise me if my alter ego's mask is near impossible to scrub off.

"Now." Aunt Pam hikes a leg to lever herself off the bean bag. "How about some dinner? You can get out of the house for a bit and grab us a burger from Bruno's."

My face scrunches up at that idea. The last time I stepped foot in Bruno's, back in high school, the smoky bar had sticky floors and reeked of stale beer and armpits. I'm a little skeptical about eating food from there.

"It's changed," she assures me. "Many things around here have. And so will your outfit before you leave this house."

She floats from the room as I glance down at myself. Wool socks, boxer shorts, and my dad's favorite flannel shirt —which now has a million holes in it—are perfectly fine for hunkering down. But I wouldn't be caught dead in public dressed this way, so I give myself a pep talk while changing into black leggings, an oversized sweater, and sneakers. Wishing I felt as comfortable and relaxed on the inside as I look on the outside, I take a deep breath and step onto the porch.

It's time to face Walford.

~

My aunt's neighborhood sits behind the main strip in town, so it's only a short trek to reach all the businesses along Main Street. Christmas decorations adorn the shop displays and storefronts, setting the holiday mood. Garland and twinkling lights wrap around the lamp posts lining the brick sidewalks. The only thing missing from the picturesque, wintry setting is the snow.

When I push through the door at Bruno's, my jaw drops at the overhaul done to the place. The long bar made of wood and gleaming brass appears to be the only original fixture remaining. But nothing surprises me more than the muscled, tattooed man behind said bar.

"Jensen?" My eyes become the size of dinner plates.

Jensen's wearing dark jeans and a tight T-shirt with a bulldog printed on the chest. Bruno's Bar shares its name with every pet bulldog the owner has ever had. The bulldog is also Walford High School's mascot. But that's beside the point because Jensen Holloway is all *M-A-N*.

"Tate!" With a bright grin on his scruffy face, he hustles around the bar and crushes me in a bear hug. "Let me get a look at you." He grabs my shoulders and moves me to arm's length so he can examine me from head to toe. "Looking good, darlin'. Was hoping you'd stop by."

I'm shell-shocked by this gorgeous hunk who's now, what, thirty-one? Thirty-two? The pectoral muscles, the biceps, the ink. Thick, dark wavy hair flowing past his ears and those piercing green eyes that see inside your soul. And ever the charmer with that smooth, Texas drawl. He's a hottie, for sure.

"You still work here?" I ask the obvious, given his black shirt with the Bruno's logo. And the fact he was manning the bar not five seconds ago. Jensen started working at Bruno's when he finished high school, long before I moved to Walford.

His grin stretches with pride. "I own the place. Bought it a few years ago and made some changes."

With his hands gripping my shoulders, I crane my neck to assess the space. "I can see that."

The scuffed hardwoods are gone, leaving behind stained and polished concrete floors. Bar-height tables are scattered around, and a small stage sits opposite the front door. The aesthetic is more Restoration Hardware than the seedy joint I remember. It's incredible. One thing is glaringly obvious though: the lack of customers.

"Is business good?" I ask.

How did I not know Jensen owns Bruno's Bar? Oh, that's right. I banned Maisy and Aunt Pam from talking about anything or anyone in Walford because my regret outweighed my curiosity. *Geez, I'm an a-hole.*

Jensen chuckles, placing a hand on my back as he ushers me to a barstool. "Business is great. Everyone will be here after the football game. Have a seat, and I'll get you a drink. Beer? Cocktail?"

"Water is fine," I say, climbing on the stool.

His steps falter, as does the smile on his face. "Shit. I'm sorry."

I wave a dismissive hand. "Don't be. It wasn't as bad as the media made it seem," I lie, having no desire to delve into my recovery.

He grabs a water from the fridge, twists the cap off, and

hands me the bottle. "You hungry?"

"Aunt Pam sent me over to pick up burgers."

"I'll put the order in." Testing the stretch limit in his tight jeans, he saunters to the kitchen and returns a few moments later with a towel draped over his shoulder and a soda in hand. He cracks open the can and takes a sip. "How long are you sticking around?"

"I'm not sure yet. Maybe a couple of months or so? Can't leave the guys unsupervised at my house for too long."

"Guys?" He arches an eyebrow as thick as the edge in his tone.

"Marcus and Judge. Friends, but also my bodyguards. They live with me and Maisy in California." I assume by his narrowed eyes he's not too keen on my roommate situation.

"Is Maisy staying in California?"

"She's in Austin for a few months. Got a job working on a film production."

"Really? Great. That's great for her. Really great." He must catch the weird face I make at his reaction because he quickly collects himself and takes several gulps of soda.

"Yeah," I agree. "She's earned it. I'm excited to watch her career take off."

"Is she the one responsible for this hair?" He tugs a lock of my hair, which is a little on the greasy side and needs a wash. And my roots are showing. "I'm still not used to the blonde," he says.

"I'm thinking about dying it back to my natural color. Makenzie doesn't belong in Walford."

That statement alone kills our attempt at light-hearted chit chat. A shadow briefly passes over his face, snuffing out his happy demeanor as the whispers of shared ghosts taunt us. The intensity in Jensen's gaze signals what's coming, so I brace for impact.

Clasping both hands together around his soda can, he rests his forearms on the bar and asks gruffly, "You see him yet?"

A big swallow of water does nothing to soothe my suddenly dry throat. "Nope. I've been busy." It's a lie, and Jensen knows it.

He studies me, probably assessing my mental state and how much information he should divulge. "He ain't the same, Tate. It was really rough in the beginning, and he's managed to make his way. But don't expect to find the Jake you knew."

My Jake was the sweetest boy with a giving heart and a big, dimpled grin that lit up the room. We were kindred spirits. Soul mates, if you believe in such a thing. And the kind of love we had could only end in one of two ways: forever or total devastation. We got the latter, and it's all my fault.

"I know he's not the same boy I left behind. And I'm aware I can't avoid him forever." Tears teeter on my lower lashes before taking the plunge. "But the guilt...the guilt has crushed me, Jensen. I'm so scared of facing him."

He hands me a napkin to wipe my wet cheeks. "We both made mistakes," he says, keeping his voice low. "Our decision to keep quiet seemed like the best thing at the time. But watching him self-destruct and saying nothing? Hardest thing I've ever done." Shaking his head, he sets his drink aside. "When he learns the truth, it could very well cost me a brother. But all choices have consequences, and I'm ready to accept mine. I've kept this secret for too long, Tate. I can't watch Jake live in the unknown anymore. It's hurting all of us."

"When did you get so chatty?" I tease, a lame effort to defuse the tension weaving between us, but it has the opposite effect.

Anger tightens his brows, forming a deep crease between them. "This ain't a joke, Tatum."

"I know it's not a joke, *Jensen*."

When planning my return to Walford, I considered the probability of confrontation, which I avoid at all costs. The people in my and Jake's shared past believed a love like ours could only be found in the movies. We represented hope after so much suffering in this town, and everyone thought we'd take the world by storm together, making Walford proud.

Coming here, I expected to be called to judgment by those who rooted for us. By those whom I failed. And I doubt Jensen will be the only person to corner me and demand answers.

We glare at each other until I deflate and lower my head, focusing on my hands as I twist the napkin around my fingers. "When you came to California—"

"Don't." His sharp command cuts in a swift slice down to my bones.

"I'm sorry. For everything," I whisper. My pleading eyes meet his hard ones. "Are you gonna tell him about that?"

Jensen inhales a steadying breath and splays his hands on the polished wood. "Jake deserves all our truths, Tatum."

He's right. Jake deserves answers. I robbed him of so much, and I can't give any of it back. I don't expect his forgiveness, and I won't ask for it.

Cheryl once said, *"The path forward begins with forgiving yourself and being okay with not receiving forgiveness from others. It's not something you can command or have any right to receive. Choosing to be at peace with your decisions, your mistakes, and the consequences they bear is the limit of your power."*

For someone who hates disappointing people and always

strives to make things right—except in Jake's case, where I avoid reality—this was the hardest lesson to grasp.

"Then how about I tell him mine, and you tell him yours. Your side of the story should come from you alone."

It's not my place to expose any role Jensen played in hurting Jake. My sense of guilt will only compound if I shift the blame to someone else.

The tension locking up Jensen's shoulders dissipates along with the strain in his eyes. "Do you ever do anything for selfish reasons?"

"What I did ten years ago was pretty damn selfish. It ruined everything."

"No. It wasn't. And it was my doing too. My job was to protect him and make sure he got everything he worked hard for. He would've blown up his future if he knew what happened." He spears a hand into his hair and sighs. "Maybe we could've handled it differently but, at heart, your idea to keep it a secret was a selfless choice."

"I don't—"

A gust of cool air interrupts my retort. We glance at the open door where a girl struggles to fit through with a giant box in her toned arms.

"I'm here, boss! Got the Christmas decorations from storage!" she shouts.

"Standing right here, Ainsley. No need to holler." Jensen makes his way over and takes the box from the girl, jerking his chin in her direction while addressing me. "This is Ainsley. She's new."

I smooth the stress from my features, unable to do anything about my puffy eyelids, and greet her with a practiced smile. "Nice to meet you. I'm Tatum."

Her chestnut ponytail swings as she brushes the long bangs out of her face, then she freezes and gapes at me. She can't be older than twenty or twenty-one, which puts her right smack in the demographic of my fan base. Judging by the way her body sways, I'm guessing she's a member of the official Makenzie fan club.

"I'm such a huge fan!" she blurts, her cheeks flushing a deep shade of pink.

"Ainsley," Jensen warns.

Ainsley takes several calming breaths that sound like something you'd learn in a Lamaze class and steadies her shaky legs. "I'm so sorry. You came out of nowhere. I wasn't ready."

I bite back a snicker. She's adorable. I'd call her innocent and sweet, but the orange-red lipstick and matching nail polish hint at her having a rebellious edge.

"You'll get used to it," he assures her. "And remember, she's just Tatum in Walford."

"Yes, sir!" she shouts with the gusto of a soldier addressing a drill sergeant.

Jensen recoils as disgust crinkles his handsome face. "Don't call me *sir*. It's weird. Now, go grab Tatum's order from the kitchen while I put this in the back."

As she scurries away, he turns to me. "Don't be a stranger. Leave your number on a napkin so I can text you mine. That way you'll have it if you need anything."

I smirk at him. "Does that line usually work for you?"

Back in the day, Jake and I gave him grief over the cheesy pickup lines he practiced on me before he'd go out with his friends. No matter how awful his lines were, he always managed to have a pretty girl on his arm at the end of the night.

He rolls his eyes, mutters, "Some things never change," and stalks down an unlit hallway.

Jensen's wrong though. *Everything* has changed.

6

JAKE

I've been avoiding Walford like the plague. On the drive home Thursday, I stopped a few towns over to buy groceries and barely made it to the football game on time. Then ducked out exactly when the buzzer sounded in the final quarter to evade Rock's pleas for me to join him at Bruno's to commiserate the team's 42–6 ass whooping.

With the weather being decent, I spent yesterday building a fence along the dirt road on the eastern border of my land. Today, I plan to install a gate at the hidden entrance leading to the northern end of the property.

Parked in a shallow ditch, I set up my tools and supplies in the bed of my truck only to discover I don't have the bolts for the gate hinges. With the sun shining and not a cloud in sight, the day's too pretty to work indoors, so I gather my courage and sneak into town to buy bolts at Menchy's.

The hardware store claims a prime location at the end of Main Street where the road starts to bend. From floor-to-ceiling windows on two sides of the building, Franklin Menchy keeps a watchful eye on Walford.

The bell over the door jingles when I walk inside.

Menchy's hunched on a stool at the cash register, chewing a toothpick while engrossed in a crossword puzzle. He dips his chin to his chest and eyes me over the reading glasses perched on the tip of his nose. "Whatcha need, kid?"

He's more than familiar with me. Besides coming in nearly every week to pick up supplies, I stocked shelves for him every Sunday night throughout high school. He's had the same shock of grey hair and a scowl on his brown weathered face for as long as I've known him. He could easily be a doppelgänger of that old boxing promoter from the '80s and '90s. Everyone calls Menchy by his last name only, and there's a long-running debate in town over how old he is.

"Hey, Menchy. Need some bolts for a gate." I shake the brass hinge in my hand to prove I have actual business here.

"Mm-hmm." He pulls a new toothpick from his apron pocket and returns to the crossword.

With our titillating conversation at an end, I begin my search for bolts. Thinking it's smart to buy things for other projects I'll work on during my self-imposed isolation, I snag a shopping basket and roam the aisles. The low shelving allows Menchy to monitor Main Street from anywhere inside the store.

I glance up from the assortment of blue painter's tape near the front window, and that's when I see her. The girl who ripped my soul from my body. She's walking along the sidewalk across the street, a moment I've envisioned a million times.

The world around me slows to a crawl. I register nothing but my shallow breaths as I catalog her every movement, like a series of still frames flashing on a screen at half speed.

Tatum glances up from her phone as an older woman approaches her. The woman waves, and Tatum fakes a smile in greeting. They exchange a few words before going their separate ways.

She dyed her hair. The honey-brown tresses I remember from when she was mine cascade in soft waves past her shoulders and reach the middle of her back. The sunlight enhances her golden highlights, giving her hair a satin sheen. My fingers gripping the shopping basket flex at the memory of the silky strands sifting through them.

Full healthy cheeks accompany her smile. They're the same rosy pink as the tip of her nose, flushed from the chill in the air. Other than being a bit thinner than she was the last time I held her, she's a replica of the girl commandeering my every thought, but she's not a teenage girl anymore. Still five-and-a-half feet of mostly legs, she's a woman now. An effortlessly gorgeous woman.

How many nights have I dreamed of her appearing before me unexpectedly? In those dreams, we'd rush into each other's arms and make solemn vows between frantic kisses to never be apart again. On the other hand, how many hours did my mind drift off during long drives, crafting all the spiteful words I'd say if I saw her again? I imagined myself drawing on the depths of my pain to hurl the most hurtful insults at her so she'd suffer an ounce of what I have suffered.

Instead of reacting in either of those ways, I'm frozen in place. Unable to tear my eyes away. She's beautiful—breathtaking, even—and I hate her more for looking like my Tatum again.

Like the first time I met her, Tatum's wearing skinny jeans and Converse sneakers. Except today, she has on a tan Camp Heartwood sweatshirt. My stomach drops at the sight of it, and a distinct *kerplunk* sound echoes in my chest cavity. A tidal wave of emotions washes over me. The primary feelings warring for dominance are extreme longing and extremely pissed off.

I can't believe she's really here. In the flesh. Flesh that I've longed to touch and taste and sink into. Soft lavender-scented flesh that my own skin itches to feel when I fall asleep at night and wake in the morning.

Tatum opens the door to the coffee shop, The Drip, and disappears inside, taking all my motor functions and fantasies of retaliation along with her.

How is she able to pierce through my defenses so easily? From a single sighting, I'm ready to abandon my hatred and race across the street into her arms. Am I really so weak?

"Hmm."

I slowly turn my head toward the sound. Menchy hovers right next to me—close enough that I smell his cinnamon toothpick—and gazes at the coffee shop. He strokes his stubbled chin thoughtfully but says nothing.

After absently staring at his profile for longer than what's considered socially acceptable, I ditch my shopping basket and flee the store through the exit leading to the alley. Thankfully, I parked along the side of the building opposite Main Street, so I'm able to avoid being seen by anyone.

I need to get the fuck out of town before I do something very, very stupid.

Sitting in the dirt—legs stretched out and ankles crossed—I lean against my truck tire and glare at the unfinished gate like it's solely to blame for all my problems.

Tires crunch on gravel in the distance. A plume of dust signals an approaching vehicle before the grill of Jensen's black Jeep Wrangler comes into view. He stops several feet away and climbs out, a plastic shopping bag in each hand.

"Brought your shit from Menchy's." He tosses the bags on the ground near my boots and remains standing, hands on his hips.

"I'll pay you back." I return my focus to the unfinished gate, unable to meet his eyes.

"He started a tab for you."

"Thanks."

"You okay?"

I attempt a shrug but lack the energy to put much effort into it. "Don't know what you mean."

Round and round we go, carrying on with the game of denial I've trained myself to play when anyone attempts to bring up Tatum in conversation. It's worked well for me in the past. They usually drop the subject and let me be. But now that she's returned, my friends and loved ones are done indulging me by playing along.

"Menchy told me what happened," he hedges.

I curl my fingers into fists, suppressing a wince when the skin stretches over the knuckles of my right hand. Hopefully, Jensen won't notice the torn flesh. Tree trunks don't have much give.

"For a man who doesn't say much, he sure likes to gossip," I respond in a flat tone.

"He's protective. Likes to keep an eye on things."

I scoff. "I'm no threat to anyone here."

Jensen's combat boots shuffle side to side in my periphery. "Yeah, well. Maybe someone in town is a threat to you."

My eyes trail upward and land on his concerned face. Gritting my teeth, I say, "I'm fine. Everyone just needs to back...the fuck...off."

It's a good thing that oak tree bore the brunt of my wrath.

If Jensen had shown up a couple of hours ago, slinging his worry around, I might've punched him instead. He finally catches sight of my bloody knuckles but, thankfully, doesn't comment on them.

With a heavy sigh, he pulls a folding camp chair from the bed of my truck. I forgot I had it with me. Otherwise, I wouldn't be sitting on the unforgiving ground for hours with an aching tailbone.

He plants himself in my direct line of sight with his elbows on his knees, loose hands dangling between them. "I talked to her."

"When?" The question comes out more demanding than I intend it to. More desperate.

"Thursday. During the game. She came by for a burger." He links his fingers together, a telltale sign of a forthcoming lecture. "Both of you are hurting, Jake. You don't want to talk to her? Fine. Whatever. But you at least need to acknowledge that she's here. Because she ain't going nowhere for a while. So stop hiding and just rip off the Band-Aid."

I jerk forward, my fingers digging deeper into my thighs as my voice rises with every word. "It's not a Band-Aid. It's a fucking tourniquet. She left me bleeding out, and I can't stop it because no one will give me any goddamn answers about why she bailed!"

The pain in my chest is so acute, I hardly feel the liquid on my cheeks. When was the last time I cried? I'll admit to being an emotional man—there's no shame in it—but I locked that shit up tight a long time ago when I learned emotions aren't necessary for survival.

Years have passed in a purgatory of unknowns. Does it matter now why Tatum disappeared from my life? Why she chose to leave me? She took everything from me except this body. This carcass, abandoned for the vultures to pick apart.

I drop my head back against the tire, exhausted from battling this heartache. My voice is rough, ragged—same as my life—when I say, "She left me for dead."

"You still love her." Jensen speaks this truth, knowing history has proven time and again my go-to rebuttal is a resounding no. But that's a lie I no longer wish to tell myself. Or him.

"I can't stop." The quiet admission is freeing. Saying it aloud eases some of the extra weight I've been lugging around. Turns out denial is some heavy shit.

"Yeah. I get it," he says.

I glance at him, curious about his implied understanding and wondering if it was an errant slip. I've never known Jensen to be in love with anyone. But he avoids my gaze and studies his unlaced boots.

"Will she come to me?" My voice trembles on a taut wire between hope and fear. He got to her first, so maybe he can prepare me for what's coming.

"Nah," he replies, shaking his head. "You know how she is about confrontation. And she probably doesn't know where you live." He gives me a knowing look.

It's obvious to everyone the house I bought might as well have Tatum's name spelled out on the rooftop in flashing neon lights. A fact I refuse to acknowledge because, again…denial.

I'll admit he's right about Tatum's fear of confrontation. She'll play peacemaker when the people she cares about are at odds, but she'll run far away from a direct fight. If she didn't have Maisy, who takes shit from no one, beside her all these years, I'm not sure she could have survived the cutthroat music business.

"I'll think about talking to her," I assure him.

He stands and reaches out a hand to pull me off the

ground. After I wipe the dirt off my jeans, he draws me into a tight hug.

"I'm here for you, Jake. Whatever you need."

"Thanks," I tell him honestly as we pull apart.

Jensen may annoy me when he tries to cross the line between the roles of brother and father, but I'm lucky to have him on my side. No better man walks the earth. On top of being my biggest supporter, he lives each day like he owes the people of Walford a debt after his best friend died in a tragic accident, sending the whole town into mourning. Jensen blames himself and constantly strives to fill the hole left in the wake of the tragedy.

The two of us have suffered enough loss, and our neighbors and friends have stood by us through it all. Which is why neither of us have ventured far from home. Although, I did consider it once.

"You heading out again before Christmas?" he asks. "The boys wanna throw you a birthday party."

"I leave tomorrow for a ten-day stretch. Last one before the holidays."

He raises his eyebrows. "I'm guessing you did that on purpose?"

"Seemed like a good plan at the time," I admit. Hard as I tried to convince them otherwise, none of my clients liked the idea of me slinking around their ranches at Christmas, disrupting their precious family time. So, ten days will be all the reprieve from Tatum's presence I get. "And tell them no party. I can't handle another year of strippers dressed like elves. Brody needs new ideas."

Jensen points a finger at me. "You tell Brody to keep his sights off Ainsley. She's too young and sweet for the likes of him. I've threatened his life, but he'll only listen to you."

Ainsley's the new waitress Jensen hired last month. Her

move to town came at the perfect time after one of his long-term employees up and quit with little notice.

I snort. "I wish. Brody only listens to the devils sitting on his shoulders."

Our easy laughter relieves some of the stress crowding my body.

Without warning, Jensen punches me in the chest. "Alright, then. See ya 'round."

"See ya," I say as he climbs in his Jeep.

After he peels out, purposely kicking up a cloud of dust in my face, I pack up all my tools and head home, resigned to finish the gate another day.

7

TATUM

A cold front came through a few days ago, plunging the temperatures to levels more fitting for the holiday season. Aunt Pam invited me to join her at the Christmas Eve bake sale taking place at the public library today. Like I've done with all her invitations—her attempts to get me to socialize and reintegrate myself into the fabric of Walford—I declined. Instead, I wrap the last of the presents on the living room floor near the lit fireplace.

Maisy promised to visit before the new year, and I hope she stays the night when she visits because I'm craving some quality time with one of my besties. If I had a driver's license, I'd be in Austin stalking her and Graham on set as often as possible. I *can* drive but haven't had to in so long, I let my license lapse. My passport has been sufficient identification for travel during tours. Of course, that's no longer a concern.

Jensen and I have texted a few times. He asks if I need anything and when I'm coming to his bar again. My replies are always "no" and "soon." It's not that I don't want to see him or learn about everything he's accomplished. I just can't handle being cornered into another conversation about Jake. I've replayed the one we had in my head many times since we talked at Bruno's.

Mulling over everything he said about Jake saddens me, and I have enough melancholy already with the Dark Days rapidly approaching. I'm clinging to holiday cheer with white-knuckled determination, desperate for any reason to feel joy before sorrow consumes me for weeks on end.

The fake tree, loaded with ornaments and too many lights, leans slightly to the right next to the cream-colored sofa. Poorly hand-sewn stockings hang from the mantle, and holiday music blares from the Bluetooth speaker on the coffee table. I hum along, wondering why I never recorded a Christmas album, when my laptop rings with an incoming video chat. A glance at the screen shows my two favorite California boys calling, so I turn down the music and click the touchpad to accept the call.

Genuine happiness tugs my lips into a smile when Marcus's face appears. As usual, he's not smiling. Taking up the space beside him is a large black-and-white image of my face with the words "Have You Seen Me?" in block letters on a white background. It reminds me of a missing person photo you'd find on a milk carton.

I frown. "What am I looking at?"

Marcus summons patience with a deep inhale before he replies. "Judge's new apron."

Sure enough, the edge of Judge's arm moves, then the image disappears off screen. He has quite the collection of aprons, but this one might be my new favorite.

Chuckling, I ask, "Did you guys get the presents I sent?"

"They arrived yesterday."

"Don't open them yet!" I rush the words out. "Tell Judge he only has to wait one more day."

Marcus shoots a *told you so* glance off to the side, presumably toward Judge, and clucks his tongue. "He opened one already. I hid the others."

"Thanks," I say. "Are you still working the gala tonight?"

Marcus despises sitting around with nothing to do, so he and Judge are taking on local security gigs to fill their time. They won't leave me until I make them, and while they seem satisfied with our situation for now, I can't keep everyone waiting in limbo for long.

"Yep," he answers. "But enough about that. I called to update you. Would've used the phone but Judge demanded proof of life." Something small bounces off his head, but he doesn't even flinch. "We've had a few perimeter breaches that set off the alarms. Activity is dying down, but there's a group camped out hoping you might show up for the holidays. So, you're better off where you are."

I might disagree with him at this point. Dodging a single person in Walford is far more stressful than hiding from a horde of paps.

"I'll set up a weekly call with you and Maisy while we monitor the situation. We all need to be in sync in case either of you decides to come home or travel for any reason. Good?"

"Good," I answer.

It's not like Marcus will accept any other response. He's the best at his job and leaves no room for error or argument.

He gives an affirmative nod. "Good. Judge, say bye to Tatum."

Judge's fingers appear, wiggle, and vanish. He's probably too emotional to show his face.

"Talk soon," Marcus says.

"Merry Christmas!" I shout as the screen goes dark. I gaze at it wistfully, wishing I was home enjoying the holidays with the guys and Maisy, when a light knock sounds on the screen door in the kitchen.

The moment I pull open the interior wood door, a loud gasp escapes me. Everything grinds to a halt, my beating heart included.

~

Jake and I stare at each other through the mesh screen as if we're both surprised deer caught in each other's headlights. He's aware I'm staying here, so *what is happening right now*?

Our gazes remain locked as a hurricane of emotions consumes me. Panic. Relief. Sorrow. Jubilation. It's such a mind fuck that I stand here completely numb and unmoving, aside from the frantic butterflies wreaking havoc in my stomach. I'm not sure if I'm going to faint or vomit.

"Hey," he says, his beautiful eyes never leaving mine.

The expression on his face lacks warmth or friendliness, but with that one word from his soft lips—after all this time—I'm seconds away from collapsing to the floor in a fetal position and bawling like a baby. I'm hanging on by a very flimsy thread here.

I can do this. I can speak to him. *Use your words, Tatum.* "Hey." We hold our stare until I gather my wits and ask, "Are you here for Aunt Pam?"

"No."

His answer sends my heart into a flurry. He came to see *me*. And the silly little girl inside who believes in unicorns and Santa Claus grasps onto the tiny ray of hope the two-letter response dangles in front of me.

The mounting pressure behind my eyes threatens to unleash years of heartache. A tear escapes, and I quickly wipe it away and press my trembling hand on the screen door in invitation. When he grabs the handle to let himself in, I retreat a few paces, allowing us both some distance and breathing room. With short hesitant steps, he crosses the threshold and leans stiffly against the wall, his hands buried deep in his coat pockets.

Throughout our cautious micromovements, we maintain eye contact and study each other. Watching for any indication that one of us might break. My single tear is all I'll allow. Not because he doesn't deserve my tears, but because I can sense he has no use for them.

Assessing eyes quickly pass over the length of my body, then return to my face. If he stood before me a few months ago, I would've ducked my head in shame. Today, however, the sickly pallor and vacant eyes are gone, leaving behind a healthier version of me.

Taking advantage of our silence, my gaze drifts over him as well. He's at least six feet tall now. His thick hair is longer on top and curls slightly at the ends, though it's still short on the sides. He never did like it touching his ears. I'm desperate to run my fingers through the wavy strands.

His stony face doesn't detract from his gorgeous features. The sharper stubbled jawline. The shallow indent from the dimple in his right cheek that never fully disappears when he's not smiling. Evidence of stress and exhaustion hardens his green eyes, but they're no less captivating. A storm of pain whirls in their depths, which he attempts to mask with a false indifference. It's impossible for Jake to truly be indifferent toward anyone. He feels too deeply.

I'm in a dream, seeing this manly version of him in a Henley, jeans, and cowboy boots, and never want it to end. Closing my eyes, I breathe in the scent of his leather jacket mixed with his familiar earthy cologne, and I allow space for my most cherished memory to run free in my mind.

"My bones are freezing," I complain through chattering teeth.

"We can sit in the truck. I'll crank the heater," Jake offers hopefully.

We're tucked under a mound of blankets in the bed of his pickup at our secret spot. Technically, we're trespassing on the Hamiltons' land. If they're aware of our frequent visits, they've never said anything.

The truck is parked on the crest of a low ridge at the northern edge of their property. The view of the hills, the open sky, the quiet…there's nowhere like it I've ever seen or been. Jake and I come here often to talk about our childhoods, our dead parents, our dreams. And we've never told a soul about our special place.

"No. I don't want to miss it," I say.

It's a cloudless night. A meteor shower will begin soon, and I'm excited to witness one firsthand. Sure, I could enjoy the show through a pane of glass, but there's something about being in the open, beneath the expanse of inky sky, that I find humbling.

"You'd think, being from Ohio, you'd know how to dress for cold weather," he says.

I have on jeans, a long-sleeved tee, and a lightweight jacket. Not nearly enough layers for thirty-degree temperatures.

Jake removes his leather bomber jacket and the hooded Camp Heartwood sweatshirt he's wearing, leaving only the T-shirt underneath. He worked as a lifeguard at the camp last summer and has loads of merch branded with its name and logo. He slips his jacket back on and zips it up to his chin.

"Here," he says, offering me the sweatshirt.

I promptly tug it over my head, cinching the hood tightly

around my face and tying the strings. He chuckles at how silly I look, but I don't care. I need the extra layer.

"Thanks."

"Want some more coffee?"

I reply with a dramatic "yes, please."

He takes a few test sips from the thermos to confirm it's still hot, and a puff of fog escapes his mouth when he releases a contented sigh. "Perfect."

The boy loves his coffee. Strong black coffee. I mostly like the taste of it on his tongue when I kiss him, but I'll drink it when the need arises. Like now, when we're trying to stay awake and keep our blood flowing.

I grip the thermos with both hands, seeking any source of heat for my frozen fingers. Right as I glance up between sips, the first bright lights streak across the sky.

"It's happening!" I yell, jolting my arms and sloshing coffee onto the sweatshirt. "Shit." I frantically swipe at the wet fabric. He loves this shirt, and I hope I haven't ruined it.

Jake pauses the breaths he's blowing into his cupped hands. "Baby, don't worry about that. Look up or you'll miss it."

Baby. Before Christmas, I persuaded Jake to try the final dance number in *Dirty Dancing* with me. He ended up with a black eye. I ended up with a sprained wrist and a new nickname.

We tip our heads back and watch the breathtaking event in awe. At some point, the thermos disappeared from my hands, which now cling to his under the blankets as we snuggle close together, relishing the heat our bodies produce.

The trailing lights become more sporadic, marking the end of the show. My gaze remains on the sky until I sense Jake's eyes on me and turn my head, drawn by the intensity radiating from him.

"You're missing it," I whisper millimeters from his mouth.

"I haven't missed a thing."

He presses his warm lips to mine. When the tip of his tongue teases my lips, I open for him, and he grabs the sides of my face and angles my head to deepen the kiss. Our tongues glide together in a slow synchronized dance, the rhythm increasing as electricity sparks between us. We've had some heavy make-out sessions before, but tonight feels different somehow. Significant.

Heat sizzles through me, igniting me from the inside out. I wrap my arms around his torso and melt into him so we're as close as possible.

Untying the strings, he loosens my hood enough to slip his fingers inside and caress my neck. I shove the hood off to give him better access to my skin, which he takes advantage of by trailing his lips along my jaw to my ear. When his teeth graze my earlobe, his nose brushes a sensitive spot behind my ear, sending shivers down my spine. But I'm no longer freezing from the glacial air. I'm on *fire*.

I slide my hands beneath his shirt to explore the soft skin on his back and drag my fingernails across his stomach. He shudders in response.

Without breaking our kiss, we shift and stretch out, our bodies cocooned in a protective den of blankets. Layers of clothing are shed. As touches and kisses wander aimlessly, a need consumes me. A need so right and so true and so urgent, it burns in my throat when I whisper, "Jake."

He slowly lifts his head from my chest. The twinkling stars fill every inch of velvet sky behind him, casting a silvery glow on his dark hair. The same desperate need consuming me shines bright in his eyes.

His low raspy voice lights up my insides when he asks, "Are you sure?"

"Yes. I'm sure."

He rids us of our remaining clothes then carefully moves up my body until he's nestled between my legs. My breath hitches, and I try not to focus on the scary things I've heard about a girl's first time.

Resting on his forearms to keep the bulk of his weight off me, he cups my face again. His steady gaze is long and loving as he gently strokes his thumbs across my cheeks. Once he's satisfied with the certainty he finds in my eyes, he kisses me passionately as a distraction while he trails a hand down my body to join us together.

He's *right there,* and I draw in a deep breath when our lips separate. The green eyes locked reverently on mine promise love, protection, honesty, devotion…the future.

Jake whispers, "I'm sorry if this hurts at first. Just focus on the sky until the pain goes away."

We gave each other our virginities that night—gave away part of our whole selves—splitting our souls in two and each trading a half with vows of safekeeping. Standing before me now, Jake's tightly coiled muscles scream of my broken vow.

Something about his expression changes, briefly tempering the impassive stare, and I wonder if he's recalling the same memory playing out in my head. The flash of desire in his eyes reveals a glimpse of the boy who once loved me. The one hiding behind the dented armor he forged to deflect life's painful blows.

He's afraid—more afraid than I am—and he's at a disadvantage. At least I have all the facts. I'm fully aware of the damage I've caused and the damage yet to come.

My heartache deepens upon realizing the truth will only add to his torment. They say the truth sets us free. While that theory may apply to the truth teller, absolving him or her of guilt, I'm certain the receiver of soul-shattering truths would firmly disagree.

We've said less than ten words in the minutes since he arrived, so I break the strained silence. "How are you?"

"Alive."

Ouch.

The implication in his terse response hits its mark. At one point, Jake didn't know if I was alive or dead. That guilt column keeps on growing.

"It's good to see you," I offer. Because…what else? You can't exactly engage in small talk with someone who'd rather be anywhere other than in your presence.

He bites the inside of his cheek as he considers his next words. "Can't say the same."

Double ouch.

My brows pinch together in frustration. "What are you doing here, Jake?"

"Getting this little reunion out of the way so we can go on with coexisting. I heard you won't be here long, but I don't want to have to duck around corners and hide in my own home until you leave."

His answer wields no emotion, but the raspy voice I've longed to hear—made slightly deeper from time and maturity—brings me comfort nonetheless. The sentiment, however, rings loud and clear as it crashes against my ears. Walford is *his* home, and I don't belong here.

Jake's surliness shouldn't surprise me, but if I had my way, this meeting would go very differently. A little less blatant contempt from him, and a little more apologizing from me. Right now, an apology is the last thing he wants.

He's right though. We do have to coexist. And now that we've seen each other and talked, sort of, I can leave the house whenever I please without fear of running into him. This encounter is a blessing and dumpster fire rolled into one.

Resigned that our conversation is going no further, I concede. "Okay. I promise to stay out of your way. I'll be gone before you know it."

"Good," he says, already pushing open the door.

"Jake?" I softly call out.

He pauses with one foot on the porch and his back to me, shoulders bunched up to his ears.

"Happy birthday."

Another pause, then he strides away, letting the screen door bang shut in his wake.

Once he's gone, the adrenaline flees my body. I close the inner door, drift to the kitchen table on unsteady legs, and drop into a chair. Knowing this might have been our one and only interaction sends me into a tailspin of misery. The dam breaks, and I welcome the flood.

I rest my forehead on my folded arms and let the sobs come freely. The release is so cathartic that when I register an older song about being celebrated while coming home playing in the background, I laugh.

8

JAKE

I make it six paces along the side of the house before wedging myself between two dormant rose bushes and collapsing against the brick. It's broad daylight, and I don't need any witnesses to my breakdown.

My fist clutches the fabric of my shirt at my chest, and I will my racing heart to slow to a normal rhythm. Counting backward by threes from one hundred in my head, I release the shaky breath I held while in Tatum's presence.

Nothing went as planned. I had every intention of letting loose all the cruel words and fury I've amassed during those long drives when I spent hours and hours thinking and plotting. Then she opened the door, smelling of lavender and wearing a fucking onesie covered in snowmen—which is just so fucking *her*—and I froze.

When her tear fell, my first instinct was to reach for her, comfort her. Reassure her that everything will be okay now that we're here, together, like we should've been all along. I've invested years into constructing this callous imitation of a heart and, thankfully, I summoned enough strength to repress those desires. I refuse to soften at the first sign of her distress.

The physical draw is powerful. The emotional draw, even more so. It would only take one moment of weakness on my part to crumble at her feet and beg her to love me again. To let me love her. And when her mind drifted? I knew exactly where she ventured in her memory bank. I visit that place more often than I'll ever admit.

The night of the meteor shower, I experienced the truest moment of my entire life. Truer than birth or death. A moment of convergence between us and the universe. A melding of souls so absolute, any separation would result in chaos, which is precisely what happened. My fragile mind and fractured heart have been stuck in a chaotic maelstrom for ten excruciating years because my soul's gone missing. Torn away without me having any say in the matter.

As my breathing levels out, the sound of Tatum sobbing drifts to my ears, muffled by the wall between us. I sober up and remind myself that I can't pity her. She made her miserable bed when she abandoned me long ago. The only path forward that will allow me to survive her presence here— given that it's short-term—is the one paved in resentment. I owe her nothing more, and it's best for me to remember that.

Damn near running to my truck, I repeat the mantra in my head that keeps me grounded. *She deserves it. She deserves it. She deserves it.*

The stripper dressed as Mrs. Claus in a sparkly red negligee, grey wig, and round spectacles shakes her ass in Brody's face as she dances to "Santa Baby." He's in heaven. It's fucking weird. The other stripper—Rudolph, judging by the red nose and broken antler headband—lounges on the couch scrolling through social media on her phone. I rejected her offer of a lap dance.

Despite making my wishes perfectly clear about not wanting a party, the second Jensen asked me to come to his house tonight, I knew what was in store.

Jensen has made a few changes to the house over the years—replacing the stained carpet with hardwoods and refinishing the nicked cabinets—but most of it remains untouched. Dark paneling still lines the walls in the living room and hallway. The bedrooms are exactly as they were fifteen years ago. He moved into the master bedroom and replaced the bedding, but the cherry furniture belonged to my parents.

He has a hard time with change in certain aspects of his life, and I won't criticize him for it.

Rock and I stand in my childhood kitchen and nurse beers while watching the nightmare before Christmas Day unfold from a safe distance. Me, because I don't want to be here. Rock, because if Lucy finds out he's anywhere in the vicinity of a stripper, she'll castrate him.

"I don't like this, man," he says, squeezing his neck and peering around to check if any cell phone cameras are pointed in our direction. Nobody here would purposely get Rock into trouble with his wife, so his paranoia is next level and wholly unnecessary. "Lucy's already pissed I'm out with y'all on Christmas Eve."

"It's my birthday."

"Doesn't matter. I have Santa duties."

"Marcella's a baby," I point out.

Rock shrugs helplessly. I have a feeling he does that a lot at home. With my beer bottle hovering near my lips, I side-eye my friend. The man must've thrown in his balls as a bonus when he exchanged rings on his wedding day.

He used to be the alpha, the team captain, the leader of mischief and mayhem. Lucy came along, and now he's buying infant tutus online and constantly checking their shared errand list on his phone. I shake my head, thankful for my freedom.

The tsunami of energy we call Brody bounds our way, all shit-eating grins and floppy hair, while adjusting his crotch. "That was awesome! Toss me a beer."

Rock jumps into action immediately, proving once again Lucy has him so well-trained, he's no longer making conscious decisions. Brody twists off the cap with his teeth, spits it on the laminate counter, and chugs. His messy blond mop falls in his blue eyes when he burps loudly. I lean sideways to peek around him when the music cuts off.

"The ladies left," he says, reading my mind. "I only paid for an hour."

Rock tilts his face to the ceiling, shuts his eyes, and lets out a long exhale. I leave him to his relief and snag a fresh beer before making a beeline for a recliner in the living room with Brody hot on my heels.

He spins the dining chair he sat in for his lap dance in the middle of the room and straddles it backward. "Why'd you turn down a free dance? Those chicks were hot, bro."

"I told you no strippers," I say, kicking up my feet.

Jensen and his friends' laughter floats from outside. They're hovering around the fire pit, saying their goodbyes before they head home to their families. I'm surprised they stopped by since it's Christmas Eve.

"They're exotic dancers," Brody argues.

I point my bottle at him. "Pretty sure Rudolph was sporting a baby bump."

We live in a small town surrounded by other small towns. It's not like the entrainment industry in these parts has high standards.

Brody's undeterred by this fact. "Pregnant women can be sexy. Lucy was sexy as hell when she was pregnant." He says this as Rock joins us, earning Brody a smack on the head.

"Don't look at my wife." Rock settles on one end of the leather couch. "But I agree, pregnant women can be very sexy." He nods slowly with a filthy smirk and glazed eyes, lost in a memory he better keep to himself.

When Jensen opens the patio door behind Brody, I decide to start shit as payback for the strippers. "So, Brody. How's Ainsley? Have you asked her out yet?"

Jensen eases the door shut and waits, arms folded across his chest and a deadly glare trained on the back of Brody's head like a sniper's laser sight. Meanwhile, my clueless friend roughly scrapes a hand through his wild hair and huffs in frustration. It's such an odd gesture for him, the rest of us glance at each other in alarm.

Brody's the easygoing guy—the life of the party who always finds a good time. Women flock to his surfer looks and carefree charm despite his crude banter and propensity to be a total airhead. The handful of rejections he's had since puberty roll right off his back. Nothing fazes him.

A negative emotion or reaction from Brody is the equivalent of a ship's Mayday signal, and he has our rapt attention. Even Jensen's militant stance eases a little.

"She's not…" Brody starts, then hesitates and wipes his palms on his khaki pants.

We collectively lean forward because a contemplative Brody is a rare sight. It's like watching a nature documentary, waiting for the lurking crocodile to suddenly lunge from the murky water and snatch its unsuspecting prey. The dude never thinks before he speaks, and our eagerness for him to finish the sentence is palpable.

He shifts in his chair. "I get the impression she doesn't think I'm smart."

We blink at him. Rock speaks for the group, voicing our shared thoughts. "That…is not what I expected you to say."

Jensen scares the piss out of Brody when he barks from the shadows. "Explain."

Brody rights himself and says with all the haughtiness of a British schoolmarm, "I'm a science teacher."

"You teach third grade," I drawl.

He lifts a shoulder. "I like kids."

Rock interjects with a solid fact. "It took you seven years to finish college."

Feathers truly ruffled, Brody glowers at Rock and says, "See how long it takes you to finish a grad program in molecular biology, complete a summer internship at a cancer research lab, then get a general education certificate so you can teach." He crosses his arms and grinds his jaw.

Meanwhile, the other three jaws in the room are firmly on the floor. *Holy shit. Is Brody secretly smart?*

Jensen lands in the other recliner as if the revelation knocked him straight on his ass. We're in shock, gawking at Brody and trying to reconcile the moron we know and love with the intellectual he claims to be. *My* mind certainly resists the idea. That resistance is validated when he speaks again.

"She said she doesn't have time for guys who only think with their dicks," he says, the corners of his lips turning down.

"You do only think with your dick," Rock mutters.

"I told you not to hit on my employee," Jensen grits out at the same time.

Brody ignores him and addresses Rock. "I think with my

brain. I lead with my dick. There's a difference." And…he's back.

Sulking like a toddler, Brody's obviously upset by Ainsley's comment. Not because she insinuated that he's a slut—a label he can't deny—but because she insulted his intelligence. Something the guys and I have done repeatedly since preschool. Which means Ainsley hurt his feelings. Which means…

"You like her," I surmise.

Brody's eyes dart to the hardwoods. His avoidance of our gazes alone speaks volumes. Women have never held his interest for more than a brief fling, and he doesn't concern himself with their opinions. Until now.

Who cares if Ainsley is on the younger side? She's an adult. If Brody finally found a woman he wants to impress and pursue seriously, who am I to interfere?

"Go for it, bud," I say, reassuring him. I'll gladly be his cheerleader right now because Broody Brody is depressing as fuck.

"Dammit." Jensen knows he'll be the one to deal with any fallout with his employee. We'll be placing bets by tomorrow on how this will end for our friend.

Rock throws another damper on my birthday fun with a swift change of topic. "You talk to Tate yet?"

Dammit. All eyes zero in on me.

"Yep." I maintain my neutral expression and stare at my empty bottle, wishing for a refill. Placing it on the floor, I recline farther in the chair, hands behind my head.

"What did she say?" A tentative thread weaves through Jensen's tone as he shifts in his seat.

"To summarize, she said hello. I told her to stay in her lane. The end."

My summary is as short as my entire conversation with

Tatum, so I'm not exactly lying. But I'm also not about to indulge Rock's latest obsession with openly discussing my feelings.

Jensen blows out a harsh puff of air.

Rock rolls his eyes, catching my preemptive strike against his emotional inquisition. He may be a brute, but he's sharp as hell.

That creepy, contemplative expression overtakes Brody's face again. "You have every right to hate her," he says. "And no one expects you to forgive her, but you deserve closure, bro. Get your answers, cut that chick loose, and find some other woman to bang forever. We're tired of watching you mope around Texas, pining for a girl who doesn't deserve you. You're seriously killing the vibe."

Rock and Jensen, surprised by Brody's bout of wisdom, bob their heads in agreement. However, which parts of his speech they're agreeing with isn't exactly clear.

I agree with one thing he implied: forgiveness and closure don't necessarily go hand in hand. Tatum's in Walford now, and once she skips town again, I may never have another shot at getting answers.

But here's the problem. If Tatum and I talk—I mean, really talk—I'll beg for her. Shamelessly beg. And my fear of her rejecting me is far more terrifying than all the unknowns combined. If I ask her for another chance, and she denies me, the destruction will be catastrophic and infinite, a fatal blow to the remaining part of me that gets me up and moving each day like a normal human. Present-day Jake is the man they need to accept long term. I can't offer more than that.

I've grown comfortable in my empty husk. Content, even. I have a decent-paying career and a house full of projects to keep me busy when I'm not working. The only thing that has been or ever will be missing from my life is Tatum Wakefield.

She's all I want—all I've ever wanted—and I just can't seem to let her go.

I glance at the familiar walls and family photos in outdated frames. At my dad's old CD player and my mom's favorite reading lamp. The remnants of my parents' lives before they died stare back at me with disappointment.

My dad was a forward thinker. A man in motion, always looking ahead and changing with the times. What would he think if he knew Jensen and I have only achieved forward momentum in our careers? In all other aspects of our lives, we're firmly stuck in place.

I need to unstick myself.

Rock clears his throat, yanking me from my thoughts. "So, how'd you feel after seeing her?"

I throw my hands up. "Really? This again?"

"Valid question," Jensen says.

I slump into the recliner and rub my forehead. Swallowing the lump in my throat, I answer truthfully, "Shitty. I felt shitty, okay?"

"Another attack?" Rock asks. They're all aware of my history with panic attacks, so he's not divulging any secrets here.

I shake my head. "No. But close."

"It's because you had eyes on her," Brody says, drawing another round of baffled expressions his way. "In the past, your concern over her whereabouts and safety ramped up the anxiety which caused the attacks. Being face-to-face, you didn't fear the unknown even though you had some residual anxiety."

I pinch my bottom lip and study him, wondering if an alien invaded his body and scrambled his brain during the summer he claims he had an internship. He hasn't been acting like himself lately. Somehow, he's making sense.

But then he asks, "She still hot?"

In unison, we each groan some variance of *shut up, Brody*.

"Maybe after you talk to Tate, you can find a way to be friends with her." Rock hefts a meaty shoulder. "After the dust settles, I mean."

Well, that's the most absurd thing I've ever heard. I can't be friends with Tatum when every piece of her should belong to me. Not to her fans, not to Maisy or anyone else. Only me. She promised to be mine forever. If I can't have all of her, then I'm resigned to settle for nothing.

They accept that I'm done discussing this topic, so we clean up the party mess and bid my brother good night.

With Brody a few paces ahead of us as we head to our cars, Rock leans in and whispers loudly, "I thought he spent that summer surfing."

"I assumed so. Did you ever ask?" I say, keeping my voice low. All Brody mentioned about his summer away was the surfing and the girls.

"No. Never asked about his major either."

"Who would've thought Brody is such an enigma?"

"Or that he'd ever use words like *molecular* and *residual*," Rock quips.

We part ways, chuckling at what terrible friends we are.

TATUM

Most small towns host holiday celebrations where citizens revel in good cheer and merriment *before* Christmas. Walford is the exception. On the Saturday after Christmas, Main Street is blocked off so families can enjoy food tents, tables with discounted shop wares, and entertainment. I've always found it odd that the decades-long tradition isn't promoted as a festival with some cutesy name.

Maisy and I linger outside The Drip, sipping hot chocolate as we people-watch. Our observations are in sync, confirmed by our shared glances and subtle smirks when we witness the same scenes.

Mayor Olson sneaks a swig from the flask hidden in his jacket, then tucks it away, smooths his silver combover, and turns to welcome a family of five.

Evelyn Truman—once widowed and twice divorced—adjusts her top to expose maximum cleavage. Her beloved toy poodle, who must be fifteen by now, wriggles under Evelyn's armpit as she fluffs her boobs. She gives Menchy a coy smile and purred greeting as he approaches. He nods once and keeps right on walking, his vigilant eyes scanning the area for trouble.

"Shameless," Maisy deadpans as I giggle.

I'm glad she's relaxing. Since the moment she arrived yesterday, she's been on edge. I loosened her up with strong margaritas to make her more amenable to my request to come to the festival. She was more than happy to guzzle the contents of the blender all by herself.

Aunt Pam said much had changed in Walford. But to me, it's like time stood still. The sights, the sounds, the people. I could be fooled into believing I never left.

A teenager with an older-model video camera pointed at the crowd stands alone farther down the sidewalk. He lowers the camera and rakes his straight blond bangs to one side while intently reviewing the footage, brow dipping in concentration. He looks familiar.

"Who's that kid?" I ask Maisy, jutting my elbow in the boy's direction.

"Danny Foster." She tosses her empty cup in the nearby trash receptacle.

"Seriously? I used to babysit him."

Danny was the only kid I babysat. His single mom, a nurse, worked double shifts at the hospital one town over, and she had a few sitters on rotation willing to watch over the sweet boy. If all kids were as easy as Danny, parents would be having babies nonstop.

He glances up from his camera and notices us watching him. With a small smile and timid wave, he shuffles over.

"Hello, Tatum," he says, his voice quiet and unsure.

"Danny! Oh my goodness!" I yank him into a tight hug, then step away for a better look. "You've become quite the handsome young man." I wink, and his cheeks flush the deepest shade of red. "What's with the camera?"

His face aflame, he rakes those bangs aside again. Must be a comforting gesture. "I'm filming a documentary for the Young Directors of Texas contest. My subject is small-town holidays. I've captured Halloween and Thanksgiving so far." He wiggles the camera in one hand. "And now Christmas."

"A filmmaker. Wow. That's impressive."

Danny blushes yet again—the cutest thing ever—and glances around, searching for rescue. He's clearly not comfortable with social interaction, choosing to hide behind a camera instead, so I give him an opening to escape.

"It's so good to see you, Danny. We'll let you get back to filming. And good luck with the contest."

He returns my smile with another shy one of his own and rushes off.

When I was that age, I knew exactly what I wanted to do with my life. If Danny has half the passion for his craft that I had at fourteen or fifteen, he'll succeed without question.

"Weird," Maisy comments, taking my empty cup and throwing it in the trash. Her grumpiness pairs perfectly with her white faux-fur coat. She's like a starving polar bear roaming the arctic in search of food.

"Not weird. He's sweet," I say. "Unlike you."

She rolls her eyes and loops our arms together. "Let's walk."

We stroll down the middle of Main Street, dodging people and making happy *ahh* sounds at every cute dog we see. Nostalgia envelops me, and longing invades my chest when I recall whose arm I clung to during so many walks along this same street.

"Move!" The brusque command comes from behind us, followed by scattering footsteps.

Turning in unison, we find Rock's hulking mass barreling toward us, pushing a baby stroller. He's wearing a royal blue

Bulldogs tracksuit and a leather…purse? The dyed leather closely matches his ginger hair.

Maisy clamps her lips between her teeth to smother her reaction. If he's the same Rock we knew in high school, nothing gets him madder than being laughed at.

He halts when the stroller wheels almost bump the toes of our shoes. "Maisy. Tate. Welcome home." Neither the dripping sarcasm nor the scornful eyes are welcoming.

"Hey, Rock," I say, padding my tone with friendliness.

His barely concealed aggression makes me want to run away and hide. Maisy nudges me, and I follow her gaze to the bundle of pink in the stroller. With so many layers of clothes and blankets, I can't tell if a baby's in there.

"When are you leaving?" Rock asks, making no effort to keep his gruff voice quiet. *No small talk or catching up. Got it.*

Maisy jumps in, ever the mama bear. "She hasn't decided." Her crossed arms and scathing glare leave no doubt she's not putting up with his rude behavior toward me.

I wish I had the courage to fight my own battles, but I'm shrinking into myself right now. People are watching us. While I'm comfortable on stage in front of thousands of cheering fans, I'm not at all comfortable being on the receiving end of public disdain, no matter how familiar the setting.

Maisy takes a slight step forward, placing herself between Rock and me. My eyes meet Rock's over her head, and I see a twinge of regret in his. Perhaps he recognizes the fear, hurt, and humiliation in mine.

We were friends once, good friends even, in the short time I lived here. But his loyalty has and always will remain with Jake. Rightfully so.

As Rock opens his mouth to respond, a loud female voice slices through the music in the background.

"Rock! Bring my wallet!"

He shoves the stroller at me, mutters, "Hold this," and scurries off toward the voice.

Maisy and I stand with gaping mouths, eyes flicking between where Rock disappeared and the stroller. A few seconds pass before a litany of words shouted in Spanish echoes above the crowd.

Then a gorgeous petite woman with black hair marches our way, a sullen Rock trudging a few steps behind her. She snags the stroller, all pursed red lips and narrowed eyes raking us over like we're conspiring to steal her stroller or her man. Recognition flashes in the scalding stare she has pinned on me, and her features instantly soften.

"Oh, hey. I'm Lucy," she says, smiling. "I heard you were in town. If you're up for it, I'd love to have lunch together sometime." Before I can react to her quick change in demeanor that has my head spinning, or respond to the unexpected invitation, Lucy shines her friendly smile on Maisy and sticks out a hand. "Hi. I'm Lucy."

Maisy mumbles "so you said" under her breath but forces a grin and reluctantly shakes the woman's hand. "I'm Maisy."

"Do you live here too? You're welcome to join us." Lucy's brown eyes widen in alarm as a faint blush tinges her cheeks. "Um. If Tatum accepts, I mean. No pressure."

"I definitely don't—"

"Lucy," Rock warns, cutting off Maisy's reply, which is probably for the best. "We're staying out of this." *Says the man who wants me to leave town ASAP.*

She sends a withering glare to her husband. "I'm just being friendly, Rock. I can't imagine you gave her a nice welcome."

"Lunch sounds great," I blurt to Lucy, which earns me an appalled look from Maisy. In my defense, she's fully aware my default setting is Do Whatever It Takes To Make People Happy.

"Perfect!" Lucy says, beaming with joy. "Let me get your number."

As she grabs for the purse on Rock's shoulder, he shifts it out of her reach.

"Okay, Mama. Time to go." He hooks an arm around her torso and moves her behind him. She's fuming as he adjusts his purse, grabs the stroller, and addresses me again. "We're all on edge, watching our friend's back. Nobody wants this to get any worse."

This. The devastation I caused Jake.

Our friend. Lines are drawn.

With those parting words and a shake of his head, Rock guides his wife and stroller through the throngs of people who witnessed our dramatic little episode.

Dumbstruck, my eyes remain fixed to Rock's retreating form until a tiny groan from Maisy draws my attention. The tightness in her features quickly dissipates as her face slips into its relaxed, unaffected mask. I spin around as Jensen approaches, his alert gaze darting between us and the space where Rock disappeared.

"All good?" he asks, concern etched on his brow.

"Yep. Just catching up with old friends." My response is way too cheerful.

"You suck at lying."

Bobbing my head, I say, "Yep."

My stomach still churns from the minor confrontation with Rock. Lucy was nice though.

"Maisy." Jensen greets her with a dip of his chin and

hooks his thumbs in the front pockets of his jeans. "Good to see you."

She doesn't respond, and I sense her thrumming with impatience beside me.

"You ready to go?" She directs the question at me, wholly ignoring Jensen's presence.

It's no secret they suffered a common loss, and I'm fully aware that shared tragedy can push people light years apart as easily as it brings them closer together. But I don't understand why she's pretending he doesn't exist.

Jensen deflates a little at her disregard for him, but he rallies enough to ask, "Y'all coming to the bar on New Year's Eve? Best party in town."

I sympathize, hearing the hope in his voice, and I'm too damn cowardly to crush it. "Maisy's heading to Austin, but I'll think about it."

He forces a smile and nods, unable to hide the defeat in his eyes. Did he not just call me out for being a terrible liar? "You do that. Doors open at eight," he says, backing away until he crashes into the person coming up behind him.

Startled, Jake glances up, his phone in one hand and a brownie in the other. A crumb sits on his lower lip as he chews slowly, eyes widened in surprise. Everyone around us fades into the background as I follow the movement of his throat when he swallows. His tongue darts out to catch the speck of chocolate, and I squeeze my thighs together.

When my gaze connects with his again, I'm unable to hide the color blossoming on my cheeks. His lips part for a moment before he shifts his attention to his phone.

"I'll call you tomorrow," he mutters to Jensen, keeping his head down as he strides in the direction from which he came.

Jensen's staring at Maisy. Maisy's pleading eyes are on

me. And mine are glued to the back of the man I want more than anything while convincing myself not to chase after him.

How will I survive the next few weeks or months with this wall between us? In all the years we spent apart, my feelings for him never changed. But I managed to power through the longing because I never had to face him. The temptation to reach for him, touch him, talk to him, wasn't there. Because *he* wasn't there. Now, the temptation is impossible to resist.

Overwhelmed with the conflicting feelings of nostalgia, yearning, and rejection from this afternoon outing, I curse my burning eyes as I try to hold in the tears.

I whisper to Maisy, "Let's go home."

Maisy's fuzzy-socked feet are planted on the wall above my headboard, knees swaying back and forth as she scrolls through her phone. 1950s doo-wop drifts from its speaker. Filming doesn't resume on Graham's movie until after New Year's, but she was ready to run after the festival today.

I persuaded her to participate in a second margarita night, offering her my irresistible puppy dog eyes and the gift of matching holiday pajamas. Green and white polka-dot pants with snug red tank tops. Hers reads "Ho! Ho! Ho!" with the last word laying on its side. Mine reads "Ho down! Call 911!"

Neither of us have mentioned our awkward moment with the Holloway brothers since we returned to my house this afternoon, but I should've known Maisy wouldn't let my encounter with Jake fade away.

"Jake turned out to be hot."

"They both did," I say, propped against the headboard as I

flip through an old notebook of song lyrics. "And I always thought he was beautiful."

"Not just beautiful. *Hot.* He's not scrawny anymore."

I frown. "He wasn't scrawny. He was lean."

"*Now* he's lean, and totally fit. Did you see his hands?"

Of course, I did. How could I not see the strong, sexy hand wrapped around that brownie? *Gosh, what I wouldn't give to be that soft brownie and feel those firm hands on me.*

"Yep," I chirp, flipping to another page and ignoring the desire stirring low in my belly.

She pokes my head with a pointy toe and, thankfully, changes the subject. "Have you heard from Pete?"

Pete Billings, my attorney with the most appropriate last name given his expensive hourly rate, speaks strictly in legalese—a ploy, I think, to have me constantly seeking clarification so the billable hours stretch on. Bette always dealt with him on my behalf.

Wiggling my toes next to Maisy's curly head, I sigh. "Yes, but I don't understand anything. *Recording this, rights that,*" I say, mimicking Pete's nasally voice.

On my video conference with Pete, I got the impression I wouldn't be allowed to re-record any music I wrote as Makenzie for a while or release those songs for profit. As long as the record label owns the recording rights, I'm at their mercy. Which is ridiculous considering *it's my music.*

Pete emailed a bunch of paperwork I signed agreeing to these terms, but I haven't read any of it yet.

"Maybe you should hire a different attorney. Someone who can explain things better." She glances up in time to see my eye roll. "You can't just stick your head in the sand, Tate."

I shrug. "What can I say? I'm a flamingo."

"Ostrich."

"Huh?"

"Ostriches stick their heads in the sand."

I give her a blank stare, the page frozen mid-turn. "Oh. Well, flamingos are cuter."

"That's just a myth, anyway. When ostriches are scared, they lie very still on the ground and try to blend in with the environment."

"I am definitely an ostrich," I mumble, tossing the notebook aside and grabbing the next one from the stack on my nightstand.

Many of the lyrics I wrote as a teenager are about my parents and Jake. Some touch on moving to a new place. The recurring themes are young love, death, and facing the unknown. The words remind me of simpler times full of optimism and innocent dreams despite the hurt. I didn't write music for most of them but always planned to.

Maisy pokes my head again, so I bat her foot away and scowl. She asks, "Where's Pam? I haven't seen her since last night."

Aunt Pam stuck around long enough yesterday to say hello to Maisy, then left. With finger quotes, I say, "She's been 'really busy.' Quite busy, I might add."

Gripping my shin, she lifts her head, eyes dramatically wide. "Does she have a boyfriend? A lover?"

"Please don't say lover."

My aunt drifts in and out of the house during the day, and we usually eat dinner together, but she's gone out a few nights with friends since I've returned. Her social calendar is full, and her glowing aura makes me wonder if her dance card is too.

Humming along to the music, I continue flipping pages and sense Maisy's eyes on me. "What?"

"You should record your old stuff. Start a YouTube channel or something."

I study her serious expression, smack her thigh with my notebook, and scoff. "I'm an international pop star."

"Makenzie was an international pop star. *Tatum* is a girl—"

"Grown woman," I correct.

"—with a guitar and notebooks full of untapped potential. Her voice has never been heard." She shrugs as if she didn't drop a sobering truth bomb on me.

Bette discovered me at an open-mic night in a tiny LA club. Everything happened in a whirlwind after she got her claws in me. I signed a contract as difficult to read as James Joyce's *Ulysses*, became a platinum blonde, and my angsty, heartfelt originals were buried to make way for sexy, shallow pop.

While I wrote most of the songs that topped the charts and carried me to fame, the music lacked the meaningful depth seeping from the pages in this stack of notebooks. I gave them just enough emotion to achieve the connection I crave with an audience. Perhaps, I subconsciously held back in my songwriting as Makenzie to avoid confronting my ghosts and to keep my fans at arm's length. A win-win, if you ask me.

If I revive or finish my teenage self's music or put my long-suppressed thoughts—the ones that are raw and honest and painful—to paper and guitar, the real me will become exposed. I'd no longer be able to conceal my true self behind tight glittery outfits and catchy stadium chants. *No, thank you.*

"I'll pass." I say, immediately shutting down her horrible idea.

Maisy accepts my ostrich-like reaction and resumes her scrolling until she gasps, "Holy shit!"

With the crap scared out of me, I abandon the song lyrics and jerk upright. "What?"

She clambers to a seated position with the phone screen an inch from her shocked face. *"Ho-ly shit.* Marzan's assistant emailed me about doing makeup for some of his videos." The sentence rushes out of her mouth like one long word.

Marion Kazan, who goes by Marzan, directed several of my music videos. He's a legend in the industry, known for utilizing costumes and makeup to create controversial imagery. He only hires the best of the best for his projects.

After a beat to process the news, we bounce on the mattress, hugging and screaming. I grab her cheeks as we cry right in each other's faces. The fact that actual tears are pouring from her eyeballs has me crying harder.

This is the second time I've ever seen her shed tears in the twelve years we've been friends. The first was a month ago when we reunited at Gateway Hills. Now, I understand why she holds it in. Gorgeous as she is, Maisy is an ugly crier.

"I'm so happy for you!" I squeal.

All she can do is nod vigorously as snot mixes with her tears.

Maisy is extremely talented in her own right, and I won't take any credit for her inevitable success. To the public, she made me appear full of life when all I wanted to do was roll over and wither away. She hid the evidence of my sleepless nights, self-destruction, and heartache for *years*, and no one was the wiser.

Until this past year, when no amount of makeup could hide my damage, I sparkled and shined under the camera flashes and spotlights through the toughest times—all thanks to Maisy. I'm humbled and honored that my face is the one she used to showcase her work.

Clinging to each other, our joyful cries morph into sad ones as we reach the same realization: it's time to let each other go, professionally. We've found shelter in one another for too long, using our working relationship as an excuse not to face the world alone as individuals. Neither of us can truly live and thrive without spreading our wings, shaking out the molted feathers, and flapping the damn things until we fly.

Strangely, I'm okay with us forging our own paths. The idea doesn't give me the anxiety it once did because I know she'll always be here when I need her, and I'll do the same for her without question.

"God, I hate crying." Maisy shoves my hands from her cheeks and rolls off the bed, landing gracefully on her feet. "Tomorrow, I'll let them know I'm busy with Graham's project until March and hope Marzan doesn't rescind the offer." She tosses her phone on the bed and physically shakes off her worries. "Let's give you a makeover and then prank call the guys."

At four o'clock in the morning, we're covered from head to toe in gold body paint we found in the back of my closet. A sleepy, pissed-off Marcus glares daggers at us from the laptop screen as we cackle like lunatics.

10

TATUM

Since Lucy and I didn't get a chance to exchange phone numbers at the festival before Rock dragged her away, she stopped by Aunt Pam's the next day with another invitation for lunch. We've been texting ever since and coordinated our first get together.

Like me, she has a lot of free time. She works three evening shifts a week and two weekend shifts a month as a nurse at the nearest hospital, which is half an hour away. Walford's too small to have anything more than an urgent care clinic and a family medicine practice.

She's already seated at a table when I enter the Noon Moon Café, which only serves breakfast and lunch. The astrological decor, complete with hanging stars and a mural of the moon phases, puts the moon in the name. Black vinyl booths line the wall beneath the mural, but Lucy chose a table in the center of the restaurant to accommodate the stroller.

My lips form an easy smile as I approach. She hasn't noticed me yet, her full attention on Marcella in her lap, waving a little, plush football in her tiny hand.

"Hey, there." I pull out the chair next to Lucy rather than

across from her and take a seat. "And you must be Marcella,"
I say, pitching my voice higher as I run a knuckle along the
adorable girl's chubby cheek.

Her soft curls are a few shades darker than Rock's—more
of an auburn color. Big brown eyes matching Lucy's stare at
me for a second before the toy hits me in the chest and
bounces to the tile floor.

Lucy chuckles and shakes her head, "I'm sorry. She
entered her throwing phase early." She bends sideways to
grab the toy, but I beat her to it.

"It's no problem. I'm sure Rock is proud." I hand the
football to a babbling Marcella. "How old is she?"

"Almost nine months," she beams, her perfect white teeth
framed by bright red lips. "And he's very proud. If she
inherits that Harrison height gene, he'll have her running
drills in the backyard by the time she's five."

"He'll probably do it regardless of her size," I tease.

Grinning, she rolls her eyes. "So true."

I've become an eager passenger on the Walford gossip
train, quickly catching up on everything I missed. When I
learned about the knee injury Rock sustained in the last game
of his final season in college, my heart hurt for him. He lived
for playing football, but coaching suits him well. As does
family life.

We place our orders with Sonja, the owner, who gives me
a long welcoming hug. She and her husband, Eddie, are in
their late sixties and have run the cafe together for decades.
Eddie's the main cook, whipping up a classic menu of eggs
and bacon, soups and sandwiches, and lots of fried food
options.

Lucy settles Marcella in the stroller with a few toys and a
bottle. "How does it feel being back here?" she asks.

I tilt my head from side to side, wondering if I should

give Lucy my usual *it's good to be back* response. She's been genuine with me, so I'm willing to offer the same authenticity. "Umm…there's good moments and not-so-good moments."

"It must be a big change of pace from what you're used to."

"It's a welcome one. I needed this break, but it's hard being away from my friends. We were together a lot."

Her eyes soften. "I get it. Before college, I was never away from my family. Then I met Rock, and the Harrisons became my family too."

Thinking about Maisy and all my California guys, I realize we've created our own little family. I have Aunt Pam, of course. We've lived apart for years and rarely see each other since she doesn't like to travel, but we stay in touch. She's always there when I need her, but my people in California are always *there*. They've been the constant, physical presences in my life until recently.

Lucy and I nibble on sandwiches and discuss everything from songwriting to nursing to life in California. All the while, I steal glances at Marcella, who sleeps soundly in her stroller.

"You can hold her if you'd like," Lucy offers.

"Oh, I don't want to wake her."

"Are you kidding? This little bundle can sleep through anything, which Rock and I really appreciate." She smirks, and my cheeks heat as curiosity takes the reins and a million questions run through my mind.

Do not ask about their sex life, Tatum. You just met this woman. Geez.

Surrounded by men, I've never had a girlfriend to talk about sex with besides Maisy, and she's not forthcoming by nature.

Lucy carefully lifts Marcella out of the stroller and hands her over, and the baby's weight in my arms quiets my curious thoughts.

With Marcella snuggled against my chest, I bury my nose in her silky hair, my eyes falling shut as the smell of baby infiltrates my cells. It's been too long since I've been close to a baby, much less held one, and I don't want to let go.

Remembering Lucy's sitting next to me, I open my eyes to find her looking at me, the pride of motherhood written all over her face. "It's the best, isn't it?"

"It is," I agree, reluctantly pulling my nose away from Marcella's hair. Her angelic face looks peaceful with her tiny rosy lips parted in deep sleep despite the clanking dishes and hearty conversation surrounding us.

Finding serenity among the chaos is a luxury reserved for infants and the elderly. In all the in-between stages of life, the chaos can become overwhelming and impossible to shut out.

"Do you and Rock plan to have more?" I ask. I'd always dreamed of having kids with Jake one day, but some dreams aren't meant to be.

She chuckles again, and the slightest shade of peach tinges her cheeks. "Ever since I was cleared for sex after Marcella was born, Rock makes it his daily mission to get me pregnant again."

"Daily?" I squeak.

Lucy seems quite comfortable discussing her sex life. The fringes of it, anyway. But when I think about this sweet petite woman getting mauled by a giant like Rock on a daily basis, I'm tempted to ask her to blink twice if she needs my help.

As if the man of the hour tracked her location, Rock flings open the door, reaching our table in a few determined strides.

"I thought we were having lunch at home," he says to

Lucy. His hardened gaze flicks to me, and he offers a curt nod. "Tate."

"I told you I had lunch plans today," she says.

He huffs, much like the bulls Maisy and I saw in Barcelona once. "You have a shift later, so you won't be home for dinner." *Oh. My. God. He wants an afternoon delight. Or a lunch delight, I suppose.*

Lucy shoves the open chair opposite me with her foot. "Have a seat, big guy."

If I hadn't noticed the tremor that rocked Rock when she called him *big guy*, the shift in the air is enough to gauge the sizzling chemistry between these two. He promptly drops into the chair, scooting it forward and caging Lucy's crossed legs between his huge thighs.

I should avert my gaze. My toenails are blushing at this point, and I'm tempted to shield Marcella's innocent sleeping eyes.

"You can drop off Marcella at your mom's and bring me dinner at work," she says. I'm pretty sure they're playing footsie, but the table blocks my view.

"Just a snack or a full meal?" Rock asks. *Is he talking in code?*

Lucy waves a hand at her half sandwich and half salad combo. "This is a light lunch, so I'll be starving by then." *They are* so *talking in code.*

Rock runs his hands up her thighs, leaning forward to whisper in her ear. But he's a rumbling giant, so his deep voice carries. I catch the words *dessert* and *vibrator* and *blindfold*.

Lucy doesn't blush or cringe or have any outward reaction to indicate embarrassment. She stares at the behemoth with the tiniest smile playing on her lips and says, "If you're a good boy, I'll let you pick."

Rock's body visibly shudders…again. *Holy fuzzballs. I feel like a freaking voyeur.*

He smacks a chaste kiss on Lucy's lips, then presses a tender kiss on top of Marcella's head before strutting from the cafe like a victor.

I'm focusing on Marcella's even breaths when Lucy heaves a big sigh. "Sorry about that. Rock is particular about mealtimes."

Testing the waters of our new friendship, I wink and say, "Among other things."

A huge smile spreads across her pretty face. "Among other things."

I want that. I want a secret language and flirty exchanges verging on unsuitable for public consumption. Despite the innocence of being teens, Jake and I had that once. We could read each other's thoughts, exchanging knowing smiles at the simplest of spoken words. I miss the bond we shared so much; it hurts.

The hurt must be written on my face because Lucy asks, "You okay?"

"Yeah. I was just remembering…" I don't finish my thought, but Lucy's expression, full of compassion and understanding, assures me I don't need to say anything more. She's obviously a woman in love. She gets it.

"I've only known him a few years, and we aren't really close, but he's always seemed like half a person to me." She rests a hand on my forearm, and I welcome the comfort. "Is that how you feel?"

"Every day," I quietly admit, pulling Marcella tighter against my chest. I'll have to let go of her soon, so I take advantage of these final minutes of our lunch date and breathe her in again.

"You let me know if I can do anything to make it better,

okay? Maybe some quality girl time will take your mind off things."

I offer her an appreciative smile. "I'd really like that, Lucy. Thank you."

11

JAKE

"She's back, isn't she?"

Kara's gentle voice pulls my attention away from the candle's flame dancing on the table. Quiet jazz and dim lights create a romantic ambiance and an illusion of privacy in the ritzy hotel lounge.

My eyes drift to her shoulder-length blonde hair, then to the hazel eyes studying me as she strokes the stem of her wine glass. It dawns on me the handful of women I've slept with over the years were all blonde. And none of them had blue eyes. *Huh.*

"Who?" I bring a glass of water to my dry lips and swallow several gulps. *It's really hot in here.*

"The woman who stole your heart." Her expression is soft, understanding.

I fuss with the edge of the black tablecloth draped over my legs to redirect my nervous energy. Otherwise, I'd be running out the door.

We've only been here for half an hour, but it's evident to Kara how distracted I am. I can't stop thinking about Tatum's rosy cheeks when I saw her at the festival. Her flushed face is like a calling card to my dick. I had to get away from her before I sprung a boner at a community gathering.

I blow out a long breath. "Kara, I'm—"

She holds up a hand and shakes her head. "No-no, Jake. People should apologize for many things, but never apologize for love."

Slumped in my chair, I shove my hands between my knees to keep from fidgeting. "It's not like that."

If her arched eyebrow is any indication, she's not buying my lie. Hell, I'm not either. I admitted to Jensen how I still feel about Tatum, but he's the only person who'll get a confession from me.

Kara takes a dainty sip of her wine. "So, tell me what it's like then."

The last thing I want to do is hash out my Tatum problems with the nice, attractive woman I persuaded at the last minute to drive an hour to meet me at this hotel. On New Year's Eve, no less. I didn't want to be tempted to show up at Bruno's where Tatum might be tonight. Pathetic, I know. What's worse, San Antonio is two hours from my house.

Twice in the past week, Tatum and I crossed paths. Staring at each other across Main Street as we went about our separate business. She tossed me a halfhearted wave and a sad smile. I choked on my need to rush over and talk to her.

She'd already been on my mind twenty-four-fucking-seven, and then the festival thing happened. It's killing me to stay away.

Amusement and candlelight sparkle in Kara's eyes. "You're still wearing your coat, Jake. Get comfy and talk me through it."

I glance at my fully zipped coat and sigh, removing it as Kara signals for the waiter. When he appears, she orders the stuffed mushroom appetizer and a whiskey for me.

At my raised brows, she explains, "Seems like you need something stronger than beer tonight." She's not wrong.

She patiently watches me spin the water glass in circles, and I sigh into the silent gap between us. "I honestly don't know where to start."

Kara and I never discuss anything beyond subjects suitable for small talk when having a few cocktails. The weather, quick updates on work life, her family's land. Her parents are clients of mine, which is how we met. She lives in a town near their ranch on the other side of San Antonio. After a couple of my on-site visits, she…erm…propositioned me.

A widow in her mid-thirties, Kara has a son who's around ten. In her proposal, she made it clear she has no interest in dating and would only meet at a hotel in the city to prevent any gossip in her hometown.

I never asked for the reasons behind her no-dating rule. It made no difference to me. When I had appointments in the San Antonio area, we would hook up.

It's been seven months or so since I've seen her. I asked for a rain check on our last meetup, which was supposed to happen, oh, around the time Tatum went to rehab.

The fact that she accepted my impromptu invitation tonight, and now wants to discuss my messed-up past, proves the type of woman she is. Kind, caring, honest, and not the least bit interested in me romantically. That confirmation is a relief.

I take in her red wrap dress and ample cleavage, her fully made-up face, how the ends of her hair are loosely curled. She came here tonight with a clear expectation, which is reasonable given the nature of our relationship. Apparently, I did not. *So, what am I doing here?*

Lounging on her side of the booth with an elbow on the table, wine glass dangling from her relaxed hand, she says,

"Let's skip the historical facts and start with why you're here with me and not out there winning her back."

"Don't want her back."

She frowns. "One rule tonight: no lies. You can say anything, knowing it will never leave this table. I've only ever been honest with you, Jake. About what this is. So, be honest with me."

"I don't know anything about you other than *this*, so that's not really fair to ask, is it?" I say, my tone hushed but harsh.

The waiter quietly sets my whiskey on the table and scurries away. He may have caught on to my prickly mood change, but Kara shows no sign of being affected.

She stares at me with pursed lips for a tick before nodding. "You're right." She places her glass on the table and leans forward on her elbows, chin resting on laced fingers. "Do you know why I picked you?"

I shift in my seat and clear my throat, avoiding her gaze. "No."

"It was the longing in your eyes. The same longing I've felt every day since my husband died. I found safety in your longing, knowing you wouldn't get attached. Because I have nothing to offer you besides a few hours of my time here and there for a couple of drinks and a physical connection. And you're exactly the same. We drink to forget, we keep our eyes closed, we say nothing, we don't caress or fully undress. I'm not paying for—"

"Please don't," I beg on a stuttering exhale, eyelids squeezed shut to block out the truth. Things aren't real unless they're spoken aloud, right? *Denial. Denial. Denial.*

I'm clutching the whiskey tumbler like it's a life raft and the only thing keeping me afloat in my turbulent ocean of shame.

Understanding my plea, Kara reaches across the table and

lays warm fingers on my wrist. "There's no shame in our kind of relationship, Jake. We aren't betraying anyone or hurting anyone. If the people we gave our hearts to abandoned us, who can we possibly hurt?"

Ourselves, I want to scream. She may try to convince herself she's not hurting every time we're together, but I call bullshit. Even when I believed Tatum would never be part of my life again, I had to force myself to bury the guilt every time I touched another woman. It hurt *me* knowing it wasn't Tatum in my arms.

I drop my head in my hands, unable to look at Kara. My voice is thick and rough as it delivers my past. "She left me a long time ago without a word. I haven't seen or heard from her since. Until she showed up a few weeks ago. And she's not sticking around." Tatum's words from the first day we met under the tree at school ring in my ears. I quietly repeat them. "It's a temporary stopover."

A platter of stuffed mushrooms lands in my line of sight, but I have no appetite.

Kara waits for her wine to be refilled before she speaks. "That's almost worse, you know? At least with death, there's often closure. You know where your loved one has gone, even if you don't understand why or want to believe it. On some level, there's comfort in the finality of death. In knowing they didn't choose to go, in most cases. When the living leaves us empty-handed, they rob us of that comfort."

We pick at the appetizer in silence for long minutes, neither of us eating, as the memories filter through my head. Since returning to Walford after college, I've never spoken to anyone about Tatum. About the wrecked man I am because of her. I shut down anyone who mentioned her name to me, including Jensen and my friends.

They witnessed my initial downfall from afar, but I only

allowed them a small peek into the real aftermath—the after that never ends. Rock believes he's seen me through the worst of the worst, but he has no idea how bottomless this dark pit really is.

The thought of exposing the soft underbelly hidden beneath my rough, scaly skin terrifies me. I've always been afraid of the possibility that someone could weaponize my pain. But it's time I finally let some of this torment go.

As I consider Kara—a stranger with a familiar brokenness —I decide to open up for the first time ever.

"We were high school sweethearts," I start, taking a fortifying swallow of whiskey. "More than that, really. Two vagrant souls that found a home in each other. We were inseparable. A perfect pairing in every way. Our dreams, our pain, our differences, our humor, our bodies. Everything fit."

I settle into my seat, legs stretched beneath the table. "We had a plan. She would head to LA after graduation, find a job, and try to get discovered. I'd stay back, earn a business degree so I could manage things when she became famous. My brother gave up everything so I could go to college, and I owed it to him to see it through."

Never have I said those words aloud, and it's pretty shitty of me to say them to Kara and not Jensen. He wanted me to graduate from college far more than I wanted it. If Jensen knew the truth, he would think I blame him for losing Tatum.

"Anyway, she promised to come home to visit, or I would visit her. We'd video chat. And we did for the first few months, then school started. The calls became few and far between, and she blamed our busy schedules. Missed calls became voicemails, then only short texts. There were no visits, no trips home."

The worry and stress I felt then—knowing Tatum was

drifting away but not knowing why—resurface now as I bare my bones in this hotel bar.

After another sip of whiskey, I say, "Right after the spring semester started, all communication stopped. Snuffed out like flipping a light switch."

"Did you look for her?" Kara asks. She's been listening so intently, I almost forgot she's sitting across from me.

"LA is huge, and I had no clue where to start. Her best friend moved to Austin for cosmetology school, but they stayed in touch. I confronted her friend over the holiday break that year to ask if everything was okay with Tatum. She said, 'she's been busy'. That's it. No further explanation."

When I later learned that Maisy joined Tatum in California, I was furious. I should've been the one by her side like we planned. Like she promised.

"Tatum?"

Crap.

I simply nod, hoping the errant slip of Tatum's name doesn't lead to Kara discovering her identity. I've already said enough for her to put the pieces together if she really tried. At this point, why the hell should I even care?

"When she cut off contact with me, I tried for weeks to reach her aunt. I finally caught her at home, and she told me to move on. That was that." I shrug, playing off the impact of Pam's words. I'll never forget the pity in her eyes when I begged on my knees for any scrap of information about Tatum. Soon after, Tatum's cell phone number was disconnected.

But that wasn't the end, not for me anyway. Madness consumed me. My grades suffered. I couldn't eat or sleep. Anxiety held me hostage, and I suffered frequent panic attacks. It took a while before I could function normally enough to survive.

I became a zombie, going through the motions of living but with no life inside me. But I don't share these details with Kara.

"One day, during my junior year of college, I saw her on the news, living her dream. Something in me snapped, and I spent the next two years self-destructing. Until my friends saved me from myself."

I'm not sure how I finished school, but I managed. My friends and brother forced me to keep going. So, I learned to fake it for their sakes, thinking she'd never return, but she has. Now, here I sit, a coward in hiding, too afraid to face the woman who broke him.

I push cold mushrooms around my plate with a fork as Kara absorbs my story. Though it's somewhat cathartic to unload my baggage, her long moment of quiet contemplation does nothing to calm my renewed urge to flee.

I'm exposed. A raw nerve on a severed finger hovering too close to a hot stove. One touch will cause searing agony.

When she sniffles, I raise my head and find tears clinging to her lashes, her hands balled into tight fists. Her voice is soft and pained when she speaks. "I would give anything for another chance with my husband. *Anything*. If something as simple as forgiveness was the only thing standing between me and my heart, I'd forgive his every transgression to make us whole again."

It's my turn to squeeze Kara's hand in comfort. She may put up a stoic front, but it's clear she hasn't recovered from the loss of her husband and never will.

"You're lucky," she says. "You still have a chance at a happy ending."

I chuckle, but there's little humor in it. "I'm not sure about that. Happy endings are reserved for good men. That's not me anymore."

"You're the best kind of man, Jake. You feel deeply and love forever. Not many women know what it's like to have a guy like that."

"But you do?"

She smiles, her glassy eyes lost to a faraway happiness. "Yes. I do."

Unsure where to go from here, I dig my phone out of my coat pocket and check the time. Almost midnight.

"Guess this it for us, then," I hedge.

"As it should be," she says.

I help Kara into her coat before slipping into mine. As I pull out my wallet, she stops me.

"I've charged it to my room."

"You didn't have to do that," I say as the countdown to a new year begins.

She shrugs one shoulder. "It's not a big deal."

The double meaning behind her flippant remark isn't lost on me. Kara's okay to pay for my part even though she didn't receive what she expected tonight, and she's okay with our arrangement being at an end.

The clock strikes midnight. I pull her into a friendly hug and whisper, "Thank you."

She kisses me on the cheek and turns to go. After a few steps, she twirls around. "Hey, Jake? Let me know how it ends?"

Forcing a smile, I nod. "Will do."

On the drive home, I'm emotionally and mentally drained. More of the burdensome weight I carry around lifted after spilling my guts for the first time. I'm not yet to the point of sharing my feelings for Tatum but voicing what happened to me chipped away some of my dogged determination to ignore them completely.

I decide to let the cards fall where they may. It's time to

back up all the brave claims I've made about not hiding from her. But I won't seek her out. If we run into each other, I'll treat her cordially. Like old friends who haven't seen each other in a long while.

If she really does love me like she used to, she'll have to make the first move.

12

TATUM

"Oh! Am I early?" I ask Lucy as she opens the door to soft background music and fewer people than I expected.

"You're right on time," she says with a nervous smile. "We're doing a thing with my family in San Antonio tomorrow, so tonight is just a small gathering." She gestures for my coat, so I hand her the bagged gift I brought while I shrug out of it.

When Lucy invited me to her birthday party, I imagined a raucous affair with a house full of people and loud conversations competing with louder music. Judging by the number of place settings I count as we pass the dining room, this is an intimate birthday dinner.

Lucy breaks off down the hallway with a "be right back, make yourself at home," leaving me to my own devices in the kitchen. But not for long.

"Tatum! Oh my word. Look at you." Mrs. Harrison, Rock's mom, pulls me into a tight, swaying hug. She's a tall, busty woman who loves wearing floral patterns. Back in high school, she was everyone's second mother. She ends the hug but grabs my hands, holding them out wide. "How are you, dear? You look fantastic. Have you been eating enough? We're about to put out some appetizers." She also likes to feed people, which makes sense considering she had to keep Rock fueled during his growing years.

When Mrs. Harrison lets me get a word in, I say, "I'm doing well. It's good to see you again." Before I can say more, Rock's dad pops into the room.

"Did I hear you right, honey? Is Tatum here? Protect your mailboxes!" As he comes in for a hug, he guffaws at his mention of when I accidentally drove over their mailbox with Jake's truck. They live outside of town, and Jake thought it would be safer for me to learn to drive somewhere with fewer obstacles and people around. He thought wrong.

"How are you, Mr. Harrison? You haven't changed a bit." He really hasn't. He's still an imposing man with a round belly, ruddy cheeks, and a huge grin. Like a giant, ginger Santa Claus. Minus the beard.

Mr. Harrison passed down his height and his red hair to both of his children. His daughter, Bree, and her husband trail in behind him.

Smiling, Bree shakes her head at her dad's corny joke and gives me a side hug. "Good to see you, Tatum. Do you remember Trent?" She gestures to her quiet husband, who offers a curt nod and a brief handshake.

"Of course. How are you two? It's been a long time."

While the Harrison family fills me in on all the fun I missed, I move to slide my fingers into my back pockets because I'm awkward and don't know what to do with my empty hands. But I'm wearing a flowing, navy dress for the occasion, so I clasp them together behind my back instead.

Lucy returned at some point and quietly moves around the kitchen, preparing platters of food. She's avoiding me. Which is strange since she sent me multiple invitations and follow-ups by text to confirm I was coming tonight.

It doesn't take long before I discover the reason for her avoidance. Rock, Brody, and *freaking Jake* burst into the kitchen, laughing and shoving at each other. Just like old times. And hearing Jake's easy laugh again? I'm a puddle of tears on the inside. And possibly a messy puddle of arousal on the outside.

Once the guys notice me standing in my pretty dress with my arms locked behind me and my ankles crossed…dead silence. The mood shift is seismic.

The Harrisons' eyes ping between me and Jake. Brody shrinks back into the living room, exiting the scene. Rock glares at Lucy, who's hiding behind a spatula. And Jake? He turns around and walks right out the patio door.

"Lucy," Rock says though clenched teeth. "Can I talk to you for a minute?"

"I have to check on Marcella," she blurts, then scurries down the hall with Rock on her tail.

The Harrisons and I stand around while crickets chirp in my head. "Maybe I should leave," I say, my tan ankle boots pointed at the front door.

"Nonsense," Mrs. Harrison says. "Help me carry the food to the table, Tatum. Food makes everything better."

Food does not make everything better. Dinner is awkward as fudge. Lucy arranged the seating so that Jake and I are across from each other, and not once do we make eye contact. Though, I don't pass up the opportunity to study his stern expression and capable hands. The rough way he handles a knife and fork should not be so attractive.

Not only is he more handsome than ever with his rugged looks and toned body that I'm eager to explore, but his eyes have a tightness to them that I yearn to soften with gentle kisses and soothing words. But he's denying me a glimpse of those green eyes as they remain glued to his plate.

I never imagined I could feel so invisible while being in his presence.

What's worse, Brody's sitting on the end between us, pretending not to examine every movement Jake and I make. Although we had the same friend group in high school, Brody and I weren't particularly close. It's hard to establish a bond with someone who constantly flirts with you and doesn't take anything seriously.

"So, Tate." He flashes a bright, flirty smile. "That was some nip shot in New York. One for the spank bank." He winks, then jerks in his seat and offers wide innocent eyes to Jake, who's glaring at him. "Sorry, bro. I'm just saying she's still hot. It's a compliment."

I roll my eyes, but inside I'm battling the urge to crawl under the table. "You have such a way with words, Brody."

His grin stretches. "Thanks. I have a master's degree."

My baffled gaze bounces between everyone watching our exchange and waiting for me to respond to his unrelated comment. "Umm…that's great." I shove a forkful of mashed potatoes in my mouth, earning giggles from Bree and Lucy.

Jake mutters to his uneaten steak, "Glad to know I'm not the only idiot in the room."

My appetite, which wasn't strong to begin with, vanishes.

The tension wafting from our half of the table kicks up a notch. Everyone fidgets in their seats, grasping for pleasant conversation. Even the jolly Mr. Harrison fakes a smile throughout the meal while I offer vague answers to their questions about the rise and fall of Makenzie.

As soon as Bree claims to have a full belly, Lucy and I spring to our feet and clear the table. Camping out at the kitchen sink, I wash the dishes as she brings them to me.

"I'm so sorry. This was such a bad idea. I honestly didn't know it would be this awkward." A wine glass trembles in her hand before I take it from her.

"You couldn't have known, Lucy." I let out a heavy sigh that has nothing to do with her plotting. "Jake and I…there's just too much time separating us."

She lowers her head. "Please don't hate me for this. I just want you both to be happy and thought a little push might help. I really do want us to be friends, and I promise never to try playing matchmaker again."

"It's fine. A situation like this was bound to happen, and I'm not going to let Jake stop me from building relationships in Walford."

"Really?" she asks, her hopeful brown eyes tugging at my heartstrings.

I place a dripping plate in the drying rack next to the sink. "Really. Let's just stick with lunch dates and hanging out with Marcella for now."

"Okay." Her relieved smile quickly fades. "I've had a hard time getting to know people here. Everyone's in the tight groups they've had since childhood, with inside jokes and stuff that I don't get. Despite what people might think, I'm actually a little shy. Except when it comes to Rock. I'm fearless around him." Lucy chuckles, knowing I've seen how she handles Rock.

I rest a hip against the counter and dry my hands. "I didn't grow up here, so I get it. But you've got me now. I'll give you the inside scoop on what goes down behind the scenes on tour. Like the time in Amsterdam when I replaced my head bodyguard's tighty-whities with silk boxers. They had a picture of his face winking at a penis printed on the butt."

Lucy barks a laugh. "I'll take it. And I can tell you about how Rock loves it when I tickle his prostate."

"Really?" I squeak, then lean closer and lower my voice. "Really? And what does that do, exactly?"

My cheeks burn from both shock and intrigue. My sexual knowledge is limited to what happens between two fumbling teenagers and the little tidbits Maisy's been willing to share. I need Lucy to tell me everything.

"I'll explain over lunch next week, but Rock can never know. Deal?"

Abso-freaking-lutely.

"Deal."

Hiding in the bathroom later, I stare at my reflection in the mirror and contemplate my next move. Should I stay and endure? It's Lucy's birthday, and she's the reason I'm here. Or should I leave and put an end to this miserable night for me *and* Jake? Lucy will understand if I can't bear this torture any longer.

"You showed up, Tatum. That's a good first step. Now, make your excuses and leave," I murmur to my reflection, summoning the courage to open the door.

But my courage isn't necessary because Jake opens it for me.

13

JAKE

I squeeze the knob and will the muscles in my face to relax, at odds with the galloping beats in my chest.

My gaze sweeps over Tatum's face and downward, stopping at the fabric covering her breasts. She's wearing a dress tonight. She never wears dresses. This one falls past her knees, revealing smooth calves that scream for my touch. And I *ache* to touch her.

Sitting across from her at dinner, while my nerves buzzed and sparked, was excruciating. Then Brody had to remind everyone—remind *me*—of her indecent exposure. I may not have any right to the jealousy the memory stirs within me, but my covetous need for her will never go away.

Adjusting to my full height, I move forward, forcing her back into the small bathroom. The lock clicking into place echoes like the final tick of the doomsday clock, signaling the end of all beautiful things.

"Why did you come here?" I ask, not one to beat around the bush.

Her confidence wavers under my hard stare, and she shrinks back a step. "Lucy invited me."

I inch closer. "Not *here*. To Walford."

When she takes too long to respond, I shake my head. But before I can voice my disappointment in her silence, she lifts her chin and says, "For you."

"Don't play games with me, Tatum." Despite my firm tone, my eyes and heart beg for this to be true.

She straightens her spine and takes a small step toward me. "I'm not. I learned a lot of things about myself in treatment. The most important thing being that I'm tired of running from my mistakes," she says, regret infusing her tone. "I wronged you, Jake. In more ways than one. But if I don't fix myself first, then I can't fix what I broke between us."

So, this is about her recovery—her path to making amends. When Maisy appeared on my porch, she said Tatum needed a place to heal. As much as I've striven to maintain my distance and the resentment I carry, a tiny ray of hope slipped through the cracks. Hope that Tatum wants to heal *us*—not simply mend the broken parts. Apparently, I'm an obstacle blocking her journey toward healing. Literally.

But I don't retreat, which leaves us less than a foot apart. Inhaling slowly, my eyelids flutter as I breathe in her scent. *Lavender.* The word nearly skims past my lips on an exhale.

"Are you better?" My fingertips ghost along her forearm like they have a mind of their own, drawing goosebumps from her silky flesh.

She grips the edge of the vanity behind her, and her breaths quicken. I swiftly withdraw my fingers, realizing their betrayal.

A tremor seeps into her strained voice when she answers. "I am. I feel better than I have in years."

"That's good," I say. My gaze caresses every inch of her

face, noting her cheeks flushed a healthy shade of pink and eyes bright with life. "You look good."

Her slender throat flexes when she swallows. "So do you."

We're dancing in a magnetic field, our foreheads almost touching. I struggle against her gravitational pull. Thousands of miles and a decade have come between us, but I'm as helpless in her orbit now as the day we met.

Several seconds pass before my raspy voice breaks the silence. "I don't know how to do this, Tate."

She's pressed against the vanity. I caged her in at some point, my hands squeezing the granite next to hers on either side of her hips. My traitorous thumb brushes the edge of her palm. The galloping in my chest becomes a chaotic drum line when her rapid breaths fan across my lips.

"Do what?"

I trail the tip of my nose along her cheek, desperate to feel her skin, but I don't make contact. Desire sneaks into my voice when I whisper, "Hate you when you're standing so close."

Her bottom lip quivers. "Don't hate me," she whispers back. Pleading dilated eyes flick between mine. *Fuck, I miss getting lost in these beautiful blue eyes.*

I can't fall into her poisonous trap. I can't allow her to suck me into her vortex, flipping and tumbling with no hope of gaining control. Until she plainly states how she feels about me, I have to be strong enough to step away. To create space and fortify the fragile wall between us.

So, that's exactly what I do, abruptly retreating and shattering the trance that had overtaken me. Unable to stomach the hurt in her eyes, I unlock the door and give her my cold back.

"Take care of yourself, Tatum."

14

TATUM

ME
What If I start a fashion line? Lots of celebs do it.

MAISY
Don't.

ME
Why not?

GRAHAM
Look in a mirror.

ME
What's that supposed to mean?

MAISY
What are you wearing right now?

GRAHAM
<GIF of a clown walking the red carpet>

ME
I have an eclectic style.

Aunt Pam kicked me out of the house. For today, anyway. Apparently, she's had enough of my growing laundry piles and half-eaten microwave dinners. It's not like I'm a slob and don't keep a clean home. It's this time of year that brings me down.

I blame my tanking mood on seasonal depression, but those closest to me know different. Maisy checks in daily. Graham randomly sends me funny memes to cheer me up despite his busy schedule. And Aunt Pam has been noticeably more present since New Year's Day, waiting to catch me if I fall into darkness.

It's coming. The darkness always comes.

Bundled in a knit hat and matching pink puffer coat, I head on foot toward The Drip. People buzz about downtown, working side by side to strip away the holiday decorations.

That's another wonderful thing about Walford. The community bands together in ownership of the town, keeping it safe, clean, and festive all year long. A deep sense of pride weaves through its residents. A pride you'd be hard-pressed to find anywhere else.

I spot Danny filming the activity and stride in his direction. When he pauses to review playback, I startle him when I speak.

"How many holidays are you covering?"

"Oh. Um. New Year's Day was the last one." He lifts a hand to brush his bangs aside, but his knit hat impedes the action. With flattened fingers, he rubs the wool against his forehead instead.

"So, what's next? When is the submission deadline?"

"Uh…next is editing. Then I have to upload it to YouTube and email the submission form by the end of February." He returns his attention to the camera: his safe place.

"Cool. If you need to screen it for anyone, I'm your girl." I wink.

One corner of his mouth tilts up, and I want to break out in a freaking happy dance.

"Thanks," he says at the same time every cell phone in the vicinity screeches with an emergency alert. Except for mine.

People pour out of stores and restaurants, joining those already huddled on the sidewalks. From the bloodlust on their faces, they may as well be carrying pitchforks and torches. Heads twist and turn in confusion once they discover no threat exists.

Mayor Olson stumbles toward us, arm outstretched with an accusatory finger pointed straight at Danny as he yells "paparazzi" over and over.

Danny's unable to move, petrified with fear and embarrassment. His red cheeks match the brick on the boutique behind him as he attempts to fade into the wall.

My eyes ping from him to the mayor to the groups of people cursing as they try to silence their blaring phones. One guy repeatedly slams his device against his palm in a futile effort to shut off the obnoxious sound.

Menchy storms out of his hardware store, a cell phone pressed to his ear as he shouts to someone on the other end of the line. Within seconds, the noise ceases abruptly, and the whole street is cloaked in silence.

All angry eyes are pinned squarely on the mayor, who's being held in a rear bear hug by Brody. He sends me a flirty wink.

"What's happening?" I whisper to Danny. We're both pressed against the building like prisoners facing a firing squad.

"Uh…" He's not going to answer. I'm pretty sure he's traumatized by all the attention on him.

"Sorry, folks," Menchy says, glaring at Mr. Olson. "We'll work out the kinks." He takes a threatening step toward the sweaty mayor and narrows his eyes. "*All* of them."

I guess not everyone supports the town's current leadership. Larry Olson was a terrible principal when I was in high school, never remembering any of the students' names and assigning detention for infractions he made up on the spot. Parents despised him more than the kids did, so I'm still not certain how he came to be the town's man-in-charge.

Brody releases Mr. Olson with a small shove and mumbles "idiot." Did *Brody* call someone an idiot? I've officially entered the twilight zone.

"What is happening?" I repeat louder to anyone who will explain.

It's Lydia, owner of The Drip, who helps me out. "Menchy's great-nephew developed an app to alert us if any paparazzi are spotted sniffing around. It obviously has flaws since any drunk fool can sound the alarm and no one knows how to shut it down." She shoots a scathing look at the mayor.

"He has a camera!" Mr. Olson protests, jabbing a finger toward Danny once again.

"He always has a camera." Menchy folds his arms across his chest. "And he's a kid."

"Well…" The mayor fizzles out as quickly as his argument. He spins and stalks away in a huff, petting his comb over as he goes. Once he's out of sight, Menchy nods curtly and heads to his store.

Realization dawns on me. "Wait. You guys did this for me?" A ball of emotion catches in my throat, causing my voice to hitch.

Lydia pats my arm. "Of course, honey. We protect our own. No way we'd allow nosy reporters to invade our privacy. We don't even like tourists rolling through town, much as we need them."

Our privacy. I'm their private business. One of Walford's own. My heart warms, and my nose stings.

"Thank you. All of you," I say, though my gratitude will never be enough.

All the high-tech security in the world could never make me feel as safe as the people in this town. It's why I chose to spend my hiatus here despite Marcus's protests about me being vulnerable and unprotected.

In all my time as Makenzie, not a single piece of gossip was ever attributed to someone in Walford. I never mentioned the town in my interviews, claiming Dayton as my home base instead. And while I assumed my decision to not take ownership of them would offend everyone here, it seems it had the opposite effect. They are protecting me in return, and I couldn't be more grateful.

"Everybody back to work!" Brody bellows, sending the horde of bodies scrambling in all directions. He notices my surprise at his authority and gives me a sheepish shrug. "I'm head of the decorating committee." *Huh.*

Danny slowly edges along the brick to extract himself

from public view, so I offer him a sympathetic smile. "Sorry about that, Danny. I didn't mean to pull you into my mess."

"It's okay," he says, then jerks a thumb over his shoulder. "I'm just gonna go."

"Okay. And I meant it about screening your film. I'm happy to do it."

He nods and slinks away, surely relieved to be out of my immediate vicinity.

I shove my gloved hands in my coat pockets and continue toward The Drip. On the rare occasion I leave the house, it's the only place I go. The coffee shop holds a lot of fond memories for me. It's also the least likely place where I might run into Jake or his friends.

Since Lucy's party, I've seen Jake twice as he was going to or from the hardware store. It was difficult to stop myself from sprinting across the street and begging him to talk to me.

Through my recent, low-key reconnaissance, I've learned Jake is rarely seen in Walford. He must live outside of town somewhere rather than in his parents' old house, which isn't too far from the high school. If Jake has a place of his own, I wonder what his home looks like on the inside. Is it warm and cozy or barren and cold? Does he entertain guests, or does he live like a hermit? But mostly, I wonder if he's lonely.

I could ask Lucy for all the details about Jake's life, but I prefer our friendship to be built on common ground rather than my need for information. Besides, she's not really the gossiping type, as far as I can tell, which is another reason I like her.

"Tate! Wait up." Brody jogs up next to me, slowing to

meet my stride. I glance sidelong at him, my hackles raised in preparation for yet another attack from Jake's camp. "Where are you headed?"

"The Drip. Care to join me?"

I might as well get this over with and complete the trifecta of Jake's defensive line. Jensen and Rock had their say. Why not allow Brody a few minutes to speak his mind? I haven't seen him since Lucy's party, when he reminded everyone of my New York incident. Although he sat next to me at the dining table, I paid him little mind because Jake's presence overwhelmed me.

"Sure." He keeps his head lowered, almost as if he's deep in thought.

My eyes swing his way again, unsure of what's happening. We don't speak the rest of the way to the coffee shop, so maybe he's waiting until we have more privacy before he admonishes me.

The electronic bell chimes when we enter, and Lydia swoops by with an empty serving tray tucked under one arm. How she got here so fast is a mystery, considering she was outside clearing decorations mere minutes ago.

"Chai tea, honey?"

"Yes, please," Brody and I say at the same time. We share an awkward giggle. Everything about this interaction is strange.

We shed our hats and coats, hanging them on the coat tree near the door. I settle into my usual corner nook by the window, choosing the gold velvet loveseat. Brody drops into one of the mismatched club chairs opposite the low table between us.

The Drip's exposed brick walls, bookshelves stuffed with donated books, and colorful vintage furniture make it a cozy spot to hang out. It's the kind of coffee shop I would expect to find close to a college campus.

In the uncomfortable silence, my gaze wanders to Lydia, who hums while preparing our drinks. She's owned The Drip for at least twenty years. Her trademark spiky hair, hoop earrings, and blinding-white teeth are staples in Walford, same as her fair-trade coffee beans. Her coffee is delicious, but I prefer tea.

"So." Brody claps his hands and rubs them together, drawing my attention to him. "How are you?"

"Um…I'm good?" I don't mean it to be a question, but his unusually high level of maturity throws me off-kilter.

His head bobs. "Good. That's good."

I search his uncertain blue eyes, a shade or two darker than mine, wondering if I need to carry the weight of this conversation. He swings his blond mess of hair to the side with a jerk of his head. It's much longer than he used to keep it, falling to his cheekbones now, though it's always been shaggy.

Other than the beginnings of a permanent line carved between his eyebrows, he looks exactly the same as he did in high school. Lean and fit, suntanned skin, preppy clothes. It's a surfer-meets-frat-boy combo that only he can pull off.

"What have you been up to?" I ask. We need to start somewhere.

"I'm a teacher. Third-grade science."

If it weren't for the pride radiating from his broad grin, I'd laugh and call him a liar. *Brody's a teacher? Someone hired Brody to teach kids?*

I manage to hide my surprise and plaster on a grin. "That's great. Must be a rewarding job."

His shoulders sag as he relaxes. "It is. Totally. People judge me for it, but I enjoy making a difference, you know?

Teachers can impact a kid's life without realizing it, and not just in the classroom."

Lydia stops by with our mugs of tea. I quickly snatch mine from her hand and blow into the mug to cool the steaming liquid, at a loss for words. Brody clearly loves his job, and I don't want to say something to imply I question his abilities. Although, I *totally* question his abilities. It's Brody!

"Science, huh?" That's the best I can do.

"Yeah. It was always my favorite subject. And STEM programs are all the rage, so I'm happy to do my part and get kids interested early. I try to make it fun."

I stare over the rim of my mug in disbelief. *Who in the fireballs is this guy?* One, he hasn't flirted with me or told me I'm hot. Two, he's talking about science stuff. And three, he's being dead serious. Now, I'm wondering if his comment at Lucy's party about having a master's degree is true.

"That's…wow. It's awesome you found your calling. Sounds like it makes you happy."

"It does." A softness I've never seen before touches his features when he smiles, and I wonder if I'm getting a glimpse at a different side of Brody. He's always been charming and likable, but he seemed *too* happy all the time. Like he couldn't turn it off.

Something outside the window snares his attention. Jensen's employee, Ainsley, hustles toward Bruno's with a large duffle bag slung over one shoulder and a giant purse in the crook of her other arm. That girl is a beast of burden, hauling stuff around all the time.

When I notice the crestfallen expression on Brody's face, I ask, "Are you okay?"

With somber eyes still tracking Ainsley, he speaks so quietly I can barely hear his mumbled words. "You ever get tired of wearing a mask?"

I shift in my seat, crossing my legs and rotating the mug in my hands to keep them busy. My palms are damp. Nerves on high alert. "What do you mean?"

He shakes his head, casting off the spell he was under, and throws me his classic smile, not a care in the world. "Oh, nothing. Ignore me. Haven't been sleeping well."

I decide not to dig further, offering an olive branch instead. "If you ever need someone to talk to, I'm around."

He waves me off. "Nah. I'm good." Brody downs his tea in four gulps and slams the mug on the table. All signs of friendliness vanish from his suddenly stony face. "So, when are you leaving?" *There it is.*

My head falls against the back of the loveseat, and I look down my nose at him. "As soon as I can."

"It's for the best. You've messed with my boy's head enough, don't you think?" He arches a golden eyebrow.

I'm flabbergasted. The one-eighty Brody pulled has my head spinning. He's changed course so many times since that flirty wink he gave me while he restrained the mayor, I'm starting to think the guy has multiple personalities.

I grit my teeth. "What I think is that it's none of your business." *Pat on the back for defending myself. Go Tatum!*

An unfriendly chuckle rumbles in his chest. "Oh-ho-ho. Jake is definitely my business. He's my best friend, and you're just the girl he had to fuck out of his system." Leaning forward, he quietly adds, "And let me tell you, he really put in the work."

Gut punch.

Brody stands and tosses a five-dollar bill on the table. With a smirk and a parting wink, he says, "See you around, *Makenzie*."

I'm too focused on the lack of oxygen in my lungs to watch him leave. Hands trembling, I set my mug on the table.

My stomach churns at the image Brody painted, threatening to reject the warm tea I drank.

Could it be true? Did Jake become the type of guy who would…? I can't think it, much less believe it. But can I honestly blame him if he chose to drown his heartache in a slew of women? If I thought the pain of losing his love was crushing, the notion that he gave his body away freely—repeatedly—without emotional investment is total annihilation.

As if the universe revels in my torment, denying me a moment's respite, the bell chimes above the door and in walks the man I no longer recognize.

I stare at the back of Jake's head and leather jacket as he approaches the counter. He pays at the register, then grabs two to-go cups from Lydia. Two cups. *Two.*

It never occurred to me he might've moved on, and that thought sends my heart tumbling down a black hole with no safe landing in sight.

15

JAKE

I drag my feet along the sidewalk, heading toward The Drip because I ran out of coffee at home and need a caffeine fix, stat. Thankfully, I scrounged together enough brain cells to think of calling ahead and placing a to-go order.

The January cold has officially arrived, so I've been holed up in my house planning future work trips and eating everything in my kitchen.

A grinning Brody gives me a high five when he walks past but doesn't say anything. Most people would consider the exchange odd or want to know what we're celebrating, but whatever. Typical Brody.

My mouth waters at the scent of roasted coffee beans and freshly brewed goodness when I enter The Drip. I shuffle to the register, pay Lydia in cash and a euphoric moan, and snatch my two cups of joe like the addict I am.

When a hush falls over a crowd, it's never for a good reason. When the energy shifts in the air, raising the fine hairs on my neck, it's for the worst reason. My muscles lock up, and I have to keep myself from squeezing the cardboard cups so hard the lids pop off.

Heightened senses alert me to the beacon in the corner before I've completed my slow turn. My eyes land on Tatum and—being the lovesick puppy I am—assess her from head to toe, seeking any cause for concern.

Someone needs to outfit me with a shock collar because I am utterly and hopelessly powerless to stay away when I register her ashen skin, blanched lips, and the dark shadows under her blue eyes. A stark difference from the flourishing woman I cornered in Rock's bathroom a few nights ago. Despite her obvious state of distress, she's beyond beautiful.

A loose braid falls over one shoulder. The baby hairs framing her face are frizzy, as if she's been wearing a hat. A black turtle-neck sweater hugs her slender body, accentuating her small breasts and slim waist.

Tatum has always dressed modestly, choosing comfort over sex appeal. To me, that makes her more enticing. Like a perfectly wrapped present, tempting me to remove each layer in order to find the surprise underneath. She only wears revealing outfits when she performs on stage as Makenzie. When I followed her career, I hated seeing her dressed that way because it's not true to who she is.

My heavy feet move forward of their own free will. A little voice in my head laughs at how quick I am to abandon —for the second time, I might add—my week-old vow to make her come to me first.

Tatum remains unmoving, hands pinned beneath her thighs as she watches me approach at tortoise speed. My stomach dips and flips with each step. Seeing her around, in the flesh, these past couple of weeks has eradicated much of my anxiety, but I'm still nervous.

Perhaps there's some truth to what Brody said about the way having eyes on her affects me. Having a full-blown conversation with her—one that I'm initiating in public—

however, is a whole different ball game. I'm overcome with a potent mixture of anticipation and trepidation with a boatload of *Oh shit! Here we go!* thrown in.

I halt next to the table and clear my throat. "Mind if I sit?"

The tiny shake of her head is hardly noticeable.

Old habit has me twitching forward in a move to join her on the loveseat. Our loveseat. The cozy spot where we spent afternoons doing homework and laughing with our legs tangled together. Lydia never seemed bothered by the scuff marks our shoes left on the table.

I stop myself and awkwardly settle into a blue corduroy chair instead. Gripping my cups, I rest one on each thigh to occupy my hands.

I want to touch her.

The low buzz of chatter resumes around us, and muffled murmurs bounce off our insulated corner bubble. We stare at each other for an uncomfortable length of time, neither of us knowing what to say.

My brows furrow at the anguish swirling in her eyes as she examines me like I'm unrecognizable. Unfamiliar. A stranger she's never seen before.

Two weeks ago, standing in her aunt's kitchen, she looked at me like it pained her not to jump into my arms. A pain I, too, felt in my marrow. In Rock's bathroom, her body hummed being near mine. Now? Her scrutinizing gaze makes me want to scream, *It's me! Your Jake! I'm still here. I've always been here.*

Maybe she doesn't know me anymore. We've grown and changed, for better or worse, as people do. And perhaps I'm blinding myself to the truth and want so badly for her to be the girl who loved only me. If she replaced me, what am I so desperately holding on to?

"Was there someone else?" I blurt, barely fending off the panic edging its way inside.

Her head jerks back. "What?"

"Did you meet someone? Is that why you stopped taking my calls?" *Please say no.*

"No." Her voice is soft, but her answer is firm. Almost believable as sorrow steals across her face. Her reply brings me tremendous relief and more questions.

"What about the actor? You were engaged," I say, the accusation clear in my tone.

They were Hollywood's golden couple, and their relationship lasted years longer than ours did.

"It wasn't—" She shakes her head, and her gaze falls to her lap with a resigned sigh. "It's complicated."

"Complicated." My lips press firmly together at her dismissal. Explosive words coat my tongue but releasing them will only scare her away.

Her shoulders droop as defeat settles in her tired voice. "We can't do this here, Jake. I promise I'll tell you everything before I leave. Please give me a little more time. It's just… shit's coming at me from all sides right now."

I've waited ages for answers and have every right to demand them this instant, but I suppress the scathing retort aimed at her comment about needing more time. The tears threatening to spill from her pleading, shadowed eyes give me pause. She's the picture of exhaustion, similar to how she appeared in the photos after her New York concert.

I want to hold her.

The concerned part of me wants to ask what's wrong or what I can do to ease her burden, but the scorned part of me nods in silent acquiescence.

Tatum tugs her hands from under her thighs and toys with the end of her braid. "It's strange being here again. I'm not sure what I expected but, mostly, everyone's been wonderful."

"Walford is full of good people."

"You have good friends here, that's for sure. They certainly have your back." She lets out a mirthless chuckle. "Brody, especially."

"Brody?"

"I had tea with him earlier. We chatted." She glances around the coffee shop. Only a handful of customers remain, including us.

Her statement strikes me as odd. Brody doesn't drink tea, and the two of them were never close enough to warrant a catching-up chat. Their banter consisted of inappropriate comments and exasperated eye rolls.

"What did he say?" I ask.

Her gaze pings between the cups propped on my knees before she rips it away. "It doesn't matter."

I lean forward, alerted by the flash of hurt on her face. An unpleasant burn simmers below my surface. "He upset you."

I want to fight for her.

"I deserve it, don't I?" Tears carve shimmering paths along her pale cheeks. She uses a sleeve to wipe them away. "I never wanted to hurt you," she rasps.

Tatum's declaration slams me into reality. I stuff every warm unwanted feeling I have for her into the box of denial where they belong. Where they've been safely locked away and guarded in her absence. I allow my tormented demon to rear its ugly head instead.

"Hurt is too small a word to describe what you did to me." My harsh words strike where intended.

Her face crumples, and she slaps a hand over her mouth to stifle a sob. Staring me dead in the eyes, honesty punches through her fingers on a strangled whisper. "I'm so sorry."

Haven't I longed for those words to fall from her pretty lips? Haven't I waited long enough for her to seek absolution from me? In a surprising twist, I find the meaningless words have no effect on me. They don't bring me solace or open the door to reconciliation. Why? Because I don't know what the fuck she's sorry for.

Tatum's earlier observation was accurate. The Drip isn't the place to unearth our monsters. It's not a big enough space to contain them.

"I have to go," is my croaked response before I lunge to my feet and haul ass out of there.

I don't dare peek when I hustle past the window where Tatum sits on the other side. Marching toward Bruno's, I toss my full coffee cups into the nearest trash can.

The door slams open with my forceful shove, a cloud of fury swirling around me as I storm toward Rock and Brody's table. With football season at an end, they've resumed their weekly meetup for beers, so they're the only ones here at the moment.

Chomping on a handful of fries, Rock's eyes bulge at the murderous expression on my face. Brody's back is to me, so he doesn't see me coming. Good. I snatch the plastic fork from his French-fry basket and jab it under his chin. My other arm locks around his neck and squeezes.

"What…the fuck…did you say to her?" I growl the question into his ear.

"You better let go of me, bro," he says, choking as I cut off his air.

Brody and I are the same height, but he's broader and packs more muscle. However, I'm the pissed-off party surging with adrenaline in this situation, so naturally that gives me the upper hand. And how hard can it be to kick the ass of a guy wearing a V-neck sweater and khakis?

Rock's eyes bounce between us as he continues munching on fries. He doesn't move to stop my attack, probably hoping it ends in bloodshed and broken bones.

"What did you say?" I ask again, pressing the fork firmly against Brody's flesh.

He catches my thumb and bends it backward, forcing me to release the chokehold. In a matter of seconds, he's off the stool and has me bent over with my arm twisted behind me at a painful angle. I drop the fork and slap at his thigh with my free arm.

"Ow, ow, ow, ow."

I've never been in a fight in my life.

Rock mutters, "Oh shit," with a mouthful of food before leaping to his feet and coming to my rescue.

Who knew Brody was capable of such swift, violent action? He's a freaking teddy bear! Even when he played high school football, he only held offensive scoring positions and was always slow to tackle.

A shocked gasp draws our attention, and all heads snap toward the kitchen. Ainsley's face drains of color, and she covers her quivering lip with a shaky hand before spinning and pushing through the swinging door.

"Fuck!" Brody curses, shoving me to the floor. He stuffs a hand in his shaggy hair, gripping it hard as he paces back and forth with a tortured expression on his face. *What the hell is going on with him?*

Jensen bursts through the kitchen door. "What are you idiots doing?" He takes in the scene and spreads his arms, eyes wide and questioning.

I pop to my feet and massage my aching shoulder, my

scowl aimed directly at Brody. "This asshole said something to upset Tate."

Yes, I'm tattling. I need someone on my side so I can pretend my defending Tatum isn't unreasonable given our current circumstances.

"What did you say to her?" Jensen asks, having my back as always.

Brody swings an arm in my direction when he answers. "I stood up for my friend. Same as Rock did."

A menacing undertone laces Jensen's voice when he steps to Brody and repeats the question slowly, enunciating each word. "What did you say?"

Meanwhile, I lift my eyebrows at Rock. This is the first I've learned of him talking to Tatum. He rubs the side of his neck while a red flush creeps from his collarbone toward his Adam's apple.

"Let's all sit down and talk through this," he offers. What's with this guy and the therapy skills he's dying to put to use?

Brody drops onto a stool, followed by Rock. Jensen remains standing with feet planted shoulder-width apart and arms crossed over his chest. I stand beside him, hands on hips, inhaling slow breaths to regain my calm-*ish* composure.

Jensen addresses Rock first. "Since you're so eager to talk things through, start talking."

Rock shoots me an apologetic look. "I saw her at the festival and might've hinted it's best if she doesn't stick around."

"Hinted," Brody scoffs, earning a glare from Rock.

I have no comment. It's one thing for my best friends to support me like they've done for years. After all, they know the history. But it's another thing for them to charge into battle on my behalf. I bet Tatum was mortified, especially if Rock confronted her in public.

I rub my jaw and study Brody, praying whatever vitriol he spewed at Tatum wasn't worse than Rock suggesting she leave. Based on Tatum's mention of him, specifically, I suspect that's not the case.

"And you?" I ask him.

In his chill manner, he says, "I also hinted she needs to go ASAP"—he pops a shoulder—"and that you worked hard to fuck her out of your system."

"Jesus Christ!" Rock shouts, appalled by Brody's crass words. Rock is a mama's boy and would never say anything demeaning to a woman. He can be rude and gruff, but never demeaning.

"What the fuck?" This comes from Jensen, his face twisted in outrage. Size-wise, he's somewhere between Rock and Brody and could probably take the latter down if they came to blows.

I plant my ass on an empty stool and my elbows on the table and fist my hair, wondering why the hell everything has gone sideways. Rock crossing a line when he confronted Tatum. Brody's sudden Jekyll and Hyde routine, with the molecular biology and secret kung-fu skills and cruel intentions. Since when do my friends act like schoolyard bullies and keep secrets? Are these the people they became while I was frozen in my chamber of heartache, unable to let love go?

The silence and tension are suffocating as they wait for me to respond.

Jensen leans in next to me and clamps a hand on my sore shoulder. "Talk to me, Jake."

I absently shake my head. It all makes sense now. Brody's stupid high five. Tatum's distraught expression. God, what she must think of me. No wonder she looked at me like we'd never met before.

If I have the chance to undo the damage Brody caused, there's no guarantee she'll listen. She thinks I'm like him, plowing my way through women with no promise of feelings or attachments. I may have a shameful secret no one knows about that involves sex, but I've never been a promiscuous man.

Sighing, Jensen adjusts to his full height. "I'll get us a round. Brody's buying." He mutters "asshole" as he walks away.

"I'm sorry, man," Rock says from his perch across from me, the regret clear in his tone.

"Why are you sorry? We want her gone, right?" Brody grunts and curses. Rock either punched him or smacked his head.

"He's in love with her, idiot. Of course, he doesn't want her gone." Rock says to me, "We shouldn't have said anything, Jake. We were out of line."

"Damn right you were." Jensen reappears and slams three beers on the table. "Come on," he says, offering me a bottle and clapping me on the back. "We can fix this." *We?*

"Why are you so invested in them patching things up?" Brody asks him.

That's a really great question. Jensen's been on my ass about talking things over with Tatum since the day she stepped foot in Walford.

I shrug off my coat and chug my beer in one go. If I can't get my coffee fix, I might as well drink beer to survive the day and escape this nightmare.

Jensen rests his forearms on the table. Cue the lecture. "There are two sides to every story. We know Jake's side. Hell, we've lived it. But Tate hasn't explained things yet. We don't need her running off before that happens. If we want Jake to find some peace, he needs to listen to her story."

"She's been here over a month. I'd say she's had plenty of time," Brody argues. He has a valid point, but everyone at this table knows Tatum will hide until she's forced to face the music.

Rock, astute as always, homes in on a different part of Jensen's statement. "How do you know her story will give him peace?"

Jensen shifts his weight, a nervous gesture I'm familiar with, having known him my whole life. "It's just an assumption. All I'm saying is Jake can close this chapter and move on once he hears her out."

I narrow my eyes at him. He knows damn well there's no end to this chapter. Hell, it's not a chapter at all. It's a never-ending story of unrequited love. I can't be at peace without Tatum by my side. So why is he pretending otherwise?

"You've talked to her. Did she tell *you* her story?" I ask him.

All eyes are pinned on Jensen, searching for the lie. *Is that a bead of sweat on his temple?*

"I know she has a lot of regrets." His gaze sweeps over the full bottles remaining. "I'll grab another round and check on Ainsley."

Jensen bolts to the kitchen like his ass is on fire. Brody tracks his departure like he wants to follow.

"He's hiding something," Rock says, biting into three fries at once.

I'm inclined to agree. However, honoring the Walford custom of keeping lips sealed when it comes to Tatum, Jensen's not saying shit.

The three of us stew in silence until he returns. I crack open the second beer he offers and drain half before I remember I have to drive home. My thoughts drift to the state Tatum was in and the mess my friends made. She might be packing her bags as we speak, and it wouldn't surprise me.

"You should've seen the look on Tate's face," I tell them, dejected and forlorn as I slump in my seat.

Brody winces. "I saw it." At least he summoned the good sense to be a little ashamed of his actions.

"What were you thinking?" Rock presses.

"He doesn't think. That's the problem," Jensen says.

"You know, I'm sick and tired of you fuckers calling me stupid."

"Enough!" I shout. "It's done."

I have to make this right, which means I'll need to set aside my stubborn pride and talk to Tatum before it's too late. She asked for more time so she can deal with other issues before she faces the big one: me.

Well, I have a three-day trip scheduled starting tomorrow morning. That should buy me some time to corral my thoughts and figure out what to say as well. It's a win-win for us both. As long as she stays put until I return.

16

TATUM

Seated on the floor with my guitar resting in my lap, I bite my favorite pick—a glittery purple one I only use for songwriting—between my teeth and press the button on my phone to stop recording. Seems pretty pointless to record nothing but the low hum of the heater when it kicks on.

I can't find inspiration anywhere. Not from my old notebooks, not from the photo propped against my guitar case, and certainly not from within.

The other day, I called Cheryl at Gateway Hills and told her coming to Walford was a mistake. The emotional whiplash isn't good for me. One minute, nostalgia and friendly faces lift my spirits and bring me comfort. The next, poisoned memories and hurtful words leave me feeling hopeless. The conflicting sentiments are difficult to reconcile when the darkness already has its hooks in me.

Cheryl told me, *"Facing your past is like looking in a mirror. You may not like what you see, but you must accept the truth in its reflection. You can make changes today to improve what you see tomorrow, but change can never be retroactive."*

While I would give anything to rewind the past—to unmake all those poor decisions in the months leading up to the phone call ten years ago that altered the trajectory of my life—it's impossible. What I *can* do is tell Jake the truth and leave for California. Because once I deliver the final blow, all hope for us will be lost forever.

Lucy's a godsend. She's funny, informative, and lets me hog Marcella during our lunch dates. We talk about everything except my troubles, and I'm thankful for the escape she offers me. It's nice having a friend in Walford.

Maisy threatened to drive here and kick Brody in the balls after I told her what he said to me. She doesn't believe Jake's the type of man Brody claims. To be honest, it's hard to wrap my head around the idea. But rumor always carries an ounce of truth.

I'm not so naive to believe Jake spent the last ten years celibate. Humans have basic needs and moments of weakness when faced with temptation. The thought of him screwing other women sickens me, of course, but I can't hold his sexual history against him when I'm to blame for our end.

However, the thought of him *making love* to someone else shatters me. Because that's what Jake does—he makes love. It's a soulful, full-body experience born of a deep, meaningful connection. We had that connection. Selfishly, and perhaps foolishly, I want to believe he never found it with anyone else.

My laptop rings, alerting me to the weekly video call with the guys and Maisy. I click to answer before setting my guitar aside and spitting out my pick.

Maisy's face pops up in a window first, followed by Marcus's face and Judge's elbow in a separate box. "What are you wearing?" she asks.

The guys' window vanishes.

"What?" I squint at the tiny frame in the screen's corner.

"Girl, change your shirt or go put on a bra."

I finally glance down. So, remember my dad's flannel with all the holes? I've been wearing it for three days straight, and one hole in the chest area might've grown bigger. A lot bigger.

My cell phone pings.

Lovely.

It's nothing they haven't seen before. They've always tried to be respectful, but it's kind of hard not to flash a boob or a butt cheek at your team while rushing through a wardrobe change in cramped spaces during a tour. A car, an elevator, a Swiss gondola…the guys rarely left my side, so they saw a lot of skin.

I rip off the flannel, grab the first T-shirt within reach, and tug it over my head. Maisy's waiting with her chin rested in her hand while I text the guys.

"I want to come home," I blurt the second they rejoin the call.

Marcus normally starts the meetings, but everyone needs to know where my head's at. The success of me traveling to California undetected rests squarely on the guys' shoulders. They make all the security plans and travel arrangements.

Marcus shakes his head. "No can do, Tatum. Not yet. A couple of assholes showed up a few days ago demanding you show your face. Said they'd been all over Dayton searching for you. Asking a lot of questions and stirring up a lot of rumors."

"What rumors?"

My team recommended a news ban to which I happily agreed. I went an extra step with a self-imposed social media ban.

Maisy says, "Remember those bitches in Ohio who claimed you were best friends when you first got famous? Now they're admitting you moved to Texas, and no one heard from you again."

"Do they know where I am?" Panic rises with my voice.

Walford may have a faulty alert system in case the paparazzi come knocking, but that won't stop them from coming. They'll descend on the town like a plague of termites and destroy everything in their path.

"They don't know where in Texas you went. Said it started with an *M*. That should keep the paps busy for a while. In the meantime, stay put. Don't let those three jerkoffs in Walford run you off." Maisy bites into a giant cookie.

The barrel of a gun slides into view in the guys' window.

"Judge wants to know if we need to fly down there and bang a few skulls together." Marcus glances offscreen. "Or hide some bodies."

Maisy raises a hand. "I'll bring the shovel." Cookie crumbs fall from her stuffed mouth, prompting Marcus's face to screw up in disgust. He's a stickler for table manners.

Returning to the issue at hand, I ask him, "So, what does this mean? Do those paps know I'm not in Cali?"

"All cameras are pointed at Texas. My guess is they'll be casing the private airports around every major city, asking with cash if you've passed through lately."

Everyone will talk for a price. With that in mind... "The flight crew—"

He cuts me off. "Already reminded of the NDA, so you're protected. And we kept you hidden on the ground. You're safest where you are, so sit tight. I'm working on contingencies and getting more eyes on you there."

I deflate at the turn of events, though I should've expected this was coming. Not a peep has come from my camp since the message Maisy posted on social media after the New York concert four months ago. Bette used to handle damage control. Now, I have no one to pander to the press on my behalf.

Pretty soon, rumors will surface that I'm dead. In reality, I'm trapped.

Fame sucks.

"What about you, Maiz? Anyone giving you trouble?" I ask.

The public is used to seeing Maisy with me. Thankfully, she's never given an interview because she doesn't trust anyone outside our little team. So we've managed to keep her personal details and history a secret.

"A reporter covering the film production recognized me on set and tried asking questions, but Graham intervened. He joked about hiring me out from under you. Made it out to be part of a lover's quarrel." She winces. "Sorry."

I flap a hand. "It's fine. I'm not upset." Addressing Marcus, I ask, "So, what now?"

"Now you find something productive to do to pass the time." His eyes slide to the side. "Judge has taken up painting."

A canvas floats into view behind Marcus's shiny head. The scene depicts a girl on stage facing an audience in shadow. There's no microphone or band. Just her and a guitar

—all alone. It's quite good, and I'm moved by the way Judge captured my recent feelings in the image.

Wow.

Judge's rare toothy grin moves into frame, and his obvious pride halts my emotional downturn in its tracks.

"I love it, Judge. It's amazing."

A sheepish shrug accompanies his grin before he disappears.

"Anyway." Marcus rubs his temples. "Meeting adjourned. I have a date tonight. Gotta jet." Their window vanishes again.

Maisy and I stare at our screens for a beat until she mutters, "I think Marcus hates goodbyes."

"Yeah. I've noticed." Deepening my voice, I mock him. "It's always 'talk soon' or 'gotta jet' or that stupid dude nod." I try to recall a single instance in the last five years when Marcus said some normal version of goodbye but come up short. "Has he always been like this?"

"Pretty sure," she says. "He never says hello either." *Huh.*

Then she gives me a look. The one that says *I'm about to switch gears and you're not going to like it because we're ditching the light-hearted bullshit for the really real shit so buckle up, bitch!*

Her tone softens to complement her stupid, sympathetic expression. "What do you need?"

Not in the mood to rehash the last few days or wallow in sadness, I scrub my hands over my face and groan long and loud. "Reinforcements." Throwing puppy dog eyes in the mix, I beg, "Come see me?"

She smiles. Such a simple movement of facial muscles she doesn't execute often enough. "I'll see what I can do."

~

Unable to tolerate being cooped up another second, I came to Bruno's to keep Jensen company. Aunt Pam and I played cards over breakfast and a riveting game of Yahtzee before lunch, but then she had errands to run and business to attend to. She invited me to come along, but her to-do list sounded as boring as watching a documentary about rock formations.

The bar's been slow for the past hour, allowing me plenty of time to talk Jensen's ear off before the working crowd trickles in. He's checked on me via text, but we haven't seen each other since the festival.

I swirl a fry in mustard and share some unsolicited business advice. "You should serve peanuts like those steakhouses where people drop the shells all over the floor."

Jensen wipes the condensation ring left behind after my third Shirley Temple, then tosses the damp rag in a bucket. "Nope. Hannah Sutton's son has a peanut allergy." He mixes my fourth sugary drink.

"I'm sure he's too young to frequent a bar." I jab a fry in his direction. "Extra cherries!"

He rolls his eyes and plops three more cherries in the pink concoction. With the flair of a true barman, he slides the drink along the shiny surface. It stops right in front me.

"Customers would track peanut dust all over town. He could come into contact with it anywhere. It only takes a small amount." He shakes his head. "Not on my watch."

"Fair point."

Gosh, he's a good guy, always looking out for everyone else. I know from personal experience Jensen will drop everything to help someone in need, no matter the cost to himself.

I sip my drink and glance around the room while he stacks glasses. "What's with the stage?"

"It's for the usual shit. Karaoke once a month. Trivia

nights. Live music when I find someone good enough to book." He pops me with a rag and winks. "You gonna play for us, Tate?"

"Pfft. Not a chance. I'm on vacation." I stick the straw in my mouth and examine the fizz in my glass while Jensen chuckles and saunters off to do whatever bar owners do.

The stage doesn't bring me the sense of longing I thought it would. I don't miss performing at all. What I do miss is the dopamine rush I get when an audience feels my music.

I've always found the power of words remarkable. Wielding that power, even more so. Being the one to put smiles on people's faces or tears in their eyes—being the reason two lovers' gazes meet in silent communication as a shared understanding passes between them—is pure magic. It's an addiction that will never go away.

The door flies open, and Rock and Brody pour through in a tussle of limbs as they curse at each other.

"Idiots," Jensen mutters, reappearing behind the bar with a pencil tucked behind his ear, which I find oddly attractive. Maybe because it reminds me of when Jake would slide a pen behind his ear while he studied.

Rock and Brody cease the horseplay when they notice me, both hesitating for a beat. Surprisingly, it's Brody who leads the charge as they approach. He's wearing a purple polo and dark khakis while Rock sports his typical tracksuit. Today's color choice is grey.

"I want to apologize," Brody says, sounding like the serious man I caught a glimpse of in the coffee shop. "What I said was way out of line. I won't make excuses for why I said it. I'm ashamed of myself because, honestly, I despise bullies. And that was a bully move."

It doesn't escape my notice that he took back the words, but he's not refuting them. With no rebuttal forthcoming, what he said about Jake's history with women might still be true.

"I'm sorry too," Rock says, stepping up beside Brody. "I was an ass."

I quirk an eyebrow. "That sounds like Lucy talking."

"And she's right." He grabs the fountain soda Jensen prepared for him. "Enjoy your mustard fries."

Brody hangs back and searches over my head while Rock claims a table.

"She's not working tonight," Jensen tells him, and I'm certain he's referring to Ainsley.

"Oh." Brody masks his disappointment with a lazy shrug. "Whatever." He accepts the water bottle Jensen offers and orders chicken wings and fries before joining Rock.

"What's up with that?" I whisper to Jensen, curious about Brody's obvious interest in Ainsley.

"I have no idea, but he's gonna scare her away if he doesn't back off. And I'd hate to lose a good server." He gets back to work and leaves me to my liquid sugar.

Twenty minutes or so pass when I sense a presence behind me. I subtly glance at the mirrored wall behind all the liquor bottles, careful not to let on that I'm aware of my surroundings.

A tall man wearing an enormous cowboy hat, aviator sunglasses, and a hunter green pea coat buttoned up all the way to his neck hovers a couple feet away. The wide brim of the hat hides his face as he tucks his chin. I stiffen, worried the paparazzi finally found me.

Jensen must sense my discomfort because he steps over and sharpens his tone when he asks the man, "Can I help you?"

A baritone voice, smooth as silk, replies, "What potato options are on the menu?"

I'm out of my seat so fast the stool tips over, slamming to the floor. Happy tears—no, scratch that—tears of overwhelming relief spill from my eyes. I scale Graham's body like he's a climbing wall, knocking his hat off in the process. His easy laugh rumbles when he hoists me up by my thighs until I'm wrapped around him in a tight koala hug.

He presses a chaste kiss to my neck. "How's my little potato?"

Graham has called me *Tot*, or his *little potato*, for as long as I can remember. I don't recall how or when the nickname originated. Knowing him, he wanted to one-up Maisy by giving me a nickname cuter than Tate.

I hold on to him, unable and unwilling to let go. It's been nine months since I've seen him, which is the longest we've ever been apart. He smells like bergamot and musk and comfort on the darkest days.

When I have my blubbering under control, I wipe my nose on his coat and slide down his body until my feet hit the floor. Chuckling, I undo his top buttons. "You look ridiculous. What are you doing here?"

He removes his sunglasses and spins in a circle with his arms spread wide. "You asked for reinforcements. Here I am."

A genuine smile overtakes my face. Despite being ragged, exhausted, and battered from the sad memories plaguing me day and night, I'm incredibly overjoyed right now. Running my fingers along his smooth jaw, I take in his sandy-brown hair, full upper lip, and amber eyes with tiny wrinkles at the corners.

"Gosh, I've missed you," I say on a sigh.

Graham and I met in the early days of our fledgling careers. I was recording my first album, and he attended casting calls for every minor role he could find. Which is how he ended up cast as the love interest in my first music video. We hit it off instantly. And the rest, as they say, is history.

Tabloids and fans went crazy, calling us Hollywood's "It Couple" years later, but my earliest fans knew our connection predated our fame. Once they spread the word, the media spun a tale of the most romantic rags-to-riches love story ever told. Two starving artists who stood hand in hand, supporting and loving each other unconditionally as they ascended to stardom.

All of that is true, minus the romance.

Jensen clears his throat, reminding me we're not alone.

"Oh! Sorry. Graham, this is Jensen Holloway. Old friend and owner of this fine establishment." Waving a game-show arm at Graham, I say, "Jensen, this is Graham Kingston. Wannabe director and apple of my eye."

Graham snorts.

Jensen isn't laughing…at all. Lips pressed in a flat line, he tips his chin in greeting and busies himself behind the bar without saying a word.

"Not a fan of my work?" Graham stage-whispers.

I frown at Jensen's rudeness. "Guess not."

"Don't worry, love. I'm sure that won't be the only unwelcome reception I get in this town." He tugs me into his arms and sways our bodies in a slow dance despite the upbeat rock song playing in the background. "Speaking of…where the hell are we? There's, like, ten houses. And what are you wearing?"

He crinkles his nose at my lime green, oversized sweater and black-and-white plaid leggings. I disregard his comment on my fashion choices.

"This town is small, yes, but it's a vault. Nobody here spills secrets beyond its borders. And no one will harass you."

He glances around at the few bar patrons. I do the same, hoping my declaration rings true. My gaze lands on Brody's narrowed eyes assessing Graham. Rock's eyes bulge out of his head while a fry dangles from his mouth. Ignoring them, I shift my gaze to the group of women at the corner table. Judging by the blushing cheeks and frantic whispers, they recognize Graham, but no one makes a move to approach.

"I'll be damned," he mutters. With his level of fame and gorgeous looks, he's often mauled anywhere he goes outside of Hollywood. Women and men swoon over him, but he won't have that problem in Walford.

"How about we order some food to go? I'll take you to my favorite spot, and we can eat while we catch up."

A cabinet door bangs shut. A glass shatters. Jensen curses.

Graham eyes him warily. "Lead the way."

17

TATUM

I never would've imagined Graham sitting on a rusty tailgate, legs swinging, as he eats a greasy cheeseburger under the stars. He's more relaxed than he's ever been. Nestled beside him with our thighs pressed together, my legs swing in tandem with his.

We faced two obstacles and made one pit stop on our way to the ridge.

First, when we stepped onto the sidewalk outside Bruno's, Menchy marched toward us with a crowbar, a roll of duct tape, and a length of rope coiled over one shoulder. Graham froze mid-step when he saw the violent intention on Menchy's face.

"You a reporter?" he barked at Graham.

Graham remained fully exposed since he hadn't put his hat or glasses on. His incredulous eyes slid my way, silently asking *does he really not know who I am?*

"Uh…"

"He's my friend, Menchy. In town for a quick visit," I said to defuse the situation.

Menchy assessed Graham with narrowed eyes and a

pinched mouth. "Mm-hmm. Well, we haven't fixed the alert system yet, so I'm on watch." I almost pointed out that Menchy's always watching but held my tongue.

"Alert system?" Graham asked.

I whispered, "I'll explain later."

Menchy gave us another head-to-toe perusal before marching back to his store.

"Doesn't that guy remind you of that boxing promoter?" Graham asked as he watched Menchy's retreating form.

I chuckled, hooked an arm in Graham's, and dragged him to Aunt Pam's house, which was our pit stop. His rental car couldn't handle the rough, gravel roads we would be taking, so we borrowed my aunt's work truck. Yes, I'm an unlicensed driver, but these are familiar streets so it's fine. I also grabbed a warmer coat, a hat, and a pair of gloves in case I needed them.

The second obstacle came in the form of a gate, which confused me because the hidden road leading to the back end of the Hamiltons' land has always been accessible. The gate wasn't locked, and I didn't see a No Trespassing sign, so I concluded that we were free to enter. Graham disagreed, but he stopped complaining once we crested the hill, and he saw the amazing view.

He balls up his food wrapper and stuffs it into the empty bag. "There's something about this place. I can see why you love it."

I'm not sure if he's referring to Walford or the secluded ridge where we're parked. "It's definitely special," I say, referring to both.

The twinkling sky above us awakens my fondest memories. I rest on my palms and loll my head to the side, embracing the tranquility.

"I don't think I've ever seen so many stars." A touch of awe laces his voice as he gazes at the heavens.

The soft glow of a small flashlight offers enough light to see our faces without encroaching on the velvet darkness enveloping us. On a moonless night, the Texas sky holds an infinite number of stars. In my head, I sing a slow rendition of "Deep In The Heart of Texas" as I stare at the shimmering wonder above.

Graham tucks a lock of hair behind my ear. "Talk to me."

I inhale a deep breath and release it slowly, then I tell him about the disastrous tour that ended with both the record label and Bette dropping me. I talk about Gateway Hills and Cheryl. About the reasons behind my decision to come to Walford instead of staying in California.

He listens with quiet patience while I describe the warm welcome I've received here, mostly, and the town's efforts to conceal me. We both chuckle when I explain the alert system Menchy spoke of when we encountered him. I gloss over the more unpleasant details from my run-ins with Jake and his friends.

When I finish, he pinches my chin between his thumb and forefinger, turning my head so I'm forced to meet his eyes.

"Now tell me how all of that made you feel. And how you feel right now."

Graham's right. I've given him the chronological rundown of events, but in a detached way.

"I guess I feel lots of things. Ashamed for letting myself get so out of control. Embarrassed by my behavior and how I disrespected my fans. Grateful for having people who supported me and stood by me through it all…and still do." I lift a shoulder. "Sad that I can't right certain wrongs."

He wraps an arm around me, and I rest my head on his chest. "Have you talked to him?"

Him. Jake.

My heart seizes at the memory of what he said to me at the coffee shop. Hurt *is* too small, too hollow, a word to describe his pain. I've seen the intensity of it lurking in the depths of his green eyes and struggling against his controlled movements, fighting to break free and rage at me.

"We've spoken some. Not about…" I trail off. Graham's privy to my history. He's been my rock and my shield on the worst days. I've always been able to rely on him, Maisy, and Aunt Pam to see me through them. "I promised him I'd tell him everything soon."

"Good." Graham squeezes me before he lets me go.

Ready to move on to happier subjects, I lace our fingers together. "How's the film going?"

He bobs his head, a hint of pleasant surprise in his expression. "Great, actually. It's refreshing to work with unknown actors. They're eager. Doing it for the experience, not just the money. I admire their hunger and focus. It reminds me of how determined I was at their age."

"As opposed to the diva you are now?" I tease, nudging his ribs.

His laugh echoes around us. "It's been eye-opening, for sure. No frills or extra perks. My budget doesn't even have room for catering, so I keep my trailer stocked with sandwich stuff and bags of chips for the cast and crew. It's more of a pantry than a workspace."

"Get out. The great Graham Kingston browses grocery aisles now? How pedestrian of you."

He scoffs dramatically. "Never. The groceries come to me."

"Of course, they do."

Gosh, it feels good to joke and laugh. Graham always lifts my spirits, and he couldn't have shown up at a better time.

"Seriously. I'm so happy, Tot. I pinch myself every morning to make sure it's not a dream."

Graham went into acting with the sole purpose of learning everything he could about directing since he wasn't able to afford film school. He didn't expect to become a mega movie star, and he gained invaluable experience while working for the best directors in the business.

I beam with pride and happiness for him. "You've worked so hard for this. You're gonna be great."

"I couldn't have done it without you," he says, his mood turning serious.

The sincerity in his tone makes me twitchy, so I bump a shoulder against him. "Oh, stop. I'm just a fantastic cheerleader."

He draws his brows together, indignation overtaking his features. "You're so much more than that. I would be nothing without you. *You* made success possible for me. Don't diminish your own worth by refusing to accept my gratitude."

Chastised, I mutter an apology, which earns me an exasperated eye roll.

"You would apologize for existing if you could. Just say 'okay, honey' and take the compliment."

My lips curve up at the mention of my pet name for him. "Okay, honey."

"Better." Raising our joined hands, he kisses each of my knuckles. "You know I love you, right? You mean everything to me."

"I love you more," I tell him.

"This is private property."

I jump out of my skin when the low icy voice pierces the night air. Flattening a hand on my chest, I try to steady my erratic heartbeats.

Graham, not the least bit startled, glances over his left

shoulder for the source of the disruption. Gripping his arm, I peek around him, fearful of confronting the man I'm sure to find.

Jake steps out of the pitch black, silhouetted by the night like some kind of shadow beast cornering its victims. He's never seemed more threatening. A ball cap sits low on his forehead, shielding his face from the stars' illumination. Curled fists restrain the anger in his tightly coiled body as he awaits our response.

I'm too stunned to speak, so Graham tucks me under his arm and responds in a ridiculous Southern drawl. "Sorry, friend. My girl, here, wanted to show me her favorite place. Make a new memory or two before I leave town." He winks for added effect.

I can't decide if he's aware this man is Jake and is intentionally messing with him, or if Graham's oblivious and trying to smooth-talk our way out of this predicament. Either way, he's playing with fire, and my heart hammers quadruple time.

"Well, *friend*. You'll have to take *your* girl somewhere else. As I said, you're on private property. And this spot, in particular?" Jake's voice drops low, along with my heart. "Only nightmares are made here."

Chest...meet dagger.

What was I thinking? Clearly, I wasn't. Internally, I'm slapping my palm against my forehead repeatedly. *Idiot. Fool. What a dummy!*

It didn't occur to me that bringing Graham here might be a colossal error in judgment given the time that's passed. Jake has a right to be furious. This ridge was our special spot, a sacred place known only to us. Somehow, I continue to hurt him at every turn.

Pressure instantly builds behind my eyes, and I silently beg for the sky to open up and swallow me whole.

Graham's body stiffens, and I'd say he figured out the shadow man is Jake. I spent countless hours telling Graham about the nights Jake and I spent on this ridge, so the harsh words and blatant animosity directed at us serve as plenty of evidence for him to reach this conclusion.

Being the skilled actor he is, Graham decides playing along is a fantastic idea. He ignores Jake's obvious fury and nuzzles my neck, pressing a kiss there.

In his huskiest bedroom voice, he says, "It's okay, love. We can leave. I've been dying to get you home and take you to bed."

My heart pounds violently, and nausea creeps into my belly. *What is he doing?*

A muted, inhuman sound—like the fading guttural moan of a dying animal before it takes its final breath—comes from the deadly shadows. As much as I don't want to face him, I can't leave Jake suffering with this misunderstanding hanging between us.

Keeping my firm gaze on Jake's silhouette, I say, "Graham, can you please give us a minute?"

Without hesitation, he hops off the tailgate and climbs in the passenger seat, cranking the ignition to warm the interior. With nerves gripping me, I slide to my heavy feet. Thankfully, the night conceals Jake's face so I'm unable to get a clear view of his expression.

"Look..." I inhale deep breath. "I'm sorry for bringing Graham out here. It was inconsiderate of me. And what he said...that's just him trying to make light of the situation." I fight the urge to ramble, but I lose. "What are you doing out here, anyway? And why did the Hamiltons put up a gate? There wasn't a lock or a sign stating the area was off limits.

Are they out of town? Are you keeping an eye on their place for them?"

"Something like that," he mutters quietly, not moving a muscle.

"Anyway, I'm sorry." When Jake still doesn't speak or move, I lower my head in shame, ready to flee toward the driver's door.

But something reaches out and stops me. Something a little bit like…courage. It's not a familiar friend, but I accept its proffered hand and draw my shoulders back.

Turning sharply on my heel, I face the shadowy past with my spine straighter and my chin angled higher. "You know what, Jake? I'm not sorry. This place is special to me, and I wanted to show it to someone who's important in my life. That may upset you, but it's been *years* since you and I claimed this spot. *We* claimed it, so it's my spot too. And I have every right to be here."

"You're trespassing," he says tightly. I imagine his jaw locked with tension.

"So are you," I argue. "We've always trespassed here."

"You're trespassing on my *life*," he hisses, fists held firmly to his chest. Pain cracks his voice open and spills to the rocks and dirt beneath our feet. The step he takes closer allows me to witness his face wrenching in agony. "You can't possibly know how it feels to live with a ghost haunting you every single fucking day while wishing it would come back to life. I mourned you. I let you go. Yet, you *still* haunt me. You haunt this place"—he points to the hallowed ground—"and now you've desecrated it."

I suck in a sharp gasp, my lungs burning when they meet the bitterly cold air.

Has he finally confessed he doesn't want me anymore? If I still haunt him, then he hasn't truly let me go. Right?

Confused, I scrounge around in my soul until I find an equivocal confession of my own to share. "I know exactly what it's like to wish for something you can never have. To stand before your angriest ghost, powerless to ease the pain."

It doesn't take a genius to realize that Jake feels alone in his suffering. From what I can tell, he no longer opens up to the people who care about him. But I chose to lean on others, and I'm lucky to have people who love me enough to help me battle my ghosts while cherishing them at the same time.

"I won't apologize for bringing someone I love to a place he's helping me fight for," I say, slamming the tailgate shut. "He's earned it."

Leaving Jake stunned and speechless, I join Graham in the truck without shedding a single tear. And I don't glance in the rearview mirror to peek at the wretched man lurking in the dark.

On the highway leading to town, Graham breaks the heavy silence. "That was fun."

I can count on one hand the number of times I've been mad at Graham Kingston, and my anger never lasted more than five minutes. It was always over dumb stuff, like the time he ate the last of my favorite lemon cookies, which are only sold once a year. Or the time the beard he grew for a movie role was in that itchy phase, and he told Marcus and Judge that I gave him crabs on his face.

What he did tonight extends far beyond the realm of *dumb stuff*.

"Why did you do that?" My emotions have been strangling me for the last fifteen minutes, so the words are gritty in my throat.

"I had to confirm something." His nonchalance has me itching to smack him and shove him out of the moving vehicle.

My temper rises, a rare occurrence, and I let loose my pent-up frustrations. "And what would that be, huh? That Jake hates me and wants me out of his life for good? That I'm the biggest loser on the planet because all these years I've held on to something invisible, and I'm too pathetic and scared to let go?"

Graham squeezes my thigh. In his gentlest tone, brimming with certainty, he says, "That he still loves you."

Neither of us speak the rest of the way home.

18

JAKE

I'm a glutton for punishment. A masochist, through and through. Otherwise, I wouldn't be lightly knocking on Pam's kitchen door at seven o'clock in the morning. Being here is nothing out of the ordinary for me. Pam and I discuss all her land business over a cup of coffee at her breakfast table since we're both early risers. But I've come here this morning to get some answers.

When my phone blew up yesterday with calls and texts from Jensen, Rock, and Brody— all saying Tatum was grinding on her movie-star lover in Bruno's and taking him to her "favorite spot"—I raced home. By the posted speed limits, I was two hours away. I made the drive in one hour and fifteen minutes, then parked my truck in the driveway and hoofed it on foot to the ridge.

The ten-minute walk in the dark felt like an eternity. My mind conjured up all kinds of images of what I'd find, each one adding fuel to my fire. The audacity of her bringing him to our place. It wasn't a slap in the face, no, it was a swift kick to the nuts that had my stomach twisting.

"You know I love you, right? You mean everything to me."

"I love you more."

Tatum's melodic voice drifted through the quiet night. Those words spoken to someone else punched into me with a deadly force. Unable to bear hearing more of their affectionate declarations, I made my presence known. Everything said or done after that? It would hurt less if I was lying in the dirt, bloody and near death, while being kicked in the ribs with steel-toe boots.

My only saving grace was the surprised—and not a happy one—expression on Tatum's face when that asshole mentioned taking her to bed.

Which brings me here. I'm eager to see their dynamic up close and in the light of day. Like I said, I'm a glutton for punishment.

I lay awake all night, mulling over Tatum's parting words.

"To stand before your angriest ghost..."

The ghost she's referring to is me. It has to be. We continue to haunt each other, which means there's a chance she still loves me. At Lucy's party, she said she came back to Walford *for me*. I assumed she meant as part of her recovery steps—to make amends. But what if I've been missing the signs?

I need to figure out her and Graham's relationship status before I make a bold move or another misstep. I need to know, firsthand, what they are to each other. Are they friends with benefits? Are they rekindling their relationship after the breakup? Are they exes who sleep together on occasion?

That's what I'm here to suss out. Is it him or me?

The inner door swings open and Graham Kingston, mega movie star and international heartthrob, appears wearing nothing but purple boxer briefs. *What a douche.* And his brown hair is too perfectly tousled to be natural morning hair.

You know when women drool over sharp angles, lean muscles, and defined six-pack abs? This is the guy who leaves them slobbering all over the place. I have abs I'm pretty proud of, but mine don't have those deep ridges between them, each one shaped like a Nutter Butter wafer.

His weird amber eyes reveal no hint of surprise, as if he expected me to show. It must be hard to catch him off guard because he didn't flinch last night either when I snuck up on him and Tatum.

Graham rubs his stupid abs as he saunters into the kitchen. I let myself in and take a seat at the breakfast table while he starts a pot of coffee. Then he leans against the counter and crosses his arms. Neither of us say a word. I sip coffee from my travel thermos. He waits me out.

Despite the lights being off, the halfway-open blinds allow the morning light to filter into the room. With my chair strategically situated, I'm partly concealed by a fiddle-leaf fig tree, my back to the corner. I have a clear view of the kitchen, living room, and hallway leading to the bedrooms.

At the sound of shuffling feet, I shift my focus to the hallway. Graham's steady gaze remains fixed on me as Tatum drags herself toward the kitchen.

She's never been a morning person. Her eyes are closed, and her pink lips turn down in a severe pout. Strands fall from the crooked, messy hair knotted on her head, and a Bob Marley T-shirt reaches the middle of her bare thighs. My gut clenches knowing she has on nothing but panties underneath, and she slept like that. With him.

It's like I'm watching a movie in slow motion, a well-rehearsed scene where Graham steps forward with his arms out. Tatum melts into his embrace and plants her forehead on his hairless chest, arms hanging loosely at her sides. She stands like that while he reaches around with his long, spray-tanned arms and pours her a cup of coffee.

He kisses the top of her head and says, "Morning, love."

She groans, and he chuckles.

Graham nudges her and pushes the mug into her waiting hands when she leans away. His hands run along her sides while she takes a sip. Not once has she opened her eyes.

She hums in pleasure, and my skin prickles at the memories the sound conjures. In a raspy voice, thick with unfinished sleep, she says, "Sorry I kept you up so late."

"We both needed that." His paws never…stop…touching…her.

She nods her agreement.

I'm white-knuckling my thermos.

"I'm going to hop in the shower. You coming?" he asks her.

I never played baseball, but right now I'm wondering how accurate my throwing arm is. If I hurl my metal container the twenty-foot-or-so distance to where they're standing, what are the odds it would hit him in the head? It is a travel thermos, after all. Let's watch it travel.

Tatum takes another sip and shakes her head. "I'll go after you."

He pecks her on the neck and waltzes off, tossing me a wink over his shoulder. *Is he messing with me on purpose?* I never got the impression—last night or this morning—he knows who I am. But that intentional little gesture has me sitting up straighter. The thump of my thermos on the table startles Tatum.

Her head snaps in my direction, eyes widened in alarm.

"Son of a biscuit!" she yells, clutching the mug to her heaving chest. "Jake? What are you doing here?"

Her panicky eyes dart around, searching for the reason I'm sitting in her kitchen. Or, more likely, searching for an escape.

"I'm meeting with Pam," I lie. "Business matters."

"Oh." She blows out a breath of…relief? Disappointment? "Well, she's not here. She's spending the day shopping with friends. She'll be back this evening." *I'm fully aware.*

In an unaffected tone, I say, "Must've read my calendar wrong."

Tatum remains nervous under the weight of my stare. She fidgets with the hem of her shirt, takes frequent sips of coffee, and her gaze wanders aimlessly to avoid my penetrating one. I don't relent, keeping my focus on her until she's forced to break our silence first.

"Graham's heading back to Austin today. He's shooting a movie there and came to visit because we haven't seen each other in a while. It was a surprise, really, him showing up. Maisy's working on the film too, doing wardrobe and makeup and stuff. I've been wanting to go see them, but my team doesn't think it's safe to travel yet. That's why I'm still in Walford."

She cuts off her word vomit abruptly, and a pink blush tinges her cheeks before she hides behind her mug.

"Cool," is my response.

Our eyes remain locked as we nurse our coffees. Several minutes pass before Graham strolls in with wet hair. He's carrying a fancy leather bag in one hand and wraps his free arm around Tatum.

"I need to head out," he says.

"Want me to drive you to your car?" she asks. A hint of

desperation seeps into her eyes, as if she's begging for an opening to get away from me.

I'm not sure why I haven't moved. We've already established that my fake business with her aunt is a no-go.

"No. I'm okay to walk. The fresh air will do me good before the long drive."

A snide remark about the drive only being an hour sits on the tip of my tongue. Then I recall their earlier conversation about them both needing whatever went down during their late-night rendezvous, and the remark dies a quick death. Instead, a buzzing noise starts in my ears as I picture what that late night entailed.

"Ok." Tatum moves to snuggle deeper into his side, but she stops short and briefly glances my way. "I'm glad you came. Don't wait so long before the next visit."

"I'll try." Graham kisses her neck...*again*. "See ya, Tot." *Tot?*

"See ya."

Why the hell am I sitting here? I'm pretty sure I already got my answers. And as soon as he walks out that door, I'll be alone with Tatum, and that won't do.

My chair scrapes against the tile floor when I stand and say to Graham, "I'll give you a ride. I'm headed that way."

The sheer panic on Tatum's face bolsters my last-second decision. I'll use this opportunity to confirm, once and for all, their relationship status. The thought of intimidating him a little adds weight to my haphazard plan. Until I see the satisfied smirk on Graham's face.

"That'd be great, man." He claps me on the back as we both reach the door.

I have a sneaking suspicion I'm being played. I mean, he *is* an actor. But that doesn't stop me from pushing through the screen door with him following close behind.

The trip from Pam's house to Bruno's takes less than two minutes by car. I take the long route, looping through the neighborhoods surrounding Main Street at ten miles per hour. Most everyone's at school or work already, so I shouldn't raise too much suspicion cruising around residential streets in my big black truck with dark tinted windows.

Graham looks far too relaxed in my passenger seat. Far too confident. I discreetly check out his distressed denim pants and clean white sneakers. Aviator sunglasses hang from the neckline of the tan sweater beneath his green coat.

He's the poster boy for easy sophistication and style. Meanwhile, I'm in dirty jeans, my faded leather jacket, and a baseball cap. My boots have certainly seen better days.

At least the inside of my truck's clean. I'm meticulous about that.

With a lazy elbow propped on the door frame, Graham grazes his knuckles along his jaw. "Where do you want to start?"

Here we go, I guess.

Keeping my eyes on the road, I say, "Let's start with why you're here. I thought you and Tatum broke up."

He shrugs while staring out the windshield. "I care about her. Had to see for myself how she's doing after everything that happened."

I scoff, annoyed by his million-dollar voice and his nonchalance, as if he's only halfway invested in her well-being. "Took you long enough. She's been here for weeks."

"I'm a busy man. She understands."

"Now I get why y'all called it quits," I grumble. A few beats pass before I toss out my intimidation plan and show all my cards instead. "Are you here to win her back?"

His head whips in my direction, and a wicked grin stretches across his face. "You threatened by me, Jake Dylan Holloway?"

I do a double take when he calls me by my full name. It makes sense Tatum would mention me while they were together, but using a middle name is kind of intimate. Unless you're a pop star.

"Yeah. Tatum told me all about you. Your favorite foods, your favorite color, your obsession with strong coffee and sunrises. The tiny birthmark shaped like a diamond on the inside of your right thigh. How you cradle her head when you pound into her."

Shock. A shock to the system so unexpected, I nearly choke to death on my saliva in front of a celebrity.

"Why would she tell you that?" I ask as my eyes water.

Graham's intense stare bores a hole in the side of my head. Gone is the pretense of nonchalance, replaced by a seriousness that demands my full attention.

"Why wouldn't she? We've spent years together. We have no secrets between us."

I wince at his mention of years. I also noticed…

"You used the present tense. Which means you still love her."

"I'll love Tatum forever. She's a beautiful, selfless human who puts aside her own happiness to ensure everyone else's. She's sacrificial." He points a finger at me. "And that, my friend, is her fatal flaw, considering it cost her the love of her life."

I flick my turn signal before making a left at a stop sign. It's my fourth left turn. And I'll keep turning left until I get to the root of what he's trying to say.

If I'm reading between the lines of his cryptic words correctly, and I'm to believe he's referring to *me* as the "love of her life," then Tatum sacrificed her happiness for mine. If true, her plan backfired in spectacular fashion. I haven't been happy for a decade.

However, she told him things about me—deeply personal, private things. Why would she do that if she didn't think of me, if she didn't love me, all this time? And if she has loved me all this time, why did she stay away?

This conversation isn't going at all like I planned or expected. My whirling thoughts hinder my ability to focus on driving, so I take one final left and park behind the only car outside the bar.

Graham's measured words bounce around in my brain. Brows drawn together in concentration, I study him hard, searching for whatever angle he's playing. He gave me a fucking bone. This guy, who claims to love my girl, is trying to help me out here.

He said they don't have any secrets between them. Which means…

"You know why she didn't come back to me." My grip on the steering wheel tightens. Learning another person knows why she left me, when I'm still clueless, sets me on edge.

He rubs his fingers across his lips, thinking and thinking and fucking thinking while he stares at my profile. "Not my story to share. I would never betray her by revealing her darkest secrets."

I huff in frustration. *Okay.* So, if he's not spilling the beans, what is he alluding to? He's so careful and deliberate in his phrasing, especially the part about her secrets being dark.

"Can I give you some advice?" he asks.

I glance at him. "From the guy who clearly knows her better than I do? Sure. Why not?"

He frowns, shaking his head at my petty remark. "The

Dark Days are here, Jake, and this is the first time Maisy and I won't be around to help her through them. So either give her some grace or leave her the hell alone." Graham's defensive tone proves he truly cares about Tatum, yet everything he says leaves me feeling more confused.

What the hell are the Dark Days?

I rack my brain, analyzing every detail I recall from my recent run-ins with Tatum. How exhausted she looked at The Drip a few days ago. The shadows under her eyes, and how she begged for more time because she's going through something hard right now.

Right now.

The timing can't be a coincidence. It's January, almost ten years to the day since Tatum and I last spoke. Before she vanished without a trace or so much as a *fuck you.*

Despite trying to convince myself otherwise, the one thing I've been sure of all these years is that Tatum loved me back then. She would never hurt me on purpose. She'd never cheat on me or lie to me. And she damn sure wouldn't abandon me without a really good reason.

Understanding hits so hard, it sucks the air from my lungs. My eyes remained fixed to the emblem on the steering wheel as my hands squeeze it to death. Tiny prickles of anxiety spread across my skin, and my breaths become shallow, more rapid. I don't like this feeling. It's too familiar and wholly unwelcome.

"Something happened to her." The words feel like sawdust in my mouth, impossible to scrape off my tongue.

When she disappeared, my instincts told me something terrible happened. They were right. She may be alive and present, but a thousand other horrific incidents could've led to her separation from me, including if some monster…

"It's not what you're thinking," he says, clocking the worst of my rampant thoughts.

His assurance should bring me relief, but I'm processing too many emotions at once. I'm hot. Anxious. My world's been knocked off its axis as a grim picture forms in my mind.

"Why are you telling me this?" I whisper.

Graham doesn't benefit from me and Tatum mending the gaping wound between us. So, what's his game?

He leans on the center console, too close for comfort when I need space to *just fucking breathe*. "I'll share something with you that, in all honesty, could destroy my career. But Tatum's happiness is important to me, so I'm willing to roll the dice. For her."

The sound of his throat clearing is the first sign of hesitation or uncertainty he's shown since I stalked out of the shadows last night.

"Because of Tatum, I spent four wonderful years with the man I love. Coming out would've been suicide for my acting career. Tatum and I let the media say whatever they wanted and never disputed a word. If anything, we leaned into it to protect my secret. In the end, Miguel left me anyway because he got tired of hiding our relationship. Hiding in plain sight is exhausting."

I can relate on some level, but Graham's hiding from something much more impactful with far-reaching consequences. I'm only hiding from my feelings. His truth, and more so his willingness to share it with me, floors me.

He continues. "The only way to win him back is to take an enormous risk. And, honestly, I'm scared as shit. But it's a risk I'm willing to take."

After taking a moment to absorb the magnitude of his revelation, I nod. "Thanks for sharing that with me. I promise I won't tell a soul."

What else can I say? Talk about full disclosure. This morning has been one secret reveal after another, and Graham's secret changes everything for me.

He awkwardly bops my arm and flashes a winning smile. "I know you won't. Tatum loves me, and she'd never forgive you."

"You're right. She wouldn't." I let out a halfhearted chuckle, but it's quickly smothered by my looming panic. I'm still lost, clueless, and now my enhanced worry over Tatum's past has me in a chokehold.

"She's afraid, Jake, but coming here was a huge step in the right direction for her." He pops the door handle and quirks an eyebrow. "Which direction are you headed?" Grabbing his bag, he slides out of the truck and says, "Good luck, friend."

Pondering which direction I'm heading next, I stare at the empty parking space where Graham's rental car sat, then I cruise around for another half hour, repeating our exchange in my mind.

Nothing about the last ten years appears as I imagined. It's possible Tatum never stopped loving me and didn't *want* to leave me. She still owes me an explanation, but I'm willing to be patient with her. If I don't allow my stubborn and selfish ways to control me, I'm confident I can gently coax the truth from her.

I have a chance at keeping her here—at making her mine again—but this only works if I'm cautious and protect what's left of my heart while reclaiming hers.

Something unlocks in my chest. A deluge of repressed emotions sweeps away my resentment, making way for anticipation as I build the courage to ask the one question I should've asked weeks ago. The only question that matters.

Does she still love me?

My lungs and sweat glands work overtime when I flick my turn signal one last time.

I'm about to find out.

19

TATUM

Holy crap. Holy crap. Holy crap.

That's been the only phrase running through my head since Jake and Graham left over an hour ago. Since I managed to unglue my feet from the kitchen floor and stumble into the shower.

Why did Graham agree to go with him? What could they possibly talk about besides me? I'm tempted to call or text Graham to find out what was said between them.

We stayed up all night while he talked me off the ledge after our tense encounter at the ridge. I was a mess, over-analyzing all the ways our presence there may have affected Jake. I don't want to hurt him more than I already have, but he has no right to hoard our memories like they're his alone.

After my shower, I slip into panties and a Prince T-shirt. Unable to tame the rat's nest on my head, I give up on trying to make my messy bun less messy. My feet trudge across the hallway to my bedroom with the intention of crawling back into bed.

I'm rubbing my favorite lavender lotion on my arms when the screen door bangs. Aunt Pam won't return for hours, and only Maisy, who is in Austin, would let herself in without knocking. Moving quietly, I grab the ukulele laying on my desk and inch toward the small closet, the only hiding place available.

Just as I'm twisting the knob, my bedroom door creaks open. I freeze on the spot with the ukulele raised high, ready to throw it across the room at the intruder.

"Tate?"

Jake's voice, low and hesitant, fills the quiet space. The door swings wide, and I gawk in disbelief as he enters my room.

His face is flushed, chest rising and falling like he ran miles to get here. He discarded the cap he wore earlier, leaving dark hair flattened against his forehead.

The most striking thing, however, is the morning sunlight reflecting off the shine in his forest green eyes. Eyes brimming with unrestrained emotion despite the hands fisted at his sides.

Lowering my weapon, and too stunned by his unexpected arrival to form words, I wait for him to speak.

"Do you love me?" he asks, eyes pleading with my disbelieving ones. My heart lurches at the nervous tremor threading through his voice. "Say you love me."

My bottom lip quivers, and tears coat my lashes. My entire body trembles as I fight the urge to fling myself at him. A hard swallow fails to coax the thickness from my throat.

"Yes, I love you. Every minute of every day, I love you."

The pounding in my chest grows more and more violent with each deliberate step he takes toward me. Stopping inches away, he pries the ukulele from my tight grasp and places it on the desk.

Taking my hands, he links our fingers and palms together, holding them between our chests. He presses his forehead to mine and releases the longest sigh. An exorcism of so much pent-up emotion occurs in that single, full-body exhale.

He's shaking, or I'm shaking, or we both are.

We stand with our eyes closed, inhaling one another and just...*breathing*. He releases my hands and gently cradles my head, tilting it so he can gaze into my eyes.

I grip the pockets of his coat, afraid he'll disappear if I don't grab him somewhere—anywhere—and hang on tight.

His thumbs dance across my cheeks, wiping away the tears. A small sob escapes me at the familiar, comforting gesture. When his lips softly brush mine, my heart goes into free fall.

"I've been stuck here. Lifeless and alone." He peers into my soul while gently stroking my face with calloused fingers. A fractured breath fills his chest before he whispers the most desperate plea. "Give me life."

I surge forward, pushing our lips together with equal desperation. When he opens for me, I savor every stroke of his tongue against mine. He tastes like coffee and salt and my Jake. He tastes like home.

Our slow melding of tongues builds to a frenzy of lips and hands and relieved sobs. I unzip his jacket while he toes off his boots. His shirt is next to go. I only have a second to admire the muscles he's developed since we were teenagers as he quickly sheds his jeans and socks, leaving him in a tight pair of black boxer briefs.

He tugs me against his hard chest and trails kisses along my neck, the stubble on his jaw prickling my smooth skin. Warm breath tickles my ear when he begs, "Tell me you want this."

"I want *you*, Jake." *Always and only you.*

Misty eyes ensnare mine when he grips my thighs near the hem of my shirt. With a firm, possessive touch, he slowly runs both hands over my hips, along the curve of my waist, up the sides of my ribs and breasts—pushing up the fabric as he goes.

He no longer has the soft hands of a studious teenage boy. Now, they're the strong, rough hands of a man who works hard.

With a sharp intake of breath, his movements halt with my T-shirt bunched over my breasts.

"Baby," he chokes, the nickname I've longed to hear a balm to my aching heart.

Bending down, he grazes gentle lips along the tattoo near my left breast. The elegant script surrounded by three stars across my ribs reads "focus on the sky."

He told me once to "focus on the sky until the pain goes away." I look to the sky often. Sunrises, sunsets, cloudy days, starry nights…they've kept Jake close to me all these years.

He nuzzles his face between my breasts before continuing the reverent journey, his hands coasting up my raised arms. He doesn't stop when the shirt pops over my head, and I arch into him. Our gazes locked, he doesn't stop until the sleeves of the fabric whisper past my fingertips, the shirt falling to the floor.

Goosebumps coat my heated flesh. Wearing only a pair of cotton panties, with Jake's hands holding my arms in the air by my wrists, he kisses me with so much passion I could burst. I've never felt so desired.

He breaks our kiss and locks my wrists together with one hand while freeing my hair with the other, the tresses spilling down my back. Then he reverses the journey, running steady hands down my body and grabbing my thighs to lift me. I wrap my legs around his trim waist as he moves the short distance to the bed.

Straddling him, I circle my arms around his neck and rest

my cheek on the top of his bowed head. My eyes fall closed on a sigh as I relish the precious moment. It's indescribable how good it feels to have him in my arms again.

"I miss you," I say.

Jake shakes his head—in denial or disbelief, I'm not sure—holding me tight as a quiet sob quakes his shoulders. He brands my electrified skin with tear-stained kisses and whispered words of agony.

He licks the hollow of my throat. "You took my heart…"

Kisses the swell of my breast. "You took my soul…"

Caresses the tattoo of his words. "All the light…"

Nuzzles the flesh over my thundering heart. "You forgot to take my body…"

Raises despairing eyes to mine. "I'm empty without you, Tate."

I palm his wet cheeks and fuse our mouths together, reassuring him with another fervent kiss that we belong to each other. We always have and always will.

Shoving my fingers in his thick hair, I drag my nails along his scalp, eliciting a groan from him. It's a simple touch that turns him on and eases his stress in equal measure.

With a firm tug, I tilt his head back and gaze upon the devastation I caused. A decade's worth of shackled heartache pours freely from his tortured watery eyes. The sight of them cleaves my soul. The very soul that he claimed ownership of years ago.

In a tone as fierce as my love, I say, "I failed you. I failed *us*. And not a day goes by that I don't regret running away. We can never have those years back. But I'd sacrifice all my years to come to hear you say you love me, just once, even if you never forgive me."

He doesn't say it, and my hope falters, allowing a shadow of doubt to creep in. But I convince myself he's simply maintaining his guard, and he'll let it down when he truly feels safe with me again.

Instead, he slips his hands inside my panties and squeezes my ass while trailing his lips and tongue down my neck and chest. Grinding against his erection, I gasp when he pulls a taut nipple in his mouth and sucks hard. He soothes the pain with his velvety tongue, and my toes curl in response. Arching my back, I offer him my other breast for the same treatment. He doesn't disappoint.

His mouth finds mine again before protective arms lock around me, and we fall to the bed. We grind into each other, stoking our fiery kiss until he rolls us over so I'm underneath him. Bracing himself on his forearms, he places chaste pecks to the tip of my nose and the corners of my mouth.

"You're as beautiful as you were the day we met," he says, eyes teeming with longing and lust. "And I've been dying to get my hands on you."

He imprisons my gaze and slides down my charged body, peeling my panties off as he goes. Lying with my legs hanging off the bed, my hungry eyes watch as he shoves off his boxer briefs. His beautiful erection juts out proudly as if saying *long time, no see*.

A tiny voice in the dark recesses of my brain repeats Brody's accusations from the coffee shop. Before the worry can take root, Jake falls to his knees and yanks my hips to the edge of the mattress, and I forget all about them.

With strong fingers clamping my thighs in place over his shoulders, he ravages me with his wicked mouth. Sucking and biting and plunging and worshipping as he laps up every bit of my arousal. My nerve endings sizzle each time his stubbled jaw scrapes my tender flesh. I moan and writhe and twist the sheets in my hands, holding on for dear life.

My legs shake, and my throat burns from crying out in

ecstasy. With a final, firm suck on my sensitive clit, he sinks two fingers inside me and applies the perfect amount of pressure. I squeeze my eyes shut when the mind-bending orgasm seizes my every muscle, silencing me.

Cloaked in a blissful haze, I hardly register Jake moving me so I'm lying fully on the bed, my head resting on a plush pillow. Only the symphony of our rapid breaths disturbs the quiet.

The mattress shifts from his weight. As my vision clears, a captivating picture sharpens into focus. Kneeling at my feet, fully naked in the daylight, Jake strokes his hard length. Messy hair, parted lips, glistening chin, green eyes filled with a love so intense it thrums between us.

He's glorious.

And I realize he doesn't have to say the words. His love flows through every starving touch and every shining teardrop

I part my legs, bent knees falling away as I expose myself to him. A pained groan claws its way from deep inside his chest, as if this is all a dream and he could awaken any second.

I reach out a hand to assure him this is real. *I* am real.

Aligning our bodies with our foreheads joined together, he guides himself inside me so…very…slowly. Our shared moans are evenly matched in their intense pleasure and profound relief at this single moment of homecoming.

The way he fills me so completely, I'm in heaven. My insides ache happily with each steady thrust.

The comforting scents of earth and trees after a spring rain infuse my lungs each time I inhale, and my eyelids flutter from the tickle of his warm breath skimming across my lips.

It's been *so long* since I've felt him, and if I died—right here, right now—it would be the most peaceful of deaths.

Jake moves in an unhurried rhythm, reveling in our reunion. Our fingers laced tightly together, he whispers sweet nothings between passionate kisses, euphoric moans, and long, languid thrusts.

"Baby, I've missed you."

"You feel so good. So perfect."

"You love me."

"You've always loved me."

"Never leave me again."

These last words are punctuated by the demand in both his voice and his hips as he quickens the pace. He slides his arms underneath me, curling them around my back and shoulders until my head is cradled in his hands.

Buried deep inside me, he shifts his weight so he's slightly balanced on his knees, which push against my hips, effectively bracing me at both ends.

A thrill rushes through me, knowing what's coming and how magnificent it will be. Muscle memory takes over. I dig my heels into his thighs and thread my fingers through his sweat-dampened hair, gripping it hard. My breathing speeds up, the anticipation keeping me on edge.

"Hold on, baby. Don't let go of me," he says.

With our bodies caged in, Jake unleashes years of burning need. He burrows his face in the curve of my neck and hammers into me with sharp, brutal thrusts. It's a claiming on both our parts, and we surrender to it.

My tender nipples rub against the smattering of hair on his chest with each punch of his hips.

"Jake," I moan. It's the only word I can manage amid our animalistic grunts, but it conveys everything I'm feeling. Elation. Perfection. Completion.

When he fists my hair, the delicious tug stinging my scalp, I know he's close. Muffled murmurs of "baby, baby,

baby" warm my neck before his body stiffens, and a long, low groan signals his release.

He collapses on top of me as if I'm made of soft marshmallows rather than pointy bones. We regain control of our breathing and untangle from our human puzzle, and I exhale a satisfied sigh.

Brushing away the hair stuck to my face, he stares deeply into my eyes and says, "This is what I dream of every night. But dreams don't do it justice."

"I can't agree more." I capture his lips and hum into our lazy kiss, which makes him chuckle. And that chuckle vibrates through me, causing a gush of...

We freeze, wide eyes pinned on each other's in alarm.

"Fuck," he whispers. "I'm so sorry."

"Takes two to tango," I tease, an attempt to hide my panic. "It's okay."

It's not okay. It's definitely not okay.

Jake can read me like a book, so he doesn't buy the lie I tell through the forced smile on my lips.

A hint of insecurity flashes in his eyes before he hangs his head and sighs. "I'll get something to clean us up."

He pulls on his underwear and fetches a damp washcloth from the bathroom. I'm too stupefied to move, so I let him deal with the mess between my legs. Once he disappears into the hallway again, I kick the top sheet off my bed, slip into my T-shirt and fresh panties, and curl up against the headboard, knees pulled to my chest.

The realm of my stupidity knows no bounds. Forgetting about protection was a foolish risk. Not only because Jake has a questionable sexual history, but because I'm not on birth control.

"I brought gifts." He pauses in the doorway, noticing my worried expression, then sets a can of Pringles on the nightstand and passes me a bottled water before settling next to me on the bed, legs stretched out and crossed at the ankles.

"Thanks." I sip the water and fiddle with the lid while we wait each other out.

We took a gigantic leap, going from a few tense encounters to sex without having a proper conversation in between. All actions have consequences, and I'm not only referring to the unprotected sex. Taking this intimate step before resolving our issues has the potential to make everything between us much, much worse when he learns the truth.

Jake finger-brushes his messy hair. By the pinched expression on his face, he either regrets what just happened and is trying to find a gentle way to backtrack, or he's also worried about the myriad of consequences.

He clears his throat, and I brace myself for the worst. "I know what Brody said to you." *Not what I expected him to say.*

I cap the bottle and set it aside, giving him my full attention. "Jake, you don't have to—"

"No, let me speak. Please."

He links our pinkies the way we used to when we had serious conversations about our dreams and our future together. The physical connection reinforced our soul-deep one, reminding us that the endgame behind everything we did was…us.

"I spent two years worrying about you, then I became angry. I got carried away with partying and drinking and, yes, I made a few bad choices. But I swear to you, baby, it was nothing like Brody suggested. And I have *never* not been safe. You have to know I wouldn't do anything to put you at risk. Even if I can't claim to be a good man anymore."

He fidgets with the hem of my shirt and nibbles the inside of his cheek. Recognizing the old habit, my heartbeats quicken. He does this when he's considering his words or trying to hold them back altogether.

"I need to tell you something," he says.

My stomach twists when I read the fear in his eyes. Whatever he wants to tell me will hurt him and me both. He swallows hard, physically keeping that fear at bay.

"After college, I was alone for a long time until I met the daughter of a client. She's a widow, a few years older than me." *I don't want to hear this.* "Every few months when I traveled her way, we'd meet up. She insisted on paying for everything—the drinks, the dinners, the hotel room. I'm not too naive to understand what it was." His eyes close, head bowing deeply in shame.

"I sold my body," he rasps, his voice cracking as tears leak from his eyes. "It was the only part of me you left behind —the last piece of me you owned—and I sold it."

I've cried so much this morning; it shouldn't be possible for my eyes to well up again. My voice trembles with both heartache for him and fear of his answer when I ask, "Is it over?"

Much to my relief, he nods. I lace my fingers through his and squeeze. Cupping his chin with my free hand, I bring us eye to eye.

"Hey," I whisper. "You've done nothing wrong. And whatever happened while we were apart…happened. I won't ever hold it against you." *But I'm shattered that I forced you to be with other women.*

As I've said before, Jake isn't wired to have sex without emotion. While his confession is shocking, to say the least, I can't help but wonder if the shame he carries distorts his perception of the arrangement he mentioned. *He* believes the interactions with the woman went against his values, and I won't belittle his reality by offering empty platitudes.

I think back on the couple of sexual encounters I attempted since him, which ended with me in tears. As luck would have it, being a busy, famous pop star makes it difficult to have relationships or random hookups, so I used my fame as an excuse to refrain from both.

Since we're trading confessions, I admit, "I wasn't a perfect angel, even though I tried to be."

His face crumples with undiluted anguish. "Don't. Please don't tell me anything. I can't bear it. Just let me pretend you've only ever been mine." *I have only ever been yours.*

"Okay," I concede, grazing my thumb along his stubbled jaw. After a long minute of me comforting him in silence, I tentatively ask, "So, what happens now?"

He blows out an unsteady breath. "We have a lot of baggage to sort through, and I'm under no illusions it will be pretty or easy. We'll take it one day at a time. But baby?" Determination erases the misery in his eyes. "Whether you stay or go—no matter if we work out or we don't—you *will* tell me everything."

My hearts stalls in my chest, and it's my turn to swallow the fear. "I promise."

20

JAKE

It's been less than a week since the wall separating me from Tatum came crashing down—since I laid everything on the line—and she's already pulling away. The chasm between us may not be as wide as it was before, but it's damn deep and still too treacherous to cross.

The first two days, we hung out at her house, not ready to make our reconnection public. We talked about our day-to-day lives. Tatum told me about the countries she visited on tour and the pranks she and Maisy pulled on her bodyguards. I told her about my consulting work and my decision to double major in business and land management.

The differences between her exciting life and my boring one are pretty stark.

Don't misunderstand. I enjoy my work. Helping ranch owners optimize land use and increase profits is rewarding. It's the travel that busts my balls. So yesterday, I posted a summer internship opportunity with my former alma mater. Figured I could offer an upcoming graduate some field experience at little cost to me. I'd been considering it for a while.

The blooming hope that Tatum might stick around and my

need to spend more time with her reinforced my decision. Spring classes already started, and the official deadline passed, but the head of the Agriculture and Natural Resources Department always liked me and allowed my late submission. With my luck, the best students already secured internships, and I'll be stuck with someone who's near the bottom of the class.

Tatum and I avoided serious topics during our visits, always keeping things at surface level. She was tired, falling asleep with her head in my lap at the end of both nights, so I'd kiss her forehead and leave her sleeping on the couch. Whatever she's dealing with, I wish she'd talk to me.

On the third day, I left for a business trip. I wish I could cancel all my appointments for the next month while we work through the issues dividing us. Splitting my time and focus between her and my job is difficult when my mind is always on her. While I was away, we exchanged a few brief calls and texts. But she's distant.

Pam crept around the house while I sat with Tatum those first two days, offering me sympathetic smiles and pitiful eyes. It was the same pity she showed me when I came knocking after Tatum disappeared. And it's the same damn pity she offered me this morning when I stood at her kitchen door and she turned me away.

My brain went on high alert, worried Tatum snuck away to California before I returned home last night. Pam must've sensed my distress, and she assured me that Tatum was sleeping and didn't want to be disturbed today. Pam's request for me to give Tatum some time, along with her ominous warning for me to be careful, is why I'm in a foul mood as I swing my hammer.

Be careful.

Be careful with who? Tatum or myself? I'm sick and tired

of being the only one on the outside, but I constantly remind myself of my self-made promise to be patient.

"You know they sell these cool things called nail guns. They make jobs like this easier." Rock's gruff voice interrupts my internal pity party.

He's helping me install the hardwood flooring in my loft. His job is to cut the boards; mine is to nail them down. My eyes flick to his royal blue sweatpants. I swear the guy owns nothing but Bulldog-themed athletic wear.

"There's one in the garage."

He drops a stack of pine boards in a corner. "So, why aren't you using it?"

"I like to keep a weapon on hand in case you piss me off. Which you're prone to do," I say dryly.

He huffs and grabs the extra measuring tape before heading downstairs. He's already misplaced two, and we've only been working for an hour.

"Sorry I'm late," Jensen yells from the foyer. "Brought beer."

Rock's faint grumbling about beers and hammers and my face reaches me before a door slams. Jensen's heavy boots pound up the steps.

"Where have you been?" I ask, a nail pinched between my lips as I line up the next board. He's an hour late, which is unlike him.

"Had to take care of something." He drops a twelve-pack of beer on the floor, twists open a bottle, and hovers over my hunched form like the micromanager he is. "Why don't you use the nail gun?"

"Why don't you fuck off?"

I realize I'm being prickly. Six days ago, I was making love to Tatum. Now, it's radio silence, sending me back to square one.

"Whoa," he says. "What crawled up your ass?"

I'm focused on placing the nail, but I sense his stare aimed at my head. I'd bet a thousand bucks he's wearing his Mr. Concerned face right now, along with skin-tight jeans and a black Bruno's T-shirt.

Jensen, Rock, and I have little variety in the fashion department. Brody's the one who views clothing as more than skin covering.

"Nothing," I mutter, swinging the hammer and cursing when it strikes the edge of the nail head and bends the nail.

Jensen moves toward the round window, gazing at the clouds while I hammer away in peace. That is until Rock bounds up the steps mere minutes later.

"Lost the tape measure. Third strike…I'm out. Pass me a beer," he tells Jensen, who wrestles one out of the pack and lobs it to him. With his unearned reward, Rock sprawls on the section of flooring where I'm working and hikes himself on an elbow. "What's up with your hair?"

I glance at Jensen's hair, which looks extra fluffy, sticking out in all directions like he ran out of gel this morning.

"What?" He combs it with his fingers, revealing the red tips of his ears when he brushes his wavy locks behind them. Red ears are a dead giveaway that he's embarrassed or flustered under his otherwise cool, steady demeanor.

"Looks like you just rolled out of bed." Rock lifts the bottle to his smirking lips. "A woman's bed."

"Whatever," Jensen mutters before changing the subject. "Brody coming?"

"He's busy today," I say. "Besides, I'm still mad at him."

Rock can't stand dissension among the ranks and jumps into peacemaker mode. "Come on, Jake. He apologized to you *and* Tate."

Brody reached out to me after our fight and apologized, but I didn't know he also apologized to Tatum.

"She didn't mention that to me."

"You talked to her?" Jensen plants a shoulder against the wall and sips his beer. His posture may seem casual, but his features tighten just enough for me to tell he's anxious about what happened between me and Tatum.

I shrug a shoulder and keep my tone neutral despite my cheeks heating up. "Not really."

He and Rock share a look. They're not even subtle about it.

Rock's the one who voices their shared, and accurate, conclusion. "Holy shit, you slept with her. What the hell is wrong with you?"

That's the problem with lifelong friends. You can't sneak anything past them.

"It just happened." Feeling defensive, I glower at Jensen. "We ripped off the Band-Aid like you said."

He pins me with a stony glare in return. "That's not what I meant, and you know it."

"Well, we're talking now, so you should be happy." My snarky attitude doesn't make this sudden turn of events with Tatum seem like a good thing.

"Then why are you in such a pissy mood?" Jensen asks.

"Because she won't talk to me."

Rock frowns. "I'm confused." *You and me both, buddy.*

Ditching the hammer, I rise to my feet and slouch against the drywall. I jerk my chin at Jensen, signaling for him to hand me a bottle.

"Things have been going good. Slow, but good. But when I stopped by to see Tate this morning, Pam slammed the door in my face."

"Pam wouldn't do that. She's way too nice," Jensen

argues despite the obvious exaggeration in my retelling of events.

"She turned me away. Same difference. Said Tatum wants to be left alone today." Tipping my head back, I blow out a long breath. "I don't know what's going on with her, man. She's always tired. And quiet. Like she's depressed or something. Her actor friend said this is a difficult time of year for her, which is coincidentally the same time of year when she ghosted me. The Dark Days, he called it." My eyes drift to Jensen and hold firm. "He implied something bad happened in California, but he wouldn't say what."

He stares out the window with a pensive expression on his face. I wonder, yet again, if he knows more than he's letting on.

"I failed you. I failed us."

I'm certain the words Tatum said the other day are significant. They're embedded so deep in my brain; I give myself migraines trying to figure out their hidden meaning. I consider myself a fairly smart guy, but I don't like games or riddles. If everyone would say what they mean, I'd sleep better at night.

"Are you talking about that guy who showed up at Bruno's?" Rock perks up, his interest piqued at the prospect of maiming and mayhem. In his football days, he was known to start a brawl or fifty on the field.

"Mm-hmm." My voice pitches high, but luckily neither of them notices.

"How'd things go with him, by the way?" There's no mistaking the bloodlust in Jensen's eyes. For me, he'd go toe to toe with anyone on my signal.

Jensen was furious on my behalf when Graham publicly groped Tatum, but he doesn't know the truth behind their relationship. I'm not telling him. Graham trusts me to keep his secret, which was a complete game changer for me and how I view Tatum. If not for him swooping in and opening my eyes, I'd keep pining for her from a distance. Now, I can be close to her…when she lets me.

I nod and say, "He's a decent dude," which earns me a quizzical look from Rock.

"So, aside from the mysterious Dark Days and you becoming BFFs with her ex, why is she shutting you out?"

I tilt my head to one side and study my boots. "Not sure. We didn't use a condom, so that could have something to do with it."

"TMI, dude." Rock scrunches his nose in disapproval. He's not a big fan of kiss and tell.

"Jesus Christ." Jensen's face pales in horror, a reaction that's a touch dramatic if you ask me.

I shrug a shoulder. "She played it off like it wasn't a big deal, but I could tell she was worried. I thought she was freaking out because of what Brody said, and she was afraid I might give her an STD or something. But I cleared up that misunderstanding."

Silence. Rock's most likely battling his need to gag at my overshare while Jensen broods.

Back in high school, Tatum and I always tried to be responsible and use condoms. And I've never been with another woman without protection. I should ask her if she's on birth control. I hope so, because I love being inside her bare. On the other hand…

"I've had a few days to think on it, and I honestly wouldn't mind a happy accident," I say, mostly to myself.

I smile as I imagine a mini-me or a mini-Tate toddling around with my dark hair and her blue eyes. Knowing Tatum, our kid would be named after a famous songwriter from the '60s. I could get behind that idea.

When we planned our future together, kids didn't come into the picture until we reached our thirties. I recently turned twenty-nine, so we're pretty close on the timeline.

"A baby," Rock deadpans, interrupting my daydream.

"Would that be so bad?"

"You want to trap her with a baby." He speaks slowly, eyebrows high on his forehead, like maybe I don't understand the simple little words he's stringing together.

I point my bottle at him. "Lucy trapped you with a baby."

He scowls at me. "Dude, we were married for two years before she got pregnant."

"My bad. She trapped you with a ring first." I polish off my beer, ignoring Rock's aggressive posture.

He's the perfect football coach. Strung so tight, he's only one penalty call away from blowing his top. I really love to push his buttons, and he bristles as expected when one of us teases about Lucy's power over him.

"Screw you. I love my wife."

"I think you're moving too fast, Jake," Jensen cuts in, killing a good time as always. Did I ask for his opinion? No. Is he going to give it to me, anyway? Not if I can help it.

Pushing off the wall, I step into his space. "You told me to go to her. *Repeatedly.* So I did. And you know what? For the first time in forever, I have moments of happiness. It's a fragile happiness, yes, but it's nice to feel something good again. She's finally within reach, which isn't a luxury I had when everything went to shit years ago. And I'm prepared to fight to keep her here. So screw you for criticizing me after I took *your* goddamn advice."

"But will she fight for *you*?" There goes Rock, finding the weak spots and punching holes in my argument.

I'm not prancing into this situation on the back of a unicorn with a blank slate and heart eyes, acting like nothing ever happened. My guard is up despite my optimism. But having them voice the doubts I've been replaying in my mind over and over doesn't help matters.

I want to move forward with Tatum, not backward. And I need these guys supporting me, not working against me.

Rock raises his hands in surrender when I send him a scathing look. "Sorry, man. We want this for you. We do. Just make sure you keep your head above water."

Jensen stuffs a hand in his jeans pocket and levels me with the same pitiful eyes Pam gave me this morning. "You need to be careful, Jake."

Hearing the warning for the second time in one day pisses me off. Not because I naively expect everything to work out with Tatum, and I'm throwing all caution to the wind. I'm mad because those exact words of foreboding have been niggling at my mind already.

I do need to be careful. After all, she ruined me before. My own insecurities are reason enough for me to tread carefully. Being cautioned by Jensen and Pam further amplifies my own doubts and fears that I wish didn't exist at all.

Tatum may be dealing with something really hard right now, but I refuse to let her cast me aside again. Like Graham said, when it comes to her, I need to be on board or hop off the train.

Well, she better be ready because I'm coming for her.

Needing to take my mind off heavy things, I set the empty bottle on the floor and scoop up the hammer. "Let's get this done."

"Jensen's cutting," Rock declares as he twists open a second beer.

I wish Jensen luck with finding one of the three missing measuring tapes as he bounds down the stairs. No telling where Rock hid them to avoid doing actual work.

21

TATUM

I wipe my eyes with the Snuggie I've had since middle school. It's tradition on this day to watch the sappiest romance movies of all time. Maybe not the best movie genre on an anniversary like today, but it's nice to imagine Jake and me overcoming the odds and living happily ever after. Depressing, I know. Hence, the box of tissues on the coffee table next to the pile of used ones.

Aunt Pam appears from the kitchen, the soft glow from the hallway framing her silhouette. The flickering TV provides the only source of light in the dark living room, splashing cool hues across her delicate features.

"What do you need, sweetie?"

Jake.

That's the honest answer. Every year, when this day rolls around, I want and need Jake. He's finally within reach, but I instructed Aunt Pam to turn him away.

When I don't respond, she glides into the living room and gestures with a slender hand for me to shift over on the sofa. She squeezes in next to me, and I lay my head in her lap, closing my eyes as she gently works the tangles from my hair.

"You can't ignore him for long. That boy is persistent." Aunt Pam has a light, airy voice that soothes. I've never heard her raise it in anger to anyone. She has the patience of a priestess and the heart of a saint. "You've let him in. And with you two, there's no such thing as halfway. The sooner you tell him what happened, the better for both of you. Give him the chance to make an informed decision before he dives in headfirst."

I'm tempted to tell her we dove straight into the deep end a few days ago, but that truth's a little too scandalous for my aunt's innocent ears.

I promised Jake that I would tell him everything, and I will. After living without him for years, I want to savor this moment and hold on to him a while longer. It's selfish and against my nature, but I've sacrificed so much. I've earned a few days or weeks to soak in the magic of our revival, even if it's temporary.

Wiping my chapped nose with a tissue, I say, "I'll tell him. Soon."

A few minutes pass before Aunt Pam clears her throat. "I want you to know how proud I am of you. For getting help. For facing everything." Her fingers continue their soothing strokes through my hair. "I don't know that I tell you that often enough."

"Thank you. And you don't have to say it. I already know."

"It's important that you hear it. I may not be your parent, but I'm just as proud as yours would be. And they would've told you so every day."

I sit up and twist so I'm facing Aunt Pam, needing her to

see the sincerity in my eyes. "You *are* a parent. And a darn good one, considering everything I've put you through."

She pats my hand and gives me a watery smile. "Aside from watching you suffer through so much, I wouldn't change a thing." I hand her a tissue, and she wipes her nose. "Can this old lady give you some parental advice?" My aunt is fifty-eight. Hardly an old lady.

"Of course."

"You made a mistake, but Jake loves you enough that he'll understand *why* you did what you did. If you push through your fear, and he sets aside his pride, I have faith that you'll both be fine. But you owe him the truth and the chance to forgive if you really want to be with him."

Unable to respond to the indisputable facts she laid out, I swallow the ball of emotions in my throat and rest my head in her lap again. "Thank you. For sticking by me."

"There's nowhere else I'd rather be."

She offers to reheat leftover lasagna from last night. Not having an appetite, I decline. So, we sit quietly, lost in cinematic heartache until the kitchen door opens and closes.

"Ugh. Why do you do this to yourself?" Maisy stomps into the room in her white fur coat, shiny black leggings, and red Doc Martens.

"Why do you hate love?" I ask.

We have the same argument every year. Maisy has no tolerance for sappy romance. Or any romance, for that matter.

"Here." She forcefully places a to-go cup on the coffee table. "Got you a chai tea." *Well, she's in a mood.*

My eyes drift from her zebra-print shirt to her scowling face. She looks like a glam-rock pixie who found out someone stole her fairy dust. Her clothes are slightly disheveled and her...

"What happened to your hair?" The curls on her head are wild and frizzy. Very untamed for the tame Maisy Donovan.

"I had the windows down. Needed some fresh air." She swats at my feet. "Move over."

"It's the middle of January." I bend my legs to make room for her. She sheds the coat, tosses it in a nearby chair, and falls onto the sofa.

"I got hot in my coat. Now shut up and watch your dumb movie." She crosses her arms and feigns interest in a film she despises, avoiding my gaze, which means she's hiding something. *Interesting*.

I'm not buying the open windows line for a second. Maisy hates the wind blowing her hair about as much as she hates romance.

"Stop looking at me," she says.

With my head in Aunt Pam's lap, I examine Maisy's perfect face, looking for clues. When I spot her signature "Murdered Merlot" lipstick—so dark red it's almost purple, like blood—smudged at the corner of her mouth, I internally shout *Eureka!*

"You've been kissing someone!" I lunge forward with an accusatory finger pointed a millimeter from her bottom lip and my first smile of the day, then flap my hands. "Tell me, tell me, tell me."

"You have serious problems," she grumbles.

"We know this. Now tell me who was worthy enough to taste Crazy Maisy's luscious lips." I'm smiling so hard I probably look like a crazy person.

Maisy glowers at me for using the nickname her brother's friends gave her when she was a child. "Don't call me that."

Aunt Pam heaves a weary sigh, lightly pats my back, and rises from the sofa. "I'll leave you girls to your drama."

"Love you," I tell her. She pecks the top of my head and practically sprints to her bedroom. My attention on Maisy, I order, "Spill. I need details."

"You first," she counters with a bratty smirk.

I told her that Jake and I had sex, but it was more of a *holy crap, I'm panicking over here* disclosure than an *it was so amazing, let me give you the play-by-play* one.

I thump her boob. She slaps my arm, then we giggle, and it feels so good to forget the reasons I'm sad today. Our laughter fades, and we sink into the cushions, facing each other while the forgotten movie plays in the background.

Maisy's eyes drift to the coffee table, which lacks the booze and pills that used to help me through this day. "How are you holding up?"

What she's really asking is if I'm managing without my usual coping mechanisms, but I'm not offended. It's a known fact within my little circle that I used to drown my sorrows in vodka and downers.

"Honestly? I'm doing okay. I had a long conversation with Cheryl yesterday. Told her I was worried about raw-dogging it today—"

"That doesn't mean what you think it does," Maisy interjects, her sculpted brows raised in amusement.

I wave a hand. "Whatever. I feel good. Well, not *good* but at least less miserable than usual."

She nods, accepting my answer as the truth. Thanks to everything I learned in therapy, I'm not allowing the pain to incapacitate me like it used to. Recovery wasn't easy in the beginning, when everything came crashing down in an emotional tsunami. Now, I tackle the past in smaller chunks, giving each breaking wave of pain the care and attention it deserves until it settles.

For the first time, I haven't fully succumbed to the darkness. The most significant improvement is that I no longer need to rely on others. I'm stronger than ever, but I'll always cherish my friends' and Aunt Pam's support.

A deep crease forms between Maisy's brows when her gaze locks on my face.

"What's wrong?" I ask.

She hesitates, then her breath hitches before her strong, husky voice comes out small and feeble. "Did I enable you?"

I jerk my head back. "What?"

"All those years, when you were spiraling and kept getting worse, did I really do anything to try to help you? Or get you help? I feel like I stood by and watched you fall but did nothing to save you. Your career wouldn't have ended if I had—"

"Maisy." I frown at my best friend. The strongest, most formidable tree in my little family grove. "Where is this coming from? Do you really think anything I've done to myself is your fault?"

"I should've said more. Or done more," she argues, and her bottom lip quivers for the first time ever.

When I snag her hand, she doesn't immediately tug it away. The fact that she needs my comfort right now means her distress has reached critical levels. "You've done more for me than anyone. I know about your texts to all the guys and Aunt Pam, telling them I had a problem. I know who trashed the bottles and flushed the pills while I was passed out. And who kept 'forgetting' to bring wigs on our tours so I couldn't disguise myself and go to the hotel bars.

"And when none of that worked, who held my hair and cleaned me up? Made me eat"—I point at the table—"and brought me tea whenever I was sad? *You* did. You had an entirely separate, thankless, pro bono career behind the scenes that no one knows about. But *I* know. And I'm grateful for you beyond words for keeping me alive long enough to finally want to help myself. If that's not saving me, I don't know what is."

Maisy driving from Austin to be with me tonight, despite her disdain for Walford, and bringing my favorite tea is the perfect example of her character. She's not warm and fuzzy with soothing words and long hugs, but her actions speak volumes. And she's the most loyal person I know.

"Now hug me." I open my arms in invitation.

She scowls as tears trickle down her face, but she finally caves and melts into my embrace. "You're such a bitch."

"I know, but I didn't make you cry on purpose." I squeeze her tight before letting her go. "I love you, Maiz."

"Whatever. I love you too." She lifts the edge of my Snuggie to wipe her snotty nose. "Drink your nasty tea and watch your stupid show."

I increase the volume on the TV, and she lets me snuggle against her while I get lost in a love story. Chewing her bottom lip, she stares intently at me while I sip my…very cold tea.

With narrowed eyes, I say, "You *will* tell me who ruined your lipstick. But I won't force you to talk about it now."

"You can't force me to do anything."

Holding the cup toward her, I say, "I can force you to reheat this tea."

Sighing, she rises to her feet and snatches the cup. "Fine. But turn off this god-awful movie and put on something about vampires."

~

The dog barking next door disrupts my fitful sleep. I close my eyes and wait for it to stop, but tapping on my window joins in the noise. I kick off my blankets, shuffle to the window, and slide open the curtains.

Jake presses a palm to the glass, his face as distressed as the faded hoodie he's wearing. "Let me in?"

On the nights he snuck into my window in high school, he managed stealth, slipping in and out without a sound. He could easily use the kitchen door now that we're adults. And to avoid riling up the neighbor's dog while speaking at full volume.

I unlatch the window and push up the lower pane. The bent screen leans against the brick behind a shrub where I left it years ago. Aunt Pam knew Jake came to me some nights, but she never said anything.

I'm drained from crying all day, so I shuffle back to bed in my sleep shorts and long-sleeved tee and climb under the covers. Jake quietly shuts the window and tugs off his sneakers and hoodie. In grey sweatpants and a white T-shirt, he crawls into bed behind me.

He nuzzles his face in the crook of my neck and wraps an arm around my waist, spooning me with our legs bent at a matching angle. My chest expands and deflates from the deep, relieved breath I take.

I've missed the way our bodies naturally fit together like we're a single entity. Even with the inches added to his height, his body molds to mine perfectly.

"What can I do?" he asks, his tone full of worry I want to ease but can't. Whether I hold back the truth or tell him everything, he'll find no solace.

I slide my hand beneath his and link our fingers together. "You're doing it."

Aunt Pam gave me the encouragement I needed today. Maisy distracted me. But Jake…he's my sanctuary.

"Please don't shut me out," he whispers. "Leave the door open just a crack so I can see you."

"You've always been able to see me." My voice trembles, but I manage to suppress the tears.

"Not when you're hiding from me in the dark."

We hold each other for a long while, his controlled breathing a telltale sign that he's still awake, his mind spinning.

"We need to talk about something important."

I stiffen, assuming he'll press me for answers about why I rejected him this morning. I've had enough emotional turmoil for one day and don't have the energy to deal with anymore.

"It's not bad," he assures me. Aside from our lips forming soft words, we haven't moved. "It's about what happened the other day. When I came inside you."

Flustered by his candid words, heat floods my face. "Okay?" I drawl.

"Are you on birth control?"

Rather than voicing my answer, I shake my head, drawing a long, disappointed sigh from him.

"I'll keep condoms on me," he grumbles.

A smile plays at the corners of my mouth, my mood lightened by the unexpected topic of conversation. "End of the world."

He groans and presses in closer. "You have no idea. Being bare inside you is the best feeling ever."

My thighs squeeze together like they enjoy his provocative words, so I elbow him in the stomach. "Don't talk like that."

"Like what? Like I love how you feel wrapped around my

dick?" The teasing lilt in his husky voice gives his game away. He's aware how embarrassed I get from dirty talk.

I wriggle around to face him, shifting closer so our bodies are flush from chest to toes. His erection digs into my stomach, and he flexes the fingers squeezing my hip.

In a breathy voice, I speak against his lips while squirming just enough that his hips rock forward. "Do you have a condom with you?"

His grip on me tightens along with his voice. "No."

"Hmm. Shame." I rub my cheek on his sternum and tuck my arms between us, settling in for a comfy snuggle.

His chest bounces when he chuckles. "You don't play fair."

"I'm just playing by your rules, so you can't complain."

He brushes the tendrils of hair that fell out of my bun off my neck, and my eyelids flutter closed. I'm exhausted anyway, and his soothing touch will easily knock me out.

"Remember when we used to talk about kids? You wanted enough to form a football team." His thumb grazes the sensitive spot behind my ear, and I shiver. "Do you still want them?"

"Someday. Do you?"

"Maybe someday."

Since he brought up the subject, I expect him to expand on his thoughts of creating a family, but he doesn't. He simply holds me while I breathe in the coffee stain on his shirt.

"I'll get on birth control," I murmur into the fabric.

"Okay."

As he strokes a hand along my back, I drift off to sleep, unclear on Jake's position on having children. Or having them with *me*. Yes, it's too soon for thoughts about a future with him, but these are resurrected dreams and discussions we had as teenagers.

People and priorities change, and I wonder if we've changed so much as individuals that we're on different pages now.

Time will tell, I guess.

22

TATUM

Aunt Pam was right about Jake's persistence. Every morning, he knocks on the door at sunrise with coffee in one hand and chocolate croissants in the other.

I'm not a morning person, but I indulge him as we chat over breakfast at the kitchen table. He leaves an hour later, only to return in the evening for dinner. Afterward, we lounge on the sofa, and I pick at my guitar while he answers emails on his phone.

We've repeated this routine every day for the past week, and he starts each morning by asking me, "How are you feeling today?" We don't touch aside from cuddling and quick hello/goodbye kisses, and I'm okay with that…for now. His presence is enough to keep me in the light.

While Jake's off doing whatever he does during the day, I've been writing songs. Being with him again, feeling the love he's yet to put words to, allowed me to find my spark. The one that's been missing for too long. The notes and lyrics pour out of me. Old songs, new songs, or a blending of the two…I've finished at least a half-dozen already.

It's amazing to regain this momentum. Like my heart is open and ripe with meaningful music to share.

I tap the pencil on my notebook while crafting a melody in my head, searching for a happy medium between somber and hopeful to express the lines on the page properly.

Jake places a mug on the table and settles at my side on the loveseat at The Drip as a rich, coffee aroma permeates the air. I untuck my legs and rest my calves on his knees. The movement comes so naturally, I don't realize what I've done until Jake starts rubbing my shin.

I glance at him, my lips pursed to keep from smiling. The corners of his mouth tilt up in a timid grin. I'm not accustomed to his insecurity. It's adorable, but unnecessary.

This is our first public outing together, and I swear Lydia sighed dreamily with hearts dancing around her head when we walked through the door. She's always been one of our biggest supporters, allowing us to loiter in our little corner for as long as we want. I'm certain she's a hopeless romantic who creates fairy-tales in her mind about me and Jake while she brews her beans.

I crane my neck to peek at the antique cuckoo clock on the wall behind me, impressed that it continues ticking even though the cuckoo stopped working ages ago. Noting the school day has ended, I bop Jake on the head with my pencil and say, "I'm meeting with Danny soon."

He nods while slurping his coffee.

I told him about Maisy's YouTube suggestion. After chewing on the idea, I've decided to take the plunge. If anything, the channel can serve as a vault to store my new music for posterity.

A couple of days ago, I stopped by Danny's house with a job proposal. His mom, Julia, answered the door in a bathrobe and pajamas, and I felt terrible for interrupting her nap between shifts. She works at the same hospital as Lucy, who told me Julia takes on more hours than any other nurse on staff.

Danny stood frozen like a red statue while I laid out my proposal. He accepted my paying offer to record, edit, and publish my videos on YouTube—with full director and producer credits—and Julia was beyond thrilled. Danny and I exchanged numbers to coordinate our schedules. Turns out, he's much better at texting than talking.

Someone on the sidewalk across the street catches my attention. "That's the second time Menchy's walked by since we got here." Earlier he strolled by on this side of the street. It's like he's on patrol. Or being nosy.

"I find it's best to just ignore him." Jake jerks his chin at the notebook. "What's this one about?"

I poke him in the chest with the eraser. "Stop asking. You'll hear them soon enough." Every day, he asks what my songs are about, but I'm keeping them a secret for now.

Expecting my dismissal, he shrugs it off. "What did your new lawyer say?"

I fired Pete Billings and hired a new attorney—Katherine Yost. She's a no-nonsense bulldozer, originally from Boston, who eats entertainment contracts for breakfast. Bette always intimidated me a little, but Katherine's razor-sharp claws make Bette seem like a toeless kitten. However, despite her endless knowledge of contract laws and loopholes, Katherine did not have good news for me.

"She said I made a rookie mistake when I signed. The label owns all recording rights."

If I want control over my songs and who gets to use them, I'll have to re-record each one from scratch. What's worse, I have to wait five years before I'm able to do so.

Jake abandons his mug on the table and turns his full

attention to me, draping an arm over the back of the loveseat. "But you're the original artist."

"Tell the label that. I own the songs, but not the recordings." Swiping my mug of tea from the table, I bring it to my nose, breathing in the scent of savory chai seasonings.

"Let me guess. Your old manager worked this deal and takes a cut every time the label lets someone use or record Makenzie's music."

"Yep."

I hold my breath, waiting for the blow which he delivers by gently saying, "I never would've let that happen. I would've fought for you."

He's never shy about looking me in the eye when he speaks heavy truths. But I falter under their weight because they serve as blatant reminders of the truth I'm withholding, which is heavier than all of his combined.

"I know you would have."

Biting my lip to prevent an episode of word vomit and apologies, I glance at the words on the page and think about that stupid contract signed by an ignorant nineteen-year-old.

A part of me is fine with letting the issue go. There's well over a hundred completed recordings, some which never made it on an album. Recording them again—even a portion of them—would require a lot of work.

I'll still earn my cut as long as the label owns the rights. And if, someday, they stop trying to profit from them, oh well. I'm ready to move on from Makenzie. I've never felt the songs I wrote as her were my best work anyway.

My eyes meet Jake's, needing him to understand how sincere I am when I say, "I'm ready to put Makenzie behind me, Jake. I want a normal life. One where I don't have to sneak out of hotel basements and have my every move planned days or weeks in advance. Where I don't have cameras shoved in my face and my name splashed across headlines. I want to be spontaneous and free like I used to be."

He skims the pad of his thumb along my neck, and I'm tempted to curl my body toward his steady comfort.

"It'll be a while before you have that kind of freedom again, Tate. If you do this YouTube thing, the fame won't go away. It'll just be Tatum Wakefield getting all the attention."

"Yes, but I'll be in control of it. The music will be for me, and my fans can enjoy it from a distance if they choose to stick around."

I'm giddy about the idea of feeling no pressure to perform or make records. I could release new songs on digital streaming platforms as often or as little as I want. If no one downloads them, I'm okay with that. It's never been about the money. All I want to do is write music and share it with people.

A wistful smile graces my lips. "It would be nice to say, 'here's my music…enjoy,' and leave it at that. It sounds simple—too simple, I'm sure—but I could really, really use some simple in my life."

Tucking my hair behind my ear, he asks, "What can I do to help?"

The day we met, Jake asked what he could do to help me become a star. After all this time, him asking how he can help me be *Tatum* again reminds me why I fell in love with him in the first place.

While Jake's been out of town, I've busied myself with ordering the video equipment Danny recommended and deciding which songs to record for my channel.

"What got you interested in making movies?" Maisy asks Danny.

We ended our weekly security update with Marcus and Judge, and Maisy hasn't disconnected from the video call. She's stuffing her face with potato chips while Danny sets up for our first recording session in my kitchen.

His eyes drop to the tripod he's carrying. "Watching Makenzie's music videos."

"Aww, Danny," I preen. He's so good for my self-esteem.

"Who's making movies?" Graham pops into frame over Maisy's shoulder.

Danny freezes, turning an alarming scarlet color. Being the standup guy he is, Graham doesn't make a big deal of Danny's reaction and breezes ahead.

"Ah. You must be the famous Danny Foster I've heard so much about. Tatum told me about your video contest. Hope you win, man."

"Thanks," Danny squeaks, raking his bangs to the side.

"Let me know if you need any pointers. I'm happy to help." Graham gives Danny his signature wink, blows me a kiss, and disappears.

I chance a peek at Danny to make sure he's still breathing.

Maisy chimes in with her mouth full of chips. "They're regular people, kid. They shit like the rest of us."

I cough to smother my laugh when an awkward giggle escapes Danny. Maisy grins at me and winks. We've just secretly agreed to make it our mission to bring Danny out of his shell. Her brand of crude, dry commentary should do the trick.

"I'll let you get to work," she says. "Later, bitch."

"Bye." The video call ends, and Danny startles when I clap my hands once and shout, "Where do you want me, Director?"

We fall into a routine. From morning until school's out, I practice my songs and put the final touches on them. When Danny arrives, dressed in his daily uniform of a long-sleeved tee and joggers, he sets up the equipment and records me as many times as necessary to complete a full song without mistakes.

He edits the videos at night and uploads them to a shared folder in the cloud for me to review and offer feedback. Once we have a small backlog of videos, he'll start publishing one each week.

On the fourth day of our sessions, Jake shows up. He sneaks in quietly through the screen door and leans against the wall, arms folded across his chest. His penetrating gaze stays on me while I sing about big dreams in a small town. It's a song I wrote in high school and was always one of Jake's favorites.

When the song ends, he waits a few beats before saying, "Sounds even better than it used to."

Danny jumps a foot in the air in fright.

Jake steps forward, keeping a straight face, and slaps him on the back. "Sorry about that." He smothers the urge to laugh as he heads for the full pot of fresh coffee.

Danny mumbles something under his breath and sends a text on his phone before packing up the equipment. I glare at Jake, silently berating him for ruining the progress I've made toward getting Danny to relax. Jake's brows bunch in confusion when I give him the evil eye. He hasn't been around lately and isn't aware of my master plan.

"I'll wait outside for my ride," Danny says, slinging his backpack over a shoulder. We leave the recording gear in the corner of the breakfast nook—much to Aunt Pam's dismay—since we use it daily.

"You can hang out here," I offer, laying my guitar on the table. "It's cold out."

"Nah. I'll be fine. Thanks." Danny shuffles side to side, unsure what to do next. Gripping the strap on his backpack, he tosses a thumb over his shoulder. "I'll see you tomorrow."

"Okay. See you tomorrow!" I call out as he pushes through the screen door.

Jake shuts the inner door behind him, settles in the chair next to me, and slurps his coffee.

I smack his arm. "You scared him off."

He holds his mug away to protect it from my assault. "Didn't mean to. Kid's jumpy as hell."

"He's shy, Jake, and I'm trying to build his confidence. The first step is to make him comfortable around me. If people keep scaring him to death, he'll never relax."

"If I had knocked, he would've jumped just as high."

I chuckle, thinking about the skittish kid. "You're probably right. Still, help me out here. It's important to me to keep Danny on this project. Any way I can help him fulfill his dream, I will."

"You're right. I'll do better." He places his beloved mug on the table and scoots his chair closer to mine. "Now fire up that laptop and show me what you've done so far."

I play four of the videos for him, claiming the other two need edits. In truth, those two songs reveal parts of my past I'm not ready to share with Jake. From the corner of my eye, I gauge his reaction to the music, but he gives nothing away.

He's quiet for a minute after the fourth song ends. It's a new one about searching for an anchor after being adrift for too long. It resonates with my feelings about Jake and how I was lost without him. The sheen coating his eyes, brightening the forest green irises, tells me the words ring true for him as well.

Rather than comment on the music, he throws me for a loop by saying, "You should make an intro video. Explain to the viewers what they can expect from you and the channel. Let them know why you're doing this."

I tuck my hands under my thighs to keep from tugging my hair. "No one cares why I'm doing it. And it's no one's business, really."

"The public hasn't heard a word from Makenzie since New York. You could use your channel to transition your fans by closing one door and opening another with an intro video."

I smirk. "You keeping tabs on Makenzie, Jake?"

"I don't give a shit about Makenzie," he says, the brutal truth hissing between his teeth.

I rear back as if he slapped me. The shock and hurt on my face must register because he drops his head and rubs his temples.

"Fuck." The curse punches from his lips.

I'm speechless, unblinking as Jake surges to his feet and paces the floor, examining the tiles as he gathers his thoughts. He can't look at me when he finally speaks, but I don't need to see the resentment in his eyes. It's painting every inch of the room.

"Makenzie isn't real to me, Tate. She's a fictional character. A body snatcher that took you and kept you away from me. I'll be honest, I have no love for her and never did. The pop princess that everyone else loves is not the girl I loved, and she never will be." He slices a hand through the air. "Don't ask me to treat you and her as one and the same. I'm glad you're moving on from being Makenzie. And, one day, I'll make peace with her, but it could be a while before that happens." Stopping abruptly, he faces me with hands on hips and an unmistakable challenge in his eyes. "Is that gonna be a problem?"

I clear the burn from my throat and shake my head. "No."

I've known all along that he has issues with my Makenzie persona. At any mention of the name, his body stiffens or a coldness dilutes the warmth in his eyes. He hasn't spoken about his feelings until now. To some extent, I understand why he tries to separate me from Makenzie, but his approach isn't realistic. Not in my world.

Distress overtakes his features when he returns to his seat and tugs me closer, caging my knees between his. "Baby, be patient with me while I work through all the mess in my head. I'm trying hard not to direct that mess at you, which is the only reason I'm not here every second of the day."

"What do you do all day?" I ask, curious about how he spends his time when we're not together and he's not traveling. He separates himself from me, to an extent, and I allow him that space by not prying too much into his daily life. He'll open up when he's ready, and pushing him won't do any good.

He holds my gaze for a beat before offering a vague answer. "I get work done at home."

I'm also curious about where he lives and why he's never taken me to his house, but I haven't pressed the issue. While Jake has no problem storming my castle, a moat and several walls surround his.

"I'll be patient with you as long as you're patient with me," I say.

A grimace passes over his face before he nods and leans in for a kiss. A kiss that turns heated as we unpack our emotions and declare how much we missed each other the last few days. A kiss that ends with us having sex in my aunt's kitchen.

23

TATUM

"All done?" Aunt Pam asks as she stands to clear the fajita feast from the table.

Jake lets out a content moan and rubs his belly. "Stuffed."

I snort into my glass of iced tea and offer to help with the dishes, but my aunt declines and takes our plates. She's not one to make a fuss or inconvenience anyone, happy to flitter about in the background and let us carry on. So, I show her my appreciation by cleaning the house and watering her plants while she's out being a small-town socialite.

Jake's fingers dance along my thigh. He's been extra touchy-feely this evening, leaving my skin a mess of goose-bumps. "I want to take you somewhere."

My thighs clamp together from the obvious lust in his tone, and his heated gaze drops to my mouth when I bite my bottom lip and squirm in my seat.

I want to say something sexy like *you can take me anywhere and everywhere, hot stuff*, but all I can manage when he looks at me like I'm his favorite dessert is, "Okay."

We tell Aunt Pam we'll be back later and not to wait up, ignoring the cheeky smile she's unable to hide.

Holding my hand, Jake strokes my knuckles as we pass the town's border in his truck. He's quiet, all of a sudden, and several times he starts to speak but changes his mind. When he turns on the gravel road leading to our special place, I'm nervous. Not knowing if I should expect the old Jake who kisses me under the stars or the new Jake who will admonish me for bringing someone else here.

"Why did they put up a gate?" I ask as he slides out of the truck at the gate.

He pauses and looks over his shoulder, a blank expression on his face. "To keep people out."

I don't outwardly react to his dismissive answer, but I'm wondering what happened to the flirty, affectionate man from earlier. He opens the gate and drives ahead without saying a word.

We park on the ridge, the front of the truck facing the hills instead of backing in like we used to, while country music drifts through the speakers. Chewing my lip, I glance at Jake's hands strangling the steering wheel.

"Talk to me," I say. He hasn't looked at me since we passed through the gate, and it's the first time we've been here alone with this uncertainty hanging between us.

Sighing, he drops his head to the headrest. I pry one of his hands from the steering wheel and give it a squeeze, reassuring him that I'm open to hearing anything he has to say, no matter how painful.

This has always been a safe place to release our demons and voice our dreams. Truth lives here, and I'll be devastated if I took that sense of safety away by tarnishing this place with my actions.

"Tell me, Jake. Whatever it is," I coax, softening my voice in encouragement.

He stares ahead at the shadowed hills under the moonlight, one hand firmly held in mine and the other in his lap, fingers grazing the bottom of the steering wheel.

"I never thought we'd be here again," he says quietly. "Seemed like a good idea earlier, but now I'm not sure."

The turmoil etched on his face saddens me, but I push aside my disappointment. "We can leave. Go back to my house or call it a night. Whatever you want."

When his eyes meet mine, they're as defeated as his tone when he says, "It's never been about what I want, Tate."

My chest aches at how true that statement is. The reasons for all his pain and suffering have been out of his control.

"So tell me," I urge again.

He looks away, jaw clenched and body rigid. With my free hand, I cup his face to turn his head, but he refuses to budge, so I unbuckle my seatbelt and shift onto my knees. Leaning over the console, I grip his cheeks with both hands and force him to see me. His nostrils flare, bursts of air escaping them as he clamps his mouth shut.

"Tell me," I say, more demanding than before. "Tell me what you want."

"I want to keep you," he grits out, but desperation dulls the hard edge he was going for.

I scrape my nails along his scalp at the back of his head to ease his tension, drawing a shudder from him.

"You have me. I'm already yours."

His eyes flare before he surges forward, crashing our mouths together. Pain stings my upper lip from the force of the impact. I fumble with ripping off my coat and shove it in the back seat just before he yanks me over the console so I'm straddling him. He pulls my sweater over my head, and a ripping sound reaches my ears as I hastily free my arms from the sleeves.

His mouth claims mine again in a ruthless kiss as he

unhooks my bra, tosses it aside, and roughly squeezes my breasts. I grind against him, an inferno of lust igniting my body at the urgency surrounding us.

He blazes a scorching path down my neck and chest with his lips and tongue, and I jolt forward with a pained gasp when he tugs a nipple between his teeth and bites.

"Shit," I hiss while grinding into him harder, seeking friction and wondering how something can hurt so bad yet feel so good.

I shove my fingers in his hair, gripping it hard enough that he grunts and releases my aching nipple. Jerking his head back, I force him to meet my eyes. His are wild and feral, and he looks nothing like the Jake who makes sweet love and whispers adoring words.

"What do you want, Jake?" I whisper harshly.

Eyes glassy and chest heaving, he rasps, "I want you to shut up and fuck me like you're desperate for me."

His raw, crude words shimmy between my legs, leaving desire in their wake. I *am* desperate for him, and I'm more than willing to prove it.

I unzip his coat, the smell of the leather intoxicating. Darkened green eyes never leave my blue ones while I work alone to free the coat from his body. I struggle to remove his shirt and only manage to work one leg out of my leggings and panties in the confined space.

The steering wheel digs into my ribs when I lean back to unbuckle his belt and unbutton his pants. When I tug on the waistband of his boxer briefs, the commanding whip of his voice stops me.

"Wait."

My labored panting drowns out the radio as he slowly pulls the hair tie from the end of my braid. He unfurls each strand one by one. The reverent movements of his fingers sifting through my hair contrast starkly with the dominance emanating from him.

When my hair falls down my back and over my shoulders, he runs his fingers through the strands from top to bottom before gripping my waist with both hands.

"There," he says, his tone soft and worshipful as if his prayers for deliverance were answered. Just as quickly, it turns commanding again. "Continue."

He lifts me, and his hips, enough for me to push his jeans and underwear down his thighs. Staring me down, he waits for me to take the lead. It's not often he hands over control, but the power exchange is heady.

I swipe my tongue along my upper lip, a seductive tease that draws his gaze to my mouth. I'm challenging him. Jake loves to kiss me, and the slight twitching of his lips in response tells me I'm close to shattering the controlled demeanor he's presenting.

Holding his lust-filled gaze, I curl my hand around his thick erection and give it a few rough tugs. His hands pulse on my waist, a sign of his anticipation and another crack in his facade. When I drag the swollen head through my arousal and nudge it against my opening, it's game over.

He slams me down as he thrusts into me, stealing the air from my lungs, my spine curving forward from the sheer amount of force. His head falls to my chest on a groan, and the drawn-out sound of his pleasure sends another surge of heat through me.

After a handful of breaths, he reclines in the seat and wipes all emotion from his face, though his body sings.

"Move," he orders.

Digging my nails in the firm muscles of his shoulders, I rock back and forth. Slowly, at first, then building momentum as his eyelids become heavy and his lips part in ecstasy. I lean away, angling my hips so he hits that sweet spot inside me.

Grabbing the handle above the window with one hand, I increase the pace, my moans becoming louder as I climb toward my release. At the first squeeze of my inner muscles around him, he loses the battle entirely.

Splaying rough hands across my ribs, he takes control and moves my body up and down, our thighs slapping as he rams into me from below.

"Fuck, baby. Fuck!"

"Yes!" I shout. A victorious smile teases the corners of my mouth as I hang on for the ride.

With each of his thrusts and grunts, my legs quake and my climax builds. He slides a thumb between us, coating it in my arousal, then rubs my clit feverishly.

"Come on, baby," he urges. "Come all over my dick. Make a mess of me."

My core clenches hard at his dirty words, and the noise that escapes him sounds a little surprised and little high pitched.

"You like that, huh? Dirty fucking girl." Another squeeze from me has him upping the pace. "Hold onto something."

With one hand still gripping the handle, I flatten my other palm on the ceiling to keep from breaking my neck as I bounce in his lap. It's a wild, loud, squelching ride. The soundtrack switches from country music to a ballad of lewd lyrics pouring from Jake's filthy mouth. I'll admit, each one sets me on fire in the most unexpected way.

He bobs for my nipples, and when he finally catches one and sucks hard, rapturous tingles skitter along my spine, and I come all the way apart while shouting his name.

My sated, limp body surrenders to him when he locks his

arms around me, thrusting and grunting and cursing until he comes with deep, rumbling groan.

I melt against his sweaty chest and hide my flushed face in his neck. "Holy smoke. That was—"

"The best feeling in the world," he says, panting into my hair. I register the meaning of his words when his cum trickles out of me.

Ignoring the mess in his lap that he begged for, we hold each other through the cacophony of our harsh, heaving breaths. I capture his lips with mine, exploring his mouth with my tongue and humming my appreciation for the thrill he gave me.

Jake breaks the kiss, settling into the seat and reducing the truck's heat. We both shiver when the cooler air seeping through the vents hits our damp skin. We're only partially dressed from the waist down, and he's still inside me as we stare at one another.

Alarm bells ring in my head when I realize he's biting the inside of his right cheek, the habit exposed only by the slight indentation of his dimple.

He brushes my hair over my left shoulder, and I'm overcome with a flood of warm memories when he drags two familiar fingers across my chest and stops them over my heart. "Give me a truth."

24

JAKE

Tatum's eyes glisten, my request catching her off guard. "A truth for a truth?" she asks.

"Yep. Something I don't already know."

We played this game many times when we held each other under the sun or the stars. She and I exchanged a truth for a truth, learning everything about each other from our guiltiest pleasures to our wildest wishes. Trading truths also helped us work through our grief after losing our parents.

I don't expect her to confess what happened that forced her to leave me, though my patience wears thin. Tonight, I'm merely creating an opening so she can give me something to work with. I've been floundering for too long.

"Can we get dressed first?"

The corner of my mouth lifts when she glances at our laps and cringes. I tap her thigh. "Lift up."

She crinkles her cute nose at the obscene sound of my dick sliding out of her. I wipe between her legs with my shirt and clean myself off, then toss it in the backseat.

With zero grace, she exposes her bare ass when she scrabbles into the passenger seat and gathers her clothes. She puts everything on, including her coat, like she needs the added layers of protection.

I pull up and fasten my pants, leaving my belt unbuckled, while she braids her hair, tugging roughly at the strands and huffing each time she has to start over.

"Look at me, baby." I say, handing her the hair tie I dropped in the cupholder earlier. When her eyes meet my soft gaze, her stress visibly dissipates. "Don't get flustered. I'm not pushing you for anything specific. Just a truth, like old times. Dealer's choice."

She loops the tie around the end of her braid, her tone earnest when she says, "I was never with Graham."

I stifle my grin. "I'm aware."

A thousand questions lay on the tip of her tongue about how I learned the truth of her and Graham's fake relationship. She must piece everything together on her own because, rather than asking for an explanation, she sighs and mumbles, "I thought we had no secrets but, clearly, we do because he didn't tell me *that*."

She's adorable when she pouts.

"So?" I raise my brows, urging her on. "A truth?"

The wheels turn in her mind, her eyes flicking between mine as she conjures up something to divulge. She's a terrible actress and fails to maintain a serious expression when she says the last thing I'd expect. "Rock likes having his prostate tickled."

Stunned, I gape at her. If not for her flaming cheeks and eyes the size of saucers, I'd accuse her of joking.

Pointing a finger at her, I say, "I'm not touching that one. Or the fact that you know about it." I crank up the heat because I'm shirtless, and the thought of Rock's bedroom activities makes me shiver. Not in a good way. "I meant a truth about you."

"You weren't specific," she says with a smirk. *Brat.* She's been hanging around Maisy for too long. I frown at the thought of her friend, which prompts Tatum to ask, "What's that face for?"

I've been honest with her about everything, but this might be the one topic I shouldn't broach. While I let go of most of my resentment toward Tatum, Maisy's a different story. And Tatum's protective of Maisy for reasons I no longer comprehend.

I grew up with Maisy. We were close as kids and even closer after Tatum moved to Walford and they became best friends. She betrayed me, in a sense, when she ran away to be with Tatum without telling me herself. I became jealous of her for all the years she spent at Tatum's side. In my place. It's not something I'll get over any time soon. Besides, Maisy hasn't tried to make amends, so why should I?

Forcing a grin, I say, "It's nothing. Just thinking about what a brat you've become."

"Only when I need to be." She leans over the console and plants a long, close-mouthed kiss on my lips. "Here's my truth," she whispers. "I've never had sex with anyone but you."

Instantly, my heart races, but my breathing falters as I study her face for any sign of deception. "Tell me you're not lying."

"I'm not lying," she says. And I believe her. But…

"But you said you weren't an angel. That you tried to be but—"

"You didn't want the details, remember?" She tilts her head, gauging how receptive I might be to hearing about her past. "Do you want them now?"

I swallow hard and shake my head in adamant refusal. Why would I want to shatter the illusion that I'm the only man who's ever had his hands or mouth on her body? I'm preening with the knowledge that I'm the only one who's ever been inside her.

This truth is no little nugget. It's a gold mine. *My* gold mine.

I wrap a hand around the back of her head and devour her mouth, our faces mashed together so hard we struggle to breathe. The sweet taste of her tongue and her lavender scent pull a groan from my chest.

"I want to keep you," I say, repeating my words from earlier. "All to myself. I'm a selfish bastard, baby. And I go insane when anyone else gets a sliver of your good heart or a second of your attention. But I'll learn how to share and play nice with others. That's another one of *my* truths."

Her chuckle is as musical as her laugh. "I'm not a toy, Jake."

I cradle her face with both hands and gaze deep into her sparkly blue eyes. "No. You're something precious. And no one deserves you, Tatum. Least of all me."

25

TATUM

ME

He does it on your face?

What if it gets in your hair?

LUCY

Yes. And he likes to wash my hair.

ME

He washes hair?!?

LUCY

Only mine. Well, and Marcella's.

ME

Aww. I can't imagine his giant hands being that delicate.

Did you have to teach him how?

Is he gentle with the comb?

LUCY

It's funny that you're more interested in the hair washing.

Over the next week and a half, Jake and I become closer, a dangerous yet wonderful place to be. He leaves for a few days for work, but otherwise spends his mornings and evenings with me.

We have lots of sex, making up for lost time and using it as an escape from our underlying problems. We're mature enough and damaged enough to see it for what it is.

Like old times, we hang out at the coffee shop, drive around town, and stroll hand in hand down Main Street. We laugh and joke and fall into old habits, and I almost believe we can sweep the monsters lurking in the shadows under the rug.

I avoid Jensen when possible, so we steer clear of Bruno's Bar. He's a reminder of my guilt, which I'm trying not to think about as I enjoy this time with Jake.

When I'm not with Jake, I'm joining Lucy for educational lunches and snuggle time with Marcella, or I'm recording music with Danny.

Today, he's teaching me how to use the video editing software he installed on my laptop. I'm not really interested in learning the ins and outs, but it's an opportunity to encourage him to open up. And, believe me, the kid becomes quite the chatterbox when he talks about filmmaking.

We're at the table, adjusting sound quality on the newest videos, when someone knocks on the door.

"Come in," I holler.

Of all people, Brody strolls into my house, putting me on high alert. He dips his chin at me before addressing Danny. "You ready, kid?"

"Sorry. Lost track of time." Danny shoots from his seat and gathers his belongings.

"No worries." Brody taps a finger against a thigh as he waits near the kitchen island. His blond hair is a lot shorter and neatly styled, no longer a shaggy mop hiding his face. Navy-blue eyes drift around the open floor plan, and it dawns on me he's never been inside my house. At least, not that I know of.

I break the awkward silence. "I didn't realize you two know each other."

Brody's head whips around, eyes wide, as if he's surprised that I would speak to him. "Oh. Yeah, I usually give Daniel rides to help Julia out. They don't live far from me."

Now I understand why Brody put the mayor in a wrestling hold the day he verbally accosted Danny on Main Street. Brody knows Danny and is protective of him, which is kind of sweet.

I quirk an eyebrow when I turn my head toward Danny. "*Daniel*?"

"Um…" His brown eyes flick to Brody, who subtly nods in encouragement. "I prefer to be called Daniel."

I gape at him. We've been working together for weeks, and he's let me call him by a childhood nickname that he clearly doesn't like. If anyone can relate to the identity crisis brought on by something as simple as a name, it's me.

"Well, then. Daniel it is. I'll make sure Graham and Maisy know too."

My heart flutters when Daniel gives me an appreciative grin. He's been around during several of my video chats with Maisy, and he giggles nonstop at her dry humor. Graham joins whenever possible and talks shop with Daniel, which always brings a smile to the kid's face. I accepted the fact that I'm not funny or endearing enough to get the same reactions from him. So, I'll take this one as a win.

"See you later, Tate," Daniel says, heading for the door.

Brody hands him the car keys. "I'll be right out."

Once we're alone, Brody stuffs his hands in his pants pockets and leans against the counter.

I give him my back while I put my guitar in the case, needing something to do to calm my nerves. I'm not prepared for another onslaught of vitriol from one of Jake's friends, especially with them knowing we've spent so much time together lately.

"If you're here to scare me off, don't bother. I'm not going anywhere. What's going on between me and Jake is our business, and Walford is my home too."

"I just came to get Daniel, but while I'm here…" He hesitates, and I stiffen as I prepare for the worst. "What I said about Jake that day at the coffee shop isn't true. He would never sleep around like that. I realized I didn't clear that up when we talked at Bruno's, and I wanted to make sure you know."

Facing him, I lean against the table, mirroring his pose. To my surprise, there's remorse on his face, along with a hint of dismay in his eyes. I tilt my head and really study him, realizing the Brody standing before me is the real one. The one without the mask.

"I appreciate that," I say. "What you said hurt me, but I also felt I deserved it if it was the truth. I'm glad it's not."

"No. It's not," he reaffirms.

I slip my fingers in the back pockets of my jeans. "What if we agree to not talk about Jake?"

Brody chuckles without a trace of humor. "What else would you and I ever have to talk about?"

"I think we have a lot in common, actually. You asked me if I get tired of wearing a mask all the time. The answer is yes. And I have a feeling you're tired of wearing one too. It's exhausting living a lie." Brody's features tighten, and his muscles tense, but I don't let up.

"If you want to be real with someone in this town, you can be real with me. Everyone needs an outlet…a safe place to breathe. I'm not offering advice or friendship. Heck, I may not be here for long. But I can offer a listening ear if you need someone to confide in."

He regards me for long seconds, his eyes shifting between mine, seeking trust. Finally, he bobs his head and says, "I'll keep that in mind."

Good enough for me.

Jake bursts through the door like the Dark Knight of ranchers in a black ball cap, black canvas jacket, and dark, dirty jeans. His intense gaze sweeps over me before pinning Brody in place.

"What are you doing here?"

Brody's entire persona switches on a dime. The goofy grin and cheerful personality come out in full force. "Hey, bro. I'm picking up my young protégé. Thought I'd apologize again to Tate for being an ass a few weeks ago." He winks at me. "We're all good, right?"

I don't mistake the double meaning in his question. He wants me to confirm I won't share my suspicions about him with Jake.

I force a smile. "Yep. All good." Jake glances between us, brows drawn together in doubt. "Seriously, Jake. Everything's fine. Let's just put it behind us."

"Good." He strides over and pulls me in for a kiss, his back to Brody.

I catch the slip of Brody's mask, revealing a moment of longing as he watches us before clearing his throat. "Guess that's my cue to leave. See ya, lovebirds."

Jake ignores his friend, staying wrapped around me until the screen door slaps shut. He examines my face for any sign of distress.

"You okay?"

"Of course," I say, reassuring him with another kiss. "Did you know that he gives Danny rides everywhere and that Danny actually prefers to go by *Daniel*?" Throwing my hands up, I yell, "I can't believe he never told me!"

Jake laughs and tugs me closer. "You hate not being in the know."

"I really do," I whine.

"Me too," he says against my pouty lips. Before his comment has a chance to take root and ruin our evening, he spins me around and smacks me on the butt. "We're going somewhere tomorrow, so pack a bag."

26

JAKE

The San Antonio River Walk boasts miles of footpaths along the river running through downtown. Restaurants, bars, hotels, and shops line the sidewalks on either side.

My favorite parts are the small pockets of seclusion where it feels like being alone in a private park. Each time we walk around a bend, without a soul in sight, I pull Tatum aside for a quick make-out session. Just like old times.

Although it's February, the weather is mild enough that we're comfortable in jeans and sweaters. Tatum's wearing fake, black-framed glasses to conceal her identity, like Supergirl's alter ego. I snorted a laugh when she first put them on. She looks ridiculously adorable, and her bright blue eyes sparkle through the lenses.

The River Walk is a kaleidoscope of lights, smells, and sounds as we stroll along with bellies full of good Tex-Mex food. Tatum is relaxed tonight, and my goal is to keep her smiling for the rest of our visit.

The minute we left Walford, she found a radio station she liked, kicked off her shoes, and planted her feet on my dashboard. The scent of lavender filled the cab of my truck, and I relaxed into the ride. As she belted the words to almost every song, I kept stealing glances at her to confirm I wasn't dreaming.

The exact scene played out many times when we were teenagers. We'd drive to San Antonio or Austin on the weekends to find her an open-mic night or a small venue that would book a minor so she could gain the experience of playing live. The crowds loved her. How could they not? Tatum has an aura that naturally draws people in.

She was loose and carefree during our ride here, and I felt a flicker of life in my chest like the ones I felt that first morning we made love, and as I watched her write music again, and when she discussed her future career plans with me. The pieces of my heart are falling into place, one by one. But I remain cautious.

Strolling along the lit path, I drape an arm around Tatum and tuck her against my side. "Have you given anymore thought to when you'll go to California? Or if you still plan to go?"

Her relaxed expression immediately tightens when she lowers her head. If I could kick myself in the nuts for ruining her happy evening, I would. *Way to go, dumbass.*

"I don't want to think about the future right now. I don't want to think about anything, really." She looks at me with eyes that sparkle a little less. "Let's just enjoy tonight?"

"Fair enough."

I stop us in the middle of a small bridge spanning the river. Cradling her face in my hands, I kiss her slow and deep to bring her back into the moment. A few whistles pierce through the background noise, but they're mostly drowned out by nearby music. When she finally hums with contentment and relaxes into me, I end the kiss with a smile before we continue on our way.

Thumping bass beats grow louder as we approach a popular bar, and the mischievous smirk on Tatum's face gives away our next destination. She can't pass up a live band, especially one playing covers of popular dance songs from all decades. After she tugs me to the door, I pay the cover and follow as she makes a beeline straight for the dance floor.

I move side to side on the balls of my two left feet, grinning like an idiot with no rhythm. Song after song, my hands never leave Tatum's body no matter if she's swaying, dipping, bouncing, or grinding her ass into my crotch.

The flashing strobes catch her golden highlights, and she shines like a diamond with the amount of sheer joy radiating from her. All I can do is stare, enraptured, while she dances and sings like she's the only one in the room.

She spins around to face me with the biggest smile, her cheeks flushed a beautiful shade of pink. Lifting her hair with one hand, she fans her neck with the other, and a bead of sweat trickles down her exposed throat. She's so fucking sexy. What makes her more attractive is that she's not trying to be.

Tatum is effortlessly enticing, and I'm so turned on right now, it's not funny. According to the situation making my jeans a lot tighter, we need to get out of his club. ASAP.

Grabbing her hand, I practically drag her to our hotel. As soon as the elevator doors close, and we're alone, I crowd her against the wall and invade her mouth with my tongue.

When I pop the button on her jeans and shove my hand inside, she yelps, "Jake!"

I don't give a single fuck if we're technically in public. My self-control and sense of propriety are sitting somewhere far away alongside my patience…probably sipping tea together at the bottom of the deepest ocean.

"Do you have any idea how sexy you are?" I whisper

roughly in her ear as I drag my fingers along her soaked panties and rub the fabric against her clit.

She's gripping my biceps, mouth open in shock and possibly pleasure, as if she intends to push me away but can't bring herself to do it. I'm not sure where this animal in me came from, but the arousal coating my fingertips tells me she likes him…a lot.

Less than ten seconds pass between the ding of the elevator and the door of our hotel suite slamming shut. We paw at each other, our dueling tongues only separating long enough to shed clothes as we pass through the living room. Note to self: there's nothing fast or seductive when it comes to removing cowboy boots.

By the time I have them off, I'm standing in the bedroom, shirtless. Tatum's on all fours in the middle of the bed—naked—beckoning me with her delectable ass on display. My wild gaze lands right between her thighs where she's glistening and ready for me.

She looks over her shoulder with a devilish twinkle in her eye and a filthy smirk and utters the greatest lyrics she's ever written. "Come and get me, Holloway."

My brain short-circuits. This is the hottest moment of my life. I fumble with my belt and zipper, damn close to tripping over my own feet as I stumble toward the bed.

Fucking *finally*, I shuck off my jeans and underwear, then climb on the mattress behind her with my socks still on my feet. I line us up, dig my fingers into her hips, and slam home. The force is so powerful, my eyeballs roll back in my head. I barely hear Tatum cry out my name.

I'm frozen in a state of instant bliss with my head tipped back and mouth hanging wide open. When she wiggles her ass, I whisper hoarsely, "Give me a minute."

She lets out a husky chuckle so damn sexy and deep,

she pulses around me and spurs me into action. And, boy, do I move. Pounding into her like a madman, eyes fixed on where we're joined together as I glide in and out, in and out.

The sight of us is hypnotic, and I give a silent shout-out to that dude who invented light bulbs because all the lights are on in the bedroom as I enjoy the show.

"Good goddamn, baby. Your pussy's fucking perfect."

She clamps down on me hard in response, her body reminding me how much she loves my filthy mouth, so I improvise a song made of my own explicit lyrics.

Every moan and grunt—every cry of my name from her lips—powers me on until she strangles my dick, forcing my release after a few more deep thrusts. An honest-to-god roar tears from my throat when I come, and I've never felt more alive.

We fall forward on the mattress in a sweaty heap with Tatum lying face down. I'm probably squishing her slender body, but I can't bring myself to pull out yet. I bury my face in her hair and inhale her floral scent while I try to catch my breath. Makes no sense, I know, but all sense flew out the window the second that bead of sweat trailed down her sexy neck in the bar.

Her cheek rubs against my ear when she smiles. "Four out of five stars. Not too shabby, Holloway."

Acting affronted, I scoff between panting breaths, "You're crazy. If I wasn't so spent, I'd recap all the highlights of my stellar performance."

She giggles, clenching once more around my hypersensitive dick. I groan and roll off her, landing on my back. Spread out like a naked starfish with socked feet.

Tatum drapes herself across my chest and kisses me, languid and sweet. Her satisfied hums in the afterglow let me know I did a fantastic job even if she didn't get to come…yet. I'm far from done with her.

In a teasing tone, she says, "First, a shower." *Kiss.* "Then room service." *Kiss.* "Then you can earn that extra star."

Damn right, I will.

I sigh dramatically. "If I must."

Eyes closed, my lips curve into a relaxed smile at the beautiful sound of her tinkling laughter. Another piece clicks into place in my chest.

We place our order for room service, then I do wicked things to her in the shower. After devouring some midnight snacks, we make love *our* way. And I show her exactly how much power she has not only over my body, but also my heart.

~

Something soft brushes against my lips, and they lift into a sleepy grin. Must be Tatum's hair because it sure doesn't feel like her lush mouth. When it grazes the tip of my nose, I crack an eye open.

My underwear hovers above my face, dangling from a beefy, tattooed finger that does not belong to my girl. My eyes slide to the side to find the owner of said finger—a mountain of a bald man who looks both murderous and amused.

Lightning fast, I sit up and jerk the covers all the way to my armpits to hide my nipples like a scandalized Victorian duchess, then snatch my boxer briefs from his meaty paw. Scowling, I shout, "What the fuck?"

Movement across the room catches my eye. An equally furious giant blocks the entire doorway between the bedroom and living room. No amusement to be found on that guy's face. It's *all* murderous intent. He's eyeing me like he wants to give me a gnarly scar in my eyebrow to match his. I keep my narrowed focus on him as I slip on my underwear beneath the covers.

Both men are dressed in black suits like they walked straight off a Tarantino movie set. When the bathroom door opens, they quickly turn their backs to it. At least they have respect for my woman's privacy. I appreciate that.

Tatum whispers, "Shit," and fumbles to tie her bathrobe. "Clear," she says louder.

At the single word, Furious Guy whips around and crowds her space. "*Shit* is right. What the fuck were you thinking?"

"Don't talk to her like that!" I spring out of bed, ready to defend Tatum against a dude who probably has a gun and at least seventy pounds on me while I'm in nothing but my underwear.

His head swivels toward me. In my mind, it sounds like the haunting creak of a rusty hinge as it spins on his thick neck. "My job is to protect her from what's outside. Something you both failed to do when you stupidly decided to bring her here and she agreed to come along without letting me know."

"What's outside?" I ask, wary eyes darting between the behemoths. My anxiety ratchets up because I already know the answer.

"There's a window, isn't there?" He stabs a finger toward the floor-to-ceiling windows. "Go look."

I creep over and peek between the curtains. My stomach bottoms out from the scene I find. Fans pack both sides of the River Walk, not an inch of pavement in sight. The mob carries posters with messages for Makenzie, yelling her name, cameras everywhere. Total mayhem.

"The street side of the hotel is worse," says Furious Guy.

Executioner Guy—fitting name because he looks like he'll enjoy killing me—simply grunts.

"We were careful. Her hair…" I gesture weakly at Tatum's brown hair. "And she wore glasses—"

"You were careless," he hisses, nostrils flaring like a dragon ready to set me on fire. "Your first mistake, pretty boy, was assuming she's free to roam the earth like the rest of us."

Tatum sits on the end of the bed, shoulders hunched. The carefree, vibrant woman from last night has all but vanished, leaving behind a wilted flower. I peer out the window again, and my chest tightens.

This has been her life for years. No privacy. No agency. No peace. And I dragged her out of hiding and threw her into the thick of it.

What was I thinking? How could I forget Tatum and Makenzie may not be the same person, but they share the same body? I exposed her—put her at risk—so I could relive the good old days.

The massive throng of bodies sways as a single organism, ignoring the police's efforts to control the crowd. These people not only love her, they believe they have a *right* to her. It's a situation I'm obviously not equipped to handle. So, I swallow my humble pie and keep my mouth shut, giving the men a curt nod in acknowledgment of my fuckup.

Dismissing me, Furious Guy speaks to Tatum. "My plan's in motion. I'm activating contingencies to get you to Walford undetected." His phone rings. "There's one of them now. Menchy!" he barks into the phone as he exits the bedroom. *Menchy?*

Executioner Guy takes up a protective position near Tatum, hands folded together at his waist. It's clear they care about her and take her safety seriously, something I failed to consider when I planned our weekend getaway.

I might as well smooth things over since we could be here for a while, so I stride toward him and stick out my hand. "Jake Holloway."

His light brown eyes flick to my outstretched hand, and he grunts his rejection.

"This is Judge," Tatum says, gesturing toward the man, her voice small and flat. "And the other one's Marcus, his cousin."

Judge shifts when I sit next to her.

"It's fine, Judge. He won't hurt me."

Another grunt, but he may as well have said *too late*.

When I squeeze her thigh, Judge's eyes zero in on my hand like he wants to sever it from my forearm.

"Look at me, baby." Dull blue eyes meet mine. Not a trace of sparkle remains in them. "I'm so sorry. I had no idea."

"It's not your fault. I'm the one who thought becoming famous was a good career choice." She tries to joke, but her defeated smile holds no humor.

How long has she hated this side of being a successful musician? If she's so miserable in this life, why did she live it for so long? As far as I can tell, there's nothing glamorous about it. And I'm such an asshole for not considering what would happen if someone recognized her.

Sighing, I rise from the bed and scoop my jeans off the floor. We get dressed and check our phones, finding dozens of missed calls and texts from our friends, family, and her security team. The first ones arrived after we returned to the hotel last night while we were drowning in passionate, sweet oblivion.

With nothing to do but wait, we tiptoe around the suite for

hours while Marcus makes phone calls and Judge glares at me. I fall down the rabbit hole of social media and breaking news photos of me and Tate walking, dancing, eating, and kissing on the bridge.

We were lost in the moment, the only two people in existence, unaware of people snapping photos of us. That's how it is when we're together. Our world is an island, but now it's being invaded.

A noisy shockwave rolls through the crowd outside. I check the window, looking for the source of the excitement, but find nothing. Several minutes later, Graham bursts through the door dressed like he rolled out of bed. With a wrinkled shirt, loose tie, and messy hair, he looks nothing like the red-carpet royal people expect to see. *Are those shadows under his eyes?*

Spreading his arms wide, he declares, "Your hero has arrived! Pardon the delay, I had trouble parking my trusty steed." He yanks Tatum into his arms, pecks her neck, and whispers something in her ear. She's half-smiling when he lets her go and says, "Don't mess up my makeup." He points to the dark spots under his eyes, then gives me a nod. "Jake."

"What is this?" I ask, rankled by Graham's open affection toward Tatum and the fact that he was called to the rescue while I sit here helpless. "And how does everyone have a key to our room?"

Graham shrugs as I glare at the keycard in his hand. He must've flown from Austin as soon as he wrapped on set for the day, which explains why we've been waiting around. I'm irritated that no one has shared the details of our escape plan. Tatum seems clueless as well, but she probably trusts her team to get her where she needs to go without question. Again…no agency.

"A distraction," Marcus answers. He still won't look at

me. "The media loves a good story. Heartbroken ex shows up to win the girl."

"How does that help us?" Yeah, I'm pressing my luck with the combative tone.

"We divert their attention. They saw him walk into the hotel, looking like he hasn't slept all night, so they'll wait with bated breath to see if he emerges alone or with his prize on his arm. Meanwhile, you sneak out the back."

Our cell phones ping like crazy with alerts.

"A red herring," I mutter to no one in particular.

"Exactly." Marcus focuses on his phone.

I plop onto the couch and do the same. Photos of a determined and devastated-looking Graham pushing through the crowd flood social media. He looks every bit the jilted lover on a mission to take back his girl. Damn, he's a good actor.

The captions and comments mostly favor Graham in this pretend duel.

"Go get her, Graham! Kick that country bumpkin's ass!"
"Mak and Graham are perfect together. What is she thinking?"
"Poor Graham. He looks miserable."
"Can you believe Graham flew here to fight for her? #trueloven-everdies"
"I don't know who the hot cowboy is, but if he kissed me like that, I'd ditch the movie star in a heartbeat!"

Well, the last one is nice. Though it doesn't erase the twinge of jealousy I feel, even if Graham's not an actual threat to me.

Tatum must sense my dejection and crawls onto my lap, straddling her legs over mine. She plucks the phone from my hand and tosses it on the cushion before pulling my hands to her waist.

With a gentle hold on my chin, she stares into my eyes. "Don't do this to yourself. None of it's real. The only real thing is us."

"The thousands of people holding us hostage in this hotel are very real. How have you lived like this? It's terrifying, baby. And knowing this is my fault…" I shake my head and squeeze her hips. "I'm powerless here, Tate."

"I should've known better. I *do* know better." She presses her mouth to my ear and whispers, "But last night was so worth it."

Everything in the room disappears when our lips meet, our island almost secure again. Until the couch shifts from the heavy weight of a man sitting so close his shoulder touches mine.

Judge stares at me with a straight face, his nose mere inches from mine, and makes a slicing gesture across his neck. I gulp. Graham cracks up laughing like it's the funniest thing he's ever witnessed.

"Judge, leave him alone," Tatum says, but there's humor behind her reprimand. I'm relieved her mood is lighter.

"We're rolling out in fifteen," Marcus announces, setting everyone in motion. Well, everyone except for me.

Marcus and Judge exit the suite without a word.

Tatum gives Graham a long hug. "Thank you. Sorry to drag you into this."

"Anything for you, Tot. Always." He pecks her nose and releases her.

From the doorway, Tatum smiles at me over her shoulder. "See you at home, Holloway." She blows me a kiss and follows her security team.

Home. The corner of my mouth quirks at her referring to Walford as home. Warmth floods my chest as another piece clicks into place.

Graham raps his knuckles on the door, drawing my attention. His soft expression indicates he knows exactly where my mind went.

"Good luck, friend," he says, using the same words as the last time we parted ways. Then he winks and walks out the door, leaving me standing in the middle of the hotel suite.

As instructed by Marcus, I wait long enough for the crowd to disperse before sneaking to my truck in the parking garage. I drive to Walford alone, a golden sunset in my rearview mirror. No music, no lavender scent, and no pretty girl singing her heart out in my passenger seat.

It's my punishment for exposing Tatum, and I accept it.

27

TATUM

A pop star, a football coach, and an interim mayor walk into a bar…

In reality, we stand outside the bar in a silent battle over who should go first. Larry Olson rushes to the door, but a scowling Rock intercepts him and growls at the wrinkle-suited mayor's lack of chivalry. The two men block the door and my entry.

I roll my eyes when Mr. Olson glares at Rock. Well, attempts to glare. His unfocused gaze lands on a point closer to Rock's shoulder than his face.

Fifteen seconds into their stare down, I hit the limit of my patience and shout, "Move aside or open the damn door!"

Rock fakes a lunge, causing the mayor to flinch and stumble backward, then Rock swings the door open and gestures me through. I mutter a "thanks" as I cross the threshold, but the brute steps around me and walks ahead. I shake my head while admiring his bubble butt. The black Walford Bulldogs tracksuit he's sporting tonight must be his version of dressing up. Mr. Olson crashes through the door behind us, and we all go our separate ways.

It's karaoke night, and I'm ready for the fun. I squeeze through the packed crowd toward the corner table where Marcus leans against the wall, scanning the room for threats. Graham and Maisy giggle as Evelyn Truman and her cleavage serenade Menchy with a horrid rendition of an Ariana Grande song.

"Where's Judge?" I ask Marcus while shedding my coat and hanging it on the back of an empty stool.

"Bathroom."

The guys decided to stick around for a week after the frenzy I caused in San Antonio. They're staying at a local bed-and-breakfast while coordinating efforts to throw reporters off my trail after Marcus worked his magic and got us to Walford undetected. The most exciting moment of our great escape happened when Marcus wasn't allowed past his own blockade on the outskirts of town.

It was dark outside when we were blinded by headlights and flashlights on the highway. As we approached, we found over twenty pickup trucks and twice as many people blocking the road. Marcus climbed out to announce us, but Menchy and Lydia stepped forward with shotguns at the ready. Judge rolled down the windows so we could hear them better, and I leaned forward between the front seats, eyes glued on the drama.

"State your business," Menchy said, his gruff tone demanding full compliance or else. The pockets of his apron overflowed with tools and other supplies. He's like the MacGyver of hardware-store weaponry.

Marcus lifted his hands, probably to rub his temples in agitation, but Lydia aimed her gun higher. "Don't be a fool. Answer the man."

"Menchy, I'm Marcus. We spoke on the phone five

minutes ago when I passed mile marker thirty-two like we planned."

I couldn't see Marcus's face, but his tone and tense shoulders signaled impending doom. He was getting pissed.

"Got any ID?" Menchy asked.

"Oh, for fuck's sake." Marcus's shaved head hung in defeat, more than done with this whole day.

"Watch your mouth, young man," Lydia scolded. "You may be a brawny bastard, but this buckshot will tear your ass up."

The vehicle rocked, and I side-glanced at Judge who shook in silent laughter, only the occasional grunt slipping through. I tried not to laugh with him but failed miserably.

"Should I help him?" I wheezed. Judge wiped a tear and shook his head no.

All hell broke loose when a scrawny sheriff's deputy, wearing pajamas with a badge pinned on the collar, edged through the group and yelled, "Hands up!" Menchy, Lydia, and several others turned their shotguns on the young deputy, and someone shouted at him, "Too far, Bobby!"

The rotund owner of the donut shop, Tom-Tom Lee, disarmed the deputy and wrangled him face down on the asphalt quicker than anyone could blink. Judge scrambled out of the car, drawing his weapon, and I followed close behind.

Everyone from town started shouting at each other, and Marcus used the chaos to our advantage. He grabbed my elbow, towed me to the SUV, and lifted me into the backseat.

"Get in, Judge," he barked as he circled around to the driver's side.

Judge dove in the passenger seat, and Marcus shot off before he could shut the door. We bounced through the ditch, bypassing the road blockade. When the taillights were behind us, Judge and I busted out laughing again. Marcus will deny it to his dying day, but I saw his lips twitch with amusement.

Ainsley appears, bright-eyed and grinning as always, and sets a tray of drinks on our table. "Gave you extra cherries!" she shouts at me over the music.

"Thanks!"

She rushes off, and frenzied hands start grabbing and sorting drinks. My friends ordered me two Shirley Temples, but the leftover tequila shot probably wasn't meant for me.

I crinkle my nose. "This is a weird combo."

Maisy snags the tequila shot and throws it back. "There. Fixed it." She slams the empty shot glass on the table and sips her margarita.

"Aren't you driving to Austin tonight?" I ask her.

Graham and I persuaded a reluctant Maisy to come and experience a night of Walford's finest karaoke singers. Tomorrow, they have an early call time on set, so they can't stay long. Maisy's making the most of their visit, apparently. She's pretty tipsy, if not drunk.

"I'm driving," Graham says with a glum pout, raising his glass in the air. "Water. Yay me." He brings the water to his lips but pauses when something catches his eye. "Mmm. Finally something in this town worth seeing."

Maisy and I lean to the side. Brody, dressed in a blue button-down shirt and slim-fit chinos that hug his ass, trails behind Ainsley through the sea of people. She's flustered and appears to be running away from him.

When she disappears through the kitchen door, Brody changes direction and heads toward the bar with a frustrated scowl on his face. Someone bumps into him, and he immediately transforms into the carefree guy everyone expects. His happiness appears genuine. When that person moves along, Brody loses the smile, ducks his head, and aims for the exit.

"Impressive," Graham comments after watching the scene play out. "I wonder if he's interested in acting. He's got the looks and, clearly, he has the skills."

Maisy barks a laugh. "If venereal diseases are any indication of his 'skills'." She uses finger quotes to make her point.

"Maisy!" I gape at her meanness, wondering what's gotten into her lately besides alcohol. She's always been sarcastic and sharp-tongued, but she's never been downright cruel. Her behavior changes when she's in Walford, and I need to uncover the reasons why.

"Are you shaming the man's sexual freedom? Or is our little Maisy jealous because she's not getting laid?" Graham grunts when Maisy digs an elbow into his ribs.

"Believe me, the last thing I want from anyone in the town is sex." Maisy downs another tequila shot, and I exchange a concerned look with Graham. He's spent more time with her lately than I have, but his expression tells me he's equally clueless about the reasons behind her snarky attitude and wild behavior. "And the only thing I'm shaming is the drool on your chin," she adds.

"Hey. The rest of my body may be spoken for, but my eyeballs are my own," Graham quips.

Judge's head floats above the crowd as he weaves his way toward us, and the sight of him puts a smile on my face, as always.

"Hey, handsome."

One corner of his mouth quirks up, and he takes his position beside Marcus on the wall. The guys ditched their suits tonight, trading them for military-grade cargo pants and black performance tees that flaunt their pectoral muscles. Very subtle. They blend right in with the faded flannels, Southern bling, and cowboy boots.

We're entertained by a few more singers who keep us

giggling, but Maisy's amusement dies a quick death when Jensen pops up at our table.

"Ladies. Having fun?" He gives Graham a tight smile and a curt nod.

"I need the restroom." Maisy scrambles out of her seat and flees.

I raise my eyebrows, silently asking Graham again what's wrong with her. He shrugs in response.

"What's up?" I ask Jensen.

"Was wondering if you'll be gracing us with a performance tonight."

"Ha! Pass. But I do want to talk to you soon about doing a show. Something small so I can test out my new stuff." I bounce my shoulders in excitement.

His face lights up. My show would rake in lots of business for him. "Seriously? Hell, yeah."

"You can't advertise though," I say, rushing out the words. "I'm not ready for anything big."

Sympathy replaces the excitement in his eyes. "I understand. Baby steps."

Pointing at him, I confirm, "Exactly."

Jensen purses his lips and glances at Graham to see if he's paying attention to us, which he is. It doesn't deter Jensen though. He braces his hands on the table and leans in.

"When are you telling Jake? Dragging this out won't end well, and I worry he's getting his hopes up."

Irritated that he's putting a damper on my fun night with the reminder, I lift a brow in challenge. "When you explain why Maisy ran away when you showed up at our table."

Anger pinches his face before he snaps, "Maisy always runs."

Judge shifts closer, his movement enough of a warning for Jensen to ease off.

He drags a hand through his hair. "Sorry. This whole situation with Jake has me on edge."

"Believe me, Jensen, no one understands that better than me." Blowing out a harsh breath, I plead with him. "Can we not do this tonight? I want to have a good time with my friends."

Flattening his lips into a thin line, he bobs his head. "Good to know where I stand." Jensen knocks once on the table. "Enjoy your friends."

"Jensen—" I start, reaching for him, but he's already walking away. I growl, frustrated by his tantrum and bad timing.

The walls close in on me every day, and the last thing I need is Jensen breathing down my neck. I also feel bad for implying he's not included in my friend group, which isn't true.

Graham leans in closer. "That guy really needs to get laid. Either that or find some looser jeans to give his balls room to breathe." Chuckling, I tug on Graham's sleeve, urging him to slide over and take Maisy's abandoned seat. He throws an arm around me and says, "He's right, you know."

"I know. Soon."

Soon. How many people have heard me repeat that promise? At least no one has asked me to define the word *soon*. Any time is too soon, and I'll put off telling Jake the truth as long as I can.

Maisy returns from the bathroom and occupies Graham's empty stool at the exact time Jake shows up. He swoops in for a kiss from me then shakes Graham's hand. Jake and Maisy don't acknowledge one another, which surprises me. They used to be friends, and I wonder what happened to cause this distance between them.

"You want something to drink?" I ask Jake.

"Nah. I'm good." He scoots closer, forcing Graham to remove his arm from my shoulders. "I do have somewhere I want to take you later."

He stuffs his hands in his coat pockets and shifts from one foot to the other, a nervous movement which has Marcus pushing off the wall.

"Where to, pretty boy?" he asks, the threat of bodily harm clear in his face and posture.

"Don't worry. We're not leaving town." When Marcus narrows his eyes, Jake holds up his cell phone. "Need me to send you updates?"

Marcus plucks the phone from Jake's fingers, moves his thumbs across the screen, and hands it back. "Got your location."

Jake gawks in disbelief. "Did you seriously just do that?"

"I seriously did." Marcus folds his arms across his chest and leans against the wall, resuming his version of a non-threatening stance.

"Unbelievable," Jake grumbles, shoving his phone in his coat pocket while giving Marcus the stink eye. "You know I can just unshare it."

"You know I can snap your neck."

"Okay!" I interject, sticking my hands up. "There will be no snapping things." My glare passes between them. "Marcus, we're staying close. Jake, let it go. He's doing his job."

Both men mumble under their breaths, but I don't catch what they say. Maisy must've heard Marcus because she smirks and winks at him. Glad to know a threat to Jake's life and limb is all it takes to put her in a good mood again.

By the time the current song ends, we've all calmed down. The host announces the next song as a duet.

"Rock!"

Lucy's high-pitched voice on the mic causes feedback

through the speakers. Everyone in the bar ducks and covers their ears. Rock elbows his way through the crowd and joins his tiny wife on stage, his shoulders slumping when Lucy offers him a microphone.

She's dressed in a black full-body leotard covered with red rhinestones, blinding the audience. Rock is so tall; the overhead stage lights make his red hair look like flames. He unzips his jacket to reveal a matching tank top, at which Jake murmurs, "Fucking kill me now." Rock grabs the microphone seconds before the first verse begins.

Our group sits stunned, not knowing what in the actual hell we're witnessing. Rock bends way over so he and Lucy are eye to eye while they sing off key to each other. They're dancing to a practiced routine, and Rock spins her around a couple of times.

"This is the greatest thing I've ever seen." Maisy's eyes are alight with amusement. She's seconds away from melting to the floor and howling.

Jake groans. "I honestly can't be any more embarrassed by him." He struggles to keep his eyes on the stage as his best friend, the brutish football coach with no rhythm, makes a complete fool of himself.

"Where's Daniel with the video camera when we need him?" Graham whips out his cell phone and records the disaster. When Rock lifts Lucy by the waist and twirls around, Graham gasps. "Oh, dear god."

Maisy cries, "I can't!" Her forehead smacks the table, and it shakes from her convulsions.

Behind me, Marcus says to Judge, "Where the fuck are we, man?"

Judge grunts a *fuck, if I know*.

Clamping my lips together, I peek at Jake standing beside me with his eyes closed, unable to watch this atrocious performance. I finally lose it, joining Maisy on the table.

The nightmare ends, and the halfhearted applause from the audience doesn't quite drown out the stifled laughter and baffled commentary. Rock and Lucy, beaming with pride, take a bow and leave the stage. When they make their way toward us, Maisy and Graham clasp hands in hopes they can keep their shit together.

"You guys were…wow…I've never seen anything like it. So…*so* entertaining," I say. Jake pinches my side to keep me from laughing right in their faces. It's really, really hard not to.

Lucy swipes her shiny, black hair over her shoulders and, still beaming, fans her blushing cheeks. "Thanks. We've been practicing for weeks, but I was still nervous."

Maisy and I share a glance that says *keep it together, sister,* before she turns away and pretends to talk to Marcus. She's on the verge of breaking, and I'll fall apart right alongside her if she does.

"I can't even look at you right now," Jake says to Rock. He pulls his cap lower on his head to shield his eyes. When Rock shrugs his big shoulders, Jake scoffs. "Dude. Too much."

His face dark red and sweaty, Rock lifts the bottom of his tank top to wipe his forehead, exposing chiseled abs. "The lights on stage are hot, man," he tells Jake. "I was dying up there."

Graham, ogling Rock's washboard abs, mumbles, "I'm dying too…from thirst."

I stab a pointy knuckle into his kidney, and his yelp draws Lucy's attention to him. There's no mistaking the sparkle of recognition in her dark eyes.

"*Dios mio,*" she breathes, offering a queenly hand for

Graham to kiss. Even her fingernails are covered in rhine-stones. "Lucy Garcia. Pleasure to meet you."

Wide-eyed, Graham shifts in his seat and glances at Rock. Everyone can feel the heat rolling off him, like he's about to hulk out and burn the building to the ground. Marcus and Judge inch forward, ready to protect Graham if needed.

"Excuse me?" Rock snatches her hand and glares at Graham. "Mrs. James Rockford Harrison the-fucking-third. Married woman"—he pounds his chest—"to me. And she's my baby's mama."

Jake slaps a palm on Rock's shoulder. "Chill, man. Graham's no threat to you. He's spoken for."

Rock whips his head around and pins Jake with narrowed eyes and a malicious smirk. "By your woman?"

Not passing up an opportunity to mess with his friend, Jake says with a straight face, "Yep. We have an arrangement."

When Lucy makes an *oooh* sound in interest, Rock snaps. "Don't even fucking think about it!"

He picks her up and hauls her away, leaving us all doubled over in another fit of laughter. Even Lucy's laughing while draped over Rock's shoulder. She winks at me and waves.

Graham rubs his chest as he catches his breath. "Those two are something else."

"You have no idea," Jake agrees, lips quirked to one side. His wagging head and amused expression indicate he prob-ably has a hundred unbelievable stories to tell about Rock and Lucy.

Maisy leans across Graham's lap, slurring when she addresses me. "That was the kind of shit show I expect to see back home in California."

I roll my eyes and chuckle. We witnessed some interesting performances at the small clubs around LA when I was starting out. Many of them were plain awful to witness.

Her comment about California being *home* must sober Jake up because he grabs my jacket from the back of my chair. "Ready to go?"

"Um…" I look to my crew for any sign of protest and find none. "Sure."

We say our goodbyes to the group, but before we step away Marcus warns Jake, "I can always find you."

Jake gives him a mock salute before we leave, earning him deadly glares from Judge and Marcus both.

28

JAKE

Before we left Bruno's, I started second-guessing myself. While Tatum was saying her goodbyes, Jensen's voice kept running through my head saying, *"You're moving too fast."*

Things have always moved fast between me and Tatum. For me, it was love at first sight. I'm pretty certain she felt the same, which is why I don't make room for those negative thoughts as we drive toward my house. I'm nervous, wondering what she'll think of me and my inability to let her go.

Her eyes bore into me while she's deep in thought. "What's the deal between you and Maisy?"

Hands loose on the steering wheel, I lift a nonchalant shoulder. "I've spoken to her exactly two times since high school. Neither time went well." Chancing a glance at Tatum, I find her frowning.

"She never said anything to me."

Before she can dig deeper and start questioning my encounters with her friend, something outside the truck distracts her. Her honey braid falls over her shoulder when she whips her head to look out the window, watching the

turnoff leading to the hidden entrance of the Hamiltons' land
—my land—go by.

"You passed it."

Makes sense for her to assume we're going to our spot on the ridge. The only other familiar place on this road is Rock's parents' house. Neither of us speak for the next quarter mile until we reach the end of my long driveway and turn in.

Tatum leans forward, confusion marring her brow. "Why are we here? Are the Hamiltons home?"

She searches the red brick house for signs of life. No cars in the driveway. No lights on. I'm embarrassed to admit that all my efforts have been focused on the interior, so the gardens and landscaping are barren since I dug everything up with the intention of starting over from scratch.

"The Hamiltons don't live here anymore."

As I park the truck in front of the garage and kill the engine, she stares at the house in silence, putting the pieces together.

"You live here," she whispers, gaze trained on the black front door. When her eyes slowly shift to me, they're glistening. "That's why we didn't hear you that night. You came on foot."

I nod slowly, biting my cheek and swallowing the angry words I have about her bringing someone to our special place. I don't care who it was. That spot is sacred ground, and only two people are permitted to be there.

"I'm sorry." She clears her throat and looks at the front door again. "Can we go in?"

My nerves skyrocket, but it's too late to chicken out. She's about to walk in that house and have a good look at my insides. At what I eat and breathe and dream of to stay alive.

Tatum's going to see that my life force is *her*.

"Come on." Ready to get this over with, I lumber up the porch steps with my head down as Tatum follows.

"Jake." She covers my hand, the one trembling as I struggle to fit the key in the lock. "Look at me."

I tilt my head toward hers but don't meet her eyes. She removes my ball cap and runs her fingers through my hair, dragging her sharp nails along my scalp. My eyelids flutter, and I inhale the lavender scent wafting from her exposed wrist when her coat sleeve falls.

"Tell me what's wrong," she coaxes, the melodic sound of her voice adding to her touch and scent, calming me. Settling me.

I bravely meet her eyes, the brightest of blue skies on the sunniest of days, and confess, "I never stopped thinking of you."

The question hovers on the tip of her tongue when she licks her lips, fighting to break free. She wants to ask *and is that so wrong*? She doesn't ask though, and I relax my shoulders, grateful she's not pressuring me to say things I'm not ready to say.

I unlock the door and gesture her inside. When the door closes behind us, there's a finality in the clicking sound. No turning back now.

I flick on the lights as she steps through the foyer, surveying the empty dining room and the kitchen with stainless steel appliances and a large center island covered by a butcher block surface where a big family can gather. White upper cabinets with glass doors reach the ceiling, displaying a mosaic of colorful dishes matching the backsplash. The lower cabinets are painted a matte navy blue with white granite countertops.

Tatum's kitchen.

She drags a finger along the wood slab as she circles the

island with slow steps, examining every detail. The decorative crown molding, the brushed nickel pulls, the hand-scraped hardwoods. Anything I could remember her gushing over when she flipped through her aunt's home decor magazines is in this room. I saved her favorites, thinking one day I'd need them for reference when I built her dream home. Our dream home.

Tatum stops, facing the six-burner stove with her back to me, and blows out a shaky breath. "It's beautiful."

I give her a moment to gather herself, grateful once again that she's not doing or saying anything to point out my obvious obsession with her. It's a forever kind of love. And by the slight quaking of her shoulders, she understands what I meant earlier.

I never stopped thinking of her. I never stopped loving her either.

My dad used to say, *"Love lives in the details."* My undying love for Tatum flows through every thoughtful detail and every drop of sweat I've poured into this old house. I spent years making the big changes, but I busted my ass the past few weeks perfecting the details of the work I've completed thus far.

With a thick swallow, I say, "I'll show you the rest."

She quietly trails behind me through the living room— genuine leather furniture in the soft shade of brown she prefers—to the three smaller bedrooms and two bathrooms. One bedroom serves as my office; the other two are empty.

The media room at the end of the long hallway has dimmable recessed lights. She dreamed of family movie nights with everyone snuggled on the huge modular sectional that takes up half the space. Her gaze lingers on it before we retrace our steps.

The master suite just off the kitchen stands alone from the

rest of the house. Decorated in soft greens and creams, it has a four-poster king bed and a sitting area facing the French doors which lead to a private porch overlooking the land. It's a relaxing space, and I chose the colors hoping Tatum would approve if she ever saw the room.

Apparently, she doesn't approve because she covers her mouth to contain a sudden burst of laughter.

"What?" *Holy hell, I got the bedroom all wrong.*

"I…I…It's…" She snorts and shakes her head, holding up one finger until she can speak. "We have the same bedroom." The expression on my face conveys my confusion, so she gestures at everything in the room as she explains. "My bedroom in California is the same as yours. The colors, the poster bed, the seating area, the patio doors. We match!"

Grinning, I shake my head in disbelief. We have the same master suite. All this time and all this distance, and we're still in sync.

"I'm glad you like it," I chuckle, pleased with myself.

"I love it!" she shouts, but doesn't mean to, which starts up another round of laughs from both of us. Our gazes lock as we calm down, and her wistful blue eyes tell me she misses this as much as I do. The happiness, the ease, the unabashed humor. Us.

We're smiling as we cling to the light moment before it fades. When I think of the staircase in the corner of my living room, my amusement dies. She gravitates toward me, her smile faltering as she reads in my eyes that something big is coming.

"I have one more thing to show you," I say, my heart racing in my chest.

I hold her hand as she follows me up the stairs placed in an awkward location against the far wall. The odd layout somehow works within the confines of the space and was the only solution to avoid having a staircase smack-dab in the center of my living room.

At the top step, I take a deep breath to prepare myself for the big reveal and all of her possible reactions, then move aside to let her enter the space first. There's no furniture. Only knotty pine floors, beige walls, and the window that draws a loud gasp from Tatum.

April - Senior Year

"Close your eyes and hold out your hand." Tatum presents her open hand nowhere near me. I chuckle as I snag it and bring it closer. "Don't peek." I place the little wooden box in her palm.

She wraps her fingers around it, assessing the shape, and gives it a small shake because she's Tatum and hates surprises. "Jewelry?"

I can't afford jewelry, so I tap her nose and say, "Better than jewelry. You can look now."

She flattens her hand and opens her eyes, which widen with curiosity. When she pops the lid, the biggest grin spreads across her face. The glittery purple guitar pick that reads "Always Pick Me" isn't much, but it's *her*.

She kisses me on the lips. "I love it. Thank you."

Her long legs are crisscrossed and pressed against mine, right where I like them. I run my hands along her bare thighs and jerk my chin at the box. "The other side is even better."

She flips the box over and bumps it against her palm to release the pick wedged inside the pick-shaped hole. When it drops into her hand, she finds a picture of my smiling face and throws her head back in laughter, the sweetest sound.

"So you'll think of me when you're writing all the hits," I explain.

Through her smile, she kisses me again. "I'll never stop thinking of you, Jake. It's impossible."

I squeeze her thighs and steal her lips with mine because she can never kiss me enough. "Happy birthday, baby." *Please don't leave me.*

With Tatum snuggled at my side, we sit quietly and stare across the landscape beneath the cloudy afternoon sky. Neither of us talk about her leaving for California in a month and me going to college in the fall. The guitar pick is reminder enough of how our paths will temporarily diverge. Being apart will be hard, but we have faith in our love and in ourselves. Against all odds, I'm confident we'll make it through the next four years until we reunite for good.

She shoots to her feet in the bed of the truck, hands planted on her hips in a determined stance. I spy the crease of her butt cheek under the frayed hem of her denim shorts and have to stop myself from gliding my fingers up her smooth leg.

"You know, one day, after I write a few hits and we have enough money, we'll buy this piece of land from the Hamiltons. We'll build the perfect house"—she makes a frame with both hands to capture the view—"right here, overlooking the hills. It'll have a big, round window so we can look at the stars on cold nights and enjoy the clouds on rainy days. You'll drink coffee on the porch, and I'll chase the kids all over these hills. Then at night, I'll play lullabies on the guitar while you rock them to sleep."

She looks down at me—the ends of her silky hair caught by the gentle breeze—and smiles with so much genuine belief in her dream, I can't help but buy in.

I hook her pinky with mine and return her smile. "Sounds perfect."

· · ·

Tatum approaches the round window, toying with the end of her braid and taking in the view. The moonlight drapes the hills in a silver blanket, and our favorite spot on the ridge can be seen in the distance.

With my hands shoved deep in my jeans pockets, I wait to see if she remembers her words. Everything we said—every future plan we made—was a promise. I intended to keep every one of them, and always believed and hoped she did too.

When she faces me again, her back to the window and tears streaming down her cheeks, I see the truth. She meant every word she spoke when voicing her dream that day. Her dream was as much a promise to me as it was to herself. It's a dream she still wishes for, and I've made part of it come true.

Finding this confirmation in her eyes—realizing I haven't been in this hellscape alone all these years—gives me the strength to power through and resolve whatever issues stand between us.

"You did it." She can't hold in the sob that chases her whispered words. I stride over and pull her against my chest, holding her close as she cries.

"Everything I've done…I've done because of you," I whisper in her ear.

It's a bold, broad statement that encompasses the good, the bad, and the ugly. But it's the truth, painful for both of us to hear.

Every action, every thought, every plan, every moment of revenge or weakness or self-loathing—Tatum was at the fore-front of my mind. Never at the back where I pretended to keep her locked away and forgotten. She's been front and center since the day I saw a sad girl in a Bob Dylan T-shirt with her button nose crinkled up, displeased by the sight of my Podunk high school.

She latches onto my shirt, desperation tightening her grip as she falls apart in my arms. Tears soak the fabric and seep through to my chest. Her sobs echo in the unfinished space, her broken voice crying, "I'm sorry. I'm sorry. I'm sorry," until it's almost gone.

Yet, I still can't offer her any words of comfort or forgiveness, so I rub her back and kiss her hair while she expends her regretful tears. Until I'm privy to the reasons she feels regret, I can't confess my true feelings. But I can soothe her pain with my actions.

"Let's get you something to drink."

She nods against my chest, and I twine our fingers and guide her downstairs. I pour a glass of filtered water while she settles on a stool at the island, resting her head in her hands. After placing the drink in front of her, I stand on the other side with my palms splayed on the wood.

"There's still a lot of work to do," I say.

Eyeing me over the rim of the glass, she searches my face. Unease flashes in her eyes the moment she catches the double meaning of my statement. The house is unfinished, and so are we. She forces down a big gulp of water and glances around the kitchen again.

When she licks her dry lips, I tap my finger on the wood. "Tatum."

Her gaze meets mine, and the unyielding determination she finds there tells her she better not look away.

"You can't keep stringing me along. Every sign points to you wanting us to be together again, but you're not willing to give all of yourself to me. A month ago, I told myself I would happily take whatever you're willing to give. But that's not true. I need *all* of you, Tate. The good and the bad. And until you talk to me—tell me what happened—I can't truly enjoy the good. And there's so much good between us.

So please, baby. Just get the bad out of the way. You can trust me."

She tugs her braid, her eyes avoiding mine again. "I know I can. I'm—"

"What are the Dark Days?"

Fear. A fear so deep it consumes her blue eyes that snap to mine, darkening them. What's even worse than watching her cower, overcome with this level of fear, is the fact that it's aimed at *me*.

"Who?" she whispers, but she already knows the answer. Realizing Graham's betrayal, she squeezes her eyelids shut, fresh tears slipping from the corners.

"He cares about you," I remind her.

She nods, running her hands down her face and slumping on the stool.

Seeing her in this state of distress shreds my insides. Her welfare always comes first, no matter how hard I try to prioritize myself, so I ease off a little and change tactics.

"You don't have to tell me what happened, not tonight. But can I ask you one question, and you'll answer honestly?" At her brisk nod, I take a deep breath and brace myself for the worst. "Did someone physically or intentionally harm you in any way?"

I've spent hours structuring that question over recent days, framing it in a way that encourages a truthful response. Graham implied she wasn't sexually assaulted, but there are many ways to harm another person and cause lasting damage.

"No," she whispers.

My relief is palpable, the air gusting out of my lungs from the breath I was holding.

But then she blows a puff of air past her own lips, meets my stare with her terrified eyes, and says, "I did it to myself."

My fingers curl into tight fists, the skin over my knuckles

stretching taut as I struggle to make sense of her words. Did I hear her correctly? Did she just say she hurt *herself*? I want to rant and rave and scream *what does that mean*, demanding clarification. But I've used my one question for the night. The patience I'm fighting to master fights back with a vengeance, and it's becoming too difficult to manage.

If Tatum harmed herself in some way or tried to…I can't even think it, much less speak the words. I'd never forgive myself for missing the signs. For not being there for her or getting her some help. I knew she was pulling away back then, and I begged her to talk to me. To tell me what I could do. But she assured me everything was fine. She was just busy with work and gigs.

I didn't believe her then and should've pressed harder. Got on a fucking plane and hunted her down to see for myself. God, did I almost *truly* lose her?

"Don't go there. It wasn't that," she says quietly, able to read my spiraling thoughts.

But her assurance brings me no solace. Why should I believe her? All I can do is make assumptions if she doesn't open up to me, which isn't likely to happen any time soon.

Every time I try to make her talk about the hard things, the gap between us grows deeper. Darker. Unfortunately, the only sound roaring from the abyss is the wild cackling of my cluelessness. She's certainly not saying anything.

I bow my head, close my eyes, and suck in deep breaths —unsure where we go from here. Her vague answer creates another obstacle. Another roadblock that I can't bulldoze my way through without pushing her further away from me.

At some point, I have to ask myself, *"when is enough, enough?"*

She startles me when she speaks again. "The song I'm working on…I'm so close. It's about what happened. You may not understand the lyrics if you listen to it out of context." *So, give me the fucking context, baby.* "Really, it's for me. To finally purge this pain out of me and put it into words. Turn it into something beautiful. I need this, Jake," she pleads. "Just a little more time to finish the song, and I'll tell you everything. I swear to you, it's almost finished."

Finished. The word would hold little meaning in this moment if not for the wince on her face after she spoke it. The tendrils of panic snake their way inside me, taunting me with thoughts of how badly this might end. I shake them off the only way I know how these days.

"Stay the night with me."

She starts at the request, surprised by my about-face when she expected me to pursue answers from her. When she doesn't react or respond negatively to the suggestion, I round the island, take her hand, and lead her to the bedroom.

After I show her with my body how much she means to me, I lie awake all night, mulling over her confession while she sleeps peacefully in my arms.

29

TATUM

The party at Lucy's house tonight isn't awkward. In fact, if Maisy were here, it would feel like high school all over again. Some of Rock and Brody's fellow teachers and their partners showed up. A few of them are around our age, and I remembered the names of those who went to school with us.

It's late, and most of the other couples left already, so I'm lounging on the loveseat, enjoying a familiar scene that's playing out in the kitchen.

Jake, Rock, and Brody crowd around the food on the island, arguing over which one of them scored the most points in a basketball game they played in the *fourth grade*. Apparently, it was a championship game for the record books.

"Baby!" Jake yells across the open space between us. "I scored twenty points that game!"

His big, dimpled grin draws a smile from my own lips. *This* is the Jake I always remembered when I thought of him. Laughing, joking, bright. From my comfy spot in Lucy's living room, I'm seeing the happy boy who always loved me in my dreams.

We had a rough couple of days after my misleading

confession. He withdrew emotionally but demanded more from me physically. The conclusion he drew was clear from the anguish on his face. I tried to set the record straight, but what I told him wasn't a complete lie. I *am* responsible for what happened. But anything more I could've said to ease his worries would've led to more questions.

Last night, he climbed in my window and held me in his arms until we fell asleep. His whispered, "*Don't ever leave me*," the only words spoken between us. And he woke up this morning in a cheerful mood, as if our conversation in his kitchen never happened.

Rock shakes his head with vehemence. "Not possible. You rode the bench for more than half the game."

"Truth," Brody confirms. "You weren't even tall enough to get a shot off without someone blocking it."

"Asshole," Jake grumbles as they crush his hoop dreams. I've seen pictures of them as young boys, and Jake was always the smallest in size. "At least I wasn't afraid of the ball."

"Can't help it if I've always prioritized my pretty face. That's why I chose football." Brody taps a finger on the bridge of his straight nose. "For the helmets."

"Yeah, but you had to be the last man standing before you'd make a tackle." Rock says, bumping fists with a smirking Jake.

"That's because my body is a temple I've vowed to protect." Brody winks at Ainsley, who's lingering at the far end of the island. She darts her eyes away.

Long bangs frame her natural face, and her hair's pulled back in a ponytail as usual. Other than the bright lipstick, she doesn't wear makeup. When she's not working, she ditches the Bruno's shirt and pairs a fleece pullover with her black yoga pants.

Everyone was surprised when she walked in behind Brody. She hasn't said much to anyone despite our efforts to engage, and she blushes every time I try talking to her.

At Bruno's, she's loud and full of spirit. But tonight, she's been standoffish and more reserved. Brody checks on her occasionally but maintains his distance. I can't get a solid read on their dynamic, though she doesn't seem that interested in him.

Lucy joins me on the loveseat after putting Marcella to bed. Her mouth stretches into a wide yawn as she sinks lower into the plush cushions.

"Say the word, and I'll send everyone home," I offer.

"No. They're fine." She yawns again. "I worked a shift last night, then Rock woke up when I got home. He demanded an early breakfast, and the man likes to savor every bite of his food."

I snicker at her metaphors now that I'm privy to their hidden meanings. "I don't know how you do it. Every day?"

A satisfied grin spreads across her tired face. "Every day. Unless one of us is sick, and sometimes that won't stop us."

"What about when you're…you know?" I dip my head toward her lap, praying she gets my drift so I don't have to discuss menstrual cycles at a party.

Lucy chuckles at my flushed cheeks, as usual. "Like I said…every day."

"Holy crap," I whisper. "And he's okay with that? *You're* okay with that?"

"It's just extra lubrication. Rock's obsessed with my pussy and will take it any way he can get it."

My face is on fire. I can't believe she just dropped *that* word so casually into the conversation. Am I a prude? Absolutely. Especially when it comes to dirty talk. And Lucy has taught me all kinds of dirty things that I haven't told Jake about because how in the world would I get the words out without dying from embarrassment?

"You never cease to amaze me, Lucy Garcia-Harrison. I hope one day I'll be able to shock you for a change."

"I doubt it." She smirks at me, confident that day will never come.

Tearing my gaze from Lucy's filthy mouth, I spy Ainsley wrapping miniature pigs-in-a-blanket in a napkin. From beneath long lashes, she glances around the kitchen before she slips them into her giant purse. I can think of a few reasons why someone would squirrel away food, and the only good one involves having a pet that loves appetizers.

I peek at Lucy to find compassionate eyes that witnessed the same thing.

"The party's dying down," I say, keeping my voice low. "What do you say we pack up the food and send leftovers home with everyone?"

"Sounds like a great idea. Otherwise, all of it will go to waste." She nudges my arm in solidarity as we rise from the sofa. "Exit the kitchen, boys. We're packing it up!"

The guys grumble and grab fistfuls of hors d'oeuvres, then head for the back porch as they say goodbye to the two remaining couples who take Lucy's announcement as their cue to leave. I bid them goodnight as Lucy walks them to the door.

Brody stops in his tracks and whirls around, hands full of food. His uncertain eyes land on Ainsley. "Are you ready to leave? Or is it okay if I hang out with the guys for a bit? We can go if you want, or you're welcome to come outside with us."

Because she looks seconds away from bolting for the door, I jump in before she can answer. "We'll get out of here faster with an extra set of hands to clear all this away. Would you mind?"

Her alert brown eyes bounce from me to Brody. "Not at all." She sets her bag on a chair and joins me near the sink. "I'll just wash my hands first. Habit of being a server." She flips on the faucet and scrubs her hands until her skin turns bright pink.

"Come get me when you're done," Brody says, frowning at her abused hands.

Ainsley nods without looking at him.

His glum face is difficult to take in, especially since it's not an expression we expect to see from Brody. But I've noticed it a few times now. I offer a gentle smile when he catches me studying him, and he returns it with a sad one of his own before walking away. Poor guy.

Lucy pulls a stack of plastic containers and lids from a bin in a lower cabinet. "Pack up whatever you want. There's plenty to go around." She places a few containers next to the sink. "You too, Ainsley. Take anything you or Brody might like. I can't imagine he's able to cook anything for himself that doesn't come with heating instructions." She chuckles at her joke, and I join her. Our eyes meet when Ainsley relaxes, a small grin tugging at the corners of her poppy-colored lips.

"Thanks," she says. "I'm surprised he hasn't gained thirty pounds eating at Bruno's almost every night."

"I'm sure he's not there for the food," Lucy teases.

Under her breath, Ainsley mutters, "No. He's not."

Lucy and I share another concerned glance. Not wanting to dig further into Ainsley's business, worried she might scurry away like a frightened mouse, we get to work sorting food and snapping on lids. We manage to shove five fully packed containers into Ainsley's arms and insist that she take them home, not giving her a chance to refuse.

Twenty minutes later, the kitchen sparkles, Lucy can't stop yawning, and Brody's walking out the door with Ainsley and her spoils.

Jake comes up behind me and rests his chin on my shoulder as I stare at the closing front door. "What's wrong, baby? You look sad."

A long exhale leaves my lungs. "Something's going on there, and I'm trying hard not to stick my nose in their business."

"With Brody and Ainsley?" he asks, wrapping his arms around my middle and pressing in closer behind me.

"Yeah. Has he said anything to you about her?"

"Not much. But he's been acting different lately. Not like himself."

I spin around and circle my arms around his waist. "You've noticed that too?"

"I have. But let them deal with whatever it is themselves," he says, brushing the hair away from my neck. I shiver when his fingertips graze my skin. "If they need our help, they'll ask."

By *our*, he means *mine* because he knows I'm a big softie and want everyone around me to be happy.

"Fine," I concede. "Lucy's dead on her feet, and Rock's glaring at us from the living room because we're keeping him from his wife's pussy. So let's get out of here."

Jake pins me against the counter with his lips against my ear. "What did you just say?" he breathes.

Holy smudge fudge.

"Umm…let's get out of here?" I turn away to hide my flaming cheeks and pretend to search for the purse I didn't bring while he laughs at me.

30

JAKE

Tatum spent the past week getting ready for her return to the stage. She kicked me out every time she wanted to practice, saying I'd heard enough. The rest of the songs on her set list are meant to be a surprise.

She's seemed lighter in recent days, like a weight has been lifted from her shoulders. I wanted to point out the noticeable change and ask if she finished the song that she mentioned the night I first showed her my house but decided to wait and see.

Pam, Maisy, and Graham are pre-gaming in the kitchen with margaritas and finger foods while we wait for Tatum to finish getting dressed.

"We're going to be late." Pam wipes stray salt crystals from the counter into her open hand. "Someone go check on her?"

Graham stares me down while he sucks on a straw, hollowing out his cheeks. Maisy snickers as she polishes off her second margarita.

"What?" he asks, batting innocent eyes at me. "A piece of ice was stuck in there."

I shake my head at his antics and stroll toward Tatum's bedroom. "Are you ready?"

She's standing in the doorway of her closet in nothing but black panties, her back to me. "I don't have anything to wear," she whines.

Clothes are stuffed along the upper and lower rods on both sides of the small, narrow closet. It's a wonder she can find anything in the mess.

I shut her bedroom door and walk up behind her. Wrapping an arm around her waist, I stroke my thumb along her soft stomach. "What's wrong with what you have on?"

She shivers and nudges her back against my chest, a lame attempt to shove me away. "Stop. I'm being serious. I don't want to look like a slob, but I also don't want to look like I'm trying too hard. This isn't a Makenzie show."

I bite my cheek at the mention of the name I've grown to despise. It's unfortunate that it's still Tatum's middle name; otherwise, I'd insist on never hearing it again.

But I've figured out that, while I don't have to like her Makenzie persona, I have to respect it. I felt like total shit for exposing Tatum in San Antonio, and I learned a valuable lesson that day. Every action comes with extremely high consequences when you're famous, regardless of the name your fans call you.

"Hmm. Let me think." I drag my nose along her neck and slide my other arm around her waist. "What would Tatum wear? From what I've seen, she prefers leggings and big, ugly sweaters."

She smacks my hand and laughs. "They're not ugly. They're comfortable and fun."

Trailing my fingers down her stomach, I dip them in the waistband of her panties and nibble her earlobe. "You know what else is fun?"

"Jake," she moans, and I've hardly touched her. Not where it counts, anyway. When I move her forward into the closet, she protests. "We don't have time," she says, while spinning around and tugging at my belt.

When the door shuts behind us, the automatic light clicks off, cloaking us in pitch black.

I help her undo my pants and shove them down my thighs, then tap her left leg. "Put your foot on the rod." She fumbles a bit but finds her footing. I ravage her mouth, then push her panties to the side and spread her juices around.

"Can you be quiet?" I ask, sinking two fingers inside her to get her ready for me.

"Yes," she breathes as I pump my hand at a leisurely pace. "Just hurry."

I palm my dick, giving it a couple of rough tugs, and line it up with her opening. "Hold on to me."

She grips my shoulders and digs her nails in. When I plunge into her, she gasps so loud I clamp a hand over her mouth.

"Shh. Stay quiet for me, okay?"

Her head jerks in a nod, and I release her mouth to grab her hip. Hooking her raised leg with my other hand behind her knee, I spread her open, press her body into the wall with mine, and let loose.

"Shit, Jake." Her moans are as heavenly as her lavender scent, and my eyes roll back in my head.

"Quiet, baby," I whisper against her lips.

I splay the hand on her hip wider so the tip of my thumb reaches her clit. We inhale each other's exhales as I work her to orgasm while thrusting into her with short, quick bursts of my hips.

"Fuck, you're incredible. So fucking perfect."

This is only a closet quickie, but every second spent

inside Tatum is like getting small doses of ecstasy injected straight into my bloodstream.

"Hurry," she begs as her legs start to shake. I work my thumb faster, out of sync with my pounding hips. Her body stiffens, and the cutest fucking squeak comes out of her mouth as she tries to stifle her orgasmic cry.

She whimpers when my fingertips dig harder into the thigh I'm gripping. The sound has pleasure coiling low in my gut as my release builds.

Picking up the pace, I bury my face in her neck and let the *whoosh* of her soft panting power me on until I come with a quiet groan. I go slack against her, my weight pinning her to the wall.

"God, I love you," I whisper.

She gasps, my name softly skimming past her lips.

Shaky breaths flutter against my ear as she lowers her leg and wraps her arms around my neck. Tears touch my cheek that's resting on hers. We stand in the dark, holding each other, neither of us saying anything more for what feels like an eternity of silence.

My admission was a slip, and we both know it. But we also know it's true, as much as I've fought against uttering those words to her.

"I love you," I say again, louder and with intention, wishing the lights were on so I can see in her eyes how my words affect her. "Always and only you."

"I love you too, Jake. More than anything. And I'm so scared of losing you again," she whispers, every trembling syllable wrought with pain.

"You didn't lose me. I've been here the whole time, waiting for you. Let me in, Tate. Give me a real chance to be the man you love. To love you back without any secrets between us. I've told you all of mine. Do the same for me?"

Her breath hitches. "What if you can't forgive me?"

"It's my forgiveness. Let me decide what to do with it."

She nuzzles her face into my neck and inhales, as if she's taking one last hit of my scent before she loses me forever. It's a sobering thought: that she could've done something so terrible, it would destroy us.

I squeeze her tighter and tangle my fingers in her long, silky hair. There's nothing but us and our vulnerable whispers in the dark. I'm fully clothed. She's mostly naked. Exposed to me. If only I could see inside her memories and find the fearsome truth that awaits me there.

Giggling on the other side of the closet door disrupts the charged moment.

"If you're done, we have a virgin margarita ready to calm Tatum's nerves," Graham says.

"Unless you took care of that for her already," Maisy adds.

"The virginity or the nerves?" he quips.

Their laughter fades as they move farther away.

Tatum drops her forehead to my shoulder and groans. "I really hate them sometimes."

I plant a gentle kiss on her head and crack the door enough to switch on the light, avoiding eye contact while I tuck myself away and do up my pants. Any sign of fear in her eyes will be too much for me to handle after our heartfelt confessions.

"Get dressed, baby. It's showtime."

As promised, Jensen didn't advertise the performance, but the whole of Walford is in attendance, kids included. Jensen recruited Daniel and some of his friends to help set up a video feed to neighboring businesses like The Drip, Noon Moon Café, and the donut shop. Main Street buzzes with energy as everyone awaits Tatum's hometown performance, the first in over a decade.

Jensen reserved our group a table at the front near the stage. I give Tatum a chaste kiss before she hops on the platform to get ready. The overhead lights cause the silver threads in her purple sweater to shimmer and reflect off her black leather pants.

We haven't said much since my unwitting disclosure, but all that awkwardness falls away, along with the noise in the bar, the second she perches on the stool and meets my gaze.

It's like old times, when she would search the crowd for me, needing one last boost of confidence before the show began. Like I did then, I give her a nod and a secret smile, which she returns. Another piece clicks in my chest after the familiar exchange.

Tatum adjusts the microphone and clears her throat, quieting the excited crowd. "Thank you all for coming tonight. I've gotta say"—she chuckles—"I'm pretty nervous. Some of these songs I played for many of you years ago, but I've freshened them up a bit. Gotta keep up with the times," she teases, coaxing titters from the audience. "Others are new and a little different from what you've heard from me on the radio over the years." She plucks a string. "I hope you like them."

From the first strum of the guitar, she enraptures us. If I had the strength to tear my eyes away from her, I'd find appreciative smiles, swaying bodies, and lots of tears in the audience as she sings about small towns, big love, longing, forgiveness, and coming home.

Each chord resonates in the bar, thrumming through our bodies and embedding itself into the collective soul of

Walford. The words pushed from her lips echo around us as her soft, melodic voice delivers them to our ears and hearts. She's captivating on stage, where she belongs.

I fracture at the thought, all my roughly patched cracks exposed under the power of her shining light. She's too…*brilliant* for a simple country boy like me. If given the chance, I'm not sure I could've kept pace with her shot to stardom. Perhaps, no matter how promising the future seemed to two love-drunk teens, the ending would've been the same for us.

The only thing that keeps me reaching for her with such desperation is the fact that she's always claimed to love me as much as I love her. Without that soul-deep truth binding us, I would gladly let her go so she's free to just *be*. Free to bless the world with her beauty and greatness without me holding her back.

Tatum being on stage again reminds me that her return to Walford is only temporary. Her *temporary stopover*. She never planned to stay—not then and not now—and the thought of her leaving a second time hits me with an unexpected, crushing blow as I watch her shine.

A strangled noise bursts from my chest, and I press a fist to my mouth to fight it back. Her eyes on mine, Tatum's brow furrows slightly as she sings. Someone grabs my free hand, and someone else gently rubs circles on my back.

I glance to one side to find a rare soft smile on Maisy's lips as her hand comforts me. I can't explain why I need it, but I do. And I welcome her long-lost comfort as I imagine my future slipping away again.

Maisy and I lock gazes for a moment, our watery eyes saying all the things that neither of us will speak aloud.

I'm sorry.

I miss you.

We both love her.

She needs us both.

We need her.

Thank you for taking care of her.

In that brief, wordless conversation, all the feelings of jealousy and resentment I harbored against Maisy fade away. She spent the past ten years with the person who needed her most, who *she* needed most, and who can blame her for that?

Tatum ends her show to a thunderous standing ovation, loud hoots, and sharp whistles. I grin at her with unbridled pride, clapping wildly. She smiles at me with wet eyes, then takes a few timid bows before turning away.

Chatter and praise surround me, but I keep my focus on her as she gathers her belongings. I study each facial expression to determine how she really feels in this moment. Is she satisfied? Is a tiny stage in a small-town bar enough? Or does she wish for more?

She places her pick and guitar in the case, then removes her set list from the waistband of her leggings and stuffs it behind the ripped, crushed-velvet lining. My lips quirk to one side, and I shake my head, remembering that's where she always hid her lyrics from me and wondering why she never had the lining repaired or replaced.

With her treasures tucked away, she bounds off the stage and straight into my waiting arms.

"You were amazing, baby," I praise against her smiling lips. "But I'm the only one who thought so."

She throws her head back, laughing at the joke I used to make after her early shows, an attempt to downplay how much the audience loved her. "Thank you. I'll be sure to give you a ticket to the after-party."

I dip my chin and raise an eyebrow. "The only ticket?"

She chuckles again, and we kiss until Graham pries her

off me so other people can congratulate her. Letting her go, I stand aside and bask in her glory from the sidelines.

When we get to my house later, I show her how wonderful I think she is. Once on the couch and again in the shower before we fall into bed, exhausted from the night's excitement and carnal activities.

Drifting off to sleep and snuggled against my chest, Tatum whispers, "Always and only you, Jake."

31

JAKE

Leaning against the headboard with Tatum's hair wrapped around my hand, I groan. "Baby, if you don't stop, I'm not gonna last." She giggles, and my stomach clenches from the vibration. "Baby," I warn. "Up."

Her warm mouth leaves my dick with a pop, and she gives me a teasing smile, moving lower and pressing a kiss to the small, diamond-shaped birthmark on my thigh. She winks and says, "You're a gem."

I bark a laugh. "You're so corny."

She giggles more, so I grab her under the armpits and drag her up my body until she's straddling me. I kiss her senseless, and the carnal glide of my tongue along hers quickly turns her giggles into moans. When she sinks down on me, neither of us are laughing anymore.

"What do you need, baby?" I ask, sliding my hands up her waist and higher, knowing exactly what she wants from me.

Rocking back and forth, she grips my thighs behind her and pushes her breasts toward my face. I worship them the way she likes, squeezing them while I bite and suck on her peaked nipples. Her hair brushes my knees when she drops her head back and lets out a long sigh.

"I love when you do this."

"And this?" I move one hand between us and rub her clit as I thrust up into her. The morning sunlight halos the crown of her head, making her look like an angel in my lap.

She circles loose arms around my neck, and we lock gazes. "Yes. Definitely that."

I loop my other arm around her waist, lifting her up and down as I take control of the pace while working her with my thumb until she trembles.

"Jake…right there."

Her forehead meets mine, and our bodies move together as smooth as an ocean swell. I apply more pressure on her clit and rub faster, coaxing chants of my name from her kiss-swollen lips. It's like a stadium anthem playing in my ears. I snag her bottom lip between my teeth and suck on it.

When she starts contracting around my dick, I slam her down harder and meet her halfway with each punch of my hips. "Open your eyes when you come for me, baby. Let me see you shine."

Her eyes spring open, and the sun's rays reflect off her irises, turning them a blue so bright they're almost blinding.

"Jake! Oh my—" Her orgasm cuts her off, and her mouth hangs open on a silent cry. The most beautiful cry I've ever witnessed.

I'm panting hard and grunting from the early morning exertion as I continue thrusting. My muscles scream when her body goes slack against mine, forcing me to double the work-load until I finally come, spilling every ounce of my love into her.

We hold each other, her in my lap and me inside her, as

we float down from the amazing high. Our heaving breaths mingle before she captures my lips and hums.

"Holy shit," I wheeze, toppling over sideways with her wrapped in my arms. "I'm out of shape."

Tatum grins and traces a finger along my stubbled jaw. "Good morning."

I plant my face between her boobs and croak, "Coffee," like it's a dying man's last wish.

Her laughter reaches my ears—a sound I want to hear every morning for the rest of my life—before she untangles herself from my limbs and crawls off the bed.

"I'll make coffee. You start the shower." She tosses my underwear, hitting me in the head, then slips on my T-shirt from last night.

Rolling onto my back, I whine at the full-body ache. "I think you broke me. We had sex four times in less than twenty-four hours. How is that even possible?"

"It's your superpower!" she calls out on her way to the kitchen.

I stretch out my arms and legs, naked as the day I was born, unable to move from this spot in the middle of the bed. "My superpower is drained. Dead battery," I mutter to myself, not having the energy to yell loud enough for her to hear.

She returns a few minutes later with two mugs of coffee and finds me in the exact spot where she left me. I gawk as she brings my favorite mug to her smirking lips. To really dig in the knife, she sets the other mug—the tiny, subpar one—on the nightstand out of my reach.

Squinting my eyes, I glare at her. "You're evil."

"You need to get up. I'll get the shower going for us."

I do need to get up. Work calls, and my truck won't drive itself three hundred miles today.

As she disappears into the bathroom, I say, "You go first. I don't trust you not to seduce me again."

But really what I want is to drink my coffee and not have to move. The shower turns on, and I tug on my underwear. Resting against the headboard again, I take a long, obnoxious slurp of heavenly java and sigh.

Memories of her show replay in my head, and I'm reminded of the guitar case, wondering if the lyrics to the song she mentioned are in there. I don't think she sang it last night, but she said I wouldn't understand it if she did. Straining my ear toward the bathroom, I hear the sound of her soft humming. Which means she's washing her long hair, giving me plenty of time to snoop.

Abandoning my coffee, I hop out of bed and scurry to the living room where we ditched our belongings after the show. I lay the guitar case flat on the floor, flip the latches and lift the lid, trying to be as quick and quiet as possible.

Reaching my fingers in the tear at the widest part of the case, I pinch the paper and pull it out, unfolding it to find her set list from last night. I set that aside and stick my fingers in the opening again, wiggling and stretching them until I touch something thicker than a simple sheet of paper.

When I wrangle the item out of its hiding place and examine it, confusion is the first thing that hits me, followed swiftly by nausea and dizziness. I slowly lower my ass to the coffee table to keep from fainting as my blood pressure spikes to dangerously high levels.

In the photograph in my trembling hand, a teenage Tatum —*my* Tatum—lies in a hospital bed.

Holding a baby.

She's gazing down at the bundled infant, part of her face hidden from view. I can only make out the dark tuft of hair on the top of the newborn's head.

My hands are shaking so hard, I barely manage to flip the photo over to see if anything's written on the other side. There's only a date: January 17. Ten years ago. I quickly do the math in my head and realize, with one hundred percent certainty, this is my baby.

I have a baby.

Can a man die from too much adrenaline? My chest tightens and pounds so hard that my ears pulsate. My mind spins with a speeding, dizzying carousel of scenarios and assumptions. Everything seems to be happening in a blurry nightmare, way too fast for me to process or grasp. The image on the photo swirls. Or maybe it's my vision failing the harder I stare at it.

What...the...fuck?

"Hey, where did you—"

Tatum's words cut off with a gasp, but I can't look at her. I don't want to look at her. If I do, I'm scared to death of what I'll find in her eyes. Guilt? Lies? Secrets? Betrayal? A mother?

"Jake."

The muffled sob that follows my name confirms I wasn't meant to discover this truth. Unless it was on her terms. And for all I know, her terms would've remained open-ended and amendable forever.

She's been here for months, with plenty of opportunities to reveal this life-changing secret to me *willingly*. Finding out this way, after spending the best morning I've had in ages with her in my bed?

I got played. Repeatedly.

Surging to my feet with renewed rage coursing through my veins, I wave the photo in her face and roar, "What *the fuck* is this?"

"Please, Jake. Let me explain." Tatum's eyes widen in

fear at the pure fury she sees in mine. She hugs her arms around her middle and cowers against the freshly-painted wall.

I'm so done letting her hide from me. Getting right up in her face, I unleash a decade's worth of anger.

"Ten fucking years, Tatum. Ten goddamn years I sat around wondering what I could've done so wrong to make you leave me. You broke every fucking promise you made. Lies! Every goddamn word out of your mouth is lies. I sacrificed everything for you. I bled my soul for you. I would've walked through hell for you, killed for you, done anything you asked just to have a scrap of your shitty kind of love." Spreading my arms wide, I bellow, "I built a fucking home for you!" I throw the photo at her, and she flinches hard. "But I'm not gonna be your fool anymore."

"Listen to me!" she screeches through her tears. Her face twists with agony, but this treacherous woman's pain is nothing compared to the searing, corrosive acid eating my every pore.

"I'm done listening to you! There's nothing you can say to fix this. The only thing I want to hear from you is one simple fucking truth." My chest heaves, each inhale like a metal claw ripping apart my insides. "Where's my baby, Tatum?"

She sinks to the floor, yanking her hair, and wails, "He's gone!"

He.

My body staggers backward from the forceful shock of this news. I have a son somewhere. A son I never knew about, never got to meet, and probably never will.

Does he look like me? Does he have my dark hair or green eyes? Does he have her smile and loving nature?

I look at her now, weeping and begging at my feet, and

the last thing I see is someone who's loving. She stole from me. Stole something precious I'll never get to hold.

An unimaginable realization seizes my brain, and bile rises in my throat as the bigger picture becomes clear. Her career was more important than being tied down with my child. Why else would she keep this secret from me? She got everything she wanted—minus the baggage—while I got totally fucked.

Every flimsy patch holding the pieces of my shattered heart together turns to dust. I shake my head harshly as I pace a short path back and forth in front of her, refusing to believe any of this is happening.

"Please," she begs, hands pressed together like she's praying to some god who can force me to listen to more of her lies.

But I've had enough. I march over and grab her guitar and case, not bothering to latch it, then toss them out the front door, past the porch and onto the gravel driveway. I go for her purse and her clothes, doing the same.

"What are you doing?" she cries, face etched with fright when I storm toward her.

I snatch her by the arm, and she flails trying to keep her footing as I drag her to the door. With her hair wet, and wearing only a T-shirt, I toss her out of my life.

"Jake!"

"Burn in hell, Tatum. You and Makenzie both." I slam the door so hard the tempered glass cracks. And I lock it for good measure to keep out the demon wailing on my doorstep.

Ignoring her pounding fists and keening cries, I stumble toward my bedroom, clutching my chest as the first waves of an attack set in. I make it as far as the bedroom door before I fall to the floor and fight for air.

The world closes in on me once again, and I don't even care if I survive its evil this time.

Everything I thought I knew about Tatum was wrong. Everything I held onto—all the reasons I loved her—for all these years was a fantasy. A sick fucking joke the universe played on me.

She's not the same girl who chased her dreams to California after high school. That girl wouldn't—couldn't—hurt me like this.

That girl is gone.

The woman she left behind is dead to me. And I can't stop my body from physically mourning the loss of both.

For the first time in my life, I sob—curled in a fetal position and wearing only my underwear. Which is exactly how Jensen finds me.

32

TATUM

I'm disembodied as I gather my things off the ground. I was ready to tell him. I finished the song days ago and set all my ghosts free. The truth sat on my tongue for days. But I've never been good at facing things head-on.

Pulling my phone out of my purse, I call the one person who will hold me quietly and let me cry.

"I'm surprised you're up this early."

"Pam." My voice breaks as I stumble down the long driveway to the road, sobbing with every step.

"Tatum? What's wrong?" The tremor in her voice indicates that she understands exactly what's wrong.

"He knows." She asks me questions, but they don't register through the fog in my head. "Come get me? Please?"

"I'm on my way." The line disconnects. When I reach the end of the driveway, I fall to my knees in the ditch and puke.

January – Ten Years Ago

The Uber driver's horrified expression when I open the rear door of his sedan ratchets up my panic. "You need ambulance!" he yells in broken English.

"No time. Drive." Between the tears and the sharp pain, I can hardly speak.

The driver lets out what I assume is a string of curses in his native language. Probably because I'm sure to make a mess all over his cloth seats.

"Good Samaritan?" he asks, peeling away from the curb before I've shut the door all the way or buckled my seat belt. The latter takes a full minute because my whole body shakes uncontrollably.

"*Ugh*," I groan through another sudden spike of excruciating pain and grit out, "Yes."

The hospital isn't too far from my studio apartment in Koreatown. My neighborhood never sleeps but, thankfully, the driver weaves quickly through the bit of traffic on the roads at this late hour.

Somehow, I had enough wits about me to grab my purse before I stumbled down three flights of stairs, stopping to breathe through the gut-wrenching pain every sixth step. I pull it to my soaked lap and dig out my phone.

My vision blurs when I search my contacts list. In this moment, I'm grateful I don't have many to choose from as I press Jake's name. It's four o'clock in the morning in Texas, but he answers on the third ring, his voice thick with sleep.

"Tate?"

Fear and desperation pour out of me in a jumble of broken phrases, tormented groans, and heavy sobs.

"Need you. Please. *Ugh*. Hurts. So scared." My body alternates between violent quakes and intense seizing. I do my best to ignore the blood.

When he speaks, he sounds far away, like a barrier stands

between us. "Hey, hey. Take a breath. What's happening? Where are you?"

"Hospital. Need you. *Oh god…fuck*. Help me."

"Where?" The panic in his voice rises. "What hospital, Tate? Where?"

"Give me phone!" the driver yells, stretching his hand toward me as the car careens through a red light at top speed. I should be afraid he'll kill us, but I think I'm already dying.

"G-good…Samaritan. *Ugh*. Korea…town. Hurry."

"Okay! Okay! I'm coming, Tate. I'll be there. Let me just call—"

"*No!*" I scream in both agony and protest. "No…don't tell. *Ugh*. Jake, please. Don't tell…a-anyone. P-please."

Heavy breathing comes from his end of the line during what feels like a minutes-long hesitation. "Okay."

"Promise…me."

"I promise."

"*Ugh*. Hurry. Love you."

"Fuck! Okay. On my way. Just hang on, Tate. I'll take the first flight I can. Just hang on."

The line goes dead. People are shouting. The car door opens, and I'm swiftly loaded onto a gurney and surrounded by medical personnel. I've never been so afraid or so alone.

Hours later, the golden remnants of sunset fill my quiet hospital room, offering the only source of light. I'm reclined in my bed, softly humming "Make You Feel My Love." My son is swaddled like a snug burrito and nestled protectively in my arms. I can't stop stroking his dark tuft of hair with my fingertips.

He's the most beautiful thing I've ever laid eyes on.

I wish my parents could meet him. My dad hadn't held a baby since I was born, but he would love my son. My mother would spoil him rotten. She'd also teach me how to be the perfect mom. Just like she was.

The door to my room opens. A hesitant voice pierces my peaceful bubble, bursting it with only one whispered word.

"Tate?"

I ignore it. Same as I ignore the light thudding of footsteps against the ugly tile floor. The walls are ugly too. And the bedding, and the uncomfortable-looking chairs, and the curtain hanging near the door. The only beautiful thing in the room is my son.

The shocked gasp near my bedside jolts me out of my lullaby.

"Tate. Darlin'." The strained voice is not the one I expected. It's all wrong, forcing my attention away from my baby.

"What are you doing here, Jensen?" I sound hollow. I *feel* hollow…when I'm not looking at my little boy.

"You called me," he whispers, fearful eyes darting between me and my son.

No.

"No. No, I called Jake. He promised he wouldn't tell." My eyes drift to the fine, silky hair. It's thick for a baby. Like his dad's. "Where's Jake?"

"Tatum," he rasps. "The baby—"

"He died." The declaration doesn't sound harsh in my dissociated state. It's simply the truth. My gentle stroking resumes. "They said I can hold him as long as I want. A lady came by and took pictures of us. She was nice."

Jensen's voice cracks. "He?"

"Dylan," I whisper. *Stroking. Stroking. Stroking.*

A choked sob punches through the air and obliterates my delicate veil of denial. When I gaze at Jensen again—tears streaming down his cheeks, fist pressed against his mouth, shoulders convulsing—my eyes bloom with renewed sorrow.

"Where's my Jake?" I ask again. My quivery voice and blurry eyes plead for him to say *just outside the door, darlin'*.

Jensen shakes his head, and it's then I realize my error. Jake…Jensen…brothers. Always together, side by side. And listed alphabetically in my phone contacts.

I hug little Dylan closer to my chest. Quiet cries turn into weeping sobs. A long soul-crushing wail leaves my aching body. Jensen pulls my head against his chest, and we mourn together.

He holds me long after I kiss my son goodbye, and the nurses take him away. He holds me long after the moon says farewell and the hues of a promising dawn break across the horizon. He holds me until I pass out from the kind of bone-deep exhaustion found at the small sticky center of grief's giant web, where its victims can no longer fight against it.

The last words I mumble before I find sleep are, "Promise me you won't tell."

I never expected to deliver my baby six weeks prematurely, according to emergency doctors. And I certainly never expected to leave the hospital a day later without him.

Jensen hasn't left my side. Wearing the rumpled flannel, dirty jeans, and scuffed, unlaced boots he had on yesterday, he walks alongside my wheelchair as a nurse pushes me toward the sliding exit doors. I squeeze my eyes shut against the crude daylight breaching our somber procession of three.

"I called a cab," he says.

He took the lead in dealing with the hospital staff after getting a couple hours of sleep. He made most of the easy decisions, such as trashing my blood-stained pajamas. And all the hard ones, like choosing cremation over burial. He struggled with making that particular decision on my behalf, but he made the right choice.

I haven't said much beyond repeating my demand that he can't call anyone yet, especially Jake.

We climb into the taxi and head to my apartment. Jensen has a small, hastily packed duffel with a single change of clothes and basic toiletries. I have my purse and a plastic bag containing a tiny wristband, a blue and pink knit hat, and a folder.

According to Jensen, the folder has a certificate with little foot- and handprints stamped in ink, discharge instructions, a pamphlet for free grief counseling, and information on how to apply for a death certificate. He can keep it or burn it all. Doesn't matter to me.

The photographer stopped by my room before we left and assured Jensen digital copies will be sent to my email address, which he supplied. I never want to see them.

He helps me navigate the three flights of stairs. As soon as he opens the apartment door, I aim straight for the bed with no intention of ever leaving it. The studio is small—less than five-hundred square feet. The kitchen has a sliver of counter space, and there's no dining area, so I eat all my meals on the sofa. The bathroom's a decent size. The closet is not.

Jensen dumps our pitiful belongings on the coffee table. "You need to eat."

"Not hungry." I lift my grandmother's quilt—a gift from Aunt Pam—and freeze at the sight of blood on my fitted sheet. The stain isn't big. The gush came after the cramps woke me and I reached the bathroom.

Noticing my lack of movement, Jensen steps over and eyes the stain. "Clean sheets?"

"Closet."

He goes about changing the sheets wordlessly while I

fiddle with the hem of my shirt. The hospital gave me scrubs to wear since my pajamas were ruined and Jensen refused to run to my apartment and grab me a change of clothes, afraid of leaving me alone for the half hour it would've taken him.

Finally, I gingerly slide into the comfort of my bed. Without walls dividing the would-be rooms, I'm attuned to every single one of his movements and irritated huffs. It's his nature to care for people, and he's easily frustrated when someone denies him the chance to do so.

"Got a washer?" he asks.

"Ground level."

He forcefully stuffs the dirty sheets into the laundry basket in the closet. "I'll run you a bath."

"I don't have a tub."

"A shower, then," he grits out. "Unless you want me to go first?"

I don't respond.

He sighs before the bathroom door clicks shut and the sound of running water echoes in the space. Probably should've warned him about the blood.

I fall asleep before he finishes his shower. And he lets me have fourteen hours of undisturbed rest before he comes at me the next morning, guns blazing.

Jensen shoves a bagel in my face. When I shake my head, rejecting the offering, he releases his millionth exasperated sigh and tosses the bagel on the coffee table. He persuaded me to take a shower, change into yoga pants and my favorite sweatshirt, and move to the sofa. Isn't that enough living for one day?

"Why didn't you tell anyone?" he asks.

Because I was scared and didn't want it to be real.

The little voice inside my head also reminds me I'm shunning reality even now. Otherwise, I wouldn't be having a normal conversation with him after suffering such a tragic loss.

"I was scared," I say on a shaky whisper, leaving out the uglier half of my confession.

Maisy was also concerned about my distant behavior recently, so I told her what I told Jake. That I had been busy working and playing at open-mic nights. In my mind, it was the truth.

Jensen's shoulders sag as he rubs a hand across his tired face. "You should've told us, Tate. You should've told Jake. He's been worried sick. Going out of his mind because y'all barely talk anymore."

"Maybe it's for the best," I admit quietly.

His voice rises in indignation. "What's that supposed to mean, huh? He's your baby's father. He should be here!"

"He's no one's father! There's no baby anymore!" I yell.

We stare at each other—chests heaving—equally stricken by my brutal outburst. Jensen looks like I stabbed him in the gut, he's so shocked. My hollow chest caves in, crushing me. I hurt everywhere—physically and emotionally. But, despite all the unbearable pain, I have no more tears to shed.

In all honesty, I desperately want Jake here with me. I *need* him like I need air. But I failed at making a simple phone call the same way I failed to face reality the past several months. I was so terrified of ruining all our hopes and dreams, I ignored what my body begged me to acknowledge.

When I took a pregnancy test, I convinced myself the result was a false-positive. I never even went to a doctor. If I had, I might've recognized the signs of placental abruption days or weeks in advance and sought help.

Because of my denial and delusions, I failed to bring a living, breathing baby into the world. I don't deserve Jake. And he doesn't deserve the destruction caused by my failures.

Jensen drops his head in his hands, elbows braced on his knees. A lone teardrop falls, crashing to his denim-clad thigh like a swift, silent gunshot.

"Dylan," he whispers. "My nephew."

The way he speaks the familial term out loud is intentional, repentant. He arrived at the hospital and learned I was in the maternity wing, but the nursing staff's refusal to let him see me raised his protective instincts. He sensed something was terribly wrong. So, he claimed to be my baby's father to gain access to my room, not realizing until later that both the Holloway surname and dark hair passed on to Dylan worked in his favor. It was the only way, given the delicate circumstances.

Neither of us corrected anyone who referred to Jensen as "the father." The pretense allowed him to handle arrangements and discuss medical details with staff since I couldn't. The cost of playing the role rightly belonging to Jake is the extreme guilt eating away at him. Jensen will suffer the cost for years to come, if not forever.

"I remember when Jake was born," he starts, his voice low and brittle. "I expected to find a screaming baby when Dad brought me in the room." I sense his gentle smile as he recalls the fond memory. "What I found was a quiet little observer with his eyes wide open, like everything he saw outside Mom's belly filled him with wonder. I didn't know babies couldn't see a thing. He had the fattest cheeks and so much hair, I asked if he was part monkey."

He chuckles softly before the flimsy moment of happiness fades. "Dylan looked exactly like Jake. For a moment, when I first saw the baby like…" he trails off, swallowing hard to clear the devastation he witnessed from his throat. "I thought it was my baby brother lying there, and that I failed him on day one.

"You see, I made Jake a promise on the day he was born. I hadn't even turned four yet, but I was determined to protect him from all the bad in the world, so he'd never get hurt. The only time I've broken that promise was when our parents died, even though I had no chance to stop it from happening."

Jensen hits me with piercing green eyes so fierce and full of anguish, I feel the physical impact. "So, explain it to me, Tate. Explain why I'm still sitting here—in my brother's seat —while he's a thousand miles away, completely unaware that all the bad things are happening to him *right now*. Help me understand how I'm supposed to protect him by making an impossible choice. Whichever way this goes, it'll destroy him. Convince me to live with that."

I take his hand in mine, speaking with more conviction than I feel. "I'm the one who failed him…and our baby. You've done nothing wrong. As for protecting him? You do it by letting *me* choose what happens next."

If I allow Jensen to call Jake, he'll come running to me. He'll not only be distraught over losing our baby, but he'll also find a way to shoulder the blame for me keeping the pregnancy a secret. Jake will want to stay here—by my side —while we fight through the fog of tragedy, which means he'll miss school and risk losing the full-ride scholarship he worked so hard to secure. If we don't call him, the only thing he'll lose is me.

The third alternative is to stay with Jake and pretend none of this ever happened. There's only one problem with that option: I'm terrible at keeping secrets from Jake when I have to face him. Which is exactly why my communication has been dwindling the last few months, causing him such distress. I'm only sending text messages at this point. Otherwise, I'd blurt out the truth and plunder his hard-earned success.

"His future's at stake, Jensen. Everything he worked for. And I'm not willing to let him throw that away."

"*You're* his future, Tate. Everybody knows that."

Perhaps I have some tears left in me after all. They fall in torrents down my cheeks.

"I love Jake more than anything. I love him so much that I would rather him endure a few years of heartbreak than suffer a lifetime of pain with nothing to show for it. This is all my fault, and I'm willing to carry the heavier burden for both of us." Jensen shakes his head, but I see the tentative agreement in his eyes and seize on it before he can argue. "You know I'm right. You've sacrificed too much to get him to college, Jensen. You both have."

He finally relents, promising to keep my secret for the sake of Jake's future success. We spend the day bickering over whether I should call Maisy to take his place when he leaves for Texas. After hours of back and forth, and being practically force-fed a bowl of soup, I reluctantly agree to let him call my aunt. Jensen leaves the next morning.

The day after that, Aunt Pam arrives on my doorstep, unannounced and distraught. A few weeks later, I receive a package with framed photos of me and Dylan in the hospital, along with a blue, velvet jewelry box with *Cherished Gems* printed in gold lettering on the lid. That same day, I change my phone number, severing the connection to anyone from Walford except for Maisy and Aunt Pam.

I'll always be grateful to Jensen for showing up—albeit accidentally—for me when I needed help, and for sending Aunt Pam to comfort me during the hard weeks that followed. But I'll never forgive him for the gifts representing the worst day of my life: the day I said goodbye to both Dylan and Jake.

33

JAKE

"Jake." Jensen kneels beside me and wraps a hand around my head. "Come on. Let's get you dressed."

"I'm a dad," I croak. The words scrape against my dry throat as they leave me. I've cried for so long; I can't breathe through my stuffy nose.

He lets out a sigh so shaky, it almost sounds like a sigh of relief. "I know."

I let him pull me to my feet and guide me to the bedroom. Catatonic, I sit on the edge of the bed and block out thoughts of how the morning started versus how it ended. I'll have to burn the sheets. Maybe start a bonfire and throw the whole bed in for good measure.

"Here. Put these on."

He holds out a clean T-shirt and a pair of sweatpants. The wounded little boy in me wants to ask him to dress me so I don't have to move. Movement signifies life, and I'm dead inside. I manage to lift a hand and take the clothes from him.

"I'll start you a fresh pot of coffee. Meet me in the living room?"

I nod, my unfocused gaze aimed at his boots. He hesitates for several seconds before walking away.

After I dress, I trudge to the living room and collapse onto the couch. The sound of Tatum's wails from earlier batters my head. For a moment, I believed her pained cries were for the long-lost baby and not for my hateful words and actions.

That woman has taken more from me than I ever could have imagined, and the trauma is far too big for my mortal shell to contain. A monster inside me surfaced. One I never knew existed. And he's stalking the edges of my skin like a predator, waiting for another opportunity to cause maximum destruction.

I dig the heels of my palms into my eye sockets, attempting to erase the memory of me hauling her out the door in anger.

Jensen shuffles into the living room and places a steaming mug on the end table. He sits on the coffee table in front of me, but I don't move or acknowledge him. Instead, I fixate on the swishing sound from each stroke of his hand against his short beard. It takes him a long time to speak.

The deep timbre of his voice echoes like a gong in my head when he says, "He was stillborn." My eyes snap to his. "Never took his first breath."

He stares at a photo pinched between his fingers. The photo I threw at Tatum. The photo that wrecked my world. Remorse is written all over his face. I slowly sit up, giving him my full attention.

"How do you know?"

He carefully sets the photo aside, rests one hand on each of his thighs, and looks me in the eyes. My skin burns with feral rage—the monster begging to be set free again—at what I find in his.

Resignation…and *guilt*.

"I took care of her after."

Jensen sees it coming before I do. I launch off the couch and tackle him to the floor, throwing punch after punch as I unleash the full reckoning of my pain on the one person in the world who was never supposed to fail me.

"How could you do this to me?"

"I trusted you!"

"Why didn't you tell me?"

"I should've been there!"

"I could've done something!"

"I lost *everything* because of you!"

My brother, who's bigger and stronger than me, accepts every blow from my fists and every syllable of blame I spit at him. I can't see or hear anything other than the red splashed behind my eyeballs and the fury rushing past my ears.

When I've worn myself out, I slump over him. Beaten and bloody and wheezing as he struggles to inhale, he wraps his arms around me and holds me tight while I expend the last of my energy through the endless tears.

Jensen's battered body racks with sobs beneath my broken one. "I'm sorry, Jake. I'm so sorry. I made a mistake," he cries.

But I don't want to hear it. Shoving away from him, I scramble against the couch, sitting with my knees bent as I fist my hair. I don't dare look at him, afraid of both the damage I caused and the apology on his face. I can't accept it. Not now, maybe not ever.

This whole fucking time, Jensen knew everything. He knew why Tatum left me. He knew I was ruined, locked inside my heartbreak and panic because of her. My own brother held the key to my freedom, and he didn't love me enough to unlock the fucking door and release me from my prison of agony and unknowns. He allowed me to suffer. And for what? I still have nothing in the end.

Minutes pass while he lies on the rug and I struggle to wrap my mind around all the grim, ugly truths. Their serrated edges slice through my grey matter with ease, leaving behind an incomprehensible mess. Ironically, the two people who tore my life apart are the only ones who can give me the pieces to put it back together.

"Tell me everything." I rasp the command, my throat even more raw from my latest shouting spell.

He gingerly pries his body from the floor, grunting and groaning as he positions himself next to me. Better his agony than mine. It takes him a minute to regulate his breathing before he can speak.

"She called me by accident the night she went into labor. I didn't know what was going on." From his short, stilted breaths, I assume I cracked a rib or two. "She was in pain. I could hear it. She begged me to hurry. I had no idea what I was walking into. Just knew she needed help. Made me swear not to tell anyone. I thought that included you."

"Did you make it in time? For the delivery?" I glance at Jensen and cringe at the amount of blood pouring from his nose and split lip.

His left eye is almost swollen shut—the cut on his brow weeping blood—and his Bruno's shirt is ripped at the collar. I feel a tiny flicker of shame that he bore the brunt of all my anger.

"No," he says, wheezing. "It was a shock. Seeing her lying there, stroking the hair of a lifeless baby. Humming a song for him." Sobs overtake him again, the sound more agonizing because of his physical injuries. "Dylan was the spitting image of you, Jake. It was hard to look at him."

Dylan. If only a name has the power to destroy me, this is the one.

I pick up the photo, my bruised knuckles protesting when my fingers flex, and have a clearer, more focused look at it. The photo seems somewhat professional in quality, not taken with a cell phone camera. The dim lighting softens the harsh reality in the image, which I'd rather put out of my mind forever.

"I took care of all the details. She couldn't function. And we"—he chokes back another sob and groans from the effort—"I let them believe I was his father. So I could make decisions for her, you know? I'll never forgive myself for that." *I'll never forgive you for that either.*

How many cuts can a person take before he's not a person anymore? Just a sad mush of soft tissue and shattered bones. The photo flutters to the floor between my legs. I'm seconds away from shutting down, unable to handle another ounce of the misery this godforsaken life keeps cramming down my throat.

"Why didn't she tell me? Either before or after? Why did she keep it a secret?"

"Before? No idea. She never said. After? She didn't want you to lose your scholarship. Throw away your future. Stupid"—his labored inhale stalls—"in hindsight. But I agreed with her. So I share the blame."

My head drops onto the cushion when I let loose a humorless chuckle. The fucking irony of life, right?

"You are to blame, big brother. You're the reason I went to college. I wanted to go to California with Tatum after graduation. But you worked hard to support me, and you were so proud of me, I didn't want to let you down. So I made a choice. I chose you over her. Yet, when you had a choice that affected my future, you chose her over me. And, fuck, did you ever let *me* down."

He splutters and chokes on his blood and tears. "Jake, I didn't know—"

"You need to go. Now," I bite out, jaw clenched hard to hold back another bout of rage. Fisting my hands, the pain in my knuckles distracts me from the pain of betrayal by my only flesh and blood.

A few beats of tense silence pass before Jensen manages to climb to his feet and limp out of my house, taking any bit of regret I had for kicking his ass with him.

ROCK

Where are you?

Lucy took care of Jensen. Cracked ribs. A few stitches. Nose isn't broken. He'll be fine.

BRODY

Call us. Let us know you're safe.

2 MISSED CALLS FROM PAM WAKEFIELD

BRODY

We're worried about you, bro.

5 MISSED CALLS FROM ROCK

ROCK

Jake. Answer. Please check in.

7 MISSED CALLS FROM BRODY

BRODY

It's been days. At least text us back so we know you're alive.

14 MISSED CALLS FROM JENSEN

Unlike some people, I honor my commitments, so I left for my work trip after kicking Tatum and Jensen out of my house. The time spent on the road allowed me to clear my head and decide what's best for me moving forward.

I'm selling the house. Should've never bought the damn thing in the first place. I wasted time and money on a fantasy, hoping for something that was never possible.

I considered ripping up the pine floors in the loft and destroying much of my other backbreaking work. But something stopped me from turning Tatum's dream home into bare bones—just like me—stripped of everything that gave it life. With the large financial investment I've sunk into this place, I expect to take a loss on it. And if I do, well, add it to all the other losses.

Shirtless and dripping in sweat, I haul the garbage through the patio door and toss everything into the bed of my truck. The chilly air hitting my bare skin every time I step outside doesn't affect me. I feel nothing, and it's a comfortable state of mind and body to be in.

I shut off my phone this morning, fed up with the endless calls and texts from my friends. They're relentless in trying to contact me, forcing me to pretend I'm not home in my efforts to avoid them. Rock quit pounding on my door three times a day, which I'm grateful for because I can't tolerate his need to delve into my feelings right now. Not until I can sort through them myself.

It's time for a drastic change in my life. There's nothing keeping me in Walford anymore, or in Texas for that matter. My clients are located all over the state, and with my expansion plans, I could live anywhere.

Tatum seems to enjoy running away. Perhaps I'll give it a try and find out what's so great about it. Hell, maybe I should buy one of those camper vans and live the nomadic lifestyle since I'm always on the road. Sounds kind of perfect, if you ask me.

The downside of spending too many hours in a vehicle is my mind morphing from intentional thoughts to wandering ones. On my recent trip—as on all my trips over the years— my thoughts often drifted to Tatum.

The devastation on her face that morning haunts me, as well as her fear when I directed my fury at her. My misguided fury. Like an asshole, I gave power to my assumptions, denying myself any chance at being reasonable. I refused to stop and listen.

Now that I know the truth, that all my assumptions were wrong, I feel even worse. Even less deserving of her than before.

I thought about how our lives would've turned out if I had spoken up and followed her to California after high school. Together, we would've faced her pregnancy and whatever impact it had on her music career. Whether or not Dylan lived, I would've been there to support her.

Her career…that's a whole different beast. Now that I've had a glimpse into her pop star life, I'm not sure I would have survived it. The fans, the industry executives, the team around her calling the shots…young Jake was way too selfish and needy to share Tatum with them. Part of me still feels that way.

But the *what ifs* don't matter now. Neither of us spoke up, and we both suffered the consequences.

Maybe it's time to let her go. To move on like my brother and friends have been wanting me to do for years. If all that exists between me and Tatum is pain, if all we do is hurt each other, then what's the point in holding on?

With that question in mind, I toss the last of the trash in my truck. I work best with a plan in place, and my plan is sound. It's time to move on and regain control of my life. It's time to unstick myself.

With my pity party at an end, I haul my kindling to the ridge. Tonight, I'm making a bonfire and having a beer. I'll burn down the past, scatter the ashes, and celebrate the new Jake—the one who puts himself first.

34

TATUM

When Aunt Pam picked me up from the roadside, I told her what happened. As expected, she didn't judge me for how I've handled this whole mess or Jake for how he reacted.

"I'm weak," I said to her, sniffling. "Spineless."

She rubbed my back as we lay on my bed together. "You're not weak. You're scared, but you're also strong. It takes a special kind of strength to deal with this by yourself all these years. Give him some time. He'll come around."

"You should've seen him," I cried, voice pitching high with emotion. "He was destroyed."

"Let him settle from the shock, then you can go to him and tell him the whole story."

Jake believes he has a son somewhere, which is almost crueler than the truth. He didn't allow me to explain anything at all. I've never seen him so crazed and angry, and I've certainly never been afraid of him like I was that morning.

"He's alone. He needs someone to be there for him." *I want to be there for him.*

"I took care of it," she said.

Later that day, I got a text from Jensen.

Jake is gone in more ways than one. I learned he left the day everything exploded, and no one's heard from him since. It's been almost a week, and not a single word.

Jensen came by to check on me, and my stomach swirled with nausea when I saw the stitches, bruising, and swelling on his face. Jake's hands did that to him. Jake—who would never cause harm to any living creature.

Aunt Pam and my friends have left me alone, mostly. I don't want to talk to anyone about what happened until after I talk to Jake.

I told Daniel I'm returning to California and thanked him for his help with the YouTube channel. We might continue working long distance, but I made no promises. I'm still invested in helping him pursue his dreams though. He reminds me of a young Graham, and I offered to fly Daniel to LA so he can hang out with us and learn more from his mentor. He gave me the biggest smile I've ever seen on his face.

Before the blowup with Jake, Daniel and I launched the channel with the introduction video Jake suggested, and we've posted two songs so far. It didn't take long for the view count to skyrocket once news spread that Tatum, formerly known as Makenzie, was making new music.

The channel's instant success made me queasy. Once again, I questioned my relationship with fame and if I've made the right decision with the channel. It's not *the* spotlight, but it's *a* spotlight. I'll have time to consider my path forward once I'm home.

Judge and Marcus will pick me up tomorrow and take me to the airport. When I get to California, I'll face my fans and own up to all my wrongdoings. I asked them to wait for me, and they have. I owe them closure.

I'm stuffing crap into my last suitcase when the sound of hushed voices in the kitchen draws my attention. Creeping down the hall, I hear Aunt Pam say, "Now isn't really a good time."

A higher-pitched, accented voice speaks. "I'd really like to see her before she leaves."

Lucy?

I step out from the hallway, making my presence known. Lucy's standing just inside the door with Marcella planted on her hip. Her thick hair is piled high in a messy bun, and her lips are free of the red lipstick she always wears. It's the least put together I've seen her.

"What's going on, Lucy? Is everything okay?"

She tugs me into a one-armed hug. "I'm sorry for your loss."

Patting her on the back, I respond, "Thank you."

I'm unsure how to react to condolences for something that happened years ago. Because I kept it hidden from almost everyone, only a few people were able to comfort me when I needed it most.

She sniffles as she transfers Marcella to my arms. I nuzzle

the baby's hair and caress her back while she gnaws on a fake donut, drool spilling down her chin and onto her little sweater.

I jerk my head at the table, gesturing for Lucy to have a seat, and meet Aunt Pam's gaze, silently assuring her that I'll be fine. She nods and retreats to her bedroom, giving Lucy and me some privacy.

"Jake won't answer anyone's calls or texts, and the guys have been beating down his door for days. They staked out his house last night and finally saw him in a window. While they're freaking out over him, I thought I'd check on you before you go."

"I'm okay," I lie, but my wet eyes betray me.

Her soft smile appears. "No, you're not. It's obvious how much you love each other. And now with this—" Her breath hitches, and she swipes a tear from her cheek. "We've all wanted Jake to be happy for a long time, and he's changed since you've been back. It's like you brought him to life. He needs you, Tatum. And by the changes I've seen in you since we met, I'm guessing you need him too."

"I do," I admit, holding Marcella tighter. "But he needs time to process this. I've had ten years. He's only had a few days."

I'll give Jake some space, but I have some things to say to him before I leave. I had planned to stay in Walford for a couple of months while I figured out my life. Now that I've accomplished that goal, it's time for me to return to California and put Makenzie to rest. Only then will I decide if or when I'm coming back to this town.

A question pops into my head as I stare at Lucy. "How did you find out?"

"Jensen." She clasps her hands together. "Don't be mad at

him. He was a mess when I patched him up. I think he was relieved to get it all off his chest."

"No, it's fine. He's carried this as long as I have and deserves to finally let it out."

I pressured Jensen into keeping the truth from Jake, and he's stayed loyal to me all these years despite the hurt it caused his own brother. He can confide in whoever he wants, say whatever he needs to say, while dealing with the aftermath. It was selfish of me to chain this tragedy to him. To force him to bear the burden in secret. The least I can do is step aside and let him break the chains so he can heal too.

"Rock was with me at Jensen's house, which is why Brody also knows. Those two are the biggest gossips." She rolls her eyes, but a smile plays at her lips, drawing out my own.

"They're good guys, Lucy. Especially Rock. He's soft on the inside and loyal to a fault. You couldn't have married a better man."

"Oh, I know. He cried like a baby when I proposed to him." She slaps a hand over her mouth, her eyes going so wide they might pop.

I gape at her. "You proposed to *him*?"

"Forget I said that. You can't tell anyone, Tatum. Promise me. He would be so embarrassed if his friends found out."

"I promise not to tell." I say, holding up three fingers in what I think means *scout's honor* while struggling to contain my laughter. But I have to ask… "Why were you the one to propose? He's pretty old fashioned, isn't he?"

She chuckles and rolls her eyes again. "Rock's good at reading a room. At reading between the lines. He picks up on *everything*. But he really sucks at reading women, so I have to tell him exactly what I want."

"Sounds like you two have communication down to a

science," I mutter, thinking about how I suck at communicating. Hence, the destruction of me and Jake.

Her love-struck eyes sparkle like they do every time she talks about Rock. "We really do. And it's not that hard. We mean what we say and aren't afraid to ask for what we want or need."

I lift an eyebrow. "Simple as that, huh?"

With a single nod, she says, "Simple as that." She scoots to the edge of her chair, stealing Marcella—who conked out while drooling on my chest—from my arms. "I better run. This one needs a diaper change and a nap, and Rock's probably prowling the streets looking for me. He's grumpy if he doesn't get his after-school snack."

"I can only imagine. And I have an errand to run after I finish packing, so I better get moving too." At the door, I brush Marcella's curls out of her eyes. "If I don't come back, you and Marcella are welcome to visit me in California any time. And Rock can come too, I guess."

"I'd like that." She studies me for a few seconds, a knowing glint in her eyes. "I'll tell Rock and Brody to stay away from Jake's house for the rest of the day."

I nod as we step onto the porch, relieved she can read right through me. "Thank you." With my arms wrapped around her and Marcella, I say, "I really am glad we're friends, Lucy."

"Me too." She gives me a watery smile as she backs away, lifting the fingers holding Marcella's back in an attempted wave. "Don't be a stranger, Tate."

My eyes sting watching her leave with that sweet girl in her arms. It's the first time she's called me *Tate*, and my heart could burst from how warm and fuzzy I feel.

~

The lights are off inside Jake's house. When he doesn't answer my knock on the front door, I creep around the outside to find the patio door to the master bedroom hanging open. Tiptoeing over the threshold, I hold my breath and listen for any sounds. When I'm greeted with only silence, I continue forward.

Although it's late evening and after sunset, there's enough light for me to see the destruction. The bare mattress leans against the wall, and shards of wood from the bed are scattered across the floor.

"Jake?"

When no response comes, I move further into the house. Crusty dishes fill the kitchen sink, and empty food bags and beer bottles litter the counters. In the living room, a pillow and rumpled sheets are on the sofa, his makeshift bed.

Treading quietly up the stairs to the loft, I try again. "Jake?"

Still no answer.

Through the round window, the distinct, amber glow of a fire on the ridge catches my attention, and my heart slams in my chest. He told me to burn in hell. And the fire raging on the spot where we fell into infinite love weakens my knees.

Sure, the likely bed in flames is merely a bed, but what it represents sets me in motion. He's purging me from his life. Burning me out. And tonight is my last chance to save us.

A long, heavy chain wraps around the gate, secured with a lock. I shut off the engine of my aunt's work truck, grab the box I brought with me, and scramble over the barrier. Struggling to hold back tears, I run toward the roaring flames.

Jake leans against his tailgate, his profile in silhouette against the darkening sky as he tosses a chunk of wood into the fire. He doesn't acknowledge me when I slow my approach, huffing from the mad dash.

He's shirtless, wearing only a ball cap, jeans, and boots. It's cold out here, but I guess the fire keeps him warm enough. Splintered pieces of the bed are piled in the back of the truck. Based on the small amount left, he's been at this for a while.

He brings a beer bottle to his lips and takes a long drink, his gaze never leaving the fire. "Did I hurt you? When I grabbed you?"

"Not physically, no," I say, keeping my voice steady. I can't cry tonight. I need the strength of a warrior, and warriors don't cry in battle.

He grunts in response, polishes his beer off, and tosses the empty bottle into the flames. "What do you want?"

You. Always and only you.

I place the small box I'm carrying on the tailgate, then cover my hands with my coat sleeves. If I show any signs of discomfort or distress, he'll assume I'm ready to run. For once in my life, I'm not.

"I'm going to talk, and you're going to listen." He doesn't look my way or run me off, so I continue. "Many factors played into the decisions I made, but when I strip everything away, it came down to one thing: I was afraid of ruining our dreams. I tried to do the right thing in the end, after I lost Dylan." Speaking my son's name aloud, the warrior in me falls, my sword sticking in my throat. "It's bad enough I had to live with that kind of trauma. I just wanted you to get to *live*. I thought I failed you when I got pregnant, but I felt even deeper shame and guilt from losing our son."

"That wasn't your fault," he interjects.

"It was. If I had gone to a doctor—"

"You can't say for certain the outcome would've been different," he says, turning his eyes on me. The hurt I see in them is exactly what I tried to prevent. It's a life-altering hurt that never goes away. "We could've lost the baby anyway. *We.* Because you didn't get pregnant alone. I had a right to be informed, especially because we loved each other."

Loved. Past tense.

"I tried to save you from this *because* I love you," I cry, angrily swiping at my tears, mad at myself for breaking when I vowed to remain strong. "You were happy to be in school. Happy to be away from Walford for the first time."

"The only place I've ever been happy was by your side." He sighs with a tired shake of his head. "I never wanted college, Tate."

"What?" I whisper, eyes wide with shock from this revelation.

If it's true, then every decision I made—the years of guilt and shame I endured—was based on a lie. The end of us never had to happen. All the misery tied to letting Jake go after losing Dylan was…avoidable.

"I did it for Jensen," he says. "It's my biggest regret because it took me away from you, and everything fell apart. You broke me, Tatum. For ten long years, I've had nothing here"—he presses a fist to his chest—"but pain. I was barely hanging on. But you showed up again. Told me you love me. Even as I imagined all the worst reasons why you would've left me; I was ready to forgive you for any of them."

"There's nothing to forgive when it comes to Dylan. That *wasn't…your…fault.*" The heartache choking him tries to surface, but he swallows it down. "But you should've called me when you needed me. I lived for you, Tate. For only you. And you denying me of my sole purpose in life is the one thing I don't know how to forgive."

He shifts his attention back to the hot flames, to the fire burning up a tangible thing in my place. A tear on his cheek catches the firelight, and I summon every ounce of willpower to keep from reaching out and brushing it away.

As much as I want to comfort him, I'm too pissed off right now to do so. The betrayal and anger simmering inside me after hearing his confession about college fuels my indignation, and I snap.

"Are you done? Because I asked you to listen to what *I* have to say. Give me that much respect, at the very least."

I inhale in a deep breath to calm my trembling body after the sudden boost of adrenaline. Jake's eyes flare at my stern tone, one he's never heard from me before.

"You think you know pain? Don't try to compare heartbreaks with me, Jake. You'll lose every time." He flinches at my blunt words, but I won't apologize for them. I spent a decade scaling my mountain of guilt, and I've reached my summit.

Encroaching on his personal space, I demand his full attention. "I came to Walford to fight for us—something I should've done long ago. We may have been apart, but we've always been together. Neither of us can deny that, but I *can* refuse to believe this is how we end." I jab a finger toward the cigar box on the tailgate. "I'm leaving that with you. It holds the proof of everything I love and lost. If you don't want to look, please give it to Pam for safekeeping. Whatever happens next between us is your choice but know this... you're the love of my life, Jake Dylan Holloway. End of story."

I spin on my heel and flee before the floodgates open, my strength dissolving the farther I move away from him. When the sound of another piece of wood landing on the bonfire—causing the embers to crackle and hiss—reaches my ears, I lose the fight.

The acrid scent of smoke wraps around me as tight as Jake's arms when he crawls into my bed. I didn't expect him to come to me tonight, not after seeing the resignation in his eyes. The distance within them grew with each swell of the fire's blaze.

"I'm sorry for the way I reacted. You didn't deserve that." His raspy voice, turned gravelly from inhaling smoke and despair, softly rumbles in my ear. "For years, I wanted answers. When the time came to learn the truth, I refused to listen."

Given how he discovered my secret, finding out on his own because I dragged my feet in fear, I don't think he over-reacted. He was blindsided, and his fight-or-flight instincts kicked in. He chose to fight against his perception of the truth.

"You were caught off guard—"

His nose rubs against my hair when he shakes his head. "Don't make excuses for me. I shouldn't have treated you that way. On top of yelling at you, scaring you, I hurt Jensen. *Bad*. That's not the kind of man I want to be."

Reflecting on the past few months, on how different he is now from the boy I remember—the boy I catch glimpses of from time to time—I wonder what he would be like if we had stayed together. Would his eyes shine with memories of our happy youth? Or was he always destined to resent me, or my life as Makenzie, for some reason or other?

In a quiet, tentative voice, I ask, "What kind of man do you want to be, Jake?"

He hesitates, and the long sigh he releases skims across my cheek. "A man who doesn't hurt all the time."

I can't change the past, and I can't change him. The only

way we can move forward together is if he steps out of the past with me, hand in hand, to live in the present and plan for the future.

"I'm sorry I hurt you," I whisper.

"I'm sorry you were hurt. My heartbreak could never compare." Tightening his hold on me, he rasps, "Tell me about him. Tell me everything."

So, I turn over to face him—like I should've done years ago—and tell him the whole story. We shed endless tears together while mourning the loss of our son in the dark. A shared mourning I never imagined but always longed for.

"He was perfect, Jake," I cry into his chest. "So beautiful."

He runs his fingertips along my spine. "How could he not be? He came from you."

We become quiet, each of us lost in our own thoughts. Being able to recount that time in my life through a mature lens, and with Jake's arms around me, I'm overcome with peace.

This is the healing moment I needed to ease the burden of overwhelming loss.

This is the person I needed to pull me from the dark abyss.

Jake rid himself of pain through fire. I'm choosing water, each teardrop a final farewell to the guilt and shame that weighed me down. No matter what the future brings, I'll be able to move forward with a lighter heart.

The last thing Jake says to me before I cry myself to sleep is, "I'm sorry I failed us."

When I wake in the morning, he's gone.

35

JAKE

Someone keeps stealing the For Sale By Owner signs I stuck in the ditch at the end of my driveway. Doesn't take a genius to know the thief is either Rock or Brody. I gave up replacing the signs after the sixth one disappeared.

Tatum left for California almost two weeks ago. Every day that passes, my resolve to let her go weakens. And it doesn't help that the people of Walford are conspiring against me.

Besides the sign-stealing bandit, Lydia changed the coffee beans she uses, but only for my coffee. She basically serves me brown water, so I've stocked my pantry with my favorite blend since I'm boycotting The Drip.

Menchy delivered an enclosed trailer carrying a new bed, no doubt adding the cost to my tab at the hardware store. He doesn't even sell furniture, and I could've easily ordered something online myself. And who uses a big-ass trailer to haul pieces of one bed?

I'm not sure how people found out about my bonfire. Apparently, spies are everywhere in this town.

The trailer, with the bed still inside, blocks the steps to

my front porch, which is fine by me because it's harder for anyone to come to the door. I covered all the windows with black garbage bags, so I'm able to use lights when I move about the house at night and keep my friends from finding out how badly I've trashed the place.

Since the home-improvement projects are no longer a priority, I spend most of my free time sitting on the couch, staring at Tatum's cigar box while everything she said the night of the bonfire replays in my mind.

She told me everything about her pregnancy and delivery, sparing no details. Details I wish I never had to hear and she never had to live through.

She recounted the cab ride and the accidental phone call that set everything with Jensen in motion. She explained how the hole she dug was so deep, she couldn't find a way out. How her music career would've ended before it began, and my education was in jeopardy. How she feared our dreams would go up in smoke because she failed us by getting pregnant.

On top of that, she felt ashamed because she ignored her pregnancy and lost our son. I assured her, again and again, that wasn't her fault.

Since she explained the medical diagnosis to me, I've read every piece of research I could get my hands on. Tatum's own life could have been at risk, and I'm beyond thankful she survived.

Yet, after hearing every tragic detail, I still can't bring myself to open this damn box. What if I'm not brave enough to face what's inside? It holds proof that everything she told me actually happened, and I'm scared of it.

What I'm struggling with most is guilt for not consoling her once I learned the truth. I should've gone to her straight away after Jensen told me what happened. Whether or not I was by her side back then doesn't matter. She experienced the ultimate loss—the worst thing imaginable—and I gave her rage and a cold shoulder instead of comfort.

Since the night of the bonfire, after holding each other and mourning together, I haven't reached out to her. I'm the one wallowing in shame now, afraid to come forward and make things right. Digging my hole deeper because I can't get my shit together and face my fears, which is ironic considering this is exactly the spot she was in, and I crucified her for it. *Such a fucking hypocrite.*

Settled on the couch for another quiet night of contemplation, I spring to my bare feet as soon as the coffee maker beeps, signaling a fresh pot of liquid heaven is ready. Empty mug in hand, I head toward the kitchen for a refill when the front door crashes open.

The glass shatters and flies everywhere. I duck and cover my head to avoid being hit by any shrapnel from the blast. A figure clad in black appears, so I throw my mug in self-defense, catching the intruder in the chin.

"What the fuck?" Rock shouts, rubbing his injured face.

"What the fuck?" I yell. "You broke my fucking door!"

Brody, also dressed in head-to-toe black, charges in behind Rock and runs straight for me, tackling me to the ground and securing my arms behind my back. "Grab his feet!"

"Get the fuck off me!" I squirm and try to break his hold, forgetting that somewhere along the way he developed martial arts skills and never told us. His legs and arms wrap around me from behind like a damn squid.

Rock zip-ties my ankles, and Brody does the same to my wrists before they haul me to the living room and toss me on the couch. My underwear twists to the side, and my pecker pops out the pee hole.

I kick at Brody when he reaches down to fix it. "Hands off my junk!"

"Calm down," Rock says, ripping a long piece of duct tape off the roll in his hand. "We have shit to say, and you're gonna listen. We can do this the easy way or Menchy's way."

"Menchy *is* kinda scary," Brody tugs at the leather gloves on his hands. "He's well-versed in interrogation tactics."

"This isn't an interrogation if you want me to listen and not talk, dumbass."

"True." He shrugs as if the technicalities don't matter much.

"At least let me put some clothes on."

"Been a minute since I've seen you without a shirt." Rock pokes his fingers all over my chest and stomach. "Look at all these cute, little baby muscles. You been working out, Jakey?"

"Stop fucking touching me, bro." Flapping like a dolphin, I try to get away and end up face down on the floor.

"Rock!" Lucy shouts from the front porch.

"Shit." Rock dives on top of me, covering my mostly naked body with his and crushing my wrists between us. I wheeze when the impact of his full weight knocks the wind out of me.

Lucy squeals in delight when she enters the living room and takes in the scene.

"No way. No babies allowed at the ambush," Brody chides.

Rock and I look over our shoulders. Sure enough, Lucy's dressed in all black with Marcella strapped to her chest and sucking on a pacifier.

"You were supposed to stay home and let us handle this," Rock says, glaring at his wife.

"Some matters require a woman's touch." She perches on the couch and plays with Marcella's curls. "Or a nurse's."

"Can I please put some fucking clothes on?" I shout.

Rock curses at the reminder of my nakedness and barks at Lucy to keep her eyes closed. He drags me from the floor, shoving me toward my bedroom, but I'm forced to hop because my ankles are bound.

"You've really messed this place up," Brody observes, trailing behind us through the kitchen. There's trash everywhere, my outsides reflecting my insides.

We come to a stop in the bedroom and no one moves, so I quirk an eyebrow. "Y'all gonna dress me or cut these things off so I can dress myself?"

Rock spins a fanny pack around his waist from back to front, which earns a disapproving head wag from Brody.

"You have zero cool points left, bro."

"What? It's handy." Rock pulls out a knife, flips it open, and cuts off my restraints.

I rub my wrists and glare daggers at them as they watch me pull on athletic shorts and a T-shirt. They couldn't muster enough decency to give me a little privacy, the jerks. This isn't a fucking locker room.

When Brody reaches for my arm to escort me, I yank it away and snap, "I can walk!"

The guys post up on either side of me on the couch like I'm seconds away from making my great escape. I plant my elbows on my knees, ignoring their intense stares, and tug at my bottom lip, my attention on the cigar box.

"What's in the box?" Brody asks.

"None of your business."

"You've been staring at it for days." When I raise my brows at a Rock, he shrugs. "We've been spying on you."

Of course, they have. It's like high school all over again.

Nights can be pretty boring in a small town, so you learn to make trouble. Sneaking around quietly in the dark is a skill most country boys develop at a young age. Doesn't surprise me that I never realized they were loitering outside my windows.

Deflating, I sag into the couch, my tired gaze drifting to the loft above us. "Talk."

"We have enough information to conclude that you're an idiot and an asshole." Brody points a finger, making doubly certain I'm aware he's speaking to me. "Tatum protected you. Kept you in school."

I sigh, weary over having to resurrect this particular topic. I'm not going to bother asking how they found out about everything. "I didn't want to go to college."

"Did she know that?" Brody asks, arching a regal golden eyebrow.

"Not at the time." I've told Tatum my truth, though it was delivered much too late.

"None of us did," Rock says. "We watched you study your ass off for perfect grades and do shitty jobs for tuition money. Nothing else mattered until she came along. But she wasn't a distraction. Other high school girls would've whined about not having enough of your time. But Tate was your biggest supporter. And you were hers. That's why you worked so well together."

He twists his upper body, spreading an arm on the back of the couch like we're on a movie date. "Did she fuck up by not telling you? Yes. Big time. But even I can see that she did it for the right reasons based on what she believed to be true."

Lucy's watery expression conveys deep sympathy when she adds, "She lost a baby, Jake. That's a hard thing for anyone to go through. I'm sure it was even harder for her because she walked away from you."

My skin itches as they rub reality all over me with their words. Rather than soothing the rash, they're irritating it further. My only course of treatment against the burning reminders is to throw up a shield. "I know all this. Y'all aren't telling me anything I haven't already figured out."

Tatum knew the cost of her decision when she made it, yet she was willing to take on twice the suffering to shield me from half of it by walking away.

The last, remaining argument I have sounds weak at this point when I say, "I just wish she would've called me."

"You love each other," Lucy says, sniffling. She reaches across Rock's lap to grab my hand in comfort. "Don't punish her for loving you the best way she knew how."

My throat's thick and acidic when I swallow. "I'm not. I'm punishing myself for not speaking up."

Tatum punished herself enough for the both of us. What she needed was someone—specifically, me—to let her know everything was going to be okay. To carry some of the blame. Or all of it.

She paid the price tenfold, literally, dealing with this loss and all the ramifications for ten long years. After the bonfire, I spent the first week of my miserable confinement convincing myself it's my rightful place to punish her when, really, I want to hug her. Hold her. Tell her how strong she is. How much I admire her tenacity to march toward her career goals despite her pain. Lesser people would've succumbed to their grief.

Tatum is a warrior. She deserves praise, not rebuke.

"You can let go of his hand now," Rock whispers to his wife, except he can't whisper for shit. Thankfully, she listens and saves me from more bodily injury.

"I let her go," I say, fisting my hair as the familiar buzz of panic begins. "Again."

This time, I'm the one who walked away. The night I burned everything, she told me the choice is mine now. But what if I waited too long? A lot can happen in a matter of weeks. What if she changed her mind and decided I'm no longer worth the trouble after telling me the whole story? After realizing how fucking self-centered I am, always making everything about me and my pain?

"And how does that make you feel?" Rock asks, his freckled face way too close to mine.

For once, I don't snap at him. "I feel like I fucked up. I feel like I'm done being an angry prick. And I feel lucky that y'all are my friends and you stuck with me."

Rock and Brody have stood by me through the bad times and the good ones, never wavering in their loyalty and love. I don't deserve them, but I'm glad they think I do. I'll need to work harder to earn the friendship they offer freely.

Brody grips my shoulder and squeezes, drawing my focus to him. His navy-blue eyes reflect wisdom and hardship I've never noticed, urging me to pay closer attention to the man hiding behind the preppy clothes and smiling face.

Despite the deep emotions spilling from his tender gaze, he asks, "Group hug or circle jerk?"

I hang my shaking head as my shoulders bounce with welcome laughter. "Love you too, man."

~

ME

Tate gave me a box.

I don't want to open it alone.

JENSEN

On my way.

Jensen shows up at my plywood door carrying a box of his own. "What happened here?"

"I was ambushed." My eyes focus on everything except his face, though I can see in my periphery most of the damage I caused has faded.

He nods, understanding what likely went down and who was involved without me having to spell it out.

"Want something to drink?" I ask, closing the makeshift door behind him. It's weird playing host to Jensen when he normally makes himself at home. This small wedge of formality has never existed between us.

"Nah. I'm good." He places his white box on the coffee table next to Tatum's box and gets comfortable on the couch.

He's more at ease than I am, considering I've been shutting him out for weeks. I'm mad at him, but I need him, and it's hard to reconcile the two after everything that went down.

I sit on the edge of a cushion with my elbows on my knees, ready to spring to my feet and run if things get heated. "Do you know what's in it?" I ask, jerking my chin at the cigar box.

"I have an idea." He holds my gaze for long seconds, crossing his arms over his chest. The fearful look in his eyes belies his stoic demeanor, and tension rolls through every one of his muscles. "I brought some things Tatum doesn't know I have."

Eyeing him warily, I reach for the white box. "What is it?"

"Open hers first," he blurts, making me jump.

I'm already wound tight. This whole stiff exchange with my brother—and the unknown contents of these boxes—have me tiptoeing on the edge. There's darkness on one side and metal spikes on the other, and neither option appeals to me.

Shifting forward to mirror my pose, Jensen presses laced

fingers to his mouth as if he needs prayer to help him through this.

The cigar box—old and worn, made of thin wood with a brass latch—has no markings. I unclasp the latch and flip the lid, peering over the rim like something might jump out and frighten me.

The folded sheet of notebook paper on top looks crisp and new. I unfold the page, recognizing Tatum's slanted handwriting and what must be the lyrics to the final song she wrote. The one she finished, making her feel lighter, happier. The one I grew impatient to read, causing our demise.

My chest tightens when my eyes trace the words of one particular verse.

> *The worst secret I never told*
> *The best secret I'll ever hold*
> *Looking up, I see your face*
> *You whisper words to ease the pain*

I refold the paper, setting it aside to read a million more times once I'm alone. The lyrics are private—for me and Tatum only—and a quick glance at Jensen's solemn expression assures me he won't pry.

Next, I pull out a stack of photos: a few of Tatum's parents and several of us together as happy teenagers. A thick envelope contains more pictures from the day in the hospital. It's difficult to look at the close-ups of Dylan. As Jensen said, he's the spitting image of me as a baby.

Aching pressure builds in my throat as I flip through the images, wondering what song she chose to sing to him. The pressure blooms into a choking sob when I land on the photo of Tatum's fingers stroking his thick dark hair.

Even though he was already gone, could he feel the magic

in her touch? How her fingertips instantly soothe all the pain and ease all the worries? If I close my eyes, I can feel the ghost of her touch on my own scalp, comforting me as I meet tragedy face-to-face.

I wish I could've been there. I wish, more than anything, I could've touched his soft hair and kissed him goodbye.

Jensen squeezes my knee to remind me he's right here to support me. His grip tightens when a notecard falls from the envelope.

> *Tate,*
> *You said you didn't want these, but one day you will. I have copies for Jake if you ever change your mind about telling him.*
> *Take care, darlin'.*
> *Jensen*

My eyes dart to the white box Jensen brought with him and then to my brother, the pieces coming together. He nods, confirming that my copies of the photos are in there.

I'm torn. Angry with him for keeping this knowledge and these mementos from me, yet grateful he had the foresight to realize the secret would eventually come to light. He knew I'd want to see them one day.

The last item in Tatum's box is a velvet jewelry box with *Cherished Gems* printed on the lid. Inside is a simple, silver ring with an oval stone. At first glance, it looks like an opal. Upon closer inspection, I realize it's made of glass.

"What is this?"

Jensen clears his throat, chasing down the nerves with a loud swallow. "It's a memorial ring. I had it made for her with some of Dylan's ashes."

My eyes widen as an uncomfortable feeling gnaws at my gut. "His ashes?"

In answer, he tips his head toward the white box, and my intuitive stomach plummets.

I rear back and cover my mouth to hold in a cry or a scream. I'm not sure which. "You've had my son's ashes this whole time?" The quiet question seeps between my fingers, but he hears it.

With sorrowful green eyes and a wobbly voice, he says, "She didn't want them. Tate couldn't think straight, Jake. I did what I thought was best for you both."

Not knowing what to say and tearing my shocked gaze from Jensen, I open the white box. It contains another thick envelope filled with pictures, which I set aside.

The square, marble urn with *Dylan Holloway, Son*, and the date etched on a silver plate should be devastating enough to take me to my knees. But what actually does the job is the laminated certificate with Dylan's tiny handprints and foot-prints. The final piece of cruel evidence proving he was an actual person. My son.

Kneeling on the floor, with Jensen's strong arms wrapped around me and the certificate pressed against my forehead to shield my heartache from the world, I weep.

I weep for me, missing the chance to meet my son. I weep for Dylan and the life he never got to live. I weep for my brother for unwittingly walking into the aftermath and making impossible choices.

But mostly, I weep for Tatum. And for all the years she's mourned in silence…alone.

When my tears run dry, the last of my angry fog fades away. It's replaced with profound clarity and the long-lost sound of my thriving heart.

All the feelings I harbored—hatred, resentment, indifference—were masks I wore to cover what I truly felt: loss. For a decade, Tatum mourned the loss of me and Dylan while I mourned the loss of her. Loss bound us together all these years, yet it kept us worlds apart.

Haven't we suffered enough? Don't we deserve happiness? Tatum and I will never be happy without each other.

I'm tired of holding grudges. I'm tired of pushing everyone away and never seeing past my own pain. And I'm really fucking tired of being miserable, living without the only person who lights up the dark.

It may have taken a couple of weeks for my brain to catch up with what my heart has been telling me all long, but I get it now. The only way either of us can work through the grief of all we lost—of losing our son—is by doing it together.

We mourned that night after the bonfire when I crawled through her window, but we haven't *grieved*.

I can forgive her for her part in our downfall. My forgiveness is as inevitable as my love for her, especially when she isn't the only one at fault. We had a misunderstanding with catastrophic consequences because I didn't make my intentions clear. I didn't speak up and voice what I wanted. Well… no more silence. I know exactly what I want.

"I have to go to her," I say, my eyes fixed on our graduation photo. Two smiling kids so in love and capable of weathering any storm.

"You do," Jensen agrees, clamping a hand on the back of my neck.

"I can't live without her."

"You don't have to."

The truth he speaks is as sure as the sunrise. As reliable as the sunset. As constant and as old as time.

The choice is mine now, and I choose Tatum.

After Jensen leaves, I pull up the text history on my cell

phone and take a gamble. Whoever contacted me the day before Tatum left for California remains a mystery, but I'll need that person's help to execute my plan.

ME

I'm coming for Tatum. Where can I find her?

UNKNOWN NUMBER

Took you long enough. She's been here for weeks.

A smile teases the corner of my mouth as I read the exact words I said to Graham when he first came to Walford. How can I ever repay him for helping me and Tatum reunite? More than once, he's intervened for the sake of her happiness. With the way he loves her, I have no doubt he and I are going to be good friends.

36

TATUM

Well, shit.

"Well, shit." Maisy echoes my thought aloud as we stare at the positive pregnancy test. "Why are you and Jake against using birth control? I thought you were getting on the pill."

The truth is I put off going to the doctor for longer than I should have, and Jake and I weren't always responsible about using condoms before I got on the pill. But that's not what I tell Maisy.

"I'm a flamingo, remember?"

"What?" Her brows pinch together in confusion, then she rolls her eyes. "Ugh, never mind. What are you gonna do?"

I rest my back against the bathroom mirror and plant my feet on the counter, wrapping my arms around my knees. "I'm having a baby, I guess. I'll tell Jake and let him decide if he wants any part in it."

I haven't heard anything from Jake or about him since I left Walford. The first week after arriving in California, I drowned in my despair, unable to eat or sleep as I cried nonstop. Losing him again ripped me to shreds.

I finally called Cheryl at Gateway Hills and told her

everything that happened between me and Jake. Her advice? Wait and see if he comes around. *Thanks a bunch, Cheryl. How much do I owe you?*

"Biologically speaking, he played a big part in it," Maisy says.

"You know what I mean. I won't keep secrets from him anymore."

"Good." She climbs onto the counter next to me. We've had many heart-to-hearts here over the years, most of them about Jake. Bathrooms are good at keeping secrets. "Don't expect me to babysit until the kid's old enough to drive."

"You'll be the best aunt ever." I pinch her cheek, and she slaps my hand away. "So warm and cuddly. My kid will be addicted to your hugs."

She scrunches her pierced nose. "I'm a little freaked out that you're not freaking out."

"I learned the hard way you can't really miss out on something unless you know what it's like to have it—or almost have it. I want this, Maiz. This is the second chance I never thought I'd get."

Those few hours I held Dylan, I could imagine my future as a mom. That future was what I grieved in the months following the delivery, setting aside all my other reasons to grieve. They were too painful to confront.

A dull hue washes over Maisy's eyes. "Sucks to say it, but I understand."

"What's going on with you? You haven't been yourself for months."

A long, heavy sigh passes her pouty lips. "I'm just dealing with all the changes that come with making a life of my own. It's harder than I thought it would be."

Maisy and Graham arrived in California a few days ago. Now that filming wrapped, Graham moves to the post-production phase, and she's getting ready to leave for Philadelphia in a couple of days.

Marzan is selective about whose videos he directs and doesn't take on many projects. Maisy missed one and was worried Marzan would move ahead permanently with his second choice. But he assured Maisy she has the "it" thing he needs. She seemed excited about it until now.

I nudge her shoulder with mine when she hangs her head. "You'll always have me and Graham. We won't be together every day like we used to be, but our life as a throuple wasn't sustainable. We always knew we'd go our separate ways at some point."

Looking skyward, she shuts her eyes. "That's not what that—ugh—forget it."

When she hops off the counter and stalks to my bedroom, I trail behind her. "I'm worried about you, Maiz. Please talk to me."

She dives onto the mattress and screams into a pillow. I'm frozen beside the bed as I witness her meltdown with no idea what's happening right now.

When I snatch the pillow from her hands, she blurts, "It was Jensen!"

I'm too slow to catch on, so she points to the corner of her mouth and flares her eyes, silently begging for me to understand. She points again, exaggerating the gesture, then smears her lipstick. I gasp, clutching my invisible pearls, and sit my dainty butt on the mattress.

"Jensen Holloway?" I ask, needing clarification so I can process this shocking news.

She spreads her arms wide and groans in frustration.

"Oh my gosh," I whisper. "You kissed Jensen? Why?"

"Shh!" Spittle flies out of her mouth. "Don't say it out loud," she hisses. At least her signature scowl is back.

In a whisper-yell, I repeat my question. "Why? I thought you hated Jensen. You're so mean to him."

She rolls off the bed and paces while rubbing her forehead furiously. I've never seen her this unraveled.

"That's the thing. I've tried to hate him. For the longest time, you know? But whenever I go to Walford, he's just... everywhere!" She growls and throws her hands up. "All over Main Street. At my mom's house. I can't step foot in that town without running into him. It's like I have a built-in homing beacon, and he immediately finds me. Why can't he just leave me alone, Tate? He pushes and pushes. Why can't he leave the past alone?"

My mouth hangs open when she plops down next to me. The panting, unhinged mess of emotions who can't decide if she wants to sit or stand or scream is a stranger. I blink at Maisy, my eyes resembling a fish inside a bowl, clueless about what's happening outside of it.

"Take a breath, Maiz." I would pat her back or something to comfort her, but I'm afraid she'll bite me. "Let's back it up. How long has he been...pushing you?" I almost said *stalking,* but that's a little extreme for a guy like Jensen.

Her eyes fall shut again. "Since I left."

"Which time? You've been there a lot recently."

"After high school."

I absorb this revelation in stunned silence. The tension between them at the after-Christmas festival and on karaoke night was palpable. Maisy was rude to Jensen, and I remember the dejection on his face. He asked about her often —that first night at the bar and a few times over text. And he did act weird, excited almost, when I said she was in Austin.

Does Jensen *like* Maisy? Has he liked her all these years? Or does this have something to do with her brother's accident?

"Is this about—"

"I don't want to talk about it," she mutters, her voice tired and her eyes still closed. *Is she falling asleep?*

"Seriously? You drop a bomb about kissing Jensen Holloway and then immediately shut down? No way, missy. Talk."

"Ugh." Her head lolls in my direction when she groans. "He kissed me. Then I drove around for hours trying to forget it happened. Hence the cold tea I gave you." She flaps a hand, gesturing at…nothing.

"He kissed you." I recall the state of her hair and the smudged lipstick that day and smirk. "Must've been one hell of a kiss."

"Don't remind me. Pretty sure he would've swallowed me whole if I stuck around."

"Sounds dirty." I waggle my brows. She's not impressed, if her severe eye roll is anything to go by. "Fine. Forget the kiss. Explain what he wants from you."

She falls to her back again, her gaze fixed on the ceiling. "What do all men want?"

That's a copout if I've ever heard one. Maisy's known Jensen her whole life; he was her brother's best friend. Something's not adding up, but I'll let the matter go because she's truly freaking out on me.

Maisy bottles up her emotions, and I'm not prepared for the uncontrolled fireworks if she lets them loose. The sparkler she's waving around right now might set my bedding on fire if I don't put it out.

"Whatever. Keep your stupid secrets. Let's post this farewell video, then we'll drink sparkling apple juice to celebrate the death of Makenzie," I say.

We bickered over the length of my video post for social media. She won, arguing that I don't owe my fans anything more than what I've already given them over the years, which was every part of me. And she's right. Besides, I have nothing left to give. The message I recorded is short and sweet.

The decision to put my pop star life behind me was an easy one to make in the end. It was freeing. Stardom never brought me the joy I thought it would, especially without Jake by my side. And knowing what I do now about all the downsides to being famous, I wouldn't wish that life on him, anyway. He's the lucky one who dodged the public bullet.

"Finally. I hate that bitch," Maisy says. She pulls out her phone and taps the screen a few times. "Done. RIP Makenzie."

We high-five each other with huge grins on our faces.

RIP Makenzie.

Judge squints at me in challenge. If my triple-score word is legitimate, I'll be the first opponent in history to beat him at a game of Scrabble. He quirks an eyebrow, daring me to use it in a sentence.

I mirror his squinted eyes and enunciate slowly, "Get your dirty fingers off my *qwerty* keyboard."

We both shift our eager eyes to Marcus, who's at the opposite end of the twelve-person dining table. He's acting as our Scrabble mediator, which is necessary since the games with Judge can become quite intense.

Reading his phone, Marcus confirms my win when he utters the most magical words. "It's in the dictionary."

I hoot and holler, wiggling my butt in my chair as I revel in sweet victory. Judge abruptly stands and flips the game board, sending letter tiles flying in all directions.

As he storms off, I call after him, "Really, Judge?"

A door slams. Mouth agape, I look to Marcus for an explanation.

"He's a sore loser." He shrugs as if Judge's tantrum is an everyday occurrence.

"You don't say," I deadpan. "How did I not know this?"

"Because he rarely ever loses. He'll be fine. Give him a few days."

"Days?"

Marcus shrugs again. "He's a sensitive man."

I shake my head in disbelief and rise to collect the game pieces from the floor. "What time will Roni be here?"

It took some convincing, but Marcus finally agreed to invite his girlfriend, Roni, over for dinner. He's a private person, but I want to know more about him outside of our working relationship. We've lived together for years, and this is the first time he's openly mentioned dating or being in a romantic situation. Although it's fairly new, their relationship seems serious, and I'm desperate to meet the woman who burrowed past Marcus's iron exterior.

"I'll pick her up at six," he says, checking his tactical watch.

"Are you sure you don't want me to cook? I can make my famous stacked enchiladas."

Marcus stares at me as if I'm babbling like a crazy person who should be committed to the psych ward, stat. I squirm under his scrutiny.

"What? Why are you looking at me like that?"

"You're cooking is famously terrible. Don't offer again."

Tucking in my chin, I splutter at the insult. "It's not *that* bad."

He holds his stare, so I duck my head and continue putting away the game, thinking about where Judge fits in if

Marcus ends up in a long-term commitment or married. Deep in thought, I don't realize I'm chewing my lip until Marcus barks at me.

"Ask."

"You're really creepy with that mind-reading stuff," I say, frowning. "And bossy."

"Ask," he repeats.

I huff. "Fine. How does Judge feel about…you know… you having a girlfriend?"

"Why would Judge feel anything about it?"

"Well, you two have always been together. Lived together. Will a woman change the dynamic? What if he feels left behind?"

Marcus leans back in his chair and widens his legs, more relaxed than I've ever seen him. "I'm not his keeper, Tatum. Judge is his own man and does whatever he wants to do. If he wants to go where I go, he's welcome. If he wants to take off and travel the world, I'll pat him on the back and say, 'see you around.' There's nothing wrong with him, and he's not dependent upon me. It may seem that way. But just because we like each other's company and have each other's backs doesn't mean we can't live separate lives."

What he's describing sounds like my friendship with Maisy. Perhaps we're less codependent than I thought, and we simply enjoy being together all the time. The past few months have seen a lot of changes, with her in Austin and me in Walford. We survived. And being apart only made the times we spent together more meaningful. If that's how our future plays out, I'll be okay with it and hope she will be too.

"Oh. Yeah, okay. I didn't mean to imply—"

Marcus cuts me off. "It's fine. I understand how you could reach that conclusion. Judge finds it hard to communicate, as you know. He sticks with people he's comfortable around, like me and you. He may never speak to you, but he talks to you all the time. And, what's more important, you understand him."

It's true. Judge and I communicate, and the conversations are never one-sided although I'm the only one vocalizing.

"Can he? Speak, I mean?"

I've never asked, and my face warms with embarrassment for prying. If Marcus and Judge would've wanted me to know, they would've mentioned it at some point.

Marcus's honest answer surprises me. "He can. He's just had trouble with it since Afghanistan." Leaving it at that, he rises from the table and looks at his phone. "I'll order from Gio's and pick it up on my way from Roni's place."

"Sounds good." I put the lid on the Scrabble box and start to walk away.

"Tatum." There's no bark or bite when he calls my name, which is a first.

I spin in place and meet his earnest gaze. "Yeah?"

His expression softens, but a hint of underlying pain seeps through. "Please don't bring this up again."

"Oh. Okay. Sure thing. Sorry."

"No need to apologize. You've known us a long time and, honestly, I'm surprised you've never asked before. It's obvious you care about Judge, which is why I answered your question as best I could."

I frown and tilt my head, curious if he'll ever let me breach his walls. "I care about you too, Marcus."

He stands motionless like I just tasered him, then one corner of his mouth twitches. "Ditto."

"Nobody says *ditto* anymore, old timer," I say as I walk off. The sound of his laughter has me doing a happy shuffle all the way to the game room.

Dinner is amazing, and not because of the food. All my

friends gather around the table, plus Roni, who happens to be awesome. Maisy and I granted her immediate entry into our girls' club. She's witty and playful, the opposite of Marcus in every way.

As Maisy pointed out when we set up the buffet of Italian food, Roni's personality is a perfect blend of mine and hers. Interesting that after all these years with us, Marcus would find someone who reminds him of us both. I'll tease him about it later.

I never would've pictured Marcus engaging in public displays of affection, but my gruff head of security is beyond smitten. Unable to keep his hands off Roni, he scoots his chair closer to hers and traces a finger along the exposed curve of her copper-toned shoulder. She's a Pilates instructor, and her sculpted biceps make my arms look like limp noodles.

Graham and his partner, Miguel Espinoza, discuss the benefits of moccasins versus loafers. Moccasins are Miguel's latest obsession. He claims his purpose in life is to be a trend-setter, though it's yet to happen.

The couple got back together before Graham finished filming, and I'm so happy that he took the risk. I, personally, don't think he'll face much backlash when the media finds out his truth. But if he does, I'll give him the unwavering support he's always given me.

Maisy's twirling around the table, pouring wine for everyone. She skips past me and sings, "None for you, mama," bringing the entire table to a record-scratching stop.

"Mama?" Miguel and Graham ask at the same time.

Judge's eyes are comically wide, and he places a hand over his heart.

I glare at Maisy for spilling the beans. She sticks her tongue out and keeps filling glasses. *Bitch.*

"Yes, I'm pregnant. I found out yesterday."

"Tot." The concern in Graham's tone is not unfounded. However, this time, I'm willing and more than ready to be a mom, even if Jake's out of the picture.

"It's all good, honey." I give him a reassuring smile. "This is a good thing. Promise."

"Okay." He bobs his head, coming to terms with the news. "Okay. Okay. Yeah. We're having a baby!" he yells, arms thrown in the air. A giant grin takes over his face as he hugs a squealing Miguel in celebration.

Maisy takes her seat next to Judge, who's face pinches as he fights his emotions. She comforts him with a light pat on the arm.

When I glance at Marcus, with his arm relaxed around Roni and pure joy on his beautiful *smiling* face, I burst into tears. This is my family. The unbelievable ride we've been on may be over, but my lifelong journey with them is most definitely not.

"I love you guys," I say as happiness streams down my cheeks.

Marcus, ever our leader, lifts his glass. "Cheers to baby Tatum."

"Cheers!" The sound of my friends' excitement is the best music I've ever heard.

There's only one voice missing. Maisy, Graham, and I exchange looks, able to read each other's thoughts. I nod, giving them a little smile to let them know I'll be just fine.

Miguel cuts in. "What do we think about the name Casper?"

A chorus of resounding *hell no's* fills the dining room, and I laugh knowing the great name debate has only just begun.

Now that the cat's out of the pregnancy bag, I reach for my phone to send an important text message.

37

JAKE

I've read the text messages from Tatum a thousand times since she sent them two nights ago. Dummy that I am, I haven't expounded on my eloquent response of "I'm in." *Idiot.*

My mind's been spinning in all directions. Fatherhood. My career. My brother. Walford. Tatum. A future with Tatum. Can I have it all? Do I deserve any of it? Guess I'm about to find out.

A limo picks me up at the Burbank airport, and more than

a few curious eyes watch me climb inside the swanky ride. The other passengers in first class gave me the same funny looks when I boarded the plane and claimed one of their precious seats. Guess faded jeans and dirty boots don't scream *worthy*.

The drive to my destination goes by pretty fast as I take in the terrain. I always imagined the outskirts of LA to be more of a desert wasteland, so the amount of greenery surprises me.

As the limo passes through tall iron gates, my eyes bulge at the sight of Graham's expansive split-level home with clean lines and more windows than a house really needs. My driver rounds the circle drive and drops me off between a huge water fountain of a merman and the grandiose front steps.

Massive double doors swing open, and Graham steps out wearing sweats and a tank top. A shorter man with black close-cropped hair, deep dimples, and immaculate eyebrows follows behind him.

"Welcome, friend," Graham says, reaching out to shake my hand. "You're just in time for lunch." I ate lunch on the airplane but don't mention it. Gesturing to the man next him, he says, "This is my partner, Miguel Espinoza."

I shake hands with Miguel as we exchange pleasantries.

"Come in. Come in," he says, his dark eyes lit up like Christmas morning. "Welcome to our home."

They guide me up the stone stairs to the massive combined living/kitchen space on the top level. With sparse furnishings and modern art pieces, the room feels like a ritzy museum where I'm not allowed to touch anything. Graham takes my bag and sets it near a low sleek chair.

"We'll show you to your room later. First, we celebrate," he says.

"What are we celebrating?" I ask, trailing behind him to the kitchen area. Endless floor-to-ceiling windows showcase an infinity pool and a gorgeous view of the hills.

Miguel shoots ahead of us, buzzing with energy and unable to stand still. I'm trying not to stare at his outfit, but my brain can't reconcile the bow tie and moccasins combo he's got going on. Hollywood fashion trends are far beyond my level of understanding.

"Your balls, dear Jake. We're celebrating the fact that you found them," Graham says.

Miguel flies around the kitchen, pulling things out of the refrigerator and cabinets with no handles. For all the luxury surrounding us, I'm surprised by the simple sandwich ingredients he's placing on the counter.

Graham clocks my surprise and shrugs. "Neither of us can cook, so we eat lots of sandwiches."

I chuckle, more from the opulence than the food. "Sounds good to me."

We take our lunch to the *lanai*—at least that's what Graham called it—and I soak in the view. The cloudless blue sky goes on forever beyond hills that are much bigger than the ones in my backyard.

While we eat, I wonder what it would be like to live in California. To raise a family here. From what I've seen, the areas outside of LA are decent, but it's too noisy for my tastes.

"You okay?" Graham asks, eyebrows furrowed.

"I'm trying to picture myself here."

"Ha! No way. You'd hate it. Hell, I hate it. I was actually planning to talk to you about buying a place in Walford. If Miguel agrees and likes it, I wouldn't mind escaping to the country a few times a year. It would be nice to get away from all the nonsense."

"That'd be great, man. Tatum and I would enjoy having you around." That is, if Tatum agrees to marry me and wants to live in Walford. I may be getting ahead of myself.

Miguel hasn't spoken much since I arrived, and I'm wondering if he's shy, but his eyes spark with anticipation every time I open my mouth.

"What do you do for work, Miguel?" I ask in an effort to break his silence.

"I'm an architect." His response is clipped, but not in a rude or dismissive way.

"Oh? Did you design this house?"

He scoffs. "This snow globe? Hell, no. My little graham cracker bought this horrendous glass palace before I could save him from himself."

Graham smiles and gives a sheepish shrug while I try not to snicker at his nickname. Or at Miguel's comparison of the house to a snow globe. It really does have too many windows.

We continue our quiet meal despite Miguel's fidgeting. When the lack of conversation becomes too much for me, I blurt, "Tatum's pregnant."

Miguel groans and sinks into his chair. "Oh, thank god. I was about to burst if you didn't say it first." He perches on the edge of his seat, excitement written all over his dimpled face. "What do you think of the name Mikael? It's close enough to Miguel and could work for a boy or a girl. Tatum doesn't have to know it was my idea. You can add it to your list and keep mentioning how it's your favorite until you brainwash her." He plants a fist under this chin. "Thoughts?"

"Uh…" The guy talks way too fast for me to keep up, and I only catch every third word.

Graham saves me from having to answer. "Ignore him. We found out two days ago we're going to be uncles, and he's ordered seven books of baby names so far."

"She told you?" I'm unable to hide my disappointment that I may have been the last to know. Again.

"Well…more like Maisy spilled the beans at a dinner party, so everyone knows," Miguel says, earning a scolding look from Graham.

"It was a slip, Jake," Graham says between bites of his veggie sandwich. "Tatum wasn't trying to keep it a secret from you. She texted you right after we toasted to the news. She only found out the day before, and Maisy was with her when she took the test."

I don't believe for a second that Maisy accidentally slipped the information. But I do believe Graham's telling of events and appreciate the explanation.

"It's okay. I get it. At least I know this time, right?" My joke falls *way* short, and nobody so much as smiles, so I change the subject. "Thanks for bringing me out here, man. First class and the limo…you didn't need to do that."

"I'll do anything for Tatum," Graham says earnestly. Slouching in his chair, he widens his legs and folds his hands on his stomach. "The minute I realized who you were that night, I knew you needed a push. Nothing shoves as hard as jealousy, and you had it in spades. I won't apologize for upsetting you. Someone had to force your hand so you could, in turn, force Tatum's. What split you two apart was no simple thing."

"It wasn't," I agree. "And I didn't react the way I should have when I found out. But I'm here to make it right. To get us back to where we should've been all along."

"That makes me happy, Jake," he says. "And, in case no one's said it, I'm sorry for your loss."

My nose fucking burns, but I nod, glancing between him and Miguel. These two men provided a safe haven for Tatum to mourn when I couldn't. I should resent them for it or feel jealous, but I don't.

Meeting their eyes so they understand how sincere I am, I say, "Thank you—both of you—for taking care of her. For being good friends to her. I have a lot of work to do. And I'll start by putting it all on the line and asking her to marry me… if she'll have me."

"Oh, she'll definitely have you. If not, we'll kidnap her and deliver her to your doorstep. Tatum talked about you nonstop—"

"Never shut up," Miguel adds.

"—over the years. It's too late for her to change her mind now. You two are a done deal, Jake. I have no doubts about how much she loves you, and you shouldn't either." Graham and Miguel rise and start clearing the table. "So? What's the plan?"

I help them carry everything inside. "First, I need a ring. Then I need to beg."

Miguel squeals at the mention of a ring.

Graham shoots me a big smile and winks. "Then let's go shopping."

Strolling through LA with Hollywood's biggest actor is nothing like strolling along the San Antonio River Walk with a global pop star. For starters, nobody pays much attention to Graham, as if the hat and sunglasses are enough to disguise him.

I pull my ball cap low on my forehead in case anyone recognizes me from my fifteen minutes of fame in Texas. They don't. A few photographers spot us, but none of them approach or draw too much attention our way. I expected a mob, but it seems the people here are used to celebrities milling about.

"You want the diamond to be at least seven karats. Seven is a lucky number." Miguel snaps his fingers at the saleswoman and points to a velvet tray in the glass case. "This one, please, Vivian."

It's the tenth or eleventh ring he's asked to see. The lady —Valerie, according to her name tag—hides her annoyance with a forced smile and unlocks the case. The huge ring she sets on the counter, like all the ones preceding it, looks expensive.

"There aren't any price tags." I rub the spot between my eyes to quell the creeping prickles of anxiety.

He scoffs, which he seems to do a lot. In the hours since we met, I've discovered Miguel's an extremely intelligent man, but he *kinda* has a bit of an ego that rivals the size of his brain. "This isn't a department store, Jakob."

I fidget on my feet and try not to sweat, ignoring the fact he's been calling me *Jakob* all day, which isn't my actual name. It's a guarantee there's nothing in this fancy store I can afford. When I look at all the ring options on display, none of them make me think of Tatum. A giant, flashy rock isn't her style.

"What do you have in mind, Jake?" Graham asks, unclasping the fat, gold chain he tried on. He lays it on the glass counter and waves off the salesman lurking a few feet away when the man starts to approach. "We can always find another store."

"None of these scream *Tatum*. She'd want something simple and vintage."

If I only get one shot at proposing to Tatum, I can't give her a ring that says *I don't know you but marry me anyway.* I do know her, and nothing in this store has my girl's name on it.

Graham flashes me his pearly whites and claps me on the back. "Good man."

"What?" I frown at him, confused.

"Finally! Vivian's attitude exhausts me." Miguel curls his upper lip at the perfectly kind lady and glides to the door.

"Her name's Valerie." I rush to open the door for him before realizing I've never opened the door for another dude in my entire life, unless he was in a wheelchair or really old. "I'm confused. What just happened?"

"This was a test." Miguel slides on his shades. "You passed. Congratulations." He pats my chest and struts through the door.

Graham strides alongside me after we exit. "You'll get used to his games. He's playing two of them right now. One is to find out how well you know our girl. The other is to find out how much he can get away with before you stop him. Stay alert, Jake. Miguel can trick you into anything."

"Like opening the door for him?"

"Exactly. And it'll get much worse than that. Trust me."

We step into a vintage jewelry store a few blocks over, and I instantly relax. There's brass and wood and the cloying, musty scent of antiques that almost hurts to inhale. This is exactly the kind of place Tatum would shop.

It doesn't take me long to find the perfect ring, which Graham and Miguel approve of. I don't need their approval—Tatum will love the ring I chose for her—but I appreciate their blessing nonetheless.

Unfortunately, I can't get the ring resized and engraved in a matter of hours, so I'll have to give it to her as is. Patience may be a virtue I'm working hard to master, but I'll be damned if I have to wait a minute longer than necessary to tell her, with a ring, how I feel.

I need to see her. I need to touch her face and kiss her lips and beg her to love me forever. The last two weeks felt like they went by slower than the ten years I spent without her.

"And now," Miguel says with a clap of his hands, "we find the perfect proposal outfit."

"For me?" My eyebrows shoot up, and I point to myself.

"Absolutely. Do you honestly think I'll let you swear fealty to our precious diamond in ratty jeans and those"—he twirls a finger, gesturing to my feet—"cowboy boots?" He grimaces as if the idea of cowboy boots causes him physical pain.

I'm being judged by a dude wearing blue moccasins.

"Fine. What can it hurt?" I raise my hands. "But nothing crazy, okay? I'm a simple man."

"I can do simple," he says, but I don't miss the smirk as he strolls ahead of me and Graham.

"He cannot do simple," Graham says, keeping his voice low. "No means no, Jake. Remember that when he uses you as his personal mannequin."

"I can handle him."

Graham shoots me a skeptical look, as if I'm not sturdy enough to survive the Miguel experience. "Are you sure you want to jump right out of the gate with a proposal?"

"Yep. I'm done wasting time. You just have to tell me where to find her."

"Well, that's easy. She's my next-door neighbor." His shrug indicates this is a well-known fact. It's not.

"Seriously?" I'm not paying attention to where we're going until Graham opens the door to a clothing store and a cloud of cologne blasts my face. I cough, and my nasal passages sting, which makes my eyes water.

"Yep." He shoves me into the dimly lit store. "We practically share a yard."

Excitement builds as I think about seeing Tatum again while Miguel plays dress-up with me. Thanks to the nightmare traffic in LA, it's evening by the time we return to their house. I'm so nervous, I can't eat a bite of the dinner they order. Instead, I pace around and practice my speech, and Graham forces two shots of Fireball down my throat.

With the edge taken off and a too-big ring in my pocket, I'm more than ready to claim my girl.

38

TATUM

Sprawled out on the sectional in the media room, Judge and I shove handfuls of buttered popcorn into our mouths. We're on day two of our *Love Island* marathon when the perimeter alarm blares through the house.

No sooner has Judge sprung to his feet than Marcus runs past the doorway and shouts, "Safe room!"

Judge grips my elbow and guides me to the safe room under the stairs, sliding open the false wall and punching in the code. The automatic lights turn on, and screens light up with multiple views of the interior and exterior of the house. Judge taps my arm to draw my attention and confirm I'll be okay here by myself. I nod before he shuts the door and joins Marcus.

My eyes bounce from screen to screen, looking for the intruder. It's dark outside, but the high-quality video has infrared and night vision, allowing me to spot the figure dangling from the tall fence. As soon as the figure lands in my yard and falls on his butt, I know it's Jake.

I hit the button to silence the alarm and enter the code to leave the safe room. When I reach the side of the property,

Marcus and Judge have their guns aimed at Jake, who lies face down in the grass.

"Stop!" I shout, rushing toward them. "It's Jake!"

A fuming Marcus yells at him, "Are you trying to get yourself killed?"

"Of course not!" Jake yells back. "Graham told me to take the path."

Graham and Miguel, with cocktails in hand, wander into the yard twenty feet away, using the secret path we made between our two houses. The narrow gap in the fence, hidden by foliage, is a dead zone for the alarm system. It's how we fooled the paparazzi all those years.

We would pull into either Graham's driveway or mine, then walk to our respective homes. The sizable lots sit on a curved road, which makes the houses appear farther apart than they are, and few people realized our properties are adjoining. No one questioned why we kept separate homes since we weren't married.

"You missed the path," Miguel calls out, amused by the drama unfolding on my lawn.

"No shit," Jake says, squirming beneath Marcus's boot pressing into his back.

Miguel's eyes sparkle with glee under the floodlights. "Graham and I were planning to spy as you grovel, but this is *so* much better."

"There's never a dull moment with you, is there, friend?" Graham asks, chuckling as he brings a glass tumbler to his lips.

"Let me up, asshole." Jake grunts while trying to do a push-up against my head of security's heavy leg.

"Why are you here?" Marcus demands.

I should be nervous that he and Judge still have their guns

leveled on Jake, but they won't actually hurt him. They know he's my baby's father, after all.

Jake lifts his head, wild eyes darting around the group before landing on me. "I need to talk to Tate. Alone."

"No can do, pretty boy. You're trespassing on private property. You got something to say, you say it with witnesses present."

"Fine! Just let me up." He makes it to his knees before Judge threatens him with the gun again.

"When a man begs, he begs on his knees." Marcus translates, stony-faced and not an ounce of amusement in his tone.

Jake's head falls back, his eyes closed in exasperation. Maybe it's the shock of finding him in my yard messing with my brain, but I swear he's wearing a button-down shirt, trendy jeans, and fashionable boots of the non-cowboy variety. I blame delirium for my hallucinations. Or pregnancy.

I move closer until I'm standing in front of him, trembling from head to toe. He texted me two days ago with a clipped response to my pregnancy announcement. I assumed he felt obligated to fulfill his duty as the baby's father. He left me hanging, unsure if he wants any kind of future with me, so why is he here?

Once he gathers his composure and open his eyes, the raw emotion shining from them forces instant tears to gather in mine. "We're having another baby," he says.

Biting my lips together, I respond with a vigorous nod.

He inhales and releases a deep breath before that dimpled smile appears beneath his soft, amused gaze. "I can't promise to wear matching family pajamas."

I glance down at my baggy, footed unicorn pajamas, and heat suffuses my cheeks. His bright eyes glisten when his expression turns earnest.

"I love that about you. I love everything about you. I love

your happy dances and your musical laughter. How even a PG-13 movie makes you blush. I love that you feel more like yourself in a T-shirt than a designer gown. But more than the things that make you unapologetically you on the outside, I love who you are at your core. I love how selfless you are, always putting everyone else's needs and comfort before your own. I love how forgiving you are, even when people don't deserve your forgiveness. I love how when you love, you do it with every cell in your body. And I love the warmth that hits me right here"—he points to his heart—"when you smile at me."

Anguish passes over his handsome face, and I fall to my knees to comfort him. He cradles my head in both hands, brushing my cheeks with his thumbs. Comforting me first, always.

"I know what it's like to walk the earth without that warmth. And I can't live that way anymore, baby. I can't. You're the burst of sunlight I want to wake up to every morning. Your voice is the one I want to hear singing to our other children like you sang to our son. Your smile is the one I want to come home to every day. And your hand is the one I want keeping me steady when we're old. You're it for me, Tate. You're all I want in this life. You're all I've ever wanted."

Speechless, all I can do is cry as Jake digs in the front pocket of his jeans and pulls out a gorgeous ring. A white-gold eternity band with rose-cut whiskey diamonds. He knows me better than to buy a ring with a gaudy rock in the center. And because of that, I swoon. It's a good thing I'm already on my knees.

"We'll have to get it resized," he mutters, sliding the loose ring on my finger. He laces our hands together to steady his shaky ones and clears his throat. "Not that long ago, someone told me that if something as simple as forgiveness was the only thing standing between them and their heart, they would forgive every transgression to become whole again. I don't want *anything* standing between you and me." He presses our foreheads together. "I love you so much, baby. Always and only you. Marry me. Please. Make me whole again."

"Yes!" Miguel cries from behind me, his blubbering likely muffled by Graham's chest.

It's hard to speak past the lump in my throat. Even harder to see through the flood as I look into Jake's eyes and seek deliverance. "Every second of the last ten years felt wrong because you weren't with me. You're mine, Jake Holloway. The other half of me. And I can't imagine going back to a life without you in it. You're my greatest comfort—my always and only—and I want to be yours. I'll do everything in my power to never hurt you again. And I promise you…no more secrets," I whisper the last words.

"No more secrets," he agrees, inching closer on the damp lawn so our bodies are flush from knee to chest and we're sharing breaths.

Fighting the desperate urge to kiss him, I clear my throat. "Before I give you an answer, I have two conditions, one warning, and one question."

"Anything," he vows.

"First, you'll accept my family. These guys and Maisy aren't going anywhere."

He flashes a dimple with his watery smile. "Done. Marcus and I are BFFs already."

Marcus scoffs.

"Second, you'll be okay with me being a stay-at-home mom. I'm retiring, Jake. And California is an okay place to visit, but Walford is where I want to raise our family. In a house with a big round window and the best view in the state of Texas."

The sob he chokes back draws out my own, and we tighten our twined hands.

"It won't be easy," I warn him. "Not for a long time. What you saw in San Antonio—the madness—that's my life. And we're bringing a child into the chaos. When we're not in Walford, we'll have to be diligent."

"I'll never make that mistake again, Tate. I promise to keep our family safe."

I search his eyes, brimming with determination and love. They also exude a humble quality, which is new. "I believe you."

The tension eases in his shoulders. "And the question?"

My gaze drops to his neck, and I slap on my most serious face. "Why are you wearing a bow tie?"

A laugh breaks free, and I treasure the sound of it as his green irises sparkle. "It's a long story." He releases my hands and wraps his arms around me. Staring into my eyes, he speaks low so only I can hear. "I've waited ten years, baby. Don't keep me waiting another second. Say yes."

"Yes."

He claims my mouth, drowning me in a passionate kiss. I forget we have an audience until a deep, guttural noise interrupts us. We look to the side to find Judge full-on weeping, shoulders convulsing as tears stream down his face, his gun still aimed at Jake. Marcus reaches over and flips on the safety, ensuring Judge doesn't shoot anyone.

"Is he okay?" Jake asks, his brows creased in genuine concern.

"Yeah. He reads a lot of romance novels."

"I don't know what that means."

"Doesn't matter." I steal another kiss from the man I was born to love. The only man I've ever wanted. The man who gave me the sky so I could find the comfort beyond the pain.

The zipper of my onesie sounds like a musical prelude as Jake drags it down my body. I step out of my pajamas and stand between his legs in nothing but panties. Soft lips graze my stomach, causing goosebumps to skitter across my skin.

"Do you think it's a boy or a girl?" he asks, resting his cheek on my flat belly.

I run my fingers through his hair and watch his muscles melt. "I have no idea."

Seated on the edge of my bed, he looks up at me like I'm the center of his entire world. And every bit of love pouring out of him coasts through my veins. "Our children are lucky to have your beautiful heart," he says.

"It belongs to you too." I push his unbuttoned shirt down his arms and toss it aside.

"It better." He pulls me into his lap so I'm straddling his thighs. "But I'm tying you down before you can take it back."

I hum when he captures my lips with his, our tongues gyrating to a silent, tantalizing beat. Our kiss leaves me breathless as he trails his warm lips across my jaw.

A memory flashes of a nervous, skinny boy attempting to flirt with a sad girl under a tree, trying his best to brighten her day. "Is that your secret plan? To tie me down and keep me forever?"

He smiles against my neck, and I can picture the same boyish grin from all those years ago. "Mmm…something like that. Got any rope?"

I'm too entranced by his touch to put any effort into my pretend scolding. "Stop."

His fingertips light up my body when they skim the sides of my breasts. Trapping my gaze with his shining eyes, he whispers, "I'll never stop."

"Good."

In no time, the rest of our clothes are gone, and I'm squirming with his head between my legs and his hair fisted in my hands. He nibbles on my labia, his stubble grazing my tender flesh. Parting me with his thumbs, he spears his tongue inside me before dragging it slowly through my folds.

When he tugs my clit between his lips and flicks his tongue, the only thing stopping my hips from shooting off the bed is the arm he has looped around my upper thigh. Then he sinks two fingers inside me, crooking them and rubbing that tender spot until I explode.

I'm a boneless heap as Jake lies on his back next to me, stroking himself. "We're not done yet. Hop on."

He chuckles when I whimper but climb on him anyway. My body may be mush right now, but I love being on top. And underneath. And on my hands and knees.

I dig my nails into his chest as he thrusts into me, pulling a gasp from my lungs each time he drives deep.

"Next time, you're sitting on my face."

Clench.

"Dammit," I whine, and he chuckles again.

"Think I can make you come again?" He slides his hands along my waist and ribs, and the rough pads of his thumbs brush my peaked nipples.

Flutter.

He squeezes my breasts with both hands and flicks my nipples. When he pinches them, I throw my head back with a loud moan.

"There's my girl. You want more, don't you?" His rasp stirs pleasure low in my belly.

"Yes. Do it again," I beg.

He pinches and twists my sensitive nipples, and every inch of me catches fire. I never imagined I would get so aroused by having my breasts handled roughly. Jake loves to discover all the things that turn me on. And I love to experiment with him.

He sits up and soothes my aching nipples with his tongue while I ride him with abandon.

"Oh…oh…oh…I'm close."

He grips my waist and moves me up and down faster. "That's it. Right there, baby. Fucking love when you come."

My legs tremble, and I cry out shamelessly before I go slack against his chest.

Panting, he flips us over and cages in my body the way he likes, curling his arms under my shoulders and cradling my head with his strong hands.

"Ready, baby?" he asks, jerking his hips with quick, short bursts. "Hold on to me."

I press my heels and fingertips into his lean body and hold on tight while he pounds into me. Desperation permeates every thrust. The pitch of his grunts rises each time his abdominal muscles contract.

When he buries his face in my neck, and he's near oblivion, I bite the shell of his ear. "Come for me, Holloway. Fucking love it when you come."

I'm not sure where this sexually confident and adventurous woman came from, but I like her. Apparently, so does Jake. His whole body seizes as a guttural roar accompanies his release, which seems to go on and on until he collapses on top of me, breathing heavily.

"Fuck, baby. My dirty girl."

"Liked that, did you?" I'm smiling so big, my face hurts. It's a post-coital, victorious kind of smile.

"Yes," he says, struggling to catch his breath. "So much, yes. Talk dirty to me always." He swallows my giggles with another searing kiss, then rolls off me and lands on his back with his arms stretched above his head, chest heaving. "Your house is ridiculous, but I like your bedroom. Very original."

"I thought so. It's one of a kind." We grin at each other as we joke about our matching bedrooms. I still can't believe he knew exactly what decor I would like. Or maybe I can. "And it'll be *our* house soon. I want to keep it…for a while, at least."

"Whatever you want, we'll do." He shifts onto his side, facing me with his head resting on one hand, grazing his knuckles along my stomach with the other. "When are you going to a doctor?"

"We'll find one in Walford. It'll save us from having to rent a bus to haul everyone to my appointments."

A smile tugs at the corners of his mouth, but insecurity surfaces in his eyes. "I'm glad you've had good people to care for you and protect you."

"Even Marcus?" I tease to keep him from spiraling toward that place where doubt consumes.

"Even Marcus. I may not like the guy, but I can respect him." Jake splays his hand across my abdomen. "I'm man enough to set aside my issues with him so he can teach me how to protect my family in this…climate."

He's being serious, so I flatten my lips together to keep from grinning. "Climate?"

"You know. The *famous people* climate. Marcus and Judge won't always be around, and I can't mess up again."

My heart clenches at the thought of leaving the guys and Maisy, but we can't thrive in life unless we're willing to accept some change. At some point, we have to realize we're only holding each other back. And that's not what family does.

"You won't mess up." I roll to my side and dig a finger in his dimple crease until it forces a smile. "And that wasn't your fault. Don't blame yourself for everything that goes wrong."

"I should've known—"

My fingers clamp his lips shut. "You couldn't have known. But you'll learn, and we'll be fine."

"Okay," he says, as best he can with clamped lips.

I lean forward and kiss him, chasing away the self-loathing and reminding him of what's important.

"We're getting married," I whisper, unable to suppress the giddiness that shudders my shoulders.

"We are." Jake tugs my body to his. "Soon."

He claims my mouth again in a soulful kiss that tapers off to something light and sweet. The thought of getting to feel his lips on mine every day, when he's not traveling, warms my insides. I'll love this man up close, in the flesh. Finally and forever.

Pressing his forehead to mine, he says, "I'm never letting you go again, Tatum Makenzie Wakefield. End of fucking story."

For three blissful days in California, we hold each other, grieve together, and forgive one another for our failures. We vow to move forward with honesty and trust as our foundation and repeat our promise to never keep secrets from each other again.

39

TATUM

Soon, in Jake's mind, meant one month. And I agreed. We've waited long enough.

Our guests, especially Maisy, aren't too thrilled about our wedding taking place at sunrise. It was Jake's idea. When he suggested we get married on the ridge—in the exact spot where we fell in love—I couldn't think of anything more perfect. Yes, it's six thirty in the morning, but we're serving pastries and coffee while the guests wait for the ceremony to begin. So, really, what is there to complain about?

"Disaster averted." Maisy appears frazzled as she enters the master bathroom where I'm getting ready. Her blush pink dress swishes when she hoists herself onto the counter.

"What disaster?" I ask with my mouth hanging open as I apply mascara.

"Give me that." She snatches the wand from my hand and hops off the counter. "You'd think after all these years of watching me do this, you'd know how."

"Your boobs were always in my face. How was I supposed to see what you were doing?" I roll my eyes at her.

She rolls hers back. *Copycat.* "What disaster are you talking about?"

"Judge challenged Graham to a game of rock-paper-scissors. Winner walks you down the aisle."

"But Graham's walking me down the aisle. And Judge already has a role to play."

Judge has two roles, actually. He's a bridesmaid—bridesman?—alongside Miguel and Maisy, who's my maid of honor. And he's the flower...boy. He volunteered to be the officiant as well, but the man doesn't speak.

"Exactly. And if Judge would've lost the game on top of the fact you didn't choose him..." She trails off, giving me a knowing look.

If Judge lost a child's game of chance to Graham, he would boycott my wedding.

"Thanks for handling that and saving the day."

She goes to work on my eyelashes, then re-does my entire face. "There. Now you're gorgeous."

I turn my head from side to side as I look in the mirror. "You're a miracle worker."

"I know." She kisses the top of my head. "Ten minutes to show time. Are you sure you want to do this?"

My jaw hits the floor. "Seriously?"

"I'm kidding. You could do a lot worse than a Holloway." At the door, she pauses and spins around, a rare softness in her features. "I'm happy for you, Tate. Happy that you're finally happy. You've smiled more in the past few months than you have since high school, and Jake's the reason. I'm glad everything worked out between you."

"You deserve it too, you know? Happiness. You deserve someone who makes you smile."

"Yeah, well, let's get you situated first. Then we can find

my dream man." She adjusts her cleavage. "See you in a few. I need a drink."

I can only hope she's referring to coffee or juice at this hour.

As Maisy exits, Judge plows into the bathroom. I have no clue where he and Miguel found the blush pink suits they're wearing, but I don't hate them.

Grinning at him, I say, "Hey, handsome."

He takes my hands, pulls me off the vanity bench, and assesses me from head to toe with the most tender expression on his face. Tears form in his eyes, and his lips purse together when he makes a humming sound from deep within his chest. My heart pounds wildly as I realize what's happening.

He struggles to push a word past his lips. "B-b-beauti-f-f-ful."

"Judge," I whisper, his name catching on a sob in my throat. I throw my arms around his waist. "Thank you. Thank you for always looking out for me. You're the best big brother I could ever wish for."

He sniffles and squeezes me, then lets me go to wipe his cheeks.

I laugh and dab the corners of my eyes with a finger. "Maisy's going to kill you for making me cry and ruining my makeup."

He flashes me a full smile and shrugs, saying *it's worth it*.

Judge and Marcus won't be my employees much longer. They agreed to help coordinate security for me if or when I need it in the future, but they'll no longer be on call. I'm a silent investor in their new venture: their own security company.

Marcus limited my investment to one-quarter of the startup costs, nothing more, and I didn't argue. I understand their need to make their own way. With their combined skills, I'm certain of their success. Now, we can move ahead as friends—as family —and put the formalities of a working relationship behind us.

With my bridal party loaded in the pickup truck, we drive toward the ridge. April weather can be iffy in Texas, some days cool and rainy or some days unbearably hot. However, fate intervened with mild temperatures and pale, fluffy clouds that capture the colors of the rising sun.

Opening the gate for our friends and family, allowing them access to my and Jake's secret place, feels right. Until Graham, no one but us and the previous owners had ever been here, and few people knew about it. Those who did learned about it during the years we were apart. We're ready to share it, if only for today.

A wedding arch covered with pink roses matching my bouquet is wide enough for me to hide behind. As the music starts, heralding the procession, I peek at the forty guests waiting to witness our union. They're the ones who supported us the most on our journeys together, and separately, and we're proud to celebrate this moment with them. They had faith in us, more than we had in ourselves at times, and we're grateful for each of them.

Marcus and Roni snuggle together next to Aunt Pam, Lucy, and Lydia. Seeing everyone from my before and after gathered in one place, my heart is full and exactly where it belongs.

"Ready?" Graham whispers as the music changes. I nod and take his arm. "Fuck, I'm not gonna make it all the way down the aisle without crying." He tips his head back to stop his tears from succumbing to gravity.

"Graham Kingston. Did you just say the f-word?" I say out of the corner of my mouth as the guests stand and we start our walk down the aisle. Daniel crouches to my right, filming every moment of my special day.

"The situation calls for it. Now shut up and check out your groom. He's a total snack in that outfit."

In a grey suit jacket, white shirt, and dark jeans with new boots, Jake looks ruggedly handsome. He styled his wavy hair to one side and trimmed his stubbled jaw. The dimple appears as he smiles at me, green eyes shining with love.

My Jake.

"He's perfect," I whisper as the waterworks begin.

This is really happening. A day I've dreamed about since I was a sixteen-year-old girl with plans for a big future. A future that always included Jake Dylan Holloway.

Time and bad choices may have kept us apart for a while, but nothing is powerful enough to stop true love. Our souls claimed one another years ago. We were always meant to be.

As I take the last few steps toward my forever—toward the most perfect man who waited for me—I think to myself, *How lucky am I?*

He'll never have to wait for me again. We're here, together, and our story is far from over.

40

JAKE

Can a man die from happiness? From loving someone too much? The emotions trapped in my throat might strangle me to death before the ceremony kicks off.

"She's beautiful," Jensen says over my shoulder, proudly standing beside me as best man.

We talked through our issues, and I forgave him for most of what he did. He doesn't expect forgiveness from me for the rest, but I hope he one day forgives himself. He has suffered as long as Tatum and I have. Carrying that secret around all these years had to be hard on him. Jensen can be a bit obsessive when it comes to seeking resolution. *Open-ended* is not a word in my brother's vocabulary.

Rock and Brody murmur their agreement with Jensen's comment about Tatum. Rock threw a fit because I'm wearing jeans while Tatum made the three of them wear dress slacks, but it's my wedding. They can suck it up.

Tatum glows with radiance as she floats down the aisle. The pearls on the bodice of her vintage strapless dress shimmer under the early morning sunlight. Layers of tulle end at her ankles, exposing her bare feet. My lips stretch into a wide grin when I notice them, understanding why I spent yesterday clearing rocks from the dirt path, and she laughs.

Her long honey tresses fall past her shoulders in soft waves. A beaded clip secures the front of her hair to keep it out of her gorgeous face.

I'm unable to hold back the moisture in my eyes when Tatum and Graham stop in front of me.

He places her hand in mine and says with a quiet, cracking voice, "All yours, friend."

Graham kisses Tatum on the cheek and steps toward his seat. She places her other hand in mine, and we lace our fingers together.

"Good morning," she whispers, the most beautiful smile lighting up her face.

"The best morning." I steal a kiss. "You take my breath away, baby."

"You're not too shabby yourself." She winks at me, and the familiar grin that accompanies that wink touches my soul.

"Dearly beloved…" Menchy's voice booms, and we both flinch at the unexpected volume coming from the reticent man.

Tatum giggles through Menchy's parts of the ceremony and cries as we exchange vows. My vow to her is simple. I'll love her forever, unconditionally, and always be her place of comfort and safety. Her vow to me is sacred: to always make decisions together and to never leave me again. Not even in death.

We exchange rings, and a sob-laugh escapes her when she reads the inscription on hers: "Always pick me." I slide the ring on her finger, a perfect fit.

When Menchy grants me permission to kiss my bride, I take full advantage of the opportunity, dipping her low and plundering her mouth. She's breathless and flushed when I bring her upright to the cheers and whistles of our guests.

Chest rising and falling rapidly, she whispers, "Do you think we can get, like, ten minutes alone?" *God, pregnancy hormones are the best.*

"All I need is five," I say, squirming to hide the evidence of arousal in my jeans. My boys snicker behind me like the adolescents they are.

"I'm proud to introduce, finally, Mr. and Mrs. Jake Holloway!" Menchy wipes a tear, playing it off like he's adjusting his reading glasses.

I steal another kiss before taking Tatum by the hand and dragging her down the aisle, ignoring the congratulations and people calling our names.

"We'll meet you at the house!" I yell to the guests.

"We have to take pictures," she says, huffing and puffing behind me.

"Later."

When I remember her bare feet, I sweep her into my arms and carry her the rest of the way to my truck. We head to the far edge of our property, opposite where the gate is, leaving a dust cloud in our wake. I park along the fence and leave the engine running.

"Back seat. Now."

Tatum scrambles into the back, her fluffy wedding dress drowning out the space. I clamber after her, squeezing between the front seats and landing halfway on the floorboard.

"Hurry, Jake."

"You wearing panties, baby?" I ask, breathing hard as I unbuckle my belt.

The pupils of her eyes flare with lust, leaving only a thin

ring of bright blue. With a mischievous grin, she says, "Nope."

"Dirty wife." I shift the layers of her skirt around until I find the opening. "Hold on to something."

She grips the front and back headrests, and I spread her legs apart and shove my head underneath her dress.

"Oh shit! Jake!" she squeals when my ravenous tongue begins to feast.

Okay…it was more like thirty minutes. The wedding party drank mimosas while they waited for us, so they're good and buzzed by the time we return to take photos.

The state of our appearances earns us several jokes at our expense. Maisy tries to fix Tatum's hair and makeup, but I couldn't care less about how I look. Every time I see our wedding pictures in the future, I'll chuckle inside knowing the reason for my mussed hair.

"Thank you all for being here to celebrate with us this morning," I say to the guests gathered in my backyard. The best man and maid of honor are supposed to give speeches, but they are nowhere to be found. "You're all a big part of our story, and we're thankful for the love and support you've shown us over the years. Please enjoy the breakfast buffet and don't laugh when you watch me dance in a few minutes. It's not a pretty sight." I raise my mug of coffee to the crowd. "Cheers to you. Cheers to us. And cheers to my beautiful wife, Tatum."

As the guests toast to us, I grin at my bride and clink my mug to her flute of orange juice. Then I take my seat next to her and scoot her closer for another kiss.

"Where the heck are Jensen and Maisy?" she murmurs as she smiles and lifts her flute at someone.

"No idea." I look around the yard, searching for missing pair.

"They better not be off somewhere sucking face again… or worse."

Stunned, I blink at her. "Excuse me?"

"It's a whole thing." She flaps a hand like the revelation is insignificant enough to wave off. "I'll tell you later. Let's dance."

Thankfully, Tatum didn't get some crazy idea to do a couple's routine like Lucy and Rock. Instead, we sway to a slow song, her arms draped on my shoulders and mine around her waist. Swaying, I can do.

"What's going on there?" She jerks her head to the right, where Rock and Marcus are standing nose-to-nose with their arms crossed over their chests. The two men are the same size and have the same scowl on their faces.

"I'm pretty sure they're sizing each other up. It's a thing big guys do. I wouldn't worry about it."

Tatum rolls her eyes. "Guys are weird."

"Know what else is weird?"

"What?"

"Our baby is the size of a fig." I flatten my hand across her stomach.

We had our first appointment with the obstetrician, and Tatum's eleven weeks pregnant. Full disclosure: I cried when I heard the heartbeat. But there's no shame in being an emotional man.

The doctor assured us that, despite Tatum being labeled as high-risk based on her medical history, she's not likely to have another abruption. And she'll be closely monitored throughout her pregnancy. She better be ready because I'm going to be an overbearing mess of worry for the next several months.

"I can't wait until you finally have a baby bump. You'll be so fucking sexy."

"Maybe I'll buy a reindeer headband and give you a lap dance," she says, her eyes twinkling with mirth.

"I never should've told you about that. But I'll enjoy a lap dance from my pregnant wife any time." I nuzzle my face into her neck and inhale her floral scent. "Can we kick everyone out now?"

She giggles as my breath tickles her skin. "So I can give you a lap dance?"

Dragging my lips up her throat, along her jaw and to her ear, I whisper, "No. You've already given me something much better."

She shivers in my arms. "What's that, Holloway?" Her voice is breathy and sexy and teeming with lust.

"You. Forever."

On the back porch of our dream home, in front of all our loved ones, I kiss the shit out of my wife. My soul's better half.

EPILOGUE

FOUR YEARS LATER...

JAKE

"Uncle G!"

My son's excited voice draws my attention away from Tatum's hand rubbing her pregnant belly. He jumps up and down on the large sectional in our media room and points at the television. The screen fills with a close-up of Graham's nervous face as they announce the nominees for Best Director. He's dapper in a burgundy tuxedo jacket with black lapels and a sparkly bow tie—no doubt Miguel's doing.

"That's him, little man." I shift my one-year-old daughter, who's fast asleep in my arms, and snag the back of Lennon's dinosaur pajama pants. "Come sit down. Let's watch."

Anticipation thrums around the room as we wait for the results. When the presenter announces the winner, we all groan in disappointment when Graham's name isn't called.

"He'll get it next time," Tatum says. A tear travels down her rosy cheek as she commiserates our friend's loss. It's one thing I like most about her being pregnant: the rosy cheeks.

I agree with her. For Graham to be nominated for the

second movie he's made, there's no doubt in my mind his talent as a director will earn him plenty of awards in the future.

"I'll put Van to bed if you want to start Lennon's bath." I kiss my daughter's head and scoot off the couch.

Most people assume her name is short for Vanessa, but they assume wrong. She's named after Van Morrison. Tatum wanted to name her Carole, but I balked until I got my way.

"It's late. He can take one in the morning." Rising to her feet, she stretches her back, the motion making her swollen belly more prominent. "I'll get him tucked in and meet you upstairs."

"I don't want sleepy time," Lennon whines.

He's three and has already perfected the pouty face his mother always uses against me. Both kids inherited my dark hair, and Lennon got my green eyes while Van's are bright blue like Tatum's.

"Go brush your teeth and listen to Mommy. We have a big day tomorrow, remember? Uncle Marcus will be here."

Lennon has an unhealthy attachment to Marcus, if you call worshipping the man *unhealthy*. And Marcus loves to rub it in my face. Though, I'm not too proud to use his arrival as a means to manipulate my son.

Everyone who doesn't already live in Walford will be pouring into town starting tomorrow as we get ready for the baby's birth. My selfless wife offered to be a surrogate for Graham and Miguel, but I had two conditions because, from time to time, the selfish bastard in me rears his greedy head.

First, I asked her to use donor eggs because sharing her heart with others is one thing, but parting with a biological piece of her is too much for me to handle. Thankfully, she agreed. I didn't even have to give my prepared speech to state my case.

Second, I made her promise me at least one more child of our own after their daughter is born. If I could keep her pregnant all the time, I would. Tatum's gorgeous with a baby in her belly, and she's a fantastic mother.

"Uncle Marcus!" Lennon whoops and makes a zooming sound as he races from the room.

Tatum chuckles at my crestfallen expression. "You'll be his hero one day."

"Whatever. At least Van loves me." I sniff Van's thick soft hair, enjoying the lingering scent of baby before she turns into a sticky, stinky toddler.

"Daddy's girl," Tatum says, shaking her head as she trails after our son.

"Absolutely and always."

~

TATUM

The stars twinkle in the night sky as I quietly pluck my guitar and gaze out the round window from my comfy chair. It's like looking out the porthole of a ship—albeit a big one—after a long journey and finding the sanctuary you've been searching for. A sanctuary recognizable only by the sight of beautiful hills and a comforting sky.

Jake is my sanctuary. He always has been and always will be.

My gaze falls on the solar lights forming a soft golden circle near our special place. The place where we mostly likely conceived Dylan.

We held a private memorial, just the two of us, not long after our wedding. Jake surrendered some of our son's ashes back to the earth, to the dirt and rocks and soil that lay beneath us when he was created. We both needed the moment to say goodbye, but Jake needed it most.

The past few years have brought many changes to the lives of our loved ones. Everyone is spread across the country, always on the go or starting their own families, but we come together for the important moments. Sometimes, simply because we need to be with each other.

The people who relied on me, who became my family, are now successful on their own. I cheer them on from the background as they did for me, and it's a role I enjoy way more than I ever enjoyed being Makenzie. Anything I can do to support them, I do.

Jake takes my guitar from me, sets it on the stand, then kneels between my legs. He runs his hands along my thighs, and his green eyes capture my focus. He gets more handsome with each passing year.

His consulting business has grown, and he has three employees now. One is the former intern he hired after we got married. She was a godsend from the beginning, eventually taking over much of the travel and allowing Jake to be at home more. With the two additional employees, he spends most of his time working at home, dealing with the management side of the business.

"Are you happy, baby?" he asks.

"Of course. Why wouldn't I be?" The tiny crease between his eyebrows appears, so I press my thumb on it. "What's wrong?"

"I sometimes wonder if you're missing out because of me."

When he lowers his head, I cup his chin and bring his eyes back to mine.

"Jake," I whisper, then kiss him hard to reassure him of my love.

Every once in a while, insecurity creeps into his mind, and I have to remind him I'm not going anywhere. Ever.

I kept up my YouTube channel for a while but decided I need to focus my full attention on the people in my life. Besides, it'll be impossible to escape the dregs of fame if I keep putting my face out there. If I want to travel with my family one day without being swarmed, I have to step away from the spotlight until it burns out.

Music will always flow through my veins, but the songs I write now are for me alone.

"A few years ago, I had everything most people could only dream of, but nothing that I wanted. This is all I want, Jake. You, our family, this house, this town, my music. I know what it's like to miss out. Believe me when I say I'm not missing out on a single thing. I love our life. Don't ever doubt it."

"Okay. You're right." Jake seals his lips to mine and moans when I drag my nails along his scalp. "I just love you, baby. So fucking much."

"I love you too." Nudging his side with my knee, I say, "Now be a good husband and rub my feet."

He smirks, flashing that sexy dimple, and slides his fingers beneath the hem my maternity sleep shorts. "You know how a foot rub will end."

"Exactly." I reach for his belt buckle. "And I love happy endings."

THE END

Lullaby For My Boys

I held you close in my arms
Vowed to keep you safe and warm
Promises, they fell away
Darkness was my price to pay

We never had a chance to start
But in my heart
You'll always be the

Sunshine, starry night
Rain clouds, first light
Find me, love me
Find you above me
Tonight

The worst secret I never told
The best secret I'll ever hold
Looking up, I see your face
You whisper words to ease the pain

The time has come to say goodbye
But in my dreams
I'll meet you in the

Sunshine, starry night
Rain clouds, first light
Find me, love me
Find you above me
Tonight

AUTHOR'S NOTE

You may be thinking, *How could Tatum just ignore her pregnancy?* Unfortunately, it's not uncommon for some teenage girls to conceal or ignore their pregnancies, but the actual statistics remain unknown. What is known, however, is that inadequate prenatal care can lead to health risks for mother and baby, including morbidity.

I'm not a medical expert by any means, so go easy on me. Out of respect for readers who have experienced, or know someone who experienced, a similar tragedy, I intentionally chose not to address the details surrounding Tatum's medical diagnosis. Rather, I chose to focus on her reactions, and her subsequent grief, and tried to handle the subject matter with the utmost respect and care.

Thank you for reading,
JB LaRee

ACKNOWLEDGMENTS

It would have been impossible to share Tatum and Jake's emotional story without the help and support of many people.

My family: Thank you for rooting for me even though most of you aren't allowed to read the book. It's too scandalous for the "Aunt Pams" of the world. If you're reading this page, you obviously didn't listen.

Dena and Joy, my fellow dog moms and the first beta readers: You knew about the book before most of my family, and you cheered me on from day one. I appreciate your input every time I popped up in the group chat with a random question about genitalia or a different version of the book cover. Thank you to the hilt!

Lauren, Jessica, Elise, Emily, Brianna, Jenny, Aimee, and Amber: Your feedback as beta readers played a huge part in developing the final draft, ensuring the notable details were addressed fully and the characters were lovable.

Cassie Marie, Sensitivity/Beta Reader: Thank you for the wonderful guidance you gave on character descriptions, which helped me showcase the book's diversity in a natural, subtle way. You really boosted my confidence.

Cassie Rottink, Personal Assistant/Content Creator: You're a life saver! Thank you for swooping in at the last minute and tackling my self-publishing task list so I could focus on final edits. You relieved so much of my stress, and I'm forever grateful.

Melissa McGovern, Developmental Editor: You're a

game changer! Thank you for leading me to that *Eureka!* moment when I needed help with Jake's character arc. And for brainstorming with me to change Lucy's role in the story. And for pointing out that I was a little hyphen happy in my first draft. Oh, and for the best feedback comment in a spicy scene in my draft: "Please no."

Angela Garcia, Line/Copy Editor: Thank you for not tearing my manuscript apart like I feared you would and for making a couple of emotional scenes hit harder. Also, I appreciate you removing all those extra commas I stuck in there and adding new ones where needed. The comma drama is real!

A special thanks to Mattie Jae—my Alpha—for being my sounding board and biggest cheerleader. Your optimism and encouragement kept me moving forward. All those long FaceTime calls lifted my spirits whenever I had doubts or insecurities while writing this story. You kept me on track with daily check-ins and held me accountable. Thank you for all the work you did to promote the book. And thank you, especially, for talking with me about the characters like they're real people and loving them as much as I do. We did it!

Finally, to my husband: Thank you for cooking dinner, making me laugh as stress relief, keeping the coffee pot full, taking the dogs out to pee, and going fishing on the weekends so I could write in peace. You've always supported this dream of mine, and I'm lucky to have a partner in life who stands beside me, beaming with pride, as I work toward my goals. You're the absolute best.

ABOUT THE AUTHOR

J.B. LaRee enjoys getting lost in dramatic love stories, so she decided to put her writing degree to use and bring the gripping, romantic tales in her head to life. Strong coffee and a playlist of epic love songs fuel her writing sessions. When she's not putting her characters (and readers) through the emotional wringer, she binges on books, TV shows, and jigsaw puzzles while planning her next adventure. Texas-born and raised, she currently resides in Michigan's upper peninsula with her husband and dogs.

Website: https://www.jblaree.com
Instagram: https://www.instagram.com/jblaree_author/
Facebook: https://www.facebook.com/jblareebooks
Goodreads: https://www.goodreads.com/authorjblaree
Reader Group: https://www.facebook.com/groups/jblareesreadernotes

TRIGGER WARNING

Be advised, the following list contains _major spoilers_. The sensitive subject matter experienced or referenced by characters in this book includes, but is not limited to:

- Alcohol/drug abuse and addiction
- Anxiety/panic attacks
- Depression
- Prostitution
- Stillbirth/loss of a child
- Violence/physical assault
- Sexual assault (referenced)
- Suicide/suicidal thoughts (referenced)

While this is a love story with a happy ending, your mental health is important. The author strongly advises you to proceed with caution, or avoid reading this book altogether, if the above themes or topics are triggering for you.